Praise for

The Elephant Mountain Gang

"A compelling sequel to "The Lobster Lake Bandits." Carbone combines mystery, romance, and historical fiction for addicting storytelling of a plot twist in the Maine woods. You will not want to put this book down."

- - Maine Books

"I've spent a lot of time in the Moosehead Lake area, and I can tell you, Tommy Carbone puts you right there in his new novel. But I must warn you, have plenty of time set aside because you're not going to want to stop reading. And, when you finish the book, you're going to want to visit Greenville and Moosehead Lake!"

- - George Smith
Maine's Bangor Daily News
Maine Outdoor Writer
Former Executive Director for the
Sportsman's Alliance of Maine

Elephant Mountain

Piscataquis County, Maine
Elevation approx. 2,650 ft (810 m)

A Maine Trail

The chirping of the birds.

A rustling wind through the

hemlocks.

The snap of a twig.

Is someone there?

Also by

Tommy Carbone

The Lobster Lake Bandits

Mystery at Moosehead

A Maine Novel

The story will have you in suspense trying to guess what was happening in the woods surrounding the Parker family hunting camp. The end results will keep you hooked right up until the end. It indeed is a great read.

- John Ford Sr.
- Author & Retired Maine Game Warden and County Sheriff

Growing Up Greenpoint

A Kid's Life in 1970s Brooklyn

A Memoir

"This book is a lot of fun. Carbone's stories are funny and full of heart, and he brings his childhood to life in vivid detail."

-- The Golden State Media Concepts Book Review

The

Elephant Mountain

Gang

Mystery at Maine's
Moosehead Lake

Song Playlist:
This Time of the Year, Barbara Mandrell
I've Got My Love to Keep Me Warm, Ella Fitzgerald
That Christmasy Feeling, Johnny Cash
Feels So Right, Alabama
Elvira, The Oak Ridge Boys
Auld Lang Syne, 1788 poem by Robert Burns
We're Gonna Go Fishin, Hank Locklin
You're Something Special to Me, George Strait
Orange Blossom Special / Hoedown, Gilley's "Urban Cowboy" Band
Silver Wings, Merle Haggard

Burnt Jacket Publishing
Greenville, Maine
20210707 ISPBK
Library of Congress Control Number: 2020910081

ISBN: 978-1-7347358-6-4
Also available:
    Hardcover
    eBook
    Large Print
        www.tommycarbone.com

The
Elephant Mountain
Gang

Mystery at Maine's
Moosehead Lake

by

Tommy Carbone

The second novel in the Moosehead Mystery series.

To

The Maine Wardens

The Forest Rangers

&

All First Responders

Thank you for being there as

protectors of the woods and for

those in need of your help.

Missed Call 13
A New York Morning 25
Season's Greetings 38
Almost a New Year 45
Let It Snow 49
Can't Get There From Here 62
Canucks at the Carry 73
Camp Axe 87
Skidder Donuts 97
Animal Lure 102
News from Germany 118
Wide Awake 125
Who was Eddy Walsh? 142
Hannibal's Crossing 160
The Black Ghost 164
Moose Sheds 179
Auld Acquaintance Be Not Forgot 190
A Winter Long Ago 198
Going Fishing 207
Been Skunked 213
The North Woods 226
The Moosetowner 228
Air Traffic Control 234
A Long Cold Night 251
Special Mission 263
Mountain Man 279
A Toast 292
Kettle to Kettle 301
Memorial Ride 315
Making a Getaway 327
Bourbon. No Ice. 336
Free Agent 347

A Frozen Moosehead Lake

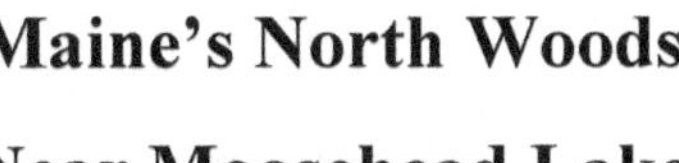

Maine's North Woods
Near Moosehead Lake

"Mayday! Mayday! Mayday!"

"Repeat – Mayday! Mayday! She's going down."

Above the whine of his chainsaw, Spencer felt a rumble in the air. He looked up. The afternoon sky was dulled by a gray overcast that was covering the tops of the mountains.

The ground started to shake. He killed his chainsaw. "Holy crud."

The plane emerged from the thick white cloudy soup above. It was only visible for a second before it disappeared into the side of the mountain. A fireball shot into the air. Black smoke rose against the snow-covered backdrop. Shocked, Spencer didn't move.

The "dee-dee-dee" song of a chickadee broke the silence. He dropped his saw, flipped off his scratched orange hardhat, and climbed into his skidder.

"Hey! Hey! Anyone! This is Spence, come in."

The CB radio crackled with static.

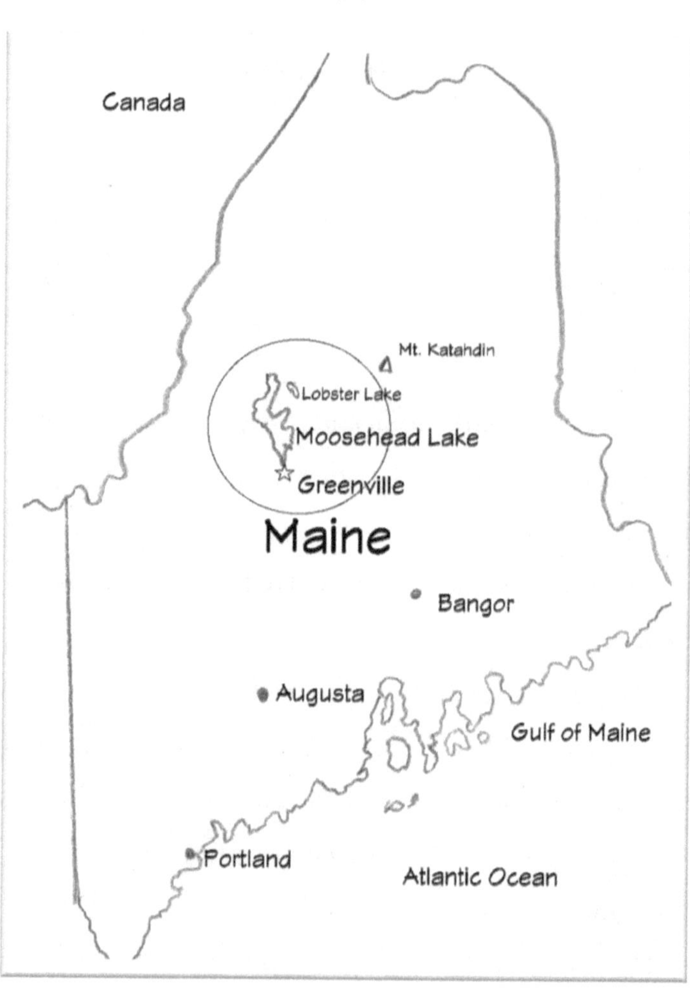

Canada
Mt. Katahdin
Lobster Lake
Moosehead Lake
Greenville
Maine
Bangor
Augusta
Gulf of Maine
Portland
Atlantic Ocean

Missed Call

Monday – October 10, 1988

Bangor, Maine

Joe woke to the sound of a tail beating a rhythm against the wall. He squinted at the clock. "It's only five. Can't you sleep in at least one day a week?" He rolled over.

Jumping up, R.C. put his front paws on the mattress.

"All right, I'm getting up." He scratched the dog on the head.

While R.C. sniffed around outside, Joe brewed a pot of his favorite eye-opener dark roast. Waiting on Mr. Coffee, he picked up the postcard from the pile of mail; he'd already read it three times before he went to bed last night.

Sitting at the kitchen table, he evaluated the skyline image of New York City and wondered how many people lived in the buildings that filled the picture. Flipping it over, he read it for the fourth time.

Dear Joe,

It was great spending time with you in your piece of the woods. I can't wait to come back in the summer and hike Katahdin with you. My neck of the woods is shown on this postcard. As you can see we have three ponds and no possible way to get lost. I was thinking, why don't you fly down to the city for the Thanksgiving holiday? (she added a smiley face) I can show you the sites here in my city. Call me when you are back from camp. I suspect by then the Red Sox will be done for another year. (another smiley face)

Warm regards,

Sarah.

To clear his head, he filled his thermos, and took R.C. for a hike around Small Pond. The October morning air was brisk and they had the trail to themselves, except for an occasional rev of a car engine and the distant roar of a plane taking off from the Bangor airport. Joe sighed; the loop wasn't nearly as peaceful as the trails near camp. Nonetheless, the canopy of brilliant red, yellow, and orange leaves gave him time to decide about going to New York. To consider his dilemma, he sat on a cement bench that was inscribed in black paint by Ricky professing his love for Julia. He watched a couple of lingering mallards floating along the shore. A squirrel, who wasn't keen on R.C. sniffing around, began chattering from a branch. The dog barked and ran in a circle through the layer of brown leaves surrounding the tree. The squirrel clung to the trunk, his tail puffed and raised.

With the peace disturbed, Joe whistled. "Let's go, boy."

Lobster Lake, Maine

The snap of a second twig in the woods behind Fred got his attention. This time his coffee mug stopped when it touched his lips. Listening, he turned his head slightly toward the sound. He knew it would be strange for a deer or another forest creature to approach his camp with the smell of a fire going, so he wondered what, or who, it might be.

Sitting still, he kept his hearing tuned for a footstep. It was still too dark beneath the canopy of pines to see into the woods; the sun was barely clearing the tip of Mt. Katahdin. With a shuffle of leaves farther down the shore, he shrugged the sounds off as probably a squirrel, or turkey, scratching for food.

With his own breakfast of black coffee and a package of Lorna Doone cookies for dunking finished, Fred broke camp. He moved from his spot, close to Ogden Point, with everything he had with him on his back. Folded in his frame-pack was a small canvas tent, along with a compass, map, matches, knife, cook kit, small axe, flashlight, rope, and two clean shirts. At the top, wrapped in a recycled piece of blue tarpaulin, his food was simple, some peanut butter, oatmeal, crackers, a can of sardines, a couple pieces of fruit, a few tea bags, and two lemons – for his tea and a garnish for fish. To catch his dinner, still an option on a few of the waters open for fishing through October, he kept his four-piece L.L. Bean fly rod bungeed to the straps of his pack.

For Fred, things couldn't get any better than a job where he got to camp and hike in the Maine woods. Not that he had to, he could commute from his house in Millinocket, but that meant less time per day on the trail, or what he told his boss he was doing, "checking operations." Which he was doing to make a living, while living life, in the Maine Highlands.

It wasn't as if he was living off the grid far from civilization, his truck was a few miles away, and in it he had plenty of supplies, but he enjoyed disappearing for two or three nights at a time into the wilderness. For Fred, the cushion of pine needles under his boots, the sound of water washing over rocks, the crackling of a fire under a night sky full of stars, were some of the reasons he had chosen this career.

Being the son of a game warden, Fred had spent the summers of his adolescent years at Clayton Lake, during which he'd disappear for weeks at a time canoeing the Allagash and surrounding waters. It was a piece of the wilderness he knew well, yet he was always discovering out of the way locations, places he wondered if anyone else had ever been.

After college, he landed a job with the Maine Forestry Service, and he'd been working the woods ever since. This was his twenty-fifth fall in his dream job, during what he considered to be the best season of the year. Not that he didn't enjoy every season in the great outdoors, it was where he wanted to be all the time, but fall, that was special.

This time of year, the sky was always bluer, no summer haze to contend with; there were fewer bugs to swat, which were the one nemesis that could drive him back to paved roads; and all the casual campers had packed up and headed south, leaving the prime camping spots open for his use. As the season wore on, and the leaves started their foliage show, he could sit on a ridge and watch the colors change almost by the hour. The first trees would begin with one or two leaves, as early as mid-August, and by the first week in October this area was often approaching peak color. As a forester, Fred could identify every tree in the forest, the deciduous almost by the color of their fall outfits.

Next to being an expert on trees, Fred's other interest was birds. And this time of year, never disappointed. Starting in late August and extending through fall, the forest birds, tourists in their own way, begin their "fall-out." Fred could sit and listen to the chorus of birds all day long, and some days he did. He could distinguish an individual bird call as easily as identifying the sounds of a feller buncher from a skidder dragging tree trunks in the woods a mile away.

With no need to rush to this morning, his mission was a bit for pleasure. Since he only had one logging operation to check over on the west side of Lobster Mountain, he meandered slowly, avoiding each twig on the trail. This morning, he had given his fieldwork the name, "Operation Songbird," with hopes of hearing a species, or two, making their way south.

Fred's choice of camp location was partly to be close to the logging site, but mostly he was wishing for a great deal of luck. At the tail end of summer a few years ago, he had been lucky to be at Ogden Point for a bird fall-out like one he had never experienced before. Walking along, he listened for birds and recalled that morning.

By the first week in September, Lobster Lake was all but deserted of people; the night before, Fred only noticed the flickering from one other campfire hundreds of yards down the shore. Bedding down between the base of Lobster Mountain and the lake, Fred rose early, and walked to a boggy area. With the sun rising, he heard the fluttering of wings. Before the birds took cover in the weeds to hunt for lingering insects and seeds, he identified several species of warbler. There were bay-breasted, black-throated greens, and the yellow-rumped that landed in quick succession. Arriving late was a group of the smallest warbler, the northern parulas. The concert began, beckoning vireos to land nearby.

A slurp of yellow-bellied sapsuckers clung to the pines, adding harmony. He almost missed seeing a charm of finches fly past the commotion. With the lake smoke rising, they rounded the point in formation singing their contact call - *po-ta-to-chip, po-ta-to-chip, po-ta-to-chip*. It was a birding day for the records, which he noted in his field journal, along with, "the way the woods should be."

Ever since that day, he had tried to find a repeat performance, but the weather, the air currents, his timing, and the internal clocks of the birds had not chosen to align. This year, he knew he was late for the largest numbers to be passing through, but he hoped if not an orchestra, at least he might be treated to an ensemble of late departure locals.

Hiking along the boggy area on course for the logging road, Fred, took a deep breath of the air that smelled of pine, dried leaves, and the freshness of north woods lake water. He had a good feeling. Last night the winds were from the northwest and the skies were slightly overcast. He had hoped those conditions proved good flying weather for songbirds, since he knew they migrated under the cover of darkness to avoid predators, while gaining the benefit of the nighttime air to keep their engines cool.

He took up a spot in the crook of a large pine tree, his pack behind his back, binoculars around his neck, and waited for the sun to brighten the sky and lift the curtain for a possible show. To pass the time, he opened his book, *Forest History of Maine – 1800 - 1950*. It was a thick volume covering the trees and logging practices of the state. He opened to the appendix that included maps of long-gone logging camps. From time to time he would explore the woods around the old camps, leading him to sometimes finding artifacts of the lumberjack life. His collection included rusted hand hooks, pieces of pike-poles, cant-hooks and a few peaveys. When he spoke at the local schools, he would bring them along for show-and-tell.

Fred closed his eyes to listen to the wake-up call of the fall forest. He passed the hour spreading an over-ripe banana, that had been squished in his side-bag, onto soggy graham crackers.

He was content reading until a noise disrupted the aria floating through the trees. The chickadees heard it first and their stanzas ceased. The hum started out low, the kind of vibrating sound you feel when a hummingbird gets close to your head. Fred sat up. When the engine passed by on the logging road a hundred yards through the brush to his west, Fred knew it was too small to have been a truck. He also knew the operation he was to check on, was marked as complete and ready for inspection, so he didn't anticipate any loggers being in the area. With the interruption and the low probability of a performance, Fred started toward the road.

At a pace better suited for a walking race, it didn't take him long to hike to the clearing he needed to inspect. All was in order with required no-cut zones, the acreage cleared matched the permit, and all brush had been hauled away per requirements – an important detail to protect against forest fires. Fred observed no sign of recent motor vehicle traffic on the sandy soil. Whoever he heard earlier must have continued along the trail-road that hugged close to the lake.

With his work done, and his stomach growling, he thought about having something more substantial to eat. Looking around, he decided a logging clearing wasn't the most appealing spot for his oatmeal and apple. Besides, open fires weren't permitted in this area and he was certainly not going to violate the law to boil water.

It was an easy decision to double back, in order to enjoy his meal at a campsite along Little Claw. Never one to move slow, he made his way down the dusty logging road at almost a full jog. He was nearly at the side trail that led to the lake, when he heard the hum again. He waited. The driver was approaching at a slow speed. Standing still in the sun, a bead of sweat rolled down Fred's back. He tried to nudge a large rock off the trail with his foot. It was too heavy. He bent down, grunted at its weight, and heaved it into the brush. His light-headedness was telling him he was much hungrier than he realized. Fred moved to the shade and leaned against a tree trunk.

The driver came around the bend and the dirt bike coasted to a stop. Fred gave a salute.

"Fancy finding you out here, Forester Fred."

"Can't say the same about you. If anyone was out this way disturbing the peace, it'd be you. I see you're still riding that noisy Two-hundred X."

"Hey, she runs and I get around faster than you on foot."

If you were to come across anyone in the vicinity of Lobster Lake or Northeast Carry this time of year, your odds were good it would be Fred or Gerry. Other than the logging outfits, they were the only two men who did business in these woods all year long.

"What are ya' doing out this way this morning?" Fred flicked his head up the trail in the direction Gerry came from.

"Ah, I went up to see if Joe was still here. He's been wanting me to put new shingles on the roof of the well house. Summer came and went, now it seems fall is going to rush by as well."

Fred sure hoped that wasn't going to be the case. "Was he there?"

"No. Looks all closed up. Except I did find something unusual. Especially for Joe."

"What's that?"

"The door to the well house was swinging in the breeze."

"Nothing to worry about there. He doesn't lock that up. He's told me to use it anytime. Comes in handy to fill my water supply." Still feeling lightheaded, Fred raised his canteen. "Wind could have blown it open."

"Not possible."

"Why's that?" Fred wiped the water droplets from his lips with the back of his sleeve.

"I fixed that door for Joe back in July, even added a barn-slide bolt latch. A racoon couldn't figure it out."

Fred screwed the cap back on his canteen. He knew Gerry had been doing odd jobs over at Joe's place for years. From what Gerry had told him, the sporting camp business wasn't what it used to be, so the extra money came in handy, and Joe had someone who kept an eye on the place.

The sun sure was hot for October. Fred removed his ranger hat and ran his hand over his sweaty forehead.

"But the door isn't what has me worried," Gerry continued.

"Why's that?" Fred perked up; his cheeks flushed.

"The rope and bucket were missing. I checked the shed, thinking maybe Joe stored it. I couldn't figure why he'd do that. He knows some of us use that old well when we're out that way. I didn't find it." He gave the dirt bike some gas. "The tarp from the woodpile near the shed was also missing. I know Joe would never leave cordwood uncovered."

Neither of them wanted to say what they were really thinking.

"Seems odd. You going to call him?" Fred had his suspicions and was concerned given what he'd been hearing lately.

"Yeah. I'm headed back to the store now. I'll call when I get there." He wiped the dust from his face with his red bandana. "Bucket could have just fallen down the well. It was on an old rope. I'll bring a tarp back out next week for the wood."

Fred nodded. "Could be. My truck's at the Penobscot Farm boat launch. I was going to stop in for some supplies before camping up on Dead Man Brook for a couple of days. It's my last checks of the season on those operations."

"That sounds like some location to camp." Gerry laughed. "I'd give you a lift, but this here's a one-man ride."

"That's fine with me. That thing is noise pollution. I prefer the peace and quiet of walking."

"Have fun." Gerry hit the gas, kicking up gravel as he peeled away. Fred turned and spit the dust from his mouth.

When Gerry was out of sight, Fred sat down on a boulder and reached into his pack. Folded between the pages of his book was a hand-drawn topographical map, a version of the one he'd been keeping since 1958. The map was coded with markings of locations and dates that started shortly after he was hired on as a forester. There were dates from the 60s, a sparse few from the 70s, but recently, since 1985, he found he was adding a new mark every few months.

He drew a circle about where Joe's camp would be, and dated it – *Monday 10/10/88*.

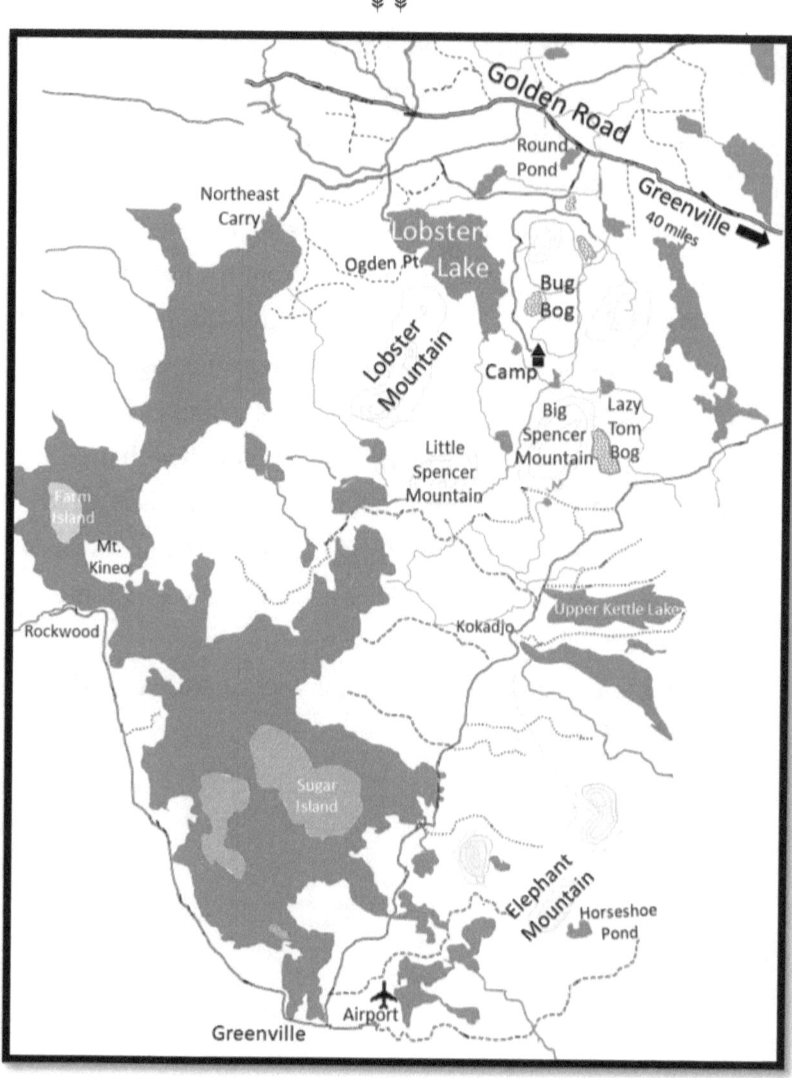

Golden Road
Round Pond
Greenville
40 miles
Northeast Carry
Lobster Lake
Ogden Pt.
Bug Bog
Lobster Mountain
Camp
Big Spencer Mountain
Lazy Tom Bog
Little Spencer Mountain
Farm Island
Mt. Kineo
Upper Kettle Lake
Rockwood
Kokadjo
Sugar Island
Elephant Mountain
Horseshoe Pond
Airport
Greenville

A New York Morning

The grinding shear of metal, followed by the shattering of glass, jolted Sarah out of a deep sleep. She rolled over to glance at the clock, the red-digit display read 6:27.

"Ah, not today."

Angry yelling exploded outside. She flipped off her comforter and pushed the matching purple-flowered curtain aside. A gray fall morning was accentuated with the lines of black, white, and general dreary car colors parked up and down the block. A box truck, with Chinese hand-painted lettering on the side, was idling in the center of the street. Behind the truck, only the back half of an MR2 was visible. Neighbors, none of whom she knew, their heads poking from random windows, were all complaining about the noise to the stranger in the closest window.

A man, pulled himself out of the wreck through the missing rear window. He was laughing. Clenched in his right-hand he waved a brown paper bag at the faces in the windows above; with his left, he jingled his car keys. He took a swig from the bag, and still looking up, licked his lips and said something to a woman in a bra peering out of a second-floor window. The truck driver, hurling a string of expletives at the drunk, grabbed the bag and flung it at the ground. Shards of green glass and liquid spread across the asphalt.

Sarah yanked the curtains closed. "And yet another reason I don't drive in this city," she heard herself say out loud. She flopped back on her bed. Thoughts of trying to go back to sleep floated across the cracks in the ceiling.

Horns blared.

She sighed.

Deciding to make the best of the early wake up, she dressed, walked right by the mayhem in the street, which by now included the officers from three blue and whites, and went for a run at River Park.

On her way home she picked up breakfast and strode along the semi desolate avenue; the Monday holiday keeping most all commuters in the outer-boroughs. On her block, the evidence of the accident had been cleared away, all but the broken glass, which had been pushed into the hydrant space. Three seedy characters were hanging out in front of the building across from hers. She quickened her pace. No matter the time of day, they always seemed to be there, always smoking something, never the same faces. She was uncomfortable as they watched her walk. The smell of something close to burning leaves filled the air.

From inside her building's entry, she peeked through the narrow frosted-glass side window to see the men passing a joint back and forth. They all resembled one another. Black leather jackets. Black leather Boots. Black leather hats. Only their facial tattoos were different. A mustached guy with straight greasy black hair, who couldn't have been more than nineteen, looked directly at the window she was standing behind. He gestured the reefer her way. She jumped back. In all the times she stared through the glass, she never realized people outside might be able to see her. As quick as she could push the key in the knob, she unlocked the inner door, and sprinted up the four flights.

In her apartment, she sat on the paint-chipped kitchen chair – one of an unmatching pair she bought from a thrift-store in the village. Her latest home improvement project had been sprucing up the chairs – they now matched her purple curtains. She untied her sneakers and flipped them to the corner. She stared out the window. Her mind drifted to the ad she originally answered for the apartment, *"with a lovely window on the bright courtyard side of the studio."* A courtyard in the city, that sounded nice to Sarah. On her way to meet the rental agent last year, Sarah imagined sitting at her window looking out over a tree and flower sanctuary where birds would sing as she drank tea. The so-called courtyard turned out to be a paved rectangle, the size of a city bus, an air shaft really, that was only bright at noon when the sun was high overhead.

Directly across, in a tinted pane, ten feet away, her reflection stared back at her. Only once had the black-frosted glass opened, and then only wide enough for someone to flick a cigarette to the cement below. Remembering this, she reached over and closed her curtain.

Sarah poured her cappuccino from the paper cup into her new favorite mug – the one with the moose Joe had bought for her at the Fly-in craft fair. *"To remember your moose sighting,"* he had said.

She ran her fingers over the glossy cover of the latest issue of *"From Here to There."* The picture on the front was the photo she took of a seaplane landing on the still waters of East Cove.

It was her first cover. Oh, how she missed waking up at the inn and looking out over Moosehead Lake. Her thoughts turned to Joe. She looked over at the answering machine – no blinking light.

She started to worry, the way she always did. Maybe she had been too forward inviting him to the city to spend Thanksgiving. Maybe it was too soon to expect him to spend a holiday together. Maybe she was making more of their relationship than was really there. Maybe there was no relationship at all. Maybe, just maybe, she should stop worrying.

She picked up the copy of the *Post* she had grabbed at the newsstand on East 14th. The headlines touted how the local politicians were going to spend Columbus Day. An entire page was devoted to how presidential candidate Dukakis was expected to march in the parade.

Flipping the paper over, she read the sports headline, "***Red Sox Out (again)***."

Hmm, Joe's going to be disappointed about that, she thought. She wondered if he had listened to the game at camp, or was already home, and if he was home, he would have received her postcard. She picked up the white paper bag from the bakery. And if he had read the postcard, why hadn't he called?

The smell of the still warm apple sharlotka escaped as she unfolded the crease. She loved the Russian bakery in her neighborhood; the tiny store was the passion of a husband and wife who did all the baking in the back room. Near the baby-blue painted frame of the window there was room for only one table, the only table in the bakery, the bench wall seat had a view of New Yorkers in a rush – going in both directions.

Some mornings Sarah would sit at that table and amongst the comforting smell of breads and pastries she'd be transported to her mom's kitchen. Sitting there, she'd hand-edit her articles, while chatting with the owner between customers. If Sarah went too many days without stopping, Svetlana would ask, "Miss Sarah, where have you been? We missed you!" The w's always pronounced as v's in Svetlana's strong eastern Ukraine accent. It was nice, in a city of strangers to be recognized – and missed. This morning, Svetlana had asked again, "So, would you move to this Maine, far from the ocean?" Sarah side-stepped the question and ordered her rogaliki, which Svetlana dusted with extra powdered sugar, to go.

Biting into the Russian cake, the taste of the cinnamon and apple, reminded her of Thanksgiving. Sarah's mother *loved* Thanksgiving. She'd start her meal planning the day after Halloween. If Joe could be convinced to travel to the city for the holiday, it would be the first Thanksgiving Sarah would miss with her mom. She realized the sooner she hinted she might be staying in the city this year, the sooner her mom would forgive her. Sarah took the receiver off the hook and dialed.

※※

Sitting at his kitchen table flipping through his latest stack of sketches. Something was bothering Joe about his sketch of the pileated woodpeckers. He took a bite of a sausage link that was hanging from the fork in his right hand.

Looking through the window, he focused on a tree, a few brown leaves stubbornly stuck to the edge of the branches. He could see the birds; it wasn't difficult to do. Back in the spring, three of them pecked at that same half-dead maple, their red crests a blur as they drilled for bugs.

Using a thick maroon pencil, he added a few strategic strokes to the male's cheek stripe. He worked on the sketch with his black, gray, and white pencils, adding in bushes, shadows, and a pair of nuthatches on a neighboring branch. He held the paper up to the window. With the scene in the background, he contemplated what the picture was missing. He pulled a blank piece of drawing paper from the stack.

Tired of staring at the blank page, he poured a cup of coffee, and looked off into space. Finally, the pencil hit the paper. "Hello, Sarah. How are you?" he printed.

He thought, *Now what? What will I say next?* He tried to think of how their conversation would go. *Yes, I got your postcard. – – Sure, Central Park looks impressive from the sky.* No, he couldn't say that, she might take it the wrong way. He tried to figure a way to tell her he wanted to visit, without seeming anxious, or apprehensive.

Crumpling the paper, he threw it in the kindling bin, and walked toward the phone. Stalling, he picked up the coffee pot and filled his mug. Tilting his head to take a sip, he saw the wall clock. It occurred to him that Sarah might not even be out of bed yet.

He sat back down at the table. He stared at the pileated sketch.

"Ah, that's what's missing," he said to himself. The pencils brushed across the paper. Red. Gray. Black. Tan. Brown. Blue. Blending the colors, he finished with a rub of his cloth drafting pad. Joe was pleased with how it turned out. He lifted his mug.

Joe's hand jerked and he spilt some coffee when the wall phone started jiggling on the holder. R.C. ran around barking.

"Calm down, boy, it's just the phone." He lifted the receiver. "Hello?"

"Hi, Joe."

On hearing Sarah's voice, Joe boomed back, "Good morning." He put his hand over the phone, "R.C., quiet!"

"I hope it's not too early to call."

"Are you kidding, R.C. woke me before sun up, we already went for a hike around the town pond." He wiped the drops of coffee with a napkin.

Sarah laughed. "And I thought I was doing good getting a quick run in this morning. When did you get back from camp?"

"Yesterday afternoon."

The corners of Sarah's mouth turned downward. She managed to ask, "I take it you watched the Red Sox game?"

"Don't rub it in."

"Oh, well. There's always next year," Sarah said, in a cheery, optimistic tone. "Did you get my postcard."

"I did."

Sarah waited, hoping Joe would say more. The second of silence seemed to last an hour. "So? What do you think?"

"I don't know, Sarah. Me, in New York City?"

"It'll be fun. I'll show you all around."

"Who'll watch R.C.?"

"How about your neighbors? You've told me how much they love him." Sarah was hoping Joe wasn't trying to find a way out. She continued, "I don't want to pressure you, but when might you decide?"

"I've already decided."

Since Joe didn't say anything more, Sarah had a sinking feeling he wasn't going to visit her. "And what's your decision?" she asked, tentatively.

"Of course, I'm coming. How could I possibly pass up spending time with you?"

"Yeah! That makes me so happy." The pitch in her voice rose two octaves.

For the next fifteen minutes they made plans for Joe's visit, and then spent a few minutes talking business.

"Joe, I don't want to seem pushy, but Barone is getting on me to finish the November issue. Is it possible you can send me your drawings this week?"

"Sure thing. I finished the final touch-ups this morning on that sketch of the woodpeckers I told you about. I almost forgot to add the yelling red squirrel. The racket outside that morning was like a construction zone – between the peckers hammering and that squirrel squealing. I think he was accusing the birds of stealing his stash. I mentioned that noisy little guy to you. Remember?"

"Yes. I remember." Sarah chuckled, amused at Joe's love for the animals. She didn't get into the wake-up call she was given. A double squelch of an NYPD siren squealed on its way up the block. She sighed, longing for the tranquil sounds of Maine.

"Listen, Sarah, is it too early to start planning for a winter trip to Maine? Maybe for New Year's? The quiet of the woods under a thick blanket of snow is only interrupted by the crackling of the fire, and an occasional boom from ice expanding out on the lake."

Sarah didn't say anything, she couldn't; the arch of her lips prevented her from talking.

"Sarah?"

Her face relaxed and she blurted, "Of course. I'd love to visit. One condition."

"What's that?"

"You have to promise to keep me warm up there in the north woods."

"Don't you worry about that. I've stacked four cords of dry wood. The camp stays toasty even on the coldest of nights."

"Oh, Joe." She brushed the crumbs from the table into her hand.

"What?"

"Nothing. Being at Lobster Lake in the winter will be magical." She dumped the crumbs in the sink. "But, back to the sketches."

"I'll drop them at the post office tomorrow."

"Okay, that's great. I'm sorry, but I've got to run. I have to be on Fifth Avenue in a little while to cover the Parade."

"Ah, you and a million of your closest friends."

Over near the door, R.C. whined.

"You might say that. And what about you?" she asked.

"I'm going over to our downtown metropolis of Bangor to watch our parade." Joe opened the back door and R.C. took off after a squirrel.

"Are there even enough people to be in it and watch at the same time?" From a drawer she pulled out a towel and headed to the bathroom.

"Funny. Keep making jokes, but the sign reads, *The Way Life Should Be*, for a reason."

"Mmm." She thought about that feeling. "Can you call me later in the week?"

"For what?" Joe realized what he had said as the words left his mouth. He clenched his jaw.

Sarah was quiet for a moment, when she answered her voice was barely audible. "Just to talk."

"Oh, sure." He smacked himself in the forehead. "How about Wednesday night?"

"Wednesday it is. Talk to you then."

"Have a great day. Bye."

"Bye." She put her cordless phone on the back of the toilet, pulled open the shower curtain, and turned on the hot water hoping there'd actually be some.

While she waited for the water to warm, she considered her feelings for Joe. Since September she wondered if what she felt was real. She thought about their letters, the phone calls, and how she wanted to get to know him more. She stepped under the spray and Svetlana's question rolled over her. *Would she ever move to Maine?*

⊰⊱

Stowing his pencils back in the chipped coffee cup, the morning paper caught Joe's eye. The hardware store was running a sale on snowblowers. Checking the time, he still had two hours before the parade.

He whistled. "Come on, boy. Let's go out to the garage and give that snow machine a tune-up."

⊰⊱

Before Gerry could call get to calling Joe, he had to feed his sled dogs. When he was finished with that four guests who were staying in one of the cabins chewed his ear off about the game laws. When he finally got around to calling, he let Joe's phone ring and ring. There was no answer. He decided to try a different route.

"Hi, Karen. It's Gerry out at Northeast Carry store. No, this won't take long. – – Yes, I understand you're busy there. But has Joe Parker been in? – – I was just at his camp. He's packed up for the season and gone. – – I know you're not his mother. Look can I leave him a message? – – I understand you're not the switchboard, but maybe you can pass it along to Don or Buddy – – Why? Because they might get a hold of him before I can reach him. – – Yes, it's important. I think. – – No I'd rather not say. – – Of course I trust you. But look, you know I still use a party line out this way. – – You can just tell Don or Buddy to tell Joe to call me. It's about Joe's well house. Thank you."

In a rush, Karen wrote down the message on the back of a customer's bill, which the woman, after paying, put in her purse along with a stack of napkins.

An hour later Buddy arrived at his usual time for his coffee break. He was still wearing his nail apron from the hardware store. Karen searched for the slip of paper. Giving up, she relayed what she could recall of the message from Gerry. Buddy didn't think it was much of a message, but he told her he'd try and call Joe later during his break. Flipping over the morning paper and reading the sports section, he relived every moment of last night's excruciating Red Sox game. It wasn't long before he was in violent agreement with everyone else who was seated at the counter, arguing about all the lousy plays and bad calls by the umps. By the time he walked across the street to finish his shift ringing up paint, screens, and leaf rakes, he had forgotten all about Karen's relayed message.

⁂

Leading up to his Big Apple visit, Joe and Sarah talked on the phone every few days. In the mailings of sketches he sent to Sarah, Joe wrote her notes about Maine – the foliage, the hikes he went on, and his trip with Charlie to the Maine Snowmobile Show down at the Civic Center.

For her part, Sarah spent the next month explaining to her mom why she wasn't coming home for Thanksgiving. Her mom encouraged Sarah to bring Joe along, "to meet the family." That wasn't something Sarah wanted to put Joe through. Sure, her family was great, Joe was great, but a family holiday together – this soon, the stress wasn't something she could handle right now. She figured it would be best to keep him a mystery a bit longer, especially given how her last few relationships had turned out – to her Mom's disappointment.

With the busy fall hunting season and his full bookings of sports 'from away' to guide, Gerry was extra busy. When he had a moment and remembered about Joe's well house and missing tarp, he decided what he discovered at Parker Camp wasn't all that big of a deal to worry about. He never got around to calling.

Season's Greetings

Lock, Stock, and Barrel

Wednesday November 23, 1988

A wreath, five feet around, hung on the bow of the Katahdin steamship. Red bows were strung on the evergreen garland that hung across Pritham Avenue. The store windows were dressed in red and green. It was the day before Thanksgiving, and Greenville was already prepared for their Christmas parade on Saturday. Karen was wearing out her Barbara Mandrell tape getting in the spirit. She had rewound the tape twice already to play, *"This Time of the Year."*

The bell on the door jingled. Buddy turned his head to see if it was Buster. Davey, a local Maine Guide, didn't look Buddy's way, rather he went directly to his typical seat at the window counter. Everyone knew he sat there to keep an eye on his Jeep. He got a kick out of people's faces when they spotted his vehicle with the moose antlers strapped on the front grill. The lettering on the doors read – *"Moose Tours – Sighting Guaranteed or Lunch is on Me."*

"I'll be right with you, Davey." Karen said. His hand went up, his gaze out the window unchanged.

She placed a Reuben in front of Buddy and whispered, "You hear the latest? This time it was pots and winter jackets."

"I heard it was the Harris place." He lifted the sandwich and took a bite.

"You know that's up near Joe's." She turned to get him a bottle of ketchup.

Hitting the side of the bottle over his fries, he said, "Ain't nobody has a camp up close to Joe's. But, you're right, the Harris camp is over on Caribou Lake. That's close enough."

"Do you think we should let Joe know?" Karen filled his mug.

"He's down in New York visiting with Sarah. Gerry usually checks on the place." With his fork, he scooped up a glob of kraut and dressing that had squeezed from his sandwich. "Besides, most of these rumors are just that – rumors. People misplace stuff all the time. Now they've got to thinking someone has taken their junk."

Her lips pursed. She placed the lime-green phone from under the counter in front of him. "Oh. Give him a ring all the same. You can leave a message."

A mechanical voice answered. Buddy hung up the receiver.

"Why didn't you leave a message."

"Can't."

Karen waited for an explanation. Buddy added sugar to his coffee. Hunching her shoulders, Karen leaned forward and slapped the counter. "Why not?"

Buddy jerked back. He pushed the sugar he spilled into a pile. "You see, Joe has had that answering machine for three, going on four years now. The tape has been full for as long as I can remember. So, unless he's home, there's no leaving him a message."

Karen wiped the counter with a towel. "Why doesn't he erase the tape?"

"Are we talking about the same Joe? He's not one for this new technology." Buddy reached for the paper. "I'll try him again next week when he's back."

⇊⇊

On a Trail – Close to Lobster Lake

The wind storm last night had dropped birch and pine trees in every direction across the trails. It was only a few weeks ago the club had finished up their fall maintenance to be ready for the season. Now they were back at it again.

Thinking about the trails over towards Parker cabin, Don yelled, "Hey, guys, I'm gonna take a run over the other side of the lake. Be back in an hour."

The three snowmobile club members didn't stop their job of loading wood into the bed of the truck. With a free hand, Bobby saluted.

Don waved back and started his ATV.

With plans made for a New Year's Eve gathering at Lobster Lake, Don had told Joe he'd have the trails in top shape for snowmobiling. All Joe had to do was to make sure Sarah didn't get cold feet about spending a week in the Maine woods, when there would be five feet of snow on the ground and temperatures were ten below zero. Don figured he had the easy part of the preparation.

After sawing up two blow-downs, Don decided to swing by the cabin. Pulling down the dirt drive, a strip of dead weeds marking the center, Don was always amazed at how neat and tidy Joe kept his dooryard. There wasn't an item out of place, or in a different location, anywhere in the pine-needle covered clearing. The rowboat was stored on a wooden rack on the right side of the shed; not one stray Adirondack chair was left out; the ashes from the fire pit had been shoveled; and even the firewood on the porch was stacked to a uniform height with each piece almost identical in length.

He pulled his ATV up to the front porch steps. His head jerked around to the left and right, almost thinking he'd hear Joe yelling to get the machine off the fieldstones and back to the driveway. A big smirk crossed his face, remembering Joe was hundreds of miles away in New York.

May as well visit Aunt Alice while I'm here, Don thought. When he came out of the old outhouse, the one Joe never bothered to tear down after installing indoor plumbing, he noticed the swing-out window on the side of the camp was open. He stepped up to the front door and checked the doorknob. It was locked. He lifted the 'Welcome to Camp,' sign away from the siding, and picked the key off the small nail that was placed in the indented space between the logs.

The camp smelled of pine. All camps did after they've been empty for any length of time with no wood smoke, no bacon frying, and no sweaty hiking clothes left on the back of a chair. It was dull inside; all but one of the curtains were drawn tight. The only light came from the window over the writing desk. Don knew Joe had a specific routine for buttoning up the camp at the end of the season, so an open window and open curtain was out of character.

Newspapers and magazines that Don knew Joe kept neatly stacked on the shelves, issues he kept for particular stories he thought were important historically, were tossed around on the writing desk. Some were on the floor. Don leaned over and looked out the window. The pop-in screen was lying on the ground. A single brown leaf had landed on top of it. *Couldn't have fallen out too long ago,* he thought.

He reached for the string hanging on the window frame and pulled it tight against the sash. The lock, was a simple hook and eye. When he slid the hook in place, there was more play in the window then he liked. To reduce the gap, he turned the hook tighter into the frame. Satisfied it was closed, he walked to the front window and threw open the winter drapes.

Making his way from the living room, to the kitchen, and the two bedrooms, he opened the remaining curtains to inspect if everything was where he expected it to be. It wasn't difficult, Joe took after his parents when it came to camp organization. The Parkers were meticulous about a place for everything and everything being in its place. For as long as Don had been coming to Parker Cabin, over thirty years now, the same cast-iron pots hung on the same hooks, plates were organized smallest to largest on the open shelf, and spare batteries were ordered triple-As to Ds in the third drawer down in the kitchen. Even the deck of playing cards had its place. The Parkers stored their cards in a faded light green Tupperware pickle container that sat in the corner of the kitchen counter. As a kid, Don thought it was neat. The container had a strainer on a handle that dipped into the deep storage to pull out a homemade pickle.

Retired from pickle storage since 1975, pulling up the handle now delivered playing cards along with pens and a small pad for score keeping.

He put his hand on the handle and pulled it up. "Huh. Guess I know one of the things to get Joe for Christmas." The last deck he knew to be in the container was the deck from the fishing vacation he and Joe took together. Alaska Airlines had given each passenger a deck during a flight delay. They had played plenty of hands of Texas Hold'em with those cards while talking about the salmon they caught up there.

Spinning around one last time, everything seemed to be where he expected it to be. He stood in the doorway of Joe's bedroom and surveyed the living room one more time. The open front door pushed in ever so slightly sending a creak from the tight, rusty hinges through the cabin. Don spun around.

Walking across the room he felt the lingering wind from yesterday's storm rushing in. He pushed the door closed and nodded. Behind it, Joe's gun safe was closed and locked. A worn-leather shotgun belt was nailed alongside. Ever since Stan had been surprised by a bear on the front porch, the Parkers left a shotgun in the safe, but they had never needed to fire a shot in warning.

Satisfied the wind must have been the culprit of the mess, he closed all the curtains and drapes. Outside, he lifted the screen back into position and with his closed fist he slammed it tight in the frame. He turned the rusty, bent, penny-nail latches inward to keep it from falling out again. He figured he'd swing back to check on things again in a couple of weeks – weather permitting.

The growl of Don's ATV faded in the distance.

It was silent – until the sound of a twig snapped, a squirrel began a continuous string of warning chatter, and the man stepped from behind the tarp-covered woodpile. He walked down the trail towards Bug Bog and disappeared into the forest.

Almost a New Year

✳

December 30, 1988

"Comin' through," yelled Karen.

From the record player under the counter Johnny Cash was singing about, "That Christmasy Feeling."

"Thank you, ma'am," said Buster when Karen placed two lumberjack lunch specials on the counter in front of him and Buddy

"How many times I need to tell you, Buster? Don't call me ma'am! Makes me sound old."

"Ah, you know I don't mean anything by it."

She exhaled. "Say it again and tell yourself I didn't mean anything by it when I throw a five-day-old dinner roll at your head." Buddy, two stools over, let out one of his, "Hee hee hee," snort-chuckles and then quickly turned away from Karen's scowl.

Buster swallowed hard. Picking up his meatloaf sandwich, he asked, "How much longer you going to be playing Christmas music? It's New Year's Eve tomorrow."

"My diner, my music." She turned and yelled, "Mrs. Claus, Comin' through." She pushed through the door back to the kitchen.

"More like the Grinch. Guess she got out of bed on the wrong side today." Taking the top bun off his sandwich, Buster slammed the side of the ketchup bottle.

"Better not let her hear you say that." Buddy shoved a fry in his mouth. "Pass me the ketchup."

"Hear anything from Joe about his trip to the Big Apple?"

"No. Haven't talked to him about it." Buddy shook the bottle over his fries.

"Everything all set for the sled dog race?"

"As best can be. We've got some icing up on the trails. But there's snow in the forecast." Buddy slurped the last of his coke through his straw.

"That ought to take care of it." Buster bit into his sandwich.

"Yep. We need a good snow pack for the dogs."

"Excuse me, gentlemen."

Buddy and Buster turned to the voice behind their stools.

Buster lifted his head upwards. "What can we do you for?"

The man's left cheek scrunched his eye half closed and he grimaced at the blob of ketchup on Buster's belly. He turned to Buddy and placed a map on the counter. "Can you tell me if there's still a camp store up this way?" He pointed to the northern end of the lake.

"The only store up that way is the Northeast Carry Store and Lodge. Been there since I was a kid – before that even."

"Is it open this time of year?"

"Sure. Open three-sixty-five."

"Does this road lead that way?"

Buster squinted to where the man was pointing and answered for Buddy. "The Golden Road? Yep, it goes that way."

"Thank you." The man picked up his map, slid it back in his pocket, dropped a folded ten-dollar bill on the table where he was sitting, and left the diner.

Buddy and Buster walked to the window. They watched him haul himself up into a lifted Ford Bronco. It was all black with windows completely tinted over. A winch, with a cable heavy enough to pull out a tank, was mounted behind a menacing looking bull bar. On the roof, six spots lights could have lit up the entire Greenville High School ballfield.

"Strange guy."

Buster nodded. "Wonder what he's preparing for."

Buddy gave Buster an elbow and turned his accent up. "I bet he's gonna be somethin' sore when he finds out he cahn't get they-uh from hee-ah, even in that there'ah monster vehicle of his. If I was you, I wouldn't want to be here when he drives back this a-way."

The growl of the truck pulling from the curb vibrated the glass. Buster wiped his forehead. "He didn't ask if he could drive there by car this time of year. He just asked if the road went that way."

The sucking of air made a whooshing whistle sound through Buddy's lips.

"Maybe you should have asked what he wanted with Gerry's store." Buster nudged Buddy back with his arm on the way back to their stools.

"You know, I could swear I've seen him someplace before." Buddy scratched behind his ear.

"From where?" Buster was skeptical.

"Not sure. It'll come to me." Buddy leaned his elbows on the counter and raised his head toward the cake platter on the back counter. "Those turnovers look pretty good."

"Yeah. You should get one." Buster never even looked over.

"Comin' through." The kitchen door flung open and Karen came through backwards, carrying a pot of coffee in each hand.

Buddy held out his mug. As Karen was pouring, he stated to Buster, "Don mentioned he and Linda are staying at Joe's camp for New Year's. Sarah will be up."

Karen stopped pouring. "Are you kidding me? With what's happening up there? And they're bringing the girls?"

Buddy coughed, and motioned to Karen with his mug that was only half full. She put the pot down; he finished pouring himself.

"Ah, you're not still believing in any of that. Are you, Karen?" Buddy wrapped his hand around the tiny stainless container, the handle too small for his fingers, and poured cream into his mug. The lid tinged closed when he set it down.

"Sure do. My cousin has a camp up off the Golden Road, close to Hannibal's Crossing. I'll tell you, what she's told me would make you wonder." The record had finished playing the last song, the staticky sound of the needle went round and round. Karen lifted the arm off the vinyl.

"Such as?" Buddy held a cold fry halfway to his mouth.

Her eyes scanned the tables of customers. She leaned in close to the guys, her voice became low and raspy. "At first, I felt like you guys. It was all in people's minds, I said. Then Di, that's my cousin,…" Karen was interrupted by a timer in the kitchen. "Oh geez, I almost forgot about the pot pies for tonight's special. I'll be right back."

Buddy, realizing he hadn't ordered his apple turnover, walked behind the counter to help himself. "I think Don said Joe was picking up Sarah this morning at the airport."

Buster was scanning the Marden's ad in the paper and didn't look up.

Let It Snow

Bangor International Airport

The cold from outside migrated to Joe's hands pressed against the large pane of tinted glass. It was hard to tell if it was morning or afternoon. The sky was gray. The fuel trucks were gray. The planes were gray. The snow on the luggage vehicles looked gray.

An announcement declaring yet another delayed flight shook Joe back to the stale, hot air, of the terminal building. On the tarmac a plane with profiles of faces in the oval windows, sat idling. The smell of exhaust seeped under the double metal gangway doors. The de-icing crew was spraying it for the second time.

The small airport was busier than usual with travelers excited to be going somewhere for the holiday weekend. However, thanks to the falling snow, there was little actual going anywhere for anyone. Waiting on the weather, some people were patiently reading, others were watching the television that continually looped a fifteen-minute clip of "Maine – Things to Do and Places to See," others were dozing off, and a young couple was desperately trying to keep their three toddlers occupied with stuffed animals, keychains, and Cheerios. Sitting across from Joe, a man wearing a UMaine Black Bear sweatshirt, had his head back, eyes closed, and was snoring louder than a diesel on a lobster boat.

To escape the chain-sawing bear, Joe paced up and down the one and only aisle of Bangor International. He paused at the arrival monitor to check it for the hundredth time. Numbers in green flickered on a black background. All, but three, of the arrivals were cancelled, and those three were late. Sarah's flight was one of them, and it was posted with a thirty-minute delay – her flight was already an hour overdue.

He started towards the gate desk, but stopped when the agent looked up and caught his eye. The agent, with her hair in one long braid that reached below her waist, was a woman of little patience. Joe had already been scolded twenty minutes ago, when she said to him, *"Sir, do you see that monitor on the wall behind me?"* Before Joe could respond, she had continued, *"You've asked me three times now. My monitor displays the same flight times you see on the arrival screens. Trust me, I have zero secret information behind this desk."*

Seeing the *"Go ahead, make my day,"* look in the woman's eyes, and not wanting to push his luck, he changed course and sat in the nearest black vinyl seat, the only one left that didn't have a tear in it with white stuffing hanging out. Within two minutes, he was anxious again. He stood. He paced.

Joe didn't need to make the twenty-minute drive to the airport as early as he did, and he certainly didn't need to leave his house the same time Sarah arrived at JFK for her 6:50 a.m. flight. But he did, and he was here now, so he worried.

He took a seat again, this time next to an older gentleman in overalls. He nodded.

The man tipped his hat. "You waitin' on a woman?"

Joe turned with a grin. "Yeah. Is it obvious? How 'bout you?"

"Son, since nineteen forty-two, I've been waiting on one woman or another." They both laughed. "Name's Floyd." The man held out his hand.

"Hi. I'm Joe. Nice to meet you."

"Where you from?"

"Right here, Bangor. And you?"

"Old Town. Today I'm waiting on my sister. She's spending New Year's with us." He pointed at the arrival screen. "As long as the Boston flight doesn't turn around."

Joe nodded. "I'm picking up my friend, Sarah. She's on the flight from New York."

"Never been that far south. How 'bout you?"

"I was there back at Thanksgiving, to visit Sarah."

"I'm getting the indication she's more than a friend." Floyd raised his head slightly in Joe's direction.

Joe thought it seemed strange to say girlfriend at his age, but he sure hoped that was the case. And besides, Sarah had introduced him as her *significant other* to a few of her friends, so he figured it was official.

He met Floyd's gaze. "I imagine your indication is correct."

Floyd knowingly grinned. "Did ya see any of the sights?"

"A few. We took the elevator up to the observation deck of the Empire State Building."

Joe was more talkative than usual, must have been his nerves. He rattled on to Floyd about the places he and Sarah went, where they ate, and her small apartment. He wrapped up with the surprise he found.

"But I tell you, the strangest find was an art shop, where they sold pictures and prints, but through a secret door, there was a bar and poolhall."

"A kind-of speakeasy?"

"Yeah, I guess so. I was looking through some old black and white photos and people kept coming through a disguised door."

"Did ya go back and have a pint?"

Joe laughed. "No. But I did buy some prints."

"Oh, yeah? Of Lady Liberty?" The man shuffled in his seat.

"No. Would you believe, places in Maine."

"You went all the way to New York, and bought pictures of Maine?"

"Do you believe in synchronicity?"

Floyd tilted his head.

Rubbing the back of his neck, Joe asked, "Can I buy you a coffee? Seeing we're both waiting."

"Sure. I've been sitting so long, these old legs have forgotten what it feels like to stand."

At the other end of the terminal, they discovered the coffee shop had closed. No sign. No explanation.

"We could get one from the machine." Joe offered.

Floyd shrugged. "Nah – that stuff is terrible." He gestured to his right. "May as well sit there. Different scenery anyway." At an empty gate they sat across from one another.

He held out a pack of gum. Joe declined. "Tell me, what was so interesting about the pictures you found?"

Joe leaned back in his seat, crossed his legs, and told a total stranger about what he discovered in the city; he only paused once when a ground crew associate leaned against a post to unwrap a candy bar. Once the man threw the wrapper in the trash and walked on, Joe finished his story. He put his hands behind his head. "And I bought six of the photos – the one of Greenville, I hung in Sarah's apartment."

The old man stared out to the gray sky. "That is some coincidence. In my younger days I spent a good deal of time fishing up in the Moosehead area, definitely a place untouched by time – in many ways." His voice trailed off thinking of a memory. "I reeled in the biggest fish I ever caught in my life near East Outlet. Ten pounder."

Joe started to respond with a fish story of his own, "My biggest fish was on a trip to Alaska . . ." The screech of an announcement drowned out his words.

"Bangor International is pleased to announce the arrival of flight 2639 from Boston. Passengers may be met at gate number two."

"That's me." The old man shimmied himself to his feet.

Joe stood to shake his hand. "It was nice talking with you, Floyd."

"Same here. Have a Happy New Year with that girl." The man left the newspaper he had been holding on the seat and with a slow limp walked to the gate.

❋

Tired of sitting, Joe went for another walk down the terminal. The flickering, "Fresh Brewed," sign of the automated vending machine, stationed outside the men's room, caught his attention. He dropped three quarters into the slot, pushed the plastic button for a black coffee, and waited for the machine to gurgle and come to life. Nothing happened. He pushed the red button for the coin return. Nothing came back.

Annoyed, he dug his hand into the left pocket of his jeans and added another quarter. This time a paper cup dropped into place behind a scratched plastic door. A stream of black liquid ran into the cup. When the dripping stopped the tiny hand-size door slid open. Taking a sip, he realized the third cup didn't taste any better than the first two he drank earlier, and this one cost him a buck. He walked into the men's room and dumped the brown sludge down the sink.

On his way back to the gate, Joe stopped. A woman, in a long silver coat, was hugging the snorer, the one in the UMaine Black Bears sweatshirt. What Joe had failed to notice earlier was the bouquet of flowers the man now handed to the woman. At the presentation of the arrangement, the woman's face lit up. She pulled the man close for a kiss.

Feeling a twinge of panic, Joe spun around and took long strides down the center of the concourse. Six seconds later he stood in the middle of, **Maine Coast to Mountain – News and Gifts**, the one, and only, shop at the airport. His head shot left and right over the short shelves. The young lady behind the counter gave him a thin smile. She knew his predicament, she'd seen it hundreds of times, no – thousands of times. There was no sense asking him if he needed help finding something, it was hopeless.

The metal racks displayed typical stuff that screamed, *"It's obvious I forgot to get you something before I arrived at the airport."* There were Maine postcards in a rotating display, boxes of salt water taffy imported from the Jersey shore, keychains with names, and sweatshirts with, *"Someone went to Bar Harbor, and I got this Great Sweatshirt."* Shelves held bottles of fruit flavored Tums (required after airport food), souvenir size Maine maple syrup (enough for maybe one pancake), stuffed lobsters (toys for children, not for eating), and ceramic loons in five sizes (all with eerie red eyes).

He picked up a pack of Tic Tacs – original flavor – for him, not Sarah – to kill his coffee breath in anticipation of a 'great to see you' kiss. For Sarah he selected a small moose. It was soft, had a welcoming grin, and was dressed in a sweatshirt with an outline of Maine on the front – corny and certainly something he figured she didn't have.

The PA speaker in the ceiling crackled. *"North Woods Air is pleased to announce the arrival of flight 44-41. Passengers may be met at gate one or at baggage claim."* Joe rushed to the register to pay and didn't even wait for his change.

He watched the plane taxi to the gate. Two ground crew workers, in orange vests and protective headphones, dragged a steep, narrow metal staircase over to the side of the plane. While one went about pulling luggage from the belly and hurling it on a cart, the other kicked the snow off each step as he climbed toward the cabin. He gave a bang on the side of the fuselage and the door swung open.

The first person to step out was a tall man who almost had to bend in half to get himself through the miniature door. Clutching a leather briefcase in one hand and a coat in the other, he paused and looked around. Realizing he'd be walking to the terminal building, he pulled on his long wool peacoat before descending the stairs. His gray hair blew in the icy wind.

Next to exit was a woman in a red coat, black scarf, and red hat that was coated in white before she reached the bottom step. More passengers followed, all shivering when they stepped into the cold. Wind blew the white flurries in swirls. Flashing red and green lights blinked along the runway. The song being piped through the terminal speakers was Ella Fitzgerald's, *"I've Got My Love to Keep Me Warm."* The scene resembled a shaken snow globe. Joe was looking forward to the week with Sarah, and keeping her warm.

Person after person cautiously stepped down the slippery stairs. In his mind, he gave each of them a reason for coming to Maine. A woman carrying a hat box, was arriving for a holiday gala. A couple in matching blue LL Bean ski jackets were here to meet family at The Loaf. The lady crying, a funeral – or maybe just happy to be back home. A college student, wearing a UMO sweatshirt and UCONN knit hat, he guessed was returning after spending Christmas with her dad and stepmom in Connecticut.

An overly happy, elderly couple stepped out arm in arm. He could hear them singing, *"Let it Snow."* They certainly were joyous for the season.

When nobody else exited, the gate employee ducked and stepped inside. Five seconds later he emerged carrying a backpack. Behind him stepped a woman in a black knit hat, puffy deep purple jacket, jeans, and winter boots. She could have been a model for an outdoor gear catalogue. Before Sarah started down the steps, she looked towards the terminal. He waved, his hand moving back and forth as if he were washing a window. She mouthed a, "Hello," and wiggled her gloved fingers.

Down on the tarmac, Sarah picked the one remaining suitcase from the rolling cart near the entry to the building, brushed the snow from it, and walked through the double doors.

"Hi!" Sarah threw her arms around his neck. "I've sure missed you," she whispered.

When Sarah loosened her hug and stepped back, Joe started to say, "Hi," but before he could get the word out, Sarah reached around his head, closed her eyes, and pulled him close for a kiss. Startled, his eyes darted around. The gate agent raised an eyebrow his way. Joe swung Sarah sideways.

Sighing, Sarah loosened her embrace, looked into his eyes, and hugged him again.

"Was the flight okay?" he asked.

She pulled him to the window. "Joe, look at the size of that can."

"Big one, eh?" He raised his eyebrows, sarcastically. He reached for the luggage and placed his hand along her lower back, leading her towards the exit.

"It held maybe sixteen people. My eardrums are about shot from the propeller noise, which wasn't near loud enough to drown out the caroling of a couple who sang the entire flight, only pausing to take sips of their drinks. I don't mean to complain, but you know how I hate flying. I had no idea it would be on a prop plane. I didn't even think they flew those anymore. And that couple sang only one song the entire flight."

"Let me guess," he sang, "*Let It Snow*."

"Yes! How'd you know?"

"I could hear them in here when they walked off the plane."

"I have to admit, they did have good harmony."

"Almost forgot. This is for you. It's not much."

"Oh, what a cute moose. He's so soft. Thank you. Do you think we'll see any real moose near camp?"

"There's always a possibility. Where we're headed there are more moose than people."

Sarah held Joe's hand as they walked. As soon as Joe stuck the key in the passenger side door, R.C. bolted awake and pressed his nose to the window.

"Hold on, boy. One second." Joe placed the luggage behind the seat and held the panting dog from tackling Sarah.

"Hi there, R.C.!" Sarah gave the dog a snuggle.

"Just nudge him over and hop on in."

When Joe started the engine, George Strait was singing about how a woman made his dreams come true. He unconsciously picked up the verse at the title line, "You're something special to me." Then turning to Sarah, he asked, "Do you like country music?"

"I like *this* song." She squeezed his leg. "And I enjoy your singing it."

"Thanks. But you'll be glad I cook better than I sing."

"I think you sing fine. And based on my last visit, I certainly am looking forward to your cooking."

"I'll do my best, but remember, we're going to be out in the middle of the woods, there won't be any gourmet meals."

"Not a problem. What do you have planned?"

"We'll be going snowshoeing, snowmobiling, and doing some ice fishing on Lobster Lake."

"All sounds good to me. I'm looking forward to this wilderness expedition away from my tiny apartment."

"And those characters that hang out across the street?" Joe asked.

"Them too. Did I tell you? The police had a sting going and turns out that gang was involved in break-ins all throughout the city."

"Does it ever worry you – living there?"

"Sure. But it comes with the territory. It's New York. Maybe I'll look for a place in Jersey. I can commute by ferry."

"Why not Maine?" Joe turned to her. His eyebrows raised, in invitation.

She wasn't sure how to respond. It wasn't as if she hadn't thought of it. But what was Joe really saying. "Where would I work?" she asked, with a look that said, I have a job, you know.

"Um, do I need to remind you, that magazine owner has you on special assignment covering Maine stories."

Sarah considered the suggestion. It's not as if she hadn't been thinking about it – a lot. Being in Maine, she'd be closer to the subject of her writing, at least while the assignment lasted. Then there was Joe; she'd wouldn't mind being closer to him. He made her laugh, he appreciated her work, she missed him when they weren't together. Oh, but could she ever leave the city behind?

She changed the subject. "How long will it take to get to camp?"

At the turn of the conversation, he kept his eyes straight ahead. "We'll be there before you know it."

In Monson, Joe pulled close to the curb along Main Street and parked. He looked down quickly when he felt the tug from Sarah's gloved hand wrap around his as they crossed the street.

She read the sign over the door out loud, "**AT Trailside Barbeque & Rooms**. That an interesting combo."

"This town is popular with hikers taking a break from the Appalachian Trail." Joe pointed at a painting of the trail on the side of a building. "It runs close to here." He held the door open for her.

"Oh, I like the north woods décor." Sarah took in the log cabin interior and log furniture.

"Hey, Joe." yelled the man who was tending the small counter.

"Howdy, Mitch. Happy New Year – almost."

"Same to you. Have a seat. And who's this?"

"Mitch meet Sarah. Sarah meet Mitch"

"Hello, Sarah. Welcome to Monson."

"Thank you. Nice to meet you."

Sarah looked for a menu. Joe took her shoulders and turned her towards a blackboard.

"Oh. What do you typically get?" Her eyes roamed over the listings.

"The pork sandwich with the slaw is a favorite of mine."

"Sounds good to me. I'm starving."

Joe ordered and they sat at the long table made from a split pine tree. The surface was coated with so many layers of varnish it reflected the moose, bear, and deer photos that hung on the walls.

When he paid the bill, on Sarah's request, he bought an extra hunk of the cornbread for the rest of the ride.

Stepping to the road, Joe yanked Sarah back to the sidewalk. A pickup truck, with a tarp flapping in its wake, came barreling down Main Street going twenty miles over the speed limit. A metal pipe bounced out of the bed and clanged its way across the asphalt. Joe squinted and made a mental note of the plate.

"That was nuts. What's he thinking?" Sarah brushed the spray of slush off her jeans.

"Some people are simply oblivious." He bent down, picked up the pipe from the road, and placed it in the bed of his truck.

Can't Get There From Here

An exhale and an "I missed Moosehead," came from the passenger seat when the truck crested the top of Indian Hill. The snow-covered East Cove was punctuated by the scraggly tops of the century-old pines growing from the small islands.

Joe twisted his head slightly. "Are you saying that view is better than a city skyline?"

Sarah felt torn between two worlds. "Yes, I have to admit it is," she answered quietly. "Although in my younger days I may have disagreed with myself."

Remembering the day they first met, Joe nodded and let out a sarcastic chuckle. "Um, you actually did." He caught her eyes doing a smiling dance.

Joe pulled into the parking lot of the North Woods Trading Post. At the entrance, he pushed Sarah a cart and took another for himself.

"Are we really going to need two carts?"

"We have to be prepared. And besides, we need enough food for us and Don and Linda." He pushed on ahead.

While Sarah was hoping to spend some alone time with Joe, she thought it would be nice to get to know his friends more. She watched wide-eyed as Joe piled groceries into the carts.

Sarah hustled along to keep up with Joe who tore through the store. "What's the hurry?"

He chucked three boxes of pasta into the cart. "The sooner we get to camp, the sooner we can get the woodstove going. It's going to be a cold night." Briefly, he contemplated two brands of instant oatmeal. He threw one of each in the cart. "I think that does it."

Outside, a few parking spaces away, two men were struggling in the wind to tighten a tarp over the bed of their pickup. A long iron pipe was protruding over their tailgate.

"Can you start the truck?" He handed Sarah the keys. "I'll give those guys a hand."

She hesitated. "Isn't that the truck that flew by us?"

"Mm. Go ahead. R.C. is waiting on you." He walked over and grabbed a corner of the tarp. "Howdy, need a hand?"

A man wearing a pair of grease-stained blue coveralls, spun around. "No!" Before he could say another word, he was bent over sneezing and spitting phlegm into the snowbank.

The other guy came around the back of the truck. "You let go of that!" He slipped his knife through a knot.

"Only trying to be helpful." Joe shrugged.

"We don't need any help." Using his hunting knife as a pointer, he motioned for Joe to take off, and he yelled to his partner. "For cryin out loud, Leont. Pull your end over more."

Joe let go of the tarp. Before the Leont person could pull it down, the wind whipped the tarp clear to the other side of the truck bed, smacking the one holding the knife in the face. Joe smirked and walked away.

"What was that all about?" asked Sarah, still looking over at the men.

"They didn't want any help." He put the truck in reverse and backed out of the spot.

"What'd they have in the truck?"

"A bunch of scrap metal." Joe drove slowly past the two men who were still yanking on the tarp.

At the Indian Store, he turned left.

Taking the Maine atlas from the door pocket, Sarah's finger traced the outline of the west side of the lake. "Aren't we on the wrong side to get to your camp?"

"Ayuh. We cahn't get they-uh from hee-ah." Joe played up a Maine accent, even more than usual.

"Why's that?"

"Too much snow. Roads are impassable this time of year. By truck anyway."

Sarah gazed out the passenger window. The snowbanks were higher than the hood of Joe's truck. "How then are we going to get there? There's snow everywhere?" Sarah's eyebrows touched the bottom of her wool hat.

"You'll see."

When they passed a sign, "*Rockwood Village – 17 Miles,*" Sarah's finger navigated the page, trying to find a possible route around the lake to Parker Cabin.

"How far past Rockwood will we be driving?"

"Rockwood is as far as we go in the truck."

"And then?"

"You'll see."

Sarah's lips tightened. She watched large flakes of snow drift from the sky, while taking a few deep breaths, trying to calm herself.

Where the road passed the East Outlet dam, the flurries turned heavier. A mile down the road, the sky cleared and the sun was out. Seconds later she sat straight up and looked back over her shoulder. "Did you just see that?" she asked, excitement in her voice.

"What?"

"Behind that snowbank. A moose with wings!"

Joe laughed, forgetting the statue surprises many first-time visitors. "Ah, yes. Rockwood's flying moose."

"Why would someone put up a life-size statue of a moose – with wings?"

"That statue commemorates a legend of the Abenaquis."

"What was it about?"

"According to the legend, Mahanak, the son of the grand chief of the Abenaquis tribe, befriended an injured young moose. After the calf was healthy, the moose rarely let Mahanak out of his sight. During the early spring, Mahanak was out hunting alone. When he was returning to camp, he slipped and fell into a river. The water was extremely cold and running high. Conditions were treacherous because the river was rushing fast due to the snowpack melting.

"The story goes, the moose dove in and swam alongside until Mahanak could climb on. But it didn't get any better, the current was too strong for even the moose to get to shore. They were swept downstream into a section of swirling whitewater. When they came to a waterfall, Mahanak called on the spirits of the forest for help. The spirits, remembering Mahanak's kindness to the moose, helped the moose descend the rushing falls. Hunters from the tribe, who were at the bottom of the falls that day, retold the story. They said the moose descended the falls on two great wings, saving the boy. And that's why the Rockwood moose has wings."

"That would make a great article for the magazine. Could you draw a sketch of that moose?"

"Won't need to. I have a few at camp. You can take your pick."

"Oh – thanks."

******

Rockwood's Winged Moose

******

Joe pulled into the town landing and put the truck in park. He pushed up his coat sleeve and looked at his watch. "We're right on time."

Sarah looked around. The lot was deserted, not another person in sight. All the vehicles were buried under a foot of white. The wind over the frozen lake was whipping snow into tornado vortexes. An ice-covered Kineo blended into the gray sky and icy landscape.

"Sure looks nasty. I can't imagine anyone being out there today." Sarah scanned the ice.

"Ah, here they are."

"Who?"

Joe pointed. Coming around the bend on the lake and roaring up the boat launch were two snowmobiles.

"Is that Don and Linda? Are we going by snowmobile?" Sarah asked, hesitation in her voice.

"Ah, yep. The only way to get there this time of year."

She stared down at the map, her eyes moved over the page to the far side of Lobster Lake. They were a long way from Parker cabin. She watched the blowing snow. "How long will it take to go around the top of the lake by snowmobile?"

Joe noticed the shakiness in Sarah's voice, and it wasn't from the cold. "We don't go around. We go across."

Sarah's mouth opened; no words came out. She had never been on a snowmobile before, and going across a lake, even if it was frozen, wasn't something she had figured on. Before she could say anything, Joe opened his door and stepped out. Sarah pulled her hat down tighter and stepped into a deep snow drift.

Don flipped the tinted face shield on his helmet up. "Hello, you two!"

"I hope we didn't keep you waiting," Linda said, swinging herself off her machine.

"No. No. We just pulled up." Joe shook Don's hand and hugged Linda.

"Hello...." Before Sarah could get her greeting out, Don lifting her off the ground and gave her a bear hug.

"Great to see you, Sarah. I'm glad you decided to join us on this winter snowmobile adventure."

"To tell you the truth, I had no idea until a minute ago." She looked at Joe, but then smiled. "I'm all for new adventures."

"Then let's get loaded up," said Joe. "I want to get over to camp before dark."

Sarah looked towards the sun that was hidden by thin clouds; It was already low in the sky. She handed Joe a bag. "How are we supposed to get there? There's only two snow machines."

"These are doubles. Plenty of room. You and I will ride on Linda's, and Linda will ride with Don. I have a sled in the garage at camp we can use once we're there."

"What about R.C.?" The dog was waiting on the front seat of the truck.

"He's probably going to be sore at you."

"What? Why?"

"He usually rides on the sled with me. You're taking his seat." Smiling, he added, "I'm kidding, he knows the drill. He rides in the tow-behind all the time."

He noticed her eyeing Linda's heavy snowmobile suit. He motioned with his finger for Sarah to follow him. From behind the seat he held up a surprise gift. "I picked this up especially for you. What do you think of the colors?"

"Wow! Yes, I love the black with the purple accents. Thank you. There's still one problem," Sarah said. "Where am I supposed to put this on?"

Joe pointed. "The truck's still running. It's plenty warm and roomy in there. The boots are behind the seat."

Once they were suited up, Joe asked, "Would you like to drive?"

"Ha ha, you're funny."

Joe started up the machine and drove down the ramp. Sarah held on tight to Joe and in a low voice, said to herself, "I hope this ice is good and thick."

She was shocked when Don's voice echoed in her helmet. "Don't worry, the ice is plenty thick."

"Don, you can hear me?" She heard him laughing so hard, he couldn't even answer.

"Sarah," said Linda, "Don can't travel in any machine without being connected. And about the ice, the temperature hasn't gone above twenty-degrees since the middle of December. Most of the lake is a foot and a half thick."

"Thanks, Linda. but what do you mean by 'most' of the lake?"

"There are sections, take for instance near the inlets and outlets, or on the Moose River, where the water is still flowing. And there is sometimes an area out near Kineo that has open water. Don knows the safe places to cross."

"Okay. But I'm not sure I like being on the ice, any more than I like flying. Can't we take the trails?"

"We'll be on the lake for the first part of the trip. After that, we'll be on solid ground until we get to Lobster Lake," added Joe.

"And then what?" asked Sarah.

"Then we'll cross over Lobster Lake. Before you know it, we'll be sitting by the fire enjoying a cocktail"

"What if these snowmobiles run out of gas?"

"That's why we packed the snowshoes," Don said, very matter-of-factly.

"He's kidding you. We have extra tanks in the sleds and I have a hundred-gallon reserve tank at the camp," said Joe.

Sarah started to relax. The snowmobile was quieter than she expected, and the heavy snowsuit was keeping her snuggly warm. With the expanse of ice and the snow-covered mountains in the distance, she felt small.

Snowmobiling Across Moosehead Lake

"We're passing Farm Island on the right," said Don.

"Is there a farm on the island?" asked Sarah.

"Not anymore, but back in the late 1800s, when the Kineo hotel was thriving, much of the food for the summer guests was grown right there."

At the end of Farm Island, Sarah was relieved to see land. "Is that the end of the lake?"

"Not yet."

When they came around a corner, Sarah exclaimed, "Ohhh." Out ahead of them were miles and miles of nothing but ice.

Linda's voice said, "Only another ten miles to the end of the lake."

To Sarah, it seemed to go on forever. The feeling that they would be completely alone in the woods started to sink in.

It was another half an hour before Joe stopped and turned off the engine. Sarah looked around. Feet from the shore there was a small log cabin with a flat roof. White smoke lazily drifted from the rock chimney. A slanted wooden dock was cantilevered over the ice. A crooked iced-over ramp led from the lake to the dock.

Standing near Joe, Sarah whispered, "What is this place?"

"This is the Northeast Carry Store and Lodging. Also, the home to Gerry Willis, the only year-round resident this end of the lake. His place is a refuge for fishermen, hikers, snowmobilers, or anyone else who feels the need to get away from it all, or needs to get some supplies while out here."

"I don't suppose he makes lattes?" Sarah asked, with cynicism, already knowing the answer.

"I seriously doubt that." Joe shook his head. "But I bet he can whip you up a wicked good mug of hot cocoa."

"That would be good, too."

Dogs, lots of dogs, were chained up in front of weathered plywood dog houses. They were barking and jumping, pulling to the end of their chains, only to be yanked back to the ground with each leap. They weren't thrilled to see R.C. being led inside.

"Why are there so many dogs here? And kept outside in the cold?"

Joe explained as they walked over the canine stained snow to the store's porch. "Gerry's a sled dog racer. A pretty good one at that. He's won races as far away as Alaska."

Inside, the place didn't look much like a store to Sarah. Rather, it more resembled a one-room camp in need of organizing. Three of the four walls were lined with shelves that held canned goods, along with an assortment of hats, rain gear, lures, ropes, cast-iron pots, and hunting knives of every size. In one corner, scattered over the floor, there were stacks of parts for boats, trucks, and ATVs.

Two men, who likely hadn't shaved or changed their clothes in days, sat at the picnic table in the center of the room. Joe caught the large-bellied one, nudge his buddy and point at Sarah. They didn't take their eyes off her as she took off her snowmobile jacket. The two of them were oblivious to Joe walking up behind them.

Canucks at the Carry

"**Y**ou two out this way ice fishing?" Joe stood at the end of the table.

The older, thinner of the two men turned. He raised his eyes taking in Joe's full height. "Nope. Stopped in for some chili is all." He pointed at his bowl, still full. "Be warned, it's spicier than a Tijuana señorita."

Joe picked up a Canadian accent and figured the man had never been farther south of the border at Kittery. Placing his hands on the edge of the table, Joe leaned in. "How about you? You up here at the lake for the view?"

The fatter one, still hadn't taken his eyes off Sarah. Without answering, his gaze moved from Sarah to a metal flask on the bench. Slowly he poured a clear liquid into the empty beer mug he was grasping in his hairy fingers.

Linda and Sarah moved to the other side of the room. They examined the selection of socks that were hanging from randomly spaced wooden pegs.

Standing opposite to Joe, Don took a whiff of the air. "That smells strong. Home brew?"

Hairy-hands swigged down his drink, not offering a reply.

Joe turned back toward the older of the pair. "I'm Joe. You seen Gerry?" He reached out his hand.

The man eyed the hand as if it were a tiger's jaw, and gave a sideways glance. Seeing his buddy distracted, downing another shot, he shook Joe's hand with a limp, tentative shake.

"I'm Heath," and pointing with his thumb, added, "Gerry went to get Axe here, another bowl of Chili."

Don snickered.

In a gravely, gruff voice, Axe scowled at Don. "Short for Axel. What's it to ya?"

While it was the name Don had in mind when he laughed, he said, "A second bowl of Gerry's chili, huh. You know, that outhouse out back is mighty cold this time of year. So, you might want to limit your intake."

"Eh?" Catching on, Heath answered for Axe, "It don't matter. We're not staying here. We're staying at a camp over on …, ow-ah!" Heath took a fist to his ribs.

"I thought I heard familiar voices. Look what the snowman dragged in." Coming through the kitchen door, Gerry held two beer mugs in one hand and a bowl in the other.

"Hey, Gerry. Good to see you're still a practicing beer maid." Don laughed at his own joke.

"Watch it, old man, or you won't be getting served in this here fine establishment."

Axe grabbed for the beer before Gerry put it down. He chugged it, and then went at the chili as if he hadn't eaten in a week.

Gerry motioned his friends towards the bench by the woodstove. "How was the trip up?" He patted Joe on his shoulder.

"No problems. The lake is smooth, made for nice sledding."

"Yeah, for the dogs too, they've been loving the clear running over the icepack." He turned to the ladies. "And how are you doing, Linda?"

"Great, Gerry."

"And I don't believe we've met." Gerry offered his hand to Sarah.

"Gerry, this is Sarah. Sarah, meet Gerry, the most social hermit in the north woods." Joe said, making the introductions.

"Nice to meet you, Gerry."

"Ah, you're the writer that's been doing all those stories about our woods. My sister, Pearl, she bought a subscription to your magazine, insists I have to hear each article…she reads them to me over the radio. No offense, the stories are fine, but unless it's about the latest rod or rifle, it's hard to hold my interest."

"No offense taken." Sarah said lightheartedly and shook her head slowly.

"What can I get for you, ladies?"

"Do you have hot chocolate?" asked Sarah.

"Fresh from the package."

"One for me too," added Linda.

"How about you two? Coffee? Beers?" He raised his head at Joe and Don.

"I'll take a coffee," said Joe.

"Same here," replied Don.

Gerry was at the door to the kitchen, when Don called out. "And, why don't you bring me a large bowl of that chili."

Gerry's hand shot up, index finger in the air. "One bowl of heat, coming up."

"And another beer here," yelled Axe.

Sarah tugged at Joe's sleeve. "I don't want to sit at that table with those guys."

There was only one table in the Northeast Carry Store, a custom-built picnic table that ran the length of the room. Gerry had built it inside and once he was done, he realized he had no room for any other tables, or any way of getting it out without the use of his chainsaw.

"This is fine right here. You ladies take the bench. Don, give me a hand with these crates." They emptied oil filters, laundry soap, and toilet paper from wooden crates and turned them over for a table and extra seats.

"Isn't Gerry going to be mad you emptied his stock on the floor?" Sarah asked.

"I'll bet you ten bucks he doesn't even notice. Watch."

Gerry set their order on the improvised table. Without a word about the new furniture layout, he dragged over a metal can to sit on.

Don and Joe told Gerry about their plans while at camp. On hearing a mention of Lobster Lake, Axe nudged Heath.

"Did you get to check that my gas storage tank was filled before the snows came?"

"Yep, Junction Oil took care of it. I saved the slip. It's somewhere. A hundred gallons ought to last you until the fall."

Axe nudged Heath again.

"Thanks. We'll need the gas with running sleds out there." replied Joe.

"Hey, Gerry, we'll give you a shout on the radio when we get to Joe's. To test the signal." Don stuck a spoonful of the chili into his mouth.

"Sure thing."

Don grabbed his mug and took a gulp. "Wow, that has some heat to it." He wiped his burning lips with a napkin. Linda shook her head.

Joe added, "It's going to take us another hour, give or take, to get to camp. And then we have to connect up the radio." At the mention of another hour, Sarah swallowed hard.

"I'll listen for you at six. That should give you plenty of time to get there. We're expecting some high winds and white out conditions tonight and into the morning. Stick to the main trail until you hit Lobster Lake." Gerry raised his hand in Don's direction. "No shortcuts. I saw some ice ridges when I was sledding on Lobster Lake the other day. Take it slow going across."

"We will," Linda stressed.

Sarah glanced out of the corner of her eye at Axe. She could tell he was listening to every word of their conversation.

"You all planning to come by and watch the sled dog race?" asked Gerry.

"Absolutely. Wouldn't miss it. I heard you're a favorite to win." Don took another spoonful of chili and then gulped the rest of his coffee. Linda rolled her eyes.

"Maybe. There's some stiff competition in the race this year. These guys are also racing." His hand motioned towards the Canadians, who had turned around to facing them, no longer hiding they were listening. Axe kept his droopy eyes glued on Sarah.

Seeing Sarah was uncomfortable being watched, Joe stood, blocking Axe's view. He put his hand on her shoulder.

Everyone turned when Axe spoke, his voice rough and gravelly. "We gotta get going. What do we owe you?"

"I'll be right back." Gerry walked up to the counter.

Axe pointed to the map posted on the wall. "Where was that trail you mentioned earlier? We might take a ride over there."

Looking up from figuring a total, Gerry traced a line on the map with his fingers. "Right about here."

"Ah. Here you go then." Axe placed a twenty on the counter. He waited for change and pocketed every penny.

Joe watched as Axe and Heath rode out on their snowmobiles. "Who are the Canuckleheads?"

Gerry sat back down. "Been coming around the past few months – hunting, sledding. I've gathered they're from around Lac Maurice Pierre. The big one's pretty gruff, but they stick to themselves. It's the first year they've registered for the race."

"That Axe fellow seems to have a problem." Linda placed the empty mugs in the brown plastic bin on the counter.

"Don't let him bother you." Gerry stood up. "The chip on his shoulder extends all the way to his Molson muscle."

"Well, he's uglier than a burnt stump anyway." Linda sat down next to Don.

"Where they staying?" Don asked.

"The Heath fella mentioned Kokadjo. When I asked where abouts, his buddy told him to shut up." Gerry scratched under his hat.

With Axe gone, Sarah walked around the small store looking more closely at the merchandise. A corkboard with pamphlets pinned on it, advertising hunting trips from Maine Guides, whitewater rafting, backcountry hiking, and fishing in the Allagash, caught her attention. "Gerry, knowing you're familiar with my articles, or at least what your sister has read to you, would you mind if I spotlighted your place in an upcoming issue? A refuge in the wild angle."

Gerry tugged his gray, brillowy beard that hung to his chest. He removed his faded red wool cap, pushed around his thinning gray hair, and gave Joe a, *"What do you think?"* look.

Joe realized he had never seen the top of Gerry's head. The man never went anywhere without a hat. Joe wondered if he slept in it. He gave Gerry a shrug, *"Up to you my old friend."*

Gerry walked to the window and spoke to the lake. "You see, Miss, this isn't the type of place most people come to for a vacation." He pointed out the large plate glass window at the lake. "Their vacation is out there. This is a simple place to dry off, have some grub, a somewhat warm place to sleep for the night, given you don't mind sleeping in your socks and with your hat on in the winter." He put his hat back on.

He turned to face Sarah. "It's not fancy. People find me by word of mouth, or they happen to stumble out of the woods and end up here. The sportsmen that stay here never complain. They're not expecting much. If you were to *'advertise'* in your city magazine, I might get people coming up here that expect five course meals, down blankets, and fancy coffee drinks. And besides, look around, I can handle about eight people at a time. I run a small no-frills outfit."

"But, Gerry, that's a great story. The article isn't meant to be an advertisement..." Seeing his serious frown, her voice trailed off.

Gerry bent down and put another log in the woodstove. "I'll think about it." He picked up the dish bin.

Linda followed him to the kitchen.

"You know I'm no busy-body, Gerry. But you might consider a write-up. It could be good for business. For the entire area."

"I know. That's what I'm afraid of."

"Huh?" Linda, poured the last of the coffee in the pot into a mug and added sugar. "Add this to my tab."

"That's old now. It's on the house." He turned on the water to fill the dish bin. "More advertising for my place, isn't necessarily a good thing. I had a family of four, from San Francisco, arrive up here last spring. Do you know what they wanted me to guide them around for?"

"I don't know. Moose safaris, ATVing, fishing, hiking. Any number of things."

"None of the above. I spent three days touring them around in my jeep for, of all things, bird watching. Not to hunt, but to watch, or mostly, listen to."

Linda snorted coffee through her nose.

"It's not funny. If anyone around here gets a whiff about it, I'll know it came from your lips. I'll never hear the end of it."

"They paid you – didn't they?"

"It actually cost me money to have 'em here. First, the beds weren't plushy enough. I had to have Folsom's fly me in a new mattress for the parents. Then they complained the no-see-ums were getting through the screens in the evening. Now how the heck would you expect me to keep those tiny things out of a cabin?"

"I don't know. What'd you do?"

"I added another layer of screening. I was out there getting eaten alive by black flies, to put up screen that wasn't going to make a bit of difference."

"I guess some guests expect different accommodations."

"Yep. And they should stay someplace else. I don't think Sarah's magazine is read by my customers, the sportsman who is seeking a place to get away from people . . . the people who want Mickey Mouse face pancakes for their kids at breakfast."

"You're probably right." Linda leaned against the sink – thinking. "I bet Joe might have a connection with *Rod, Rifle, and Arrow* magazine. Maybe Sarah and him could get a freelance piece submitted. Could be a win-win."

"Now that would be an idea. You're always thinking, Linda." Gerry placed the washed chili bowls back on the shelf.

"I'm not the president of the economic development committee for just my looks." She tossed her brown hair with the back of her hand. "What's all these supplies stacked in the corner here? And why are all the boxes taped together?"

"Those are supplies for the sled dog race lunch wagon. Cans of beans, macaroni, chips, cups, plates, etc. I secured them to make 'em harder to swipe."

"What? Who's swiping stuff from you?"

"That's what I want to know. I had a stash stored in the back hallway last week. I took the dogs out for a run, and by the time I came back, someone had rummaged through it. Some of the food was missing."

"Did you report it?"

"Nah. Not yet. Been too busy." His eyes narrowed and he stared through the window. "Maybe I already opened the boxes and forgot."

Linda sensed a strained look on his face. She remembered hearing the other day about equipment that had gone missing from the snowmobile club storage shed near Kineo. To her, it seemed there were too many reports lately of *misplaced* items. "You should inform Chief Robley, or Warden Green."

To get Linda off the subject, Gerry said, "I'll mention it to one of them when I see 'em, but I'm sure each of them got bigger fish to fry." He rinsed the mugs and left them in the sink. Linda was still staring at him. "There was one more strange thing about it."

He opened a drawer next to the sink. Pushing aside a flashlight, matches, a box of toothpicks, and a bunch of pens, he took out a folded piece of paper. "That same day, I found this lying on the counter next to my ham radio. Not only that, my dials and settings had all been messed with." He handed Linda the paper.

She unfolded and scanned the article. "What about it?"

"Who knows. I'm not a Springsteen fan and why would I have saved a piece of the Bangor paper from way back in July?"

"Joe keeps a lot of articles. I bet he'd appreciate this."

"He can have it."

Don pushed open the kitchen door and slapped a twenty on the counter. "Gerry, we're gonna top off the gas."

Gerry threw Don the key for the pump lock.

As Linda squeezed by Don, he grabbed her around the waist. "Will you stop it. Go gas up the sleds." She wriggled away and called, "Hey, Joe. Look at this." She handed him the paper.

"Oh, sure. I remember reading this back over the summer."

Sarah read the headline. "I didn't know you were a Springsteen fan."

Bangor Daily

Springsteen Rocks the Wall in East Germany

July 21, 1988   Staff Reporter: F. J. Snowe

On the 19th, Bruce Springsteen sung his anthems deep inside East Germany. Springsteen was upset on learning, at the last minute, that the East German leaders had billed the concert as a fundraiser for Nicaragua Sandinistas – a communist regime. Springsteen, not usually moved to political activism, addressed the concert goers.

"I want to tell you I'm not here for or against any government. I came to play rock 'n' roll for you East Berliners in the hope that one day all the barriers will be torn down."

Picture of the Berlin Wall on the West German side.

An ode to Reagan's 1987 speech.

"öffne dieses Tor, reiß diese Mauer nieder !!"

"I'm not. A few songs are okay. But this concert was a big deal. For two reasons. One, the fact he played in East Germany. The other, is that the concert was originally devised by the East

Germans as support for the Sandinista regime. It was billed as the "Concert for Nicaragua." But really it was in support of the communist government. Springsteen was unaware of it, until he saw it printed on the tickets. He was so ticked off, he gave that impromptu speech in rough German to make a statement of his own."

"Wish I could read what that graffiti says." Sarah was squinting at the newspaper in Joe's hand.

"It says, 'Open this Gate. Tear Down This Wall.' Obviously, a nod to Reagan's speech in eighty-seven."

Sarah gave Joe a look of wonder; her eyes were bright and her mouth slightly parted.

"Don't you remember that speech?" Joe flicked his head her way.

"Um, yes. But I didn't know you could speak German."

"I wouldn't say I can speak it, not well anyway. I can still read a little."

"When did you learn?"

"In college to satisfy my language credits." He shrugged and went to give the paper back to Linda.

Linda put up her hand. "Gerry said you can have it, for your collection."

"Don't need it." Joe placed the article on Gerry's counter. Linda gave him a curious glance.

"This is only the lead-in. I saved the whole article to eventually tape in a camp journal. It's a good piece of history. You know, I predict that wall will be coming down." Seeing Don waving from outside, Joe said, "We got to move out."

The ladies zipped up their snowsuits. Out on the porch, Sarah spotted the thermometer; the mercury wasn't even reaching twenty. The sun was getting close to the top of the mountains in the west. It was only going to get colder for the remainder of the trip.

"You two go ahead, I forgot to tell Gerry something." Joe went back inside.

"Hey, Gerry."

Gerry poked his head from the kitchen. "Yeah, Joe? You forget something?"

"No. But is everything all set for what we talked about? Out at the ice shack?"

"Sure is. Along with everything from your list, I even left a few eight-tracks out there for you." Gerry pointed at him.

Joe laughed. He knew Gerry didn't have a romantic thread in his body, he wondered what the selections might be. "Same combination for the lock?"

"Yep."

"Great. Talk to you later tonight." Joe pulled the door closed.

❦✳❦

At the Lobster Lake trail crossing, Don pulled to a stop. Ice ridges were blocking access to the lake. The men walked around in circles thinking over a plan.

"Can't sled over those," said Joe.

"Nope. Let's have a look along this trail for another spot."

Don turned and looked back at Linda, "We'll be right back."

"We're not planning on going anywhere." There was a hint of sarcasm in Linda's tone.

Joe pushed the snow covered branches out of the way. "We'll have to bushwhack through here to find a flat section of the shoreline."

"Yep. If we can't squeeze by, we'll have to head back and stay with Gerry until morning." Don looked back over his shoulder. "Let's go tell the girls."

"Umm, you know we can hear you." Linda tapped her helmet.

"We'll be on our way in a few minutes, this is a minor setback." Don grabbed a saw and handed Joe a machete for bush whacking.

While Sarah was impressed the men were prepared, she wasn't feeling too great about the situation. It was now dark and she was cold.

It wasn't long before Linda was tired of waiting around. She nudged Sarah. "I thought I saw of a side trail back a little ways. Don was going so fast, hard to tell. Maybe it leads down to the lake."

They left their helmets on the sleds and went exploring. When they hit the side trail, they both stopped. The snow was packed down from someone in snowshoes.

"Who do you think would have been out here?" Sarah asked.

Staring at the tracks, Linda had the same question. The indents were recent. She was torn between continuing down the trail to look for a clear way to the lake, or getting back to the guys.

Camp Axe

"Darn cold out tonight." Leontel pushed the door closed with his boot and set a box of supplies on the table.

"Took you long enough. Heath and I've been back for an hour with nothin' to eat." Axe held *his* elk-bone handle hunting knife in one hand, a thick maple branch in the other. Well, it wasn't originally his knife. The sentimental cutlery had been in the minister's family for seventy-five years, as the history was relayed up on West Outlet last September from Parson André to Axe. Long after Axe departed for home, the minister was on his hands and knees in the icy water, thinking he had dropped his knife sometime earlier in the frothy current.

Napolin, opened a bag of chips from the box he had carried in. He scanned the cabin as he shoved a handful in his mouth. It was obvious Axe or Heath hadn't made any attempt to even clean up the place while he and Leontel were out "collecting" and getting their dinner to boot. At least the camp, which was spotless when they 'checked in' and now smelt like a fish head left to rot in an ashtray, was warm and dry.

Axe had located their recent accommodations when his truck '*broke down*' last fall. He had asked the owners of the tiny, meticulously kept cabin if he could borrow their phone. Since he knew there was no phone lines running down the private out-of-the-way camp road, he knew the answer before the shaky seventy-five-year-old man answered him. Through the open door, Axe observed the elderly couple had been packing; Axe's truck trouble had coincidently coincided with the time of year for closing up camps.

"You two finished for the season?" Axe chewed on a whittled birch branch.

"Oh, yes," answered the frail woman. "We're headed back to Florida tomorrow."

"I noticed your shed roof is covered in moss. I could fix that for you. By the time you come back for ice fishing, it'll be fixed up good."

"Oh, we don't come back for the winter. We'll be down south until Memorial Day weekend. No snow for us." The man held himself up leaning on the doorknob.

"We're snowbirds." The little old-lady sang, proud to use the term.

Axe nodded. "Won't cost much." He turned back towards the shed. "I can clean most of that moss off, only need to replace maybe half the shingles."

"I've been meaning to get to that." The man's eyes were glossy. He knew his years of caring for the camp were behind him.

"Dear-ah, why don't you let the nice man help out." She liked Axe's red flannel shirt. He gave her the impression of someone who did fine work – a lumberjack of sorts.

They struck a deal and the couple gave Axe all the particulars, their phone number in Florida should he need to contact them (*not twenty feet down their drive on his walk back to his perfectly running truck, he had used the sheet of paper to blow his nose and tossed it in a ditch*), where they kept the hidden keys for the shed padlock (*the man said, "It's the small key, the other on the ring is for the camp. You won't need that one."*), and a signed note to use down at the lumber yard to charge to their account (*Axe had said, "Won't likely need to use it, but from my experience, a note saves time instead of you mailing me a check."*).

Before Axe left, the woman hugged him and handed him fifty dollars – "That should do nice for the supplies to give the shed a new coat of paint," she said in her shaky voice. (Axe thought it would *do nice* for a couple of two-fours of Molson and a carton of cigs.)

When Axe and the gang arrived earlier in the week, they found the keys right where they were supposed to be, hanging on a nail under the eave of the shed. With the thermometer reading ten degrees, Napolin wasn't too pleased to discover Axe had selected a camp with no woodstove, or fireplace, or any heating at all. But they were always a resourceful bunch. To remedy the situation, they located an ice shack that was no longer in need of a stove, not until the owners returned anyway to discover their lock had been cut. Since there was no chimney in the cabin, Axe knocked out a pane in a window and hung the stove pipe using metal clothes hangers. The summer clothes the old couple had left neatly hanging in their closet, came in handy as rags to wash with, as towels to clean up after scaling fish, for the dogs to sleep on, and for checking the oil dipsticks in their trucks and snowmobiles.

With the camp heating up, Axe and the gang had completed the shed improvement in less than an hour. The polished antique tables the couple had painstakingly restored by hand, the sixty-year old birch-bark canoe the man had made as a teenager, their outdoor seat cushions, the grandchildren's rubber floats, the man's fishing gear, her gardening gloves and tools, the golf clubs he planned to hand-down to his son, every little thing, even an old Christmas ornament, a glass moose in a Santa hat, was plucked from the shed and thrown into the snow.

To give Mother Nature a hand hiding the belongings until late spring, Heath started plowing the snow from the driveway up over the piles.

"Wait," yelled Axe. He pulled a hardwood toboggan with a plush red and black checkered cushion to safety. "I want this for my kids." He propped it up against a tree and stood by as Leontel and Napolin finished the burial off with shovels.

Axe then went about setting up his acetylene cutting torch in his new chop shop. When Heath walked in, Axe said, "Now this is the shed I had in mind to hide, sort, and store our haul."

Next, they set to making their sled dogs at home. The row boat and the classic Hackett mahogany motorboat were pushed from the boathouse. Chains were nailed to the shiny polyurethaned pine walls with spikes to keep the canines separated. The dogs settled into their new home, keeping occupied chewing the oars, lifejackets, wooden waterskies, buoys, dock ropes, and the set of four cedar Adirondack chairs. They only got through three of them completely. Axe won a fight with the largest husky, pulling the fourth chair away. Outside, he flung the chair repeatedly against the deck railing to smash it into pieces to use in the woodstove, along with the deck rails.

With their hide-away customized, the only thing they needed for a week in the woods was food. This morning, Axe and

Heath had taken snowmobiles over to the Northeast Carry Store for lunch and reconnaissance. While they were drinking beer, Napolin and Leontel were sent to a garage in Monson for a truck part and then a grocery run at the Trading Post. To make the trip to town worthwhile, they also made stops along the way to get started on "collecting."

"At least I see you kept busy while we were out." Napolin, opened a can of Molson, kicking the pile of shavings from Axe's whittling on his way by. "And besides running errands, we made two pickups on the way back here. Good stuff too."

"Plus, the Trading Post was packed. All these amateur fishermen showing up. Some lookers, too." Leontel, whistled.

Thirsty from sitting, Axe got up for a beer.

Napolin sat down on a kitchen chair and put his feet up on another. "Yeah. How about that good Samaritan, who was with that pretty one."

Axe spun on his boot heels. "What are you talking about? What Samaritan? I told you to keep a low profile."

"Wasn't anything we did. The wind was blowing the tarp off the back of the truck. This Main-ah decided he wanted to show he was helpful in front of his lady." Leontel laughed.

The sound of the full beer can crushing in Axe's hand coincided with his grunt. "Did they get a look at the haul?"

"No. Scared him off quick." The end of Napolin's cigarette glowed orange-red as he sucked in a breath.

Axe took another beer and slapped the case. "You only got one two-four?" He held the can to his lips and emptied it in one throw back of his head. "Well?"

"There's another in the truck. Why don't you go grab it." Napolin stared him down, his chin up, in Axe's direction.

Not one to be stared at, Axe leaned close to Napolin, his face only inches away. A foul smell came from deep within Axe when he belched.

"You're disgusting." Napolin turned away.

Laughing, Axe said, "Catch," and he threw a beer at Heath. Seeing Heath was playing solitaire and didn't see the can coming at him, it hit the table, bounced, scattered his cards, fell, and rolled across the floor.

Startled, Heath jumped up. "What the? What'd you do that for?" He tried to reorganize the card piles. He gave up and pushed them aside.

"Since I got you a beer, go grab that other case." Axe then glared at Leontel and Napolin. "You two better get that haul locked in the shed. We don't need anyone seeing it out there."

"There ain't nobody gonna be around here tonight."

"I don't want any chances. You go ahead. I'll start the chow."

"Ah, let's get it over with. You two give me a hand. Let Axe play cook." Leontel put his unopened beer on the windowsill.

Axe waited until the door closed, and then he dumped the box of groceries on the now chipped and scratched slate counter, chipped on account he used a hammer and screwdriver to make ice chips for his Crown and coke earlier. He pushed aside the canned beans, strips of jerky, bags of chips, and cigarettes until he found what he wanted. He slipped the knife from his belt holster and punctured the cellophane wrapping on the four-pound package of chop meat. Popping another Molson with his right hand, he scooped up a chunk of meat with the hairy fingers on his left. He licked his hand and swallowed the mound of meat without even chewing. Downing the beer, he watched the gang unloading the truck, his smirk reflected in the blackness of the window. The truck headlights stretched across the snow to the shed that was stuffed to the rafters with the hauls they'd collected already. He thought, if he had to be stuck with these losers as his crew, at least he didn't have to do the manual labor. He shoved another handful of meat into his mouth. He picked up the meat package, another beer, and flopped down on the couch – he wiped the mud from his boots on the beige fabric.

✸✷✸

"Hey, Heath, move it a bit. The faster we get this truck unloaded, the sooner we can get inside for those burgers," yelled Napolin.

"I was checking out this heavy piece. Where'd you get it?"

"Found it yesterday, over near Lobster Lake. At a campsite."

"It's heavy. What do you think it is?"

Napolin was carrying a length of pipe. He swung around to face Heath. Leontel ducked. "It's from a train. The front grill. Really antique." He swung back around, this time Leontel didn't see the pipe and it hit him square in his shoulder.

"Ah, what the! Watch what you're doing." He spat near Napolin's boot.

Heath propped it up against a pile of pipe. "Must be fifty pounds. Ought to fetch a good price. Right, Leont?"

Leont was the treasurer of the group, he kept a book with a list of their supply and what price they got for each piece. "I imagine, maybe thirty bucks. Can you believe it. Some idiots were using it as a grill." Leontel stood rubbing his shoulder. "There was a cabin nearby. Nice place. Real neat. Closed up for the winter. We're gonna go back there. Tomorrow. Right, Napol?"

"Sometime this week." Napolin lit a cigarette and exhaled. "Should be some good iron water pipe, the place is old school. Water pipe probably runs all the way down to the pond." He dragged on his smoke. "You about done with the inventory list, Leont?"

"Yeah. Go on in. I'll be right behind you." Once he was sure Napolin had led Heath inside, Leontel pulled a second black book from his coat – a twin of the first. He placed the two books side-by-side on the truck hood and transcribed selective entries.

"Hey, Axe you should see the …" Napolin stopped in the open doorway. The groceries were still out on the counter. No burgers were cooking. Axe was strewn out on the couch, the buzz of his snoring filling the room. The empty meat package lay on the floor next to him. His right hand hung down over the side, bits of raw meat clung to his fingernails. Three crushed beer cans were scattered across the floor.

"Can you believe this? We ought to dump his fat butt out in the snow." Napolin kicked a can at the sofa.

"You got a bulldozer to move the fat lard?" asked Heath.

Napolin threw the empty meat package at Axe's head.

"Keep it down, I'm trying to rest here." Axe rolled over, the crack of his rear-end hanging over the edge of the couch.

Heath picked up the beer that Axe had earlier thrown across the room, walked close to the couch, and popped the top. The beer exploded in a stream over Axe's back. He jumped up to grab Heath.

Heath jumped back in time to see Axe's pants fall to his knees, causing him to fall back on the couch. "I'm gonna slug you in your face."

"You ate the entire package of meat? What about us?" yelled Heath. As Axe and Heath were related, it fell to him to make this point. Napolin stood back, waiting – watching.

"You guys were taking too long." Axe pulled up his pants. "I had to eat."

Leontel entered, threw his coat on the chair, and opened the beer he had left by the window. "Isn't this typical." He had assessed the scene that seemed all too familiar.

"What are you all worried about. There's plenty of beans and jerky. Besides, with what I found out for our next score, we're going to be making a killing. You're gonna owe me big time for this one."

"Oh, yeah? What's this latest scam of yours?" Napolin ripped open a stick of jerky and bit off a piece.

"Back in the sixties I was here, working for a salvage company. I've come into some information where there's a good deal of metal sitting around, free for the taking." Axe stood up and tightened his belt. "While Heath and I are at the dog race, you two can make the pickup. I gotta hit the outhouse. I'll tell you more when I get back." On his way out, he took the half-empty exploded can of beer from Heath's hand and shook it at his brother-in-law's face. The rest he saved for his trip. The cabin shook when he slammed the door.

Heath pulled off his shirt and walked into the bedroom to change.

"Killin'. Killin'. The last time he had an idea to make us a killin', we drove six hundred miles, one way, for two hundred bucks." Napolin opened a can of beans. "And that we had to split four ways."

Responding, Leont whispered, "I told you, brother. We finish up the places here, including that place over on Lobster Lake, we'll have enough to split from this dump."

"You mean it? Enough to get home?" Napolin's spirits were lifted.

"Yep. We'll be visiting with Mama by Islander Day. As long as you make sure Axe doesn't find that other piece we collected from that yocals truck today. He doesn't need to know about it, or he'll want half the profit." Leontel left the gang's official inventory book out on the counter. He knew Axe was going to want to review the numbers. The twin, his private book, he hid under the sink, behind the empty beer cans.

Skidder Donuts

Greenville Public Safety Building

Buddy, sitting across from the chief, continued his plea for help. "Chief, you don't understand. It was my Winchester 70. The wife gave me that gun, for Christmas. I've only had it a week."

"Where were you parked, again?"

"At Upper Kettle Lake. We towed the sleds and ice fished that way."

The report the chief had taken from someone missing a woodstove from their shack up that way, came to mind. "Why'd you leave it hanging across your truck's rear window for everyone to see with the doors unlocked?"

"Are you serious? I've seen your truck, you've got three guns hanging in there."

"I'm the police chief." Robley sat back in his chair, tapping his pen on the desk. "Look, Buddy, a stolen gun is a big deal. You know I know that. I'll file a report, but there isn't much I can do about it until a clue turns up. I can't go out searching for a needle in a hardwood forest."

"For crying out loud. My initials are engraved on the stock. BB."

"I know your initials. And I told you, I'll keep a look out for it. With all these flatlanders up here for the long weekend and the sled race, I've got my hands full."

Buddy had been chewing the chief's ear for near a half hour already and the chief didn't see any point in belaboring the conversation. Wanting to move things along, he craned his neck around Buddy and waved at the next person to come on in. It was past five and he wanted to get home to supper.

Taking the hint his time was up, Buddy turned to go, talking to himself with his head hung low. "Milly had those initials inlaid with silver. She's gonna kill me." Reaching the doorway of the chief's office, he bumped right into the person entering. "Hey, why don't you...., oh, sorry, Fred. How are ya?"

Fred stepped to the side to give Buddy room to get through. "Seems better than you."

"Hmm." Buddy continued on his way, his head in a continuous slow shake.

The chief leaned around to the side of his desk and stuck a soda under the bronzed opener. The top fell into a metal trash can that was up to the rim with bottle caps. He motioned for Fred to have a seat.

"Been one after another today. I bought this an hour ago over at the gas station." He held up the bottle. "I bet it's warm now." He took a breath and chugged down a gulp. Half of the caramel-colored liquid disappeared before the bottle came down with a thud on the desk.

"Yep. Warm as Prong Pond in August." The chief eyed Fred, who was sitting relaxed in the chair, waiting. It was never good when Fred came by; it always meant more work for the chief, usually it ended up with him having to drive to some mosquito infested swampy area in the woods. At least this time of year there wouldn't be any bugs, but he envisioned Fred having some urgent need to bust someone who dropped a tree where they weren't supposed to. He took another chug of the soda and finished it off, staring down the end of the bottle at the local fire ranger. The chief's swivel-chair squeaked as he rotated around to balance the empty bottle in a wooden crate that was already full.

"What brings you in this evening, Fred? The football team have a bonfire out in a lumber pit again?"

Fred knew the chief well enough to let the comment slide. The town's only constable, Robley had held the position for twenty years. He had a big bark, but was a protector of the people, creatures, and trees all the same. The chief was an avid outdoorsman and anyone in the wrong was going to be on his wrong side, which was a side with little room – and not only because of the chief's two hundred and fifty pound frame. With the types of crime in Greenville, Robley's primary focus was on the out-of-towners who drove down Pritham Avenue past the school with a lead right foot. He was content to let the wardens and forest rangers take care of the woods.

Before the sound reached the office, through the window behind the chief, Fred saw the jacked-up 4x4 Chevy. The engine revved, the tires squealed, and the truck kicked up gravel leaving the gas station lot. The chief stood up with such force, his chair hit the crate of empties, which tipped over, slid, and spilt the entire can of bottle caps across the black and white tile floor.

"I knew it was that Rodney kid. Peels out every day." The chief was reaching for his hat on the peg when he caught sight of Fred, remembering he had a visitor. "Ah, shoot."

He picked up his chair, looked at the bottle caps, exhaled, and sat back down. "Okay, Smokey, what is it today?"

The nickname didn't bother Fred. In fact, he may have liked it; it fit his personality, a little friendly, but not to be messed with. On the friendly side, the kids over at the school were always excited when he showed up dressed as a bear. On the other hand, the loggers out in the woods knew not to poke the bear – it was best not to see that side of Fred.

Putting his hand into his coat, Fred took out a folded slip of paper. "I need a signature on this affidavit. You sent it in, but didn't sign it." He slipped the three pages across the desk to the chief.

Robley burped. "When was that?"

"Back in the fall. Court clerk down in Augusta just got around to looking through it. Sent it all back to me."

The chief had turned back to the window, his head looking down the street. "That kid'll be back this way in two minutes. Pushes every limit there is."

"If you could sign it, right there at the bottom, I'll be on my way and you can go have your high-speed pursuit."

Robley whirled back to face Fred. "You think it's funny? That kid is a menace with that loud truck." He watched the smirk on Fred grow wide. He shook his head and laughed at himself. "What was the case?"

"Last spring. You were in the wood lot behind your camp, turkey hunting, when you came across that group who had broken into a skidder. They were doing donuts through the vernal pools."

The chief put on a big grin. He had enjoyed busting that crew who suspected he was an old man out with a bow and arrow. "Those flatlanders never saw it coming. I pulled my badge and they went totally white."

Fred knew what the chief was feeling. He would have felt the same satisfaction – after he cooled down from seeing what they were doing. The chief picked up his pen and tapped the desk as he glanced over the paperwork. He was proud of how he wrote up what he witnessed. '*I snuck up on a menacing group of four, who were armed and dangerous.*' Well, they were armed – with six packs and hunting knives (who didn't carry one), and they were dangerously close to crashing the skidder they hot-wired into a pile of recently cut timber. He signed the paper and slid it back to Fred.

"Say, Fred, you spend a lot of time in these woods."

"As a forester that's what I do." He folded the pages.

Robley gave him a blank stare and nodded. "You see anything strange up near Upper Kettle Lake lately?"

Fred's hand slowed as he placed the envelope in the pocket inside his coat. He felt for his map, it was in the same pocket he always kept it. "You mean because of Buddy's rifle?"

"That, among other things."

"There's been a lot of rumors."

The chief rubbed his forehead. "More than normal. Especially up that way."

"I suppose. Maybe." Fred stood to go. "You going to be at the legion tomorrow night?"

"You bet. Best band in the county playing."

As Fred was about to say goodbye, he caught sight of Rodney's hood come to a stop at the intersection of Moosehead Lake Road. The engine revved.

The chief's chair hit the back wall. Robley grabbed his hat, "See ya, Smokey, I gotta catch that bandit."

Animal Lure

⁑

Once Linda and Sarah reported there was an unobstructed way onto the ice, they were on their way again; until they reached the far side. It took Don and Joe a few slow passes to find the narrow, unmarked trail through the woods to Joe's cabin.

"You really should stake that trail. It's tough to see in the dark." The frustration was evident in Don's voice – he was hungry, tired from chopping branches, and was bothered by the tracks Linda and Sarah had spotted.

"Not a chance. I don't want any more visitors than necessary," Joe replied.

With the snow stopped and the clouds thinning, the moon shone between the tree branches lighting the way to Parker cabin. Even though she was getting cold, Sarah found this part of the ride under the snow-covered tunnel of white and evergreen arches to be stunning. Even Don was quiet until they pulled into Joe's camp drive, then he went into Commander mode.

"We're late. We've missed Gerry's first contact. I don't want to miss the next one. I'll get to work getting the radio connected to Joe's antenna, while you three unload the sleds."

"Aye Aye, Captain," Linda said.

"How many times have I told you, that's the Navy."

"Plenty." Linda saluted. Don sighed.

R.C. circled the yard and then ran through the open camp door. He settled down on his old gray wool blanket near the woodstove, and maybe realizing the camp was as cold as a meat freezer, let out a single bark.

"All right, old man, I'm on it." After lighting the gas lights and starting up the propane refrigerator, Joe knelt and lit the fire box that was made-ready with paper and kindling since the day he'd left in October.

Sarah and Linda pulled their chairs close to the stove, not yet willing to shed their coats or hats. By the time Don had the radio connected and powered, it was past six.

"Eagle One, calling Trail Cat, come in." Don waited. Nothing. He repeated, "Eagle One, calling Trail Cat, come in."

"He might not have his radio on. You know how he is about conserving power. We did say hour on the hour, and it's now six twenty." Joe set a pot on the stove.

"You're right." Don put the mic down.

Within thirty minutes the cabin was warm enough to take off their coats. At seven on the dot, the radio crackled.

"Trail Cat to Eagle One, come in."

"I read you, Trail Cat, thanks for the check," said Don.

"You were late. What happened?" Gerry questioned.

"Some ice ridges blocked access. We backtracked to find a crossing." Don caught Linda's frown.

"Didn't I tell you to watch for that side trail?"

"No, you didn't,"

"Huh. Could have sworn I mentioned it. I forget things more easily now. Anyway, everything else in order?"

"All good. Place is warming up, Joe's making dinner, and the drinks are poured. It's going to be a great night in the woods."

"Okay then. I'll check in with you tomorrow. Maybe I'll run the dogs out that way for some exercise. Over."

"10-4." Don switched off the radio power and headed to the stove. "I'm starving. That smells good. What are you cooking up?" He stuck a spoon into the pot Joe was stirring.

* * *

Gerry went to put the mic down, and remembered he never asked Joe about the well house and bucket. He tried to get Don back on the radio, but had no luck. The sports he had for the weekend had already taken their meals and were playing cribbage or telling togue stories, so he took the time to get something to eat himself.

He was opening a can of beans, when a call came over the radio.

"Gerry, this is Warden Andy Green. You got your ears on?"

"Evening, warden. What is it?"

"I'll be making a pass over the race course tomorrow, as planned."

"Yep." Gerry didn't have much patience to be reminded of things that were interrupting his ten minutes of peace *and* his supper. The fly-over was already planned during the race committee meetings, he was well aware of it. "We appreciate that."

"There's more. I need to make a stop at the Parker camp to relay a message from Chief Robley."

Stopping his search of the shelf for crackers, Gerry stated, "I'll be talking to them I'm sure. You can leave the message with me. I'll pass it along."

"Can't do that. Not something to say over the air. If you could let them know I should be out there sometime tomorrow midday."

Curiosity wasn't Gerry's thing, he had too many irons in the fire to worry about other people's business. Besides, his sister Pearl had enough busybody in her for the two of them. "Alrighty then. I'll let 'em know. Out."

"Thanks. Over and out."

⚘*⚘

"**T**hat chowdah hit the spot, Joe. You're going to make some woman very happy one day." Don rested his hands on his belly.

"Don!" Linda gave her husband an elbow to his side.

"What?" He shrugged. "It's true." He turned to Sarah across the table to see her smirking. "Don't you agree?"

"Absolutely," She twisted toward Joe. "It was delicious." With a smile on her lips, she left an extra-long pause before adding, "And, he certainly makes me happy."

"Ahh, isn't that sweet." Don gave Linda a gentle poke in her side. "See, Linda, it's all factual information."

"Glad you all enjoyed it. I knew Sarah was looking forward to lobster, so I prepared it yesterday to bring along. My trick is to add a little more of the sherry when it reheats."

"Sherry?" asked Linda.

"Uh-huh. That was grandma's secret ingredient. The consistency of the butter, milk, and cream, is critical. And a good seafood stock is key. But it's the medium sherry that gives it the kick."

"I don't know about all that, but in my bowl the lobster was the star. There must have been a two pounder in it. You cook like this the next couple of days, and we may move in with you," said Don.

"Don't get so smug, darling. Tomorrow night it's our turn in the kitchen."

Don frowned and gave Linda a quizzical look. "You know I only do breakfast."

"If you don't shape up, you'll be swabbing the decks."

"That's the Navy!"

"Don, why don't you help me cover up the sleds." Joe figured separating his friends was the best way to avoid their quarreling over chores.

"Sure thing, buddy. I'll grab the flashlights."

While the guys were outside, Linda and Sarah organized the kitchen.

"Joe sure bought a lot of food for a few days." Linda handed three boxes of pasta to Sarah.

"I mentioned the same thing back at the store. He wanted to be prepared." Sarah placed the boxes on the shelf.

"Nothing wrong with that. And Don can work up an appetite during winter activities." Passing a can of beans to Sarah, Linda continued, "Actually, that man has an appetite no matter the season."

The wind howled. The half-century old thin-paned windows rattled in their metal frames. Sarah held the faded moose-print kitchen curtain between her fingers and pulled it aside. She watched the shadows of the guys being illuminated from the flashlights propped in the snow. The black canvas cover was being whipped from their hands quicker than they could strap it down. A flash of orange and red reflected off the glass. She turned to see Linda adding wood to the fire.

Sarah flopped down on the old green couch, put her flannel slipper-covered feet up on the dark wooden coffee table, and unwrapped the red scarf from around her neck. She quietly yawned and then sighed.

Linda sat down across from her. "You must be exhausted. Traveling from New York City to Lobster Lake in one day."

"Yep. Planes, trucks, and snowmobiles. That could be a movie." They both laughed.

Linda picked up her wine glass. "You and Joe have been seeing a lot of one another, especially seeing the distance between the two of you is so large – Maine to New York and all. You two getting serious?"

The question took Sarah by surprise. It was the same one her mother had asked her, twice already. Svetlana from the bakery had asked as well. Sarah had asked it of herself several times.

Linda pushed on. "I don't mean to pry. It's just you realize, Joe is our dearest friend. We can tell he's serious about you."

The statement took Sarah by double surprise. Joe being so reserved, she wondered how long it would take her to be able to read him. "Things between us have been terrific. We had our time in New York and he drove down for my family's Christmas party in Boston a couple of weeks ago."

Linda sat up. "What? I didn't hear about that!"

Sarah was kind of happy to hear her life wasn't the main topic of conversation. "It was a bit last minute."

"That's the tri-fecta of holidays – Thanksgiving, Christmas, and now New Year's."

"I guess that's true." Sarah could tell where Linda was headed and stood up. "You want a refill?" She picked up Linda's wine glass.

"Sure, thanks."

Sitting back down, Sarah watched the flames behind the glass door of the stove and considered the contrast to her life in the city. Here she was, in the deep woods with no connection to the electric grid, but they had plenty of light. There was no superintendent in charge of the boiler, but she was warmer than in her apartment. They had no convenience store on the corner, but they had more than enough supplies for a week. Her thoughts were interrupted when the cabin door banged open. R.C. walked over and sniffed at the pails Joe held in each hand.

From outside, came Don's yell. "Should I leave the coolers outside for the night?"

"No, too cold. Bring them in. We'll put them in the back-hall closet until the fridge kicks in. It's always an icebox out there. Besides, never know what animals may be out scrounging around." Joe pushed the door shut against the wind that was fighting to get inside.

"What's the snow for?" Sarah pointed.

He stomped his boots on the mat. "We'll have to melt it on the woodstove – for our wash water."

"Huh?"

"Darn bucket in the well house must have fallen off the pulley and sunk. I'll fish it out in the morning. This will have to do, until then."

He saw Sarah looking from the bucket to him and back to the bucket again.

"In the morning, I'll get the pump running from the newer drilled well. Can't turn it on until it warms up in here – the pipes will freeze. In the meantime, I have a holding tank up in the loft that feeds the shower. It's another ingenious invention my dad rigged up, way back when. It comes in handy as a backup. The fire melts the snow, we dump the water in the tank up in the loft, and you get a low-flow shower."

"Oh." The train scene from the movie *White Christmas* flashed before Sarah's eyes. Ever since she was a little girl, she had loved the idea of washing her hair with snow. Now she was actually going to do it.

Joe placed the metal pails on the stove. The condensation droplets snapped, popped, and sizzled.

The door opened and Don slid in two coolers. He went back out and came back in with two more buckets that he placed on the mat. R.C. stole a chunk of the snow. "Hey! It's not ice cream." The dog wagged his tail, dropped the snow on the rug, and went back for more.

With Joe tending to his snow buckets, Sarah turned to Linda. "What type of animals might be out there this time of year?"

"Don, pick those buckets up off the floor. The dog's dragging snow around."

"Yes, dear."

Linda shook her head and answered Sarah. "There could be raccoons, coyotes, and if you listen to Don, even a wolf."

"Wolves?" Sarah said it so loud, both Don and Joe snapped to attention.

Don threw his coat over the back of a chair. "Linda and I disagree on it."

"He thinks there are wolves, says he's seen them. I don't think they're back."

"Back?" asked Sarah.

Don became more animated than Sarah had ever seen him. His arms went up in the air. "Wolves, in great numbers, used to live in Maine. Hundreds of years ago. They were hunted because of their destructive nature on livestock … chickens and cows and such. As their habitat decreased, and hunting continued, the population dwindled. Some say they were eliminated, but...” He stopped and motioned to Joe, “You putting that away?”

“Why you want some now?”

“I could go for a glass to warm me up. Pour me a double.” He turned to the ladies. “Who else would like a brandy?”

“Me!” Linda replied.

“How about you, Sarah?” Don asked.

“I’m not much of a brandy drinker, but sure, I’ll try some.”

Don handed her a glass and Sarah took a sip of the coffee liquor. Joe laughed seeing her crinkle her nose.

“That’s different.” She placed the glass on the side table.

“What? You’ve never tasted the champagne of Maine?” asked Don, holding up the bottle.

“Nope. And I think I’ll stick with the wine.”

Sarah walked to the window; she ran her fingertip through the frost that coated the inside corner of the square of glass. The snow had started again and a steady wind was blowing it sideways. She stared out into the darkness.

The windows shook, a cold stream of air passed by Sarah’s ears. She squinted at what she thought was a flash, or a reflection, over near the shed. A slight tingle ran down her back. Even though she was in the wilderness, and there were no degenerates across the street looking in, she pulled the drapes closed.

The action didn't go unnoticed by Joe. The only time he closed the drapes was at the end of the season, and then it was only to keep the sun from fading the old furniture, but after all these years even that was a lost cause. "What is it, Sarah?" he asked.

She sat on the couch, pulling a blanket over her legs. "I got a chill, that's all."

Pouring another drink, Don went on about the wolves. "No way, no how, is anyone telling me the wolves ain't here. I've seen dark, gray-black animals, much darker and bigger than coyotes."

Linda seeing Sarah's surprise, calmly added, "There's strong evidence that western and Canada wolves have crossbred with coyotes. These hybrids have a larger range than wolves and thrive in the Maine wilderness. Coyote pelts, skulls, and DNA show genes from these Maine coyotes include that of the western wolf. While these animals are bigger than a coyote, and are living in the Maine woods, they are not the large wolves that once roamed the forest."

Impressed with Linda's knowledge, she asked, "Why such an interest in wolves, um, I mean coyote-wolves?"

"I found out about it from an exhibit down at the Maine State Museum in Augusta. It does a nice job covering the animal history."

"I think you should stop scaring Sarah with these tales about wolves." Joe picked up one of the coolers and carried it down the hall.

"There are no tales here. It's all factual. And something she needs to know being out here in the woods," said Don, picking up the second cooler and following Joe.

Linda opened a second bottle of wine and poured Sarah a refill.

"Thank you. Are these hybrids around here?" Sarah shuddered, only part of which was from a chill.

Before Linda could answer, Joe was back. "I've never seen any traces of the hybrid wolves around the cabin. Coyotes, sure, but nothing larger than that." Joe picked a thick maple stick from the kindling and pushed on the melting snow in the buckets. Sarah walked over, picked a stick, and stirred the other bucket.

"Joe, you up for a game of cribbage?" asked Don.

"Oh, I forgot. Have I got something to show you. It's in my bag." Joe disappeared to the bedroom and came back holding a box. From the box, he slid a black velvet bag. He untied the silver string and held the board.

Don jumped to his feet. "Wow! That's some fancy. Much nicer than that oak cribbage board we've been playing on for thirty years."

"Where'd you get that?" Linda asked.

"It was a Christmas gift from Sarah." Joe smiled her way.

"What kind of wood is this?" Don reached and touched the smooth finish.

"The sales person told me, but I can't remember right now." Sarah let out a big yawn. "The card's in the box."

Joe read, "The base is Bubinga and the inlays are white Holly with black Wenge."

"Never heard of Bubinga or Wenge." Don took the card from Joe to read it again.

"There's more." Sarah reached for the board. "You push here, and here." As she did, the block of wood separated to reveal an inside compartment. "It's a secret wood-lock."

Metal pegs in gold, silver and copper were standing on display in the velvet lined interior. Behind them was a spot for a deck of cards to fit securely in the compartment.

"It sure is a beautiful piece, it'll be fun to play on that board," said Linda.

"Fun nothing. I plan to walk away with some big winnings from Don. I'll get the cards." Joe started towards the counter.

A loud thump from the front porch made Linda and Sarah gasp. R.C. jumped up from his blanket, started barking, ran to the door, then circled back to the window and jumped up on the sill. His paws caught on the closed curtains, causing the rod to come crashing down. After he got over the surprise, he shook off the fabric and jumped back up on the sill. He held a slow, low growl looking out at the darkness.

The guys walked over to the door. Linda held R.C. by the collar. Don grabbed a flashlight. Joe looked outside as Don swung the beam of light around the porch. A few logs from the woodpile had dropped to the floor. The beam of light came to a stop on a set of boot prints leading around the side of the cabin.

"You go around that way earlier?" Joe's voice was low, he was hoping neither of the girls had heard him.

Don shrugged, "I guess. Maybe. I don't recall."

Joe closed the door. "A piece of wood fell. Must have been balancing on edge after I pulled some out earlier."

"Or maybe a racoon?" Don more asked, than stated.

A silence came over the room. The woodstove popped. Linda stood on a chair and hung the curtain rod back up.

Still holding the stick, Sarah asked, "Don't they hibernate?"

"Who?" asked Joe.

"Racoons."

"Um, well, not ..." Joe was still thinking about the tracks outside and if they were Don's or not.

"No. They don't," answered Linda. "They may stay in their winter den for weeks at a time sleeping, but they are not one of the animals that hibernate in the strict sense. They do go out for food. They may have seen an opportunity with us being here, they're not shy looking for trash or handouts."

"Glad we brought the coolers in." Don tried to lighten the mood with a laugh.

Joe nodded. "On the topic of coyotes, just so you all know, don't let R.C. out alone. I'd prefer he's on a leash, that way he doesn't wander off. When you let him out, if you're not going, there's a long rope with a collar hook hanging outside the door. Stay close by until he comes back in." He pointed. "And this is right here if you need to scare anything off." Joe swung open the safe door.

Seeing the shotgun, Sarah assumed he was talking to Don and Linda, and not her about that point.

Don turned on the CB radio. A whine of static filled the room.

"You calling out?" Joe asked.

"Figured I'd listen in for any radio traffic."

"Don, turn that thing down. The only traffic you're gonna get will be from Canada, and you don't speak French. Better yet, turn it off." Linda took a seat in a rocker near the woodstove.

Don's hand was on the off switch, when the radio crackled.

"Trail Cat to Eagle One, you there?"

Don, feeling validated, shot Linda a glance.

"Eagle One here. What is it, Gerry?"

"Hey, Don, use my handle."

Don rolled his eyes. "What is it, Trail Cat?"

"Warden Green gave me a call earlier. He's going to stop over that way tomorrow, says he has a personal message for Joe. He asked me to give you a heads up. By the way, anything missing up at your place?"

"Missing?" Don answered, looking over at Joe.

Joe shook his head and shrugged. Don handed him the microphone.

"Why would there be anything missing?" Joe was on edge.

"Hi, Lobsterman. There's been some trouble lately. I don't want to talk about it over the radio."

"Gerry, why didn't you mention it when we were down at the store?"

"Slipped my mind, Joe. Getting old ya know. Besides, I kinda mentioned it to Linda earlier."

They all looked over at Linda. "I haven't had a moment to bring it up. Didn't seem like that big of a deal," she answered their accusing stares.

"Nothing you all need to be concerned about. Trouble only seems to happen at closed up cabins. Although, earlier today..." Gerry's voice become distant, *"Hey! Hey! Darn it!"*

"Gerry?" "Gerry?"

"Got to go guys, couple of the dogs are loose, they're causing mayhem out by the kennels. Trail Cat, out."

"Gerry? Gerry? Trail Cat, you didn't finish telling us about what's going on." He was gone.

"What do you think he meant by that?" Sarah's voice trembled. She moved to the edge of the couch, her arms crossed tight. Joe saw she was shivering.

"I can't say for sure. I've heard some talk that summer places have been getting broken into the past few months. I figured people were making somethin' out of nothin," Don said.

"Why'd you think that?" asked Sarah.

"Sometimes, out here, if someone gets stranded in the winter, to stay alive until help arrives, they may need to make use of a cabin. Maybe they light a fire. Maybe they move stuff around. But lately there have been stories of things gone missing."

"What would someone find in a cabin way out here worth stealing?" Sarah looked around at the old furniture, black and white photos, and the cast iron pots and pans suspended from the black hooks hanging from the kitchen ceiling. She saw Joe frown. "I didn't mean it that way, Joe. You know I love it here. When we get a burglar in the city, he's after cash, jewelry, electronics. Things they can sell."

"I understand, Sarah. But you see, this place holds a lot of memories for me. The photos on the wall, the camp journals, even that old rocker," he pointed, "it was my mom's. If anything ever happened to any of it,..." his voice trailed off, "well these are my treasures."

"What's going on here is a little different you two," interrupted Don. "The rumors are that whoever is breaking into places isn't taking any valuables, sentimental or otherwise."

"Then what are they taking?" Sarah asked. She went around to all the other windows in the cabin closing the curtains.

"From what I've heard, the person, or persons, are taking supplies. Matches, lanterns, blankets, pots, tools." Don paused. "And propane tanks. Always the propane tanks."

"If I ever catch whoever it is, I'll give them a pot across the head. Blankets and matches are highly valuable when you show up at your cabin in the winter," Joe said.

To Sarah, suddenly her city apartment seemed pretty safe.

Joe was adjusting the woodstove when he noticed Don fiddling with the window near the writing desk.

"What are you doing?" asked Joe.

"I don't think I ever got to mention to you..." He paused.

"Mention what?" Joe walked towards Don.

News from Germany

✳✳

Cocking his head at Don, Joe asked again, "Mention what?" He raised his hands.

Don cleared his throat. "Back in November, when I was doing trail maintenance with the guys." His words came slowly, as he thought back. "I swung by this way."

"Yeah, so?"

"I just remembered something."

"What?" Joe's impatience had a sharp edge.

"Do you remember if you closed all the windows before you headed out last October?"

"Of course. You know I have a checklist of things I have to do before I leave each fall." Joe's left eye twitched. "What are you getting at?"

"It's probably nothing."

"Spit it out, Don. I want to go to sleep." Linda stood, her feet apart, hands on her hips.

"You remember, dear. I must have told you. I found that window open." He pointed.

They all turned towards the window over the writing desk. Sarah reached above the desk and pulled the curtain closed.

"You never mentioned it to me. Do you think you might have left the latch open, Joe?" Linda asked.

"I highly doubt that. I triple check every item." Joe pulled the curtain aside and jiggled the latch. "Maybe the wind blew it open." Sarah came up behind him and tugged it closed again.

"That's what I thought. I came in and checked it out. The old newspapers you keep were strewn all about." Don's right arm went from motioning at the desk, to the kindling box, to the floor. "Even the papers in your fire starter pile were spread around." Nobody said a word. Don continued. "I figured maybe you left in a rush."

"And you didn't think to call?" Joe sat back against the top of the desk.

"I told him to call you." Linda pointed a finger at Don.

Linda's head was bobbing so much, Don waited for it to fall off. He said, "It was when you were in New York, over Thanksgiving."

Joe's eyes were looking off in the distance. Don went on, "And your answering machine is full. Matter of fact, that thing has been full for over a year."

"I can't figure how to delete the darn messages. But you're only thinking to tell me about this now? While we're here." Joe sat down. Sarah sat close to him. He could feel the slight tremble of her body.

"Slipped my mind. Nothing else looked out of place, so I stacked the stuff back where it was, and made sure everything was locked up."

Leaning back and putting his hands behind his head, Joe thought for a moment. "It's possible maybe I left the window open. The wind could have blown things around." He put his arm around Sarah. She didn't think that was the case at all.

Linda yawned. "I don't know about the rest of you, but I'm exhausted. I'm going to get ready for bed."

"Me too. Can you bring me my toothbrush?"

"Did you pack it?" Linda stood at the doorway to the guest room.

"No." Don shook his head. "Figured you would."

"There's a new pack under the bathroom sink. Help yourself," said Joe.

Getting up, Sarah headed to the bedroom. "Guess, I'll get my stuff together to see how this shower contraption of yours works."

"It's not all that fancy. Linda can give you a quick rundown when she's done. Keep in mind, we've got limited water tonight. Use it sparingly." Joe lifted his right hand, showing a small space between his thumb and index finger.

"No worries. Some days I have no hot water at all in my apartment, so this could be quite luxurious."

Joe raised his eyebrows and nodded, recalling the icy shower he had the pleasure of taking at her flat.

Waiting on his turn for the bathroom, Joe took a closer look at the stacks of papers Don had haphazardly put back on the shelves. The stack contained his collection of issues from, "The Maine Daily," "The County News," "The Boston Times," and a few others. Rarely was there a full paper, mostly he saved sports articles, but mixed in were world events going back to the 60s. His dad and his grandpa had started the saving and he had done the same. Over the years, he would refer to his organized collection when working on a story, or in an argument with one of the guys over a certain Red Sox game.

He sighed. The collection was no longer in order. They were not sorted by date and all the different topics were shuffled together. Reorganizing the stacks was a project he was going to have to do before he'd be able to sleep. He took the papers to the couch and began sorting them on the pine coffee table.

When Sarah sat down in the maple rocker, she was all ready for bed. Joe thought she could be on a postcard. "Cute pajamas."

"You like?" She lifted her right arm and left leg and jiggled. "Bought them by mail-order, specially for this trip."

"The moose skiing between the pine trees goes with the setting."

She laughed and examined the moose on her sleeve. "I'll tell you, this moose can ski better than me."

"Speaking of moose, here are those sketches of the winged moose.

"Thanks." Sarah moved to the couch and flipped through the drawings. She patted him on the knee twice. "Is the rest of that Springsteen article in your stack? The one Gerry had a piece of?"

"It's here somewhere. Things are still a bit out of order." Joe felt Sarah's eyes on him as he searched through the piles. "Where the heck did it go?"

Don came out of the bathroom and stood brushing his teeth. He watched Joe rummaging through the desk and flipping through each camp journal. "What are you looking for?"

"The rest of that Springsteen article about the East Berlin concert. Sarah wanted to read the rest of it."

"Oh." Don turned back to the bathroom to rinse his mouth. When he had finished, Joe was still searching the desk. "Good night, you two."

"Night." Joe's voice had a bit of an edge.

"Don't stay up too late, I want to get an early start tomorrow."

"What are we doing tomorrow?" asked Sarah.

"We came out here to give you the grand experience. We'll be doing some ice fishing, a snowshoe hike, and of course, more sledding." The door to the guest room clicked shut.

"Ahh, sounds... fun." Sarah's voice trailed off. She was sort of hoping that getting to the camp *was* the snowmobiling tour of the backcountry. Putting her arm over Joe's shoulder, she said, "Don't worry about it. The article's not important. We should go to bed."

"You go on on. I'll be in after I get cleaned up." On his way to the bathroom Joe walked to the front door and locked it; an action that did not go unnoticed by Sarah.

Lying in bed, her leg curled around Joe, Sarah asked, "Will we be safe out on the trails tomorrow?"

"Absolutely. We'll go as far as we can on the sleds, then we'll snowshoe. Don knows these trails. He wouldn't have us sledding anywhere that's not safe."

"No. I meant from whoever else might be out there in the woods."

"Ah, that's mostly people making something of nothing." He pulled her closer.

"Ohhh," she breathed.

After, Joe's breathing became heavy and he started to slip off to sleep.

Sarah whispered in his ear. "Tell me about that name Gerry called you – Lobsterman?"

Joe took a deep breath, coming back to life. "Ahh. It's called a handle."

"Huh? When were you a lobsterman?"

"Never."

"Well I get Gerry's name, I mean '*handle*,' Trail Cat, as a Maine Guide. And Don's handle, Eagle One, being a pilot. But why Lobsterman for you?"

"I'm the only one living up here on Lobster Lake."

"Oh." Sarah stared at the knotty pine on the ceiling. The board over her head had knots for eyes and a beak of an owl.

Joe drifted off.

A few minutes passed. Sarah lightly nudged him. "Joe?"

"Yes?"

"Can I have a handle?"

An airy laugh came from Joe's nose. "Certainly. What name do you want to have? Latte Lady?"

She poked him. "No! It has to be something north woods style."

"How about Snow Bunny?"

"I like that."

"Okay. Snow Bunny it is. We'll register that in the morning."

"Really?"

"Absolutely. Goodnight." In the dim light, she couldn't see him smirking.

Sarah turned off the gas light next to the bed. Closing her eyes, her thoughts jumped around in a recap of the day, what she'd seen, who she'd met, and her travels. By the time she started thinking about Gerry's story of the person stalking the woods, Joe's breathing was steady, his mouth slightly open letting out a low whistle.

A creak from the living room caused Sarah's eyes to open to complete darkness. With no streetlamps, no car headlights, no flashing neon lights from the corner store, there wasn't a sliver of light in the bedroom.

She whispered, "Joe, you still awake?" His breathing rhythm continued with no recognition of her voice.

The floor creaked again. She slipped from under the covers, and felt around with her feet for her slippers.

Pulling back on the pine door it squeaked. She opened it only enough to peak out.

Wide Awake

✳✴

Sarah pulled her heavy sweater on and slipped out of the bedroom. A flickering of orange escaped from the embers in the woodstove. R. C. appeared from behind the couch.

In a whisper, she asked, "What is it, boy? Why are you walking around out here?" The dog looked at her blankly and settled back on his blanket.

She patted his head. "I guess I can't sleep either." She shivered. Opening the door of the woodstove, the glow reflected her crouched silhouette, on the wall behind her; R.C. growled.

"It's okay. That's just my shadow." She set two logs on the coals, and sat on the floor, enjoying the warm heat. In the stillness of the room the timbers cracked and popped, echoing through the cabin.

Reluctantly, she closed the firebox. The room went dim; her eyes tried to adjust. She felt her way to the supply box on the kitchen counter and felt for a flashlight. It was now obvious why Joe had given her the tour of the cabin and his supplies — *"for emergencies,"* he had said.

The wooden box with a hinged lid had been made by his grandfather. It contained compartments for matches, batteries, flashlights, a screwdriver, a knife, and a few loose shotgun shells, which Sarah thought was an odd place for them.

Taking the matches, she lit the kerosene lantern the way Joe had showed her. Placing the glass over the wick, the living room brightened. She turned down the flame and started toward the couch. Remembering Joe's words, she doubled back and placed the matches and flashlight back in the box.

R.C. stood up. She whispered, "Go back to sleep. It's not time to get up." He circled three times around on his blanket and laid back down.

While she had been up since four-thirty this morning, she suddenly didn't feel the need to sleep herself. The clock read eleven fifteen. She looked towards the bedroom door. Her book was in her bag and she didn't want to risk waking Joe. Lifting the lamp off the table, she walked to the bookshelf. She scanned the spines on Joe's collection of reading material. One shelf held his stacks of old magazines and yellowing papers. The other shelves appeared to be ordered by topic. There were books on birds, hunting, and how to illustrate wildlife. Above her head, on a shelf she'd need a stepstool to reach, there were classics she had read many times – Twain, Cooper, Dickens, Verne, and others. A shelf of well-worn spines held Maine titles, including, *The Maine Woods*, and *Woods and Lakes of Maine*.

The shelf at eye height gave her goosebumps as she read the titles, *The Body Snatchers*, *The House on Haunted Hill,* and *I Am Legend.* Seeing a book by an author she hadn't read in a long time, and with a faint recollection of enjoying the stories when she was in high school, she sat down and began to read.

At the passage, *"For his gold I had no desire. I think it was his eye! Yes, it was this! He had the eye of a vulture --a pale blue eye, with a film over it. Whenever it fell upon me, my blood ran cold."* She closed the book with a bang and took a breath. She quickly remembered that, *The Tell Tale Heart*, was only memorable because of a Halloween sleepover with seven other girls when they told ghost stories. She wondered how Joe, or anyone, could read arm-hair raising books out here in the deep woods.

In need of something less scary, she rose and noticed the shelf above the writing desk and the camp journals. She ran her finger across the bindings, selecting the one labeled 1956.

When she sat back down, R.C. flashed his doggie eyes her way. "Okay, boy. You can keep me company." She patted the cushion. The dog didn't need to be asked twice, he was next to her in a flash.

Sarah pulled the lamp closer. She slowly turned the pages until she found an entry she was hoping would be there.

Visitor in the Meadow — Friday July 27, 1956

Henry stopped by today. But he wasn't here to visit. He picked up a visitor we had and drove her back to town. Well, she wasn't so much a visitor, but someone who was kind of passing through. If it wasn't for the weather this week, I might have been out fishing and not up on Rum Ridge when I spotted her.

For the past week we've had thunderstorms almost every afternoon. The rain has been a pain, but it's been mostly the wind after the storms that has been messing up my time fishing. Dad hasn't wanted me out on the canoe. The lake has been an ocean — well not exactly, nothing like that day Dad and I were caught in that gale out off Hog Island, it was when we went to visit Grandma at the cottage down in Pemaquid. The wind that day would have turned Grandpa's old skiff into toothpicks if we had washed into the ledges. Those were some rough seas. I'll take the white caps on Lobster Lake any day of the week.

Because of the storm last night, the lake was still choppy this morning and I couldn't go out in the canoe. Dad cooked our breakfast over the fire pit down by the water and I fished off the dock. I didn't catch anything. It's too warm in the shallows. After a while, Dad took Sparky over to Bug Bog. He still thinks he can turn him into a bird dog. Yeah right! (I know you're reading this Dad, it won't happen.)

I was supposed to go for a run. Dad had reminded me of my promise to coach to keep up my training for track. I figured I'd go later in the day. (I did, Dad, you'll see!)

I hiked up to Rum Ridge to check the spot where I was building my hunting blind. When I reached the top, there was a storm cloud over Black Cap Mountain. The lightning was shooting down pretty good over that way. The clouds blew off to the east. When I looked down towards the meadow, that's when I saw her.

She was walking in a circle. It was obvious she was lost. I couldn't hear what she was yelling.

I left my pack and ran down the trail. I ran it, all the way. I made pretty good time too.

At the spot where the trail opened onto the meadow, I stopped to catch my breath.

That girl looked at me like I was something out of a horror movie. I guess I was sweaty and dirty. Turns out, she hated being out in the woods, and boy, was she snarky. Her parents had taken her on a hike and she got separated from them, I won't even say how she managed to do that, but wow, what a city girl.

On the bright side, she was wearing a Red Sox cap. On the down side, it wasn't hers, it was her sister's. I probably would have gotten along with her sister more. This girl didn't follow the Sox at all, or any baseball.

She wasn't much of a hiker either. Fact is, she wasn't much of a talker either, except about city life in Boston and wanting to go to New York City.

When we walked back to camp, Henry was there. He was surprised I had already found her. So was Dad.

Maybe I'll see her sometime again over the summer, maybe in town at the Dairy Shack. I don't know her name.   J. P.

Sarah was smiling when she closed the journal. R.C.'s head was on her lap.

"I wish I was as sleepy as you." She scratched behind his ear. He groaned.

She nudged him over and checked the fire. While she knelt letting the flames warm her, she thought of her own diary entry from that day in the woods, remembering she wasn't as gentle in her prose of the wilderness, her predicament, or the *mountain boy* she had met on the trail.

By the time she got back to the couch, R.C. had sprawled out lengthwise. She pushed him over, covered her legs with the quilt, and again opened the journal.

There were entries written by Joe, by his dad, and from camp guests that covered fishing, a moose who strolled by the cabin one evening, a few pages of sketched birds, and an entire page for the game when Ted Williams hit his four-hundredth home run. A note was scribbled on the paper clipping that was taped in the journal.

> We didn't know if Ted was going to play again after being called up to serve in the Korean War and then after his retiring in '54.
>
> ## Now this in '56!
>
> – Stan P.

Turning the pages, she found another entry in Joe's handwriting. She kicked off her slippers, pulled her legs up under herself, and sat back.

Stranded in the Snow – Thanksgiving 1956

What a week at camp. Dad and I came up to hunt and some strange things have been happening. Right now, Dad is with Henry and Nate P. and an FBI agent. Yep – the FBI, here at Lobster Lake. I'm stuck here because a couple of deer ran us off the road and the truck got stuck. At least I have cookies to eat, Alice sent them up with Henry. This is what happened.

Dad and I came up on Sunday. The first surprise was we caught perch in Duck Pond. Dad's going to talk to Henry about it.

Then I heard people making bird calls in the woods. That really spooked me because I didn't know who they were – could've been hunters or who knows who.

The third surprise was a man I saw in the meadow. He was smoking by a tree and watching Dad. I was up on Rum Ridge and this man was keeping an eye on Dad through binoculars.

(December 1956) I never got to finish this up at camp as we had to leave in a hurry. Dad, Henry, and the FBI man – he was the guy watching Dad in the meadow, captured the Lobster Lake Bandits and took them in. They were stocking perch in the *ponds and robbing cabins. I'm not sure what happened with the investigation on the Brink's robbery or if it was the bandits. Dad has to speak with Henry.   - - J.P.*

She turned the page and read the newspaper clipping, the one Joe had showed her back in the fall – the article written by H. Molloy. Thinking of her dad, she wiped the corner of her eye with a tissue.

Sarah couldn't tell if she was over-tired and that's why she wasn't sleepy, or if she was anxious based on what Gerry said earlier. She flipped the page.

Spring 1957 – The Trapper Cabin

From what I heard from Henry and Dad talking, Henry never could get a straight answer from the FBI on agent Jim Smith. We went with Henry to investigate over at the old trapper cabin. He and Dad had a hunch that the old place may have been what Jim Smith was looking for. When we got there, we found it was burned to the ground.

Henry walked around in circles and looked at the trees. He said it must have happened in the dead of winter. None of the surrounding trees were burned. Dad asked him if maybe it was from a lightning storm. Henry shook his head and said it was very unlikely.

I stepped on a piece of rotten wood and my leg went through. Turns out it was an old root cellar. Henry led the way with his flashlight and Dad and I followed him down the rock steps. There were some wooden shelves along the dirt wall and a workbench in the center. The mold smell was terrible. The only stuff there were some rusty tools. Henry said they were locksmith tools. He collected them and said he was going to ship them down to Augusta. The town later filled in that hole so nobody would fall in and get hurt.

We never did find out anything more. – – J.P.

Sarah closed the journal. Remembering the package of shortbread cookies she had stowed on the shelf earlier, she felt hungry. When her right foot hit the cold pine plank floor, she yanked it back and wiggled her feet into her slippers.

On her way back to the couch, she selected another journal, the cover was marked, 1972 - 1974. Opening the book, she saw a woman's writing and the initials on the entries that could only be Ellen's. Joe had only briefly talked to her about Ellen, and she was intrigued to learn more. She took the book and sat down.

This morning, Joe and I were on the canoe near Sunset Point and what a surprise we had. I counted twelve loons in a raft-up. It was the most wonderful parade I've ever seen in my life. They were singing to us with their tremolo call. We drifted not more than thirty feet as they glided by. We spent more than an hour watching them.

Joe wasn't as thrilled as I was, he'd seen plenty of these gatherings before. He wanted to fish, but he was a good sport and reeled in his line. I used up my entire roll of film.

Joe and I whispered possible reasons for the normally territorial loons to socialize in such a large group. We hypothesized it had to do with the end of the nesting season, or preparing for their coastal migration. I liked the best guess from Joe, he said they were trying to pair up their youngsters for the next year. That seems as *good an explanation as any to me – match making in the north woods.*

   E.M.P. August 25, 1972

Taking another cookie, the package crinkled. R.C.'s ears twitched. She handed him a piece.

Flipping through the pages, she realized that midway through the 1973 entries, there were no further writings with the initials *E.M.P.*

"Sarah? Is everything all right?"

She hadn't heard Joe enter the living room. She tried to force a smile, but couldn't. Her lips quivered, enough for him to notice.

"Are you cold?" He put his hand over the stove. He leaned over and opened the firebox. "I see you've been stoking it."

It was Joe, she thought, who should be cold. He had no socks on and was wearing only his boxers and a t-shirt. He nudged R.C. with a, "Get down, boy," and sat next to her on the couch.

He asked, "What's wrong?" Then he noticed the journal she held in her hands. He hadn't opened a journal from those particular years in a long time. It didn't matter, he knew each and every entry by heart. His head moved up and down, almost imperceptibly. He knew he would have to tell Sarah more about Ellen, he only wished he had prepared for doing so.

"I need some water. You want some?" He kissed her forehead and went to the kitchen.

In the shadowy darkness, she watched him pour two glasses from the jug. She wondered if she should have been reading Ellen's entries. Her concern was heightened when he handed her a glass and sat in his rocker, and not next to her. She took a sip and swallowed. The sound reverberated in her ears.

"I guess it is chilly in here. Be right back." Returning from the bedroom, he was wearing his jeans and a flannel shirt.

This time, he sat next to her. "Ellen and I were friends through high school and started dating in college. My mom had died when I was young. Then what happened to Ellen. It was tough." His eyes were locked on hers. "I want you to understand that knowing you, I've been happier than I've been in a long time."

She nodded, but held back telling him she felt the same, she didn't want to interrupt.

"Ellen was a nurse. She loved her job. It was her calling. When the hospital asked for volunteers for hurricane relief efforts, she didn't hesitate." His eyes didn't leave a painting on the wall of a loon couple approaching one another in a pond; Ellen had painted it. "I only talked with her once while she was there. The phone line went dead before we said goodbye."

Sarah wanted to reach out, to pull him close, but he reached for his water glass and stood up. She scrunched the blanket in her hands, and pressed it tight to her chest. The shadow of the flame from the lantern bounced off the wall.

He walked to the window, and pulled the drape aside. Lifting his glass, he finished his water in one long drink. His eyes adjusted to the darkness over the ridge to the north. "What I was told, three days later, was her group was headed to the foothills, west, in Veracruz, the roads were washed out and muddy. It was a narrow pass when the jeep lost traction . . ."

The gasp of air Sarah sucked in caused Joe to stop. "I'm sorry, I didn't mean to upset you."

Her eyes closed. She didn't want to see the pain in his eyes, or for him to see the pain in hers. She wished she could take back the last ten minutes, to not have asked her question.

Joe reached out and her fingers slipped within his, she felt herself rising.

"I want to show you something." His voice was low. He took her coat from the hook and held it open for her.

"Outside? Now? It's *freezing*."

"Trust me. It'll be worth it."

Her eyes were still wet with tears. She dried them with her sleeve, slipped her arms into the coat, stepped into her boots and pulled on her hat.

He buttoned his field coat and his hand reached for the door knob. "Close your eyes."

"Joe..."

"It's fine. Hold my hand." He led her to the front porch. She began shivering.

"Keep your eyes closed."

"Okay!"

He stepped behind her and wrapped his arms around her chest. It felt good, but she was still freezing.

"Open your eyes."

She went to turn towards him.

"No. Look out there. Towards the break in the clouds. Let your eyes adjust to the darkness."

The ultra-cold air, the dark sky void of all light pollution, and the location of Joe's cabin, were the perfect combination to see the waves of greens and pinks shimmering amongst the stars in the blackened sky.

"Are those the northern lights?"

"Sure are."

"I didn't know you could see them from Maine."

"From *this Maine*, you can."

"I've never seen them before. Obviously. The colors are so bright."

Sarah felt Joe's arms tighten around her. She no longer seemed cold. There wasn't a sound to be heard. The dancing swirls of color had her mesmerized. "Does this happen all the time here?" she asked.

"No. The conditions have to be right for the spirits to be in a dancing mood."

She nudged him.

"I don't claim to understand when or why the charged particles in the atmosphere tend to collide. But I do enjoy it when it happens."

"It is beautiful." Her head leaned back into his shoulder.

"Best movie we have out here."

They stood in silence for a few minutes. When her body quivered, he guided her back through the door. He helped her out of her coat, took her hand, and led her to the bedroom.

She stopped. "What about R.C.?"

"Come on, boy." Joe picked up R.C.'s blanket and the dog followed behind him.

With her arms wrapped tightly around Joe, Sarah wasn't sure when she fell asleep, but it wasn't long before she melted into a dream. Neither they, or R.C., heard the crunching of snow from out near the shed.

The roaring wind and the moonless night, thanks to the thick clouds, provided the perfect cover for the gang to go on a night excursion to scout their latest collection point. Napolin and Leontel had found the place a few days earlier, a closed-up camp down a dead-end close to where they found the heavy iron grill. Aside from a lot of old metal pipe they wanted, there was a large gas tank, enough to supply them for the rest of their trip.

The four snowmobiles made their way over the nine miles of trails under the cover of darkness. It was a little before five a.m. when Napolin stopped along a narrow camp road. The others pulled in behind him. Strapping on snowshoes, he and Leontel went ahead to ensure there was no one around. They were back in fifteen minutes.

"Is it clear?" Axe asked, smoking his third cigarette, he hadn't moved from the seat of his sled.

"No. There are sleds there now. Can't chance it." Napolin started to get on his snowmobile. "We hiked in there for nothin'."

Annoyed his crew were giving up so easily, Axe jumped up, grabbed two red five-gallon cans from the pull-behind and started down the tracks the other two had made. "We may not get the metal, but that gas is easy taking."

"You want to walk in there to siphon out a few gallons of gas?" asked Heath.

"Num-nut. Can't you multiply? Four of us, each carry two five-gallon cans that's ..." Axe coughed and spit at a tree. "That's a good haul."

"You expect each of us to carry over forty pounds of gas? It's starting to snow again!" sniped Napolin.

"What are ya? A little girl? Man up. We're gonna make somethin' from this trip. Each of you grab those cans. The sooner we're done, the sooner we can get to breakfast. Besides, when else might we have a chance for fresh snow to fill in our tracks by daylight."

The gang made it back to their sleds without being detected. Axe, who was completely winded, said, "See – told ya. Easy taking." He plunked the cans in the tow sled.

✻✻✻

"**Y**ou hear that?" Linda nudged Don.

"What?" Don rolled over, stretching his legs under the covers.

"Sounds like a snowmobile."

"What time is it?"

She reached over him for his watch on the nightstand. He grumbled.

"Close to six," she said. Don didn't move. She poked him. "Don't you think you should check?"

Don couldn't hear anything, but sitting in the cockpit of a prop plane for thirty years will do that to you.

"Probably a plane. Sounds in the atmosphere travel far on cold nights."

"Sounded close."

"Maybe someone's out on the lake for ice fishing."

"Sounded closer than that."

"Is the sun up?" Don growled and pulled the comforter over his shoulders.

"No."

"Wake me when it is."

Linda knew it was no use. A few glasses of Allen's at night and the bear wasn't rising until he was good and ready. She pulled on yesterday's clothes and left him slumbering.

Who was Eddy Walsh?

New Year's Eve - Morning

A thin strip of sunlight breaking through a slit in the curtains shone on Sarah's eyes. She slipped out of bed, pulled on her thickest, heaviest, sweatshirt over her pajama top, and parted the winter drapes an inch. A low, "Ooh," escaped from her lips.

Beyond the window an open sloping field of pristine white extended all the way to the frozen stream. Daylight was cresting in a red-orange line between the clouds and the mountains that framed the view. Icicles, the clearest she'd ever seen, hung down from the edge of the roof, glistening in the first rays of morning sun. Fluffy snow from the tips of the evergreen branches shimmered to the ground in slow motion, a glitter reflecting rainbows of color floating in the wind.

Closing the drapes, Sarah turned. The rise and fall of Joe's chest under the blanket was barely visible. In need of her morning coffee, she lifted the latch on the knotty-pine door, the creak of the hinges caused Joe to groan. He rolled on his side.

She stepped into the hall; R.C. pushed his way through behind her. Looking back in at Joe, she recalled a trick she and her sister learned when they were young to sneak through doors. Quickly she pulled the door to her, almost slamming it shut. The creak was barely audible. She lifted the black iron latch into place.

"Good morning, boy." Without an acknowledgment, he walked to the stove and curled up tight with his nose buried under his belly.

Tiptoeing across the wide-plank pine floor, the cold penetrated the wool socks she had slept in. She placed her hands over the woodstove; there was a disappointing amount of heat emanating from the metal. Lifting a log from the stack near the brick hearth, she pushed it around on what remained of the coals. The oak was too large to catch. Wrapping the blanket from the couch over her shoulders, she slipped into Joe's boots, and stepped out into the cold.

On the porch, she was putting sticks in the kindling bag when she was startled by motion she caught out of the corner of her eye. Sarah watched in a trance, suddenly oblivious to the biting cold, as four deer pranced across the snow. She stood, listening to the sound of silence. She closed her eyes and took in a deep breath of the frozen air – forcing herself to remember the nothingness forever.

Closing the door with a leg, she was greeted by the sight of Joe standing in the bedroom doorway. "Good morning. There are deer in the yard."

He eyed the armfuls of wood she was balancing up to her chin. "Good morning. I'd be surprised if there *weren't*. You're up early. And already getting wood to stoke the fire? Impressive."

"It looked too beautiful outside to stay in bed, and the wood, well it's freezing in here." She placed the smaller logs on the floor and added starter pieces to the fire. Standing to hug him, she knocked a log to the floor.

"Hey – what's all the noise out here? Oh, excuse me." Don faked shielding his eyes on his way to the kitchen.

"Morning. How'd you sleep?" asked Joe.

"Same as always, on my left side, and like a log." He filled the stainless coffee pot with water from a jug.

"Is Linda still sleeping?" asked Sarah.

"Nah. She's out taking photos. She has an addiction to early morning pictures. It's a hobby of hers."

"Oh. Wish I'd known, I would have tagged along."

"Not sure she'd have let you. I was with her a few weeks ago and I let out an almost inaudible yawn when, coincidently, a barred owl flew away. She told me from then on I had to stay home."

"That'll teach you." Joe said.

"It's not bad. I get to sleep in now." He placed the pot on the burner. From the look on Don's face, Joe got the impression that may have been his plan all along.

The warmth from the woodstove began to fill the room and when the coffee pot started to percolate, the smell drew Don to take three mugs from the shelf. R.C. decided to get up, walked over to the door, and barked. When Joe opened the door a gust of icy wind blew into the cabin. R.C, took a step back.

"Appears we have some nasty weather coming in from the north." Joe tugged the leash. "Okay, boy, let's go."

Sarah sat at the counter drinking her coffee and watched Don mix up pancake batter.

"Are you worried with Linda being out alone?"

"What? Why?"

"With what Gerry said about someone sneaking around."

"Anyone would be crazy to mess with that woman. The camera isn't the only thing she takes along on her photoshoots that shoots." Don noticed Sarah's raised eyebrows. "These are the woods. She has to be prepared."

"I guess my city girl is showing through, huh?"

"A little bit."

Stamping the snow from his boots, Joe said, "Look who we found outside."

"That dog flushed me out of a perfect picture taking spot," said Linda, as she walked in behind Joe.

Joe unclipped R.C.'s leash, the dog shook, sauntered to his bowl, and beckoned for his breakfast with a single "woof."

"Where'd you take pictures this morning, dear?" Don poured her a coffee and added cream and sugar.

"I started down at the lake." She wrapped her hands around the warm mug. "Then I followed a set of tracks to find a moose drinking from the outlet."

"Be careful over that way," Joe warned. "Around the outlet there's always thin ice."

"I know. I stayed on shore. The sunrise through a horizontal strip in the clouds was the perfect background for the photo. I wish I could develop it right now."

"You can't do that. But take a seat, these hotcakes are a work of art." Don placed a platter at the center of the table.

"Looks good. I see you can cook after all," said Joe.

"Breakfast is my specialty." Don carried the warmed pot of maple syrup to the table.

"When I was outside with R.C., I checked the well-house. No sign of the rope or bucket."

Sarah stopped slicing a banana. "Does that mean no water?" Her level of concern was obvious in the pitch of her question.

"No. Not at all. The water from the well house is from the well my grandfather dug by hand. It's a good emergency backup. I turned the generator on while I was outside. The new system will fill the tanks in ten minutes."

"Ah." Sarah didn't really care to understand all the details of camp plumbing, as long as she had confirmation more than a two-minute shower would be available.

"Joe, I never got to hear. How was your trip to New York City?" Linda poured syrup on her hotcakes.

With his coffee cup still at his lips, Joe's eyes met Sarah's. He contemplated how to answer without saying something he'd regret. While it was no secret he didn't care for city life, he wouldn't have passed up being with Sarah for a minute. Trying to think through his answer, he asked, "Sure, first pass me those sausages please?"

He cut up a sausage. "For one thing, I'll take the blackflies over that many people any day. The sites Sarah showed me were interesting. We went to the Empire State Building, Central Park, Times Square – you know the tourist spots. I had a New York Italian Hero – it's very different than the Maine version."

"Did you see anything that surprised you?" Linda poured a second cup of coffee.

Joe laughed. He was thinking of the guy on the subway holding a monkey in a baby carrier. Before he could tell them about it, Sarah spoke up.

"Oh, tell them about the bar."

He knew immediately what she meant. His conversation with Floyd, the gentleman at the airport, was fresh in his mind. "That was an interesting place. Remember we told you about Eddy Walsh."

"Huh? Who's Eddy Walsh," asked Linda.

He rubbed his left temple. "Hmm, that's right. We had to leave last fall when I was telling you that story. Turns out, Jim Smith, the FBI agent was really someone by the name of Eddy Walsh."

"It gets even stranger. My dad, Harry Molloy wrote several news stories about the Brink's robbery in the Boston paper."

"Now that's new news!" Linda sat up straight.

"Yeah. We ... Joe and I, have a hunch maybe my dad took my family on that Maine vacation to follow up on a lead."

"Dum da dum dum dum," Don sang. Linda rolled her eyes.

"I remember my dad saying Jim Smith, this Walsh fellow, took a lot of pictures when he was here," said Joe.

"What's this have to do with a bar in New York?"

"The bar was actually part of a print shop. Out front they sold old vintage photos. Through a hidden door, out back there was a bar."

"A modern-day speakeasy? I guess people want to relive prohibition." A sizzle came from the batter Don poured on the pan.

"Did you have a drink?" Linda raised her juice glass.

"No. But I bought a few photos."

"Of what? The Brooklyn Bridge?" Don waved the spatula and grinned.

"No. Maine."

"Maine?" Linda's cup slammed down on the table.

"Yep. Would you believe places around Lobster Lake?"

"What?" Linda used a napkin to wipe up the coffee that had jumped from her mug.

They were silent as Joe told them the story of Eddy Walsh – fake FBI agent, son of a bankrupt grocery store mogul, turned amateur photographer and Boston photo store owner.

"You see, this Eddy Walsh, must have made lots of trips to Maine, maybe hoping to find that money that was stolen from his family business. While here, it appears he took photos. He had opened a camera store. When he went out of business, he auctioned all the pictures. The speakeasy in New York, called "Prints and Pints," came to be in the possession of his stock, including the pictures he took. In the bins I found pictures with his initials - *E.W.* There were photos of McGooseley Pond, the old McGinnus cabin . . ."

The ever skeptical Don interrupted, "Maybe it only reminded you of the McGinnus place."

"I'm sure it was. Dad and I used to fish that pond. That was until the McGinnus brothers bought that camp. They had a way of making people uncomfortable."

"How?" Sarah asked.

"They'd stand in the shadows, watching us. Or they'd canoe out on the pond and throw large rocks in the water to scare the fish. The final straw was the time we went on an overnight fishing trip with Nate Philbrick. Don, you were there with us.

Remember the trees we came across the next day? Blocking Dad's truck in – on the pond road."

"Sure do. It was a heck of a mess to clean up. Your dad was something mad."

"Took us hours to get out. Dad didn't have the chain saw in the truck and he and Nate had to take turns using an axe to cut through. After that, we fished elsewhere."

Don placed a stack of hotcakes on the table. "Did your dad ever report them to Henry or the sheriff?"

"I'm sure Dad mentioned it. You know he was more the type to show he wasn't intimidated from fishing on public waters. But hacking away at a tree late into the evening wasn't his idea of fun either. A few weeks after that, I remember hearing Henry telling Dad and Nate that two wrongs didn't make a right. From what I could piece together, the McGinnuses found the end of their camp road blocked with a line of huge boulders that only an excavator could have placed there."

Don started roaring. "That sounds about right for what Nate and Stan would do."

"And there was another photo ..." Joe paused for effect.

"Of what?" Linda was halfway out of her chair.

"The old trapper cabin."

"The one that burned down? Get out!" Linda shouted and stood up.

Sarah could hardly sit still; she was finding it entertaining to see Don and Linda discovering these clues for the first time.

Joe pointed to the map on the wall. "Linda, you know the ponds and streams around here better than anyone. What's common about the McGinnus place and the trapper cabin?"

Linda ran her finger from the Golden Road, up to the Deadwaters, and back down. She bit her lower lip as her finger circled between the locations. "McGooseley!"

"That's right." Joe smiled and nodded.

"What is?" Sarah squeezed between them trying to see the old faded map.

Linda poked at the map. "You see here. That's McGooseley Pond. That's where the McGinnus place was." She moved her finger to a thin blue line lower on the map. "And this here, this is McGooseley Stream. That's where the trapper cabin was. That Walsh fellow had Joe's dad snowshoe to the wrong place with him."

"So, what did you do?" Don asked Joe.

"About what?"

"Finding all this new information?"

"I bought the photos. The one of downtown Greenville, with the original Indian Store, I gave to Sarah for her apartment." Sarah nodded. "The others are back at the house in Bangor. I'll have them framed and then hang them here at camp."

"Not about the photos. Don't you think you should report the connection?"

"Linda, this all happened back in the 1950s. Nobody is restricted from taking pictures."

"I don't know. You'd think somebody would want to know." Linda shook her head.

"From what I recall, when Henry tried to get people to take notice, he had a tough time about it. And he wore a badge."

Sitting back down, Linda said, "I suppose you're right. It's all just so strange."

Sarah spoke up. "That vacation my family took to Maine sure makes a lot more sense to me now. After I was lost, my dad went out hiking every day – on his own. He'd strap on a backpack, with a small army shovel hanging from it. He'd be gone until dinner."

"Did he enjoy the outdoors?" asked Linda.

"If he did, I never knew it. He was a reporter for the Boston News, spent his days on the phone, at a typewriter, or running around Boston's South End chasing stories. I never took him for much of an outdoorsman, but on that trip he was a modern day Henry Thoreau."

"Do you think he was looking for clues from the Brink's robbery?" asked Linda.

"Your guess is as good as mine. But the evidence lines up that way. Maybe Walsh wasn't the only one looking for the loot. I was happy to stay put at the rental cabin and read my magazines," said Sarah.

Don stood and looked at Joe. "You never heard if anyone found the money? Is that right?"

"As far as I know, nope, most of it was never found. The burned down trapper cabin and that old root cellar only add to the unknowns," replied Joe.

"Getting turned around in the woods must have been a scary experience for you as a young girl." Don picked up the plate of sausages and put them in the fridge. "It could have been a very different outcome. Probably twenty years or so before that, a young boy named Don Fendler, who was twelve at the time, was lost up near Katahdin. He was out for nine days on his own. He eventually stumbled into someone's camp. He was dehydrated, malnourished, and he wouldn't have survived much longer."

"You were lucky to end up in the Parker camp yard, of sorts, and Joe was there to see you," said Linda.

"I know." Sarah eyes glistened, locked on Joe's.

Not one to be sentimental, Don slapped the counter. "Enough talking. This breakfast has turned into a brunch."

"It's not even seven thirty." Linda stretched.

"No matter. We've got things to do." He was already pulling on his coat. "Linda, how about giving me a hand with the sled covers. We'll meet you two out on the ice." Don pointed at Joe.

Joe gave him a single head nod. Linda, in on the plan, rolled her eyes on the way out the door.

"Sarah, why don't you get ready. Put on your warmest gear. I'm going to pack up some snacks."

He watched her head towards the bathroom and he went to work in the kitchen. With his plan brewing for weeks, he selected what he needed and packed the cooler. He went over the list in his mind and was zipping his backpack as Sarah emerged from the bedroom.

"All set?"

"I guess." She was still confused as to why Don and Linda had taken off so suddenly. "What was Don's rush?"

"Oh, he likes to be out on the ice before anyone else shows up."

Leaving R.C. behind to nap, Joe opened the door and motioned to the sled. "Your carriage awaits."

⁑

As they drove onto Lobster Lake, Sarah kept a lookout to her left and right, but there was no sign of Don's sled. Joe rounded a point and pulled next to a small shed.

Sarah flipped up the shield on her helmet. "What's this?"

"This? It's an ice shack." Joe went about unloading the bags he had stowed.

"I know that. But where are Don and Linda?"

"They'll be around shortly, I'm sure." He spun the combination lock and opened the narrow door. "Give me a minute to check on things."

He ducked inside and was glad to see Gerry had left it clean. Sarah was already standing behind him when he turned to call her.

"Huh," she said; an element of surprise evident in her voice. "What?"

"It's nicer than I was expecting."

The ice shanty was finished in the same honey color pine as the inside of Joe's camp. On one side there was a built-in wide bench with a comfy futon cushion. Resting on top of a neatly folded moose-print blanket was a ripped piece of brown paper bag. Sarah could see there was a squiggly hand-printed note on it. On the other wall there was a sink, a stove top, and a table. A tiny blue-enamel woodstove, which Joe was already lighting, was vented out the back wall.

"Gerry rents this unit, and several others he has on different lakes and ponds." He closed the door to the firebox to see Sarah reading the note.

Joe — the propane tank is full, and the batteries are charged. The blanket is the one you ordered — it's new and yours to take. Pearl added clean towels and such. All the gear is where you'd expect. You didn't tell me what kind of music your lady liked, so I left you a few different tapes.

Enjoy and please log what you catch in the book — it helps with promoting the place.

--- Gerry

"Sorry, this is for you." She held out the note, her eyebrows raised high; having caught on why Don and Linda had performed their disappearing act.

"Ah, guess I'm busted." Joe pushed the paper into the firebox.

"Seems that way." Sarah's foot nudged a plate on the floor. "What's this?"

Joe lifted the black cover. "Watch where you step when these are open." The hole was closed in with a bit of skim ice. He used a metal ladle to break through.

Opening the cabinet above the couch he took out the gear and set Sarah up with two lines. He did the same on two holes for himself.

"So, we sit on the couch with fishing poles and wait for the fish to start biting?" Her eyes danced at him, expecting there was probably more to it than that.

He nodded to confirm. "That's pretty much it." "Well, that is if it's your first rodeo in a shack. Lucky for you, you have me along."

While she was occupied looking down at the dark, icy-cold water anticipating a bite, he took a look at the music Gerry had left. It was a detail he probably shouldn't have delegated, especially after seeing the three old eight tracks. His choices were *An Elvis Romance*, *80s Top Rock Ballads*, or *Country Love*. Pushing the tape in, the player hissed until the smooth voice of Randy Owen filled the tiny shanty.

"How you doing?"

She gave him a bored, blank stare.

"I know what you need. Give me a minute. No peeking."

At the counter, being sure to block her view, he went to work. He picked up the song, "Mmm, feels so right."

"What are you making up over there?"

"Never mind. You keep your eyes on those lines." He stirred the pot he had warming on the burner and placed a tinfoil-wrapped pan on the woodstove to warm.

"Joe."

"I'm almost done here."

"No, Joe, I need you now. I think I have a fish!"

He turned to see her shaking the line. "Reel it in. Slow." He turned down the burner and sat down next to her. "That's right. You got him."

The fish flopped out of the hole onto the floor. "What kind is it?" she asked.

"A togue." Joe knelt down and removed the hook. He weighed it using the gripper scale. "Eight and a half. That's a good size fish."

"What's a togue?"

"It's a lake trout. Same as you caught last fall."

"What are we going to do with it?"

"We could keep it and bring it back to camp for dinner. But let's let this one swim on and see if we can hook a salmon." He eased the fish back into the hole and let it go.

Dipping a pot into the icy water he filled it and heated it on the woodstove.

"What's in here?" She opened a door. "Oh. That's tinier than on an airplane."

"Beats finding a tree to hide behind when you're out in the middle of a lake."

"It appears this shack has everything."

"That's the objective. That couch you're sitting on is a pull-out. You want to spend the night out here?"

The answer was obvious in her expression. "No, thank you. I'd be afraid of the entire thing getting swallowed up by the ice and sinking."

"Ah, that doesn't happen until around the middle of April." She frowned.

"It's true. That's about when the ice starts to thin out. There's always a few shacks in the area that end up needing rescuing."

He washed up with the hot water, dumped it down the sink (which drained out the floor onto the ice), and returned to finishing his special surprise.

"Okay, I can't serve you cappuccino out here, but I hope this will do." On the small pine-box table in front of the sofa he placed two mugs of hot chocolate. Turning back to the counter, on two paper plates he added thin slices of a Granny Smith apple next to the warmed squares of apple-crumb cake. Over the cake and apples, he drizzled the caramel sauce he had been heating. The last of the caramel he added to the mugs.

"This looks good. Hard to top a snack like this, way out here." She plucked a large sugar-dusted crumb off the cake and slid it in her mouth. "Mmm. Did you make this?"

"Yep. My grandmother's recipe. I had to keep it hidden from Don." He pulled a can of whip cream from the cooler. "Almost forgot this."

"I guess you can *top* it." She laughed. Taking a fork she tasted the cake. The softness and sweet apples reminded her of the city bakery, which she wasn't missing at all.

"You want some on your cake *and* in your hot chocolate?"

"I see you know me well. Yes, please." She tasted the hot chocolate. "Wow, that is rich."

"It's made from Belgian milk chocolate cubes that I stirred into the warm milk."

"Mmm." She finished off her mug. "Any more?"

He took her mug and as he was spooning in the thick chocolaty drink, she said, "About last night."

She wanted to say she didn't expect him to replace Ellen's memory with her, or that she didn't expect to take Ellen's place in his mind, but she wanted a new place, she wanted to try with him.

He didn't turn. "What about it? You needed to know. I want to live in the moment with you. Not the past." He was glad he had given some thought about what to say, before she brought it up.

Placing the mug on the table, he didn't have time to sit down, she stood and kissed him. "I never did get to give you a good morning kiss," she whispered in his ear.

There was little in the way of fishing after that. An hour later, a sled buzzing by the shack woke them up. Joe looked at his watch, it was close to eleven.

"What do you say we take a little snowshoe walk around Big Island and then we'll have lunch."

"You brought lunch out here, too?"

"This man can't live on cake alone."

⚘⁎⁎⚘

Where the trail met a clearing on the far side of the island, Joe cautiously moved a hemlock branch with his hand. Cottony clumps of snow floated to the ground. The cloud-filtered midday sun was reflecting off the snow pack.

Joe pointed. At the far end, three animals were crossing between a stand of dri-ki.

"Whoa." Sarah's voice was barely audible, but it was enough to cause the mother lynx to come to a stop. Her head raised to get a scent. The two juveniles, who were following directly in her tracks, paused, waiting for guidance.

Sarah braced herself against a tree to steady her camera. She took a shot. The youngsters moved closer to their mother, who must have quickly processed there was no immediate danger, and she continued towards the dense woods. The camera clicked with each step the animals took.

"That was exciting." Sarah's eyes were wide.

"For me too," said Joe. I've never seen a lynx family, usually only one at a time. "That's a special sighting."

"I hope I got some good photos. I'm not sure I could zoom in close enough. Wait until I tell Linda." She twisted the lens cap back on.

Joe added, "I guess we had some good timing to see that. Ready to get back for lunch?"

"Sure am. What are we having?"

"I'm making you one of my specials." He couldn't tell by the look on her face if she was confused or concerned. "It's a sandwich."

"Oh." She didn't seem too impressed.

Hannibal's Crossing

⁂

He kicked snow over the fire, burying the remaining coals. With a stick, he flung the squirrel pelt far from where he had built camp. Per his usual modus operandi he never left a trace. Camping overnight was expected, he had planned on it, even after locating the Northeast Carry Store. Until he was confident his information was correct, keeping a low profile was essential.

Last night, he hadn't planned on driving directly to the store, so it didn't matter that the guys from the diner hadn't disclosed the road wasn't maintained for winter travel. What he hadn't anticipated, after the five-mile hike in the dark, was being spotted – by of all things, a pack of sled dogs. Even his methods of gathering intelligence weren't a match for twenty canine ears in the dead silence of a winter night. Improvising, he fed the last of his jerky to select dogs, let two loose, and used the created commotion to get inside. Then he checked the radio call frequency, and got back to the woods while the owner was getting his animals to settle down again.

After a couple of hours in his tent along a frozen stretch of Lobster Stream, he snared his breakfast, and hiked back to his Bronco.

⁂

"Slow down." Axe punched Heath in his side. "I said, Slow down!"

"I did."

"Turn around. There's a truck off there," he thumbed over his shoulder, "in that logging pullout. Saw it as we drove by."

Heath knew Ace could spot a woodcock in a woodpile a half mile away if it had a loonie between its teeth, so he wasn't about to argue. He pulled a U-turn and crept into the clearing. The washboard ground was a mix of ice, snow, mud, and ground up pieces of pine bark.

"Pull over there. Get the truck up along that snowbank – next to that log pile. Keep it out of sight from the road."

"Buzz off. I know how to drive."

Stepping from the truck, Axe took the last swig of his beer and then threw the bottle into the snow. The two of them snooped around the Bronco, making a pass as if it were a used vehicle for sale.

"He could be a logger." Heath glanced around, not wanting to take chances. "Might be off in the woods taking a leak."

"Stop you're worrying. We ain't doin' nothin'." Axe cupped his hands around his eyes, trying to see past the dark tint. "Must be trying to hide something valuable in there."

⁂

The man was approaching the pullout when he heard voices. He stood behind the log pile and listened to their conversation.

"That light bar would fit nicely on my truck."

"And that winch, that's heavy duty. Whoever left his truck out here must not need this stuff." Axe pulled on the door handles. "Locked up."

The man didn't have time for his plans to be delayed by two common thieves. He also didn't want to be seen.

Up front, Axe was kneeling in front of the Bronco, trying to see what tools he needed to swipe the winch. "I need the hacksaw from the toolbox." He was getting up when a gunshot sent him diving for the ground.

At the sound of glass shattering, Heath yelled, "My truck!" He went running across the lot.

Lumbering along at his fastest jog, Axe came up behind him, leaned on the hood, and bent over wheezing.

"Did you see anyone?" asked Heath.

Out of breath, Axe responded, "Nope, but you better have a look here." Both passenger tires were flat.

"And that explains the glass. Your damn bottle." Heath pointed to the green fragments near a rock.

"Someone's messing with us." Axe spun around. "Whoever is out here, I'm gonna kick your ..."

The engine of the Bronco started, growling so rough the ground vibrated. Before Axe had time to grab a rifle from his gun rack, the Bronco was bearing down; forcing them to scramble over the snowbank to escape being hit. The truck barreled past them and out onto the road.

"Who the heck was that?"

"I don't know, but when I find that truck again he'd better watch his back." Axe was feeling along the tires. "I don't see any gashes."

"Hoser must have let the air out." Heath was pulling the jack from behind the back seat.

"What sense is it gonna make changing one tire?" Axe lit a cigarette and blew out a stream of white smoke against the cold air. "Put that jack back and hand me a beer."

"What are you gonna do? Sit here smoking and drinking?"

"No stupid. It's for the walk. We're gonna have to hike it down to the Kokadjo store, or thumb a ride. We can meet Nap and Leont as planned at noon for grub. They can bring us back here and we can use their spare tire, too."

Heath grabbed a beer for himself and locked his truck. "I ain't in no mood for walking three miles. I find that Bronco, I'm slashing all four tires."

The Black Ghost

※

Fred kissed his wife, threw his pack over his shoulder, and reached for his snowshoes that were leaning against the mudroom wall. He poked his head back into the kitchen. "I'll be back by three."

His wife, sitting in the rocker near the fire, lifted her head from her book. "You really have to do this today? On New Year's Eve."

"We've been over this twice already. There's a logging operation out towards Alligator Pond. Yesterday was their last day of cutting. Won't take me long to make an assessment. I want to get a peek before it's covered in new snow."

Spotting last month's issue of, "Science Stories," on the pile of old magazines, he stuffed it in the side pocket of his pack.

"Don't forget your lunch."

"Got it. Thanks."

Bouncing over the cracked and heaved asphalt, and then onto a frozen dirt road, it didn't take Fred long to get to the harvesting area he had to inspect – not the way he drove anyway. Selective cutting had been completed and the remaining trees would be an effective crown release zone. As required, some branches and woody material were left on the forest floor. Fred anticipated this would provide good cover for salamanders and small mammals come spring. A grapple skidder and slasher were parked on the access road, the only two pieces of heavy equipment remaining at the site. He updated his permitting notes and signed the log sheet. In the margin of the yellow slip, he did something he didn't normally do, he wrote a few words to the logger praising the operation. He was softening in his aging years.

There was only one more stop he needed to make, one he hadn't told anyone about. Before driving away, he turned on the truck to get the heater going. While waiting, he ate his liverwurst and pickled red onion sandwich on rye. He thought it could have used a little more mayo, and a little less lettuce, but since he didn't have to make it, he couldn't complain and simply dropped two leaves out the window. He wiped the mayo from his fingers and lifted the magazine that was poking from his pack. He reached for a bottle of Moxie, his favorite drink, especially with liverwurst.

He opened to the cover story, "Whales Trapped in Ice — Rescued!" Although he had already read the article explaining how native Alaskan hunters, oil companies, and even Soviet icebreakers cooperated to cut a path to the sea for the stranded whales, he was fascinated by it again. He'd always wanted to see a whale. The picture of a native whaler rubbing the nose of a gray whale had captivated him. He figured it would make a nice read for someone out in the woods alone. Fred assumed the person liked reading, since he tended to find a lot of magazines and books at the abandoned camp sites; items he ended up having to haul away. He grinned at the irony that he was likely leaving stuff that he'd end up having to clear out in the months ahead. But right now, he was focused on doing a good deed.

From his jacket pocket he took out his map. The location markings he had made, and the success he had leaving items over the past two months, gave him confidence this drop would be picked up within a few days. He wasn't exactly sure where the latest camp might be, but he'd found some clues last week – an empty cigarette pack, a chocolate wrapper, the label from a B&M beans can, and a hand-tied fly, a variation of the Black Ghost. The discarded items, except the fly, were from packages Fred had left in the woods. The neat stack included a return of the pair of winter boots, size eleven; these were left with a size ten soleless shoe missing its shoelace, which seemed to have been finely separated and used to tie the Black Ghost.

***

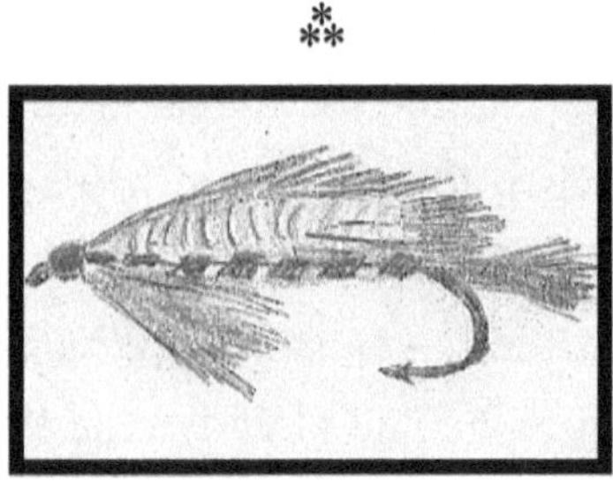

***

Today, in addition to a store of food, his pack contained a pair of boots from the church thrift shop, this time size ten, and a small book on fly-tying he had picked up from the library book sale.

He flicked the gifted Black Ghost that he had hung from the rearview mirror by fishing line. The fly was one of a half dozen Fred had 'found,' left as markers; either the person was sending Fred a thank you, or a message.

It was a well tied fly, the kind made popular in Maine back in the 20s and 30s. He had to wonder if the person saw him fishing with one of his favorite black, yellow, and white flies. Or was he sending Fred the message that he was the ghost of the night, not to be found. Whoever it was, certainly hadn't been easy to see, by Fred or anyone else. Lately, he had started to think of the hermit as 'the woods ghost.'

With a dill pickle from his lunchbox hanging from his mouth, he put the car in drive and headed to the drop point. The roads were quiet, although up this far on the Greenville Road seeing another car this time of year would be considered high traffic. Before turning left into a dead-end transfer pit, he looked in his review mirror, he didn't want to risk anyone spotting him – people always had something they thought was important to tell a ranger, and this morning he didn't have the time.

Parked in the pit there was a line of chippers, feller-bunchers, and skidders. It was where the logging company kept their equipment for easy access between jobs. A rusty field trailer sat crooked on its cinderblock supports.

He pulled his red Dodge Power Wagon, a reliable but beat-up twelve-year-old truck, around the far side of a skidder. Through the ruts he eased up to the line of boulders that had been pushed against the trees; the boulders had been there so long, the new-growth birch trees had climbed up and around the rocks.

Turning off the engine, he contemplated his off-road hiding space. His vehicle was dwarfed next to the monster skidder tires that were higher than his roof. As he had anticipated, the pit was deserted; everyone was off for the long holiday weekend and he was confident he wouldn't be spotted. Getting out and wrapping his neck with his scarf, he figured he was hidden well enough from the road. Not that he anticipated anyone poking around, and if they did, he had the perfect cover for being there – he was a forest ranger, checking a logging operation.

Strapping on his snowshoes, he only planned to hike part way to Lazy Tom Pond. His hunch was somewhere out that way, if he had days to search, he might find a few clues on where this person lived, which he had no intention of doing — not today anyway. Today his plan was to hike the two miles to the same hollow trunk he had used twice before. It was near the stream where campers had reported, back in October, their cooler had been raided and they were missing a lantern, a pair of jeans, and a windbreaker. Fred reasoned if he left supplies in the woods, people wouldn't be stolen from, although he had no evidence of a connection, only a hunch. All he knew was that someone was making use of the items he left. Secretly, well his entire operation was secret, but secretly, he hoped to find out who the person was and if they had anything to do with the abandoned camps he'd been finding over the years, or if the person was just a local down on their luck.

He made the drop and without any investigation for tracks, he immediately turned around to get back to his truck. The return hike was easy going; he had already broken the trail, and he was relaxed now that he had left the package without anyone seeing him. His breathing was noticeably slower, and he enjoyed the hiking. At one point, in an open clearing, he came across tiny arrow marks in the snow. What was likely a ruffed grouse had passed over his trail since the time he hiked by twenty minutes earlier. Ah, with it being the last day of grouse season, he had a passing idea of getting his rifle from the truck and tracking the bird, which would make a nice addition to Dot's New Year's Day meal tomorrow. This time of year, he might even find them snow-roosting. But he hadn't the time, not today.

Getting close to his truck, he had one thing on his mind – the New Year's Eve party at the legion. Tonight, "*The Backwoods Bastard Boys*," a country rock band of locals he knew, was playing. With his deep bass voice they always invited him up on stage to help them sing "Elvira." As he walked along, he practiced his chorus of "mow mows." He was feeling happy – until he arrived at the logging pit.

"What the! Who the heck did that?"

Fred circled the wagon; however, he couldn't get all the way around. Behind his truck, a Bronco was pulled so close to his rear bumper a piece of sheet music couldn't have slid between them. Along the front were the boulders he had pulled up close to. He was boxed in. His heart thumped when he heard the voice.

"Kind of strange to be working on a Saturday, seeing it's New Year's Eve. Isn't it, ranger?" The man appeared from the far side of the skidder. The white and gray of his fatigue pants and jacket, against the bright yellow of the logging vehicle, made him look like a cow posing in front of the sun. Not that Fred would say anything, the man was menacing looking.

"Good singing back there. I met one of those Oak Ridge Boys once, at a veteran concert. Really nice guy." The man approached Fred.

"Who are you? And why are you blocking my truck in?"

"Name's Frank Merrill." He took off his glove to shake hands. "And you're Fred, Fred the forester."

"How'd you know that?" Fred cautiously shook the man's hand, while considering what this was about. Over his career, Fred had met all sorts of characters out in the woods. He had his share of close calls in violent situations, but this man wasn't showing any ill-intent from what Fred could see, not at the moment.

The man held Fred's stare with a slightly friendly grin.

"Your truck gives you away," Merrill took hold of the wooden rail running along the bed. "And you're the only forester in this region. Isn't that right?"

"Yeah, that's right. I'm in charge of these operations out here." Fred had regained his composure. "So maybe, you should be explaining to me why you're trespassing if you're not from the logging company."

"Don't go getting yourself all worked up now. I'm here looking for someone."

"Who? Me?"

"No. You're easy to find." Merrill cleared his throat and spit.

Fred didn't find the comment amusing. "Then why are you following me?"

Wanting to diffuse the situation, Merrill took a different approach. "I suspect you knew Warden Henry Ford."

Fred took a step back. There were few days out in the field he didn't see something that didn't remind him of Henry. There had never been two stewards of the Maine woods any more serious, friendly, and somewhat grumpy than Henry and Fred. They made a great backwoods team – but that was back in the day.

"Henry's been gone a while now. Rest his soul." Fred's eyes looked to the tree line. "What's Henry got to do with you snooping around?"

"Henry helped me out. A long time ago. Just figured we knew someone in common."

"Look mister, you'd better be getting to your reason for keeping me standing here in the cold. I've got places to be."

"How about you first tell me who you left that pack for – back there in that tree hollow. I can't see why any animals would need a pair of boots."

Fred's mind was racing. He wondered how this person followed him to the drop and he heard nothing. And, the man had time to go through the bag and meet him back at the pit without being seen.

"What concern of yours is that?" Fred opened the door to his truck, hoping to move things along.

"Plenty. I've been searching for the person you're giving magazines to for twenty-five years." At this point, Merrill wasn't a hundred percent sure it was the same person, but he played his hand, hoping to learn something.

"Excuse me?" Fred's left eye twitched.

"That's right. Now do you know where he is?" Merrill probed Fred's face for any hint of deception.

Fred tried to evaluate the man's interest. Since he had nothing to hide, he answered directly. "Exactly? No. And besides, I've never even seen him." Fred touched his coat pocket.

"Hmm." Merrill's eyes narrowed on the edge of the paper Fred touched. "There's more to him than you know."

"What I know is up here when we have a recluse who lives alone, they're hermits. Usually harmless. This one is the most reclusive of all. Ghost like."

"Look, my senses tell me you're my best bet in finding him." Merrill had a feeling the ranger knew more about this 'hermit,' if that's only what the ranger thought he was, beyond the leaving of care packages. So, he tried a different approach. "If you're leaving him supplies, you know better than anyone the tough time he's having surviving out here. We need to find him. To get him out of these woods."

Fred wondered about Merrill's motives. He also wanted to find the hermit. Cleaning up the campsites the man left on private land got to be a nuisance. Fred also knew he'd sleep better if he knew the hermit wasn't freezing to death somewhere on a mountain. He'd already had two dreams where he came across a deserted camp, with skeletal remains wrapped in old blankets. Merrill began speaking again, interrupting Fred's thoughts, almost reading them.

"Wouldn't it be better for your neighbors if this person stopped stealing from them? If you know this person is doing that, which I think you suspect, you'll help me locate him." He paused. He stood back from the ranger truck, taking in the curve of the front bumper. "I will find him. With or without your help. This time, he's slipped up."

Fred's eyes slowly moved downward and his hand started again towards his map. Catching Merrill watching, his hand went instead to loosen his scarf.

Merrill's eyes were locked on Fred's pocket. "If you have suspicions he's a thief, why not inform the warden service or the police?"

"I tried that approach once." He shook his head. "Back in the early seventies. I was fed up finding camps on land where no camping was allowed. My biggest concern was the risk of a forest fire being started. The agencies tracked the person for six weeks. All they really did was push him deeper into the woods. He was gone, or at least he wasn't near here any longer." Fred shrugged. "This time I was taking a different approach. Stealth mode. As to whether it's the same person or not – I doubt it. That was a long time ago."

"I see." Merrill nodded, his eyes narrowing. He liked someone that took things into his own hands. "But I can guarantee you, ranger, if the person you're feeding is the one I'm after, it's been the same person all these years."

Fred closed the wagon door. If they were both tracking the same person, he needed to know more about what was going on. "You going after him tonight? By staking out that bag I left?"

"No. He's too smart for that. I need to track him. To find him by surprise, when he doesn't see me coming." Merrill noticed a twitch of Fred's nose. "What is it?"

"Why don't you tell me who you work for and why you're searching for him?" Seeing a discarded beer can, Fred took the opportunity to bend down and pick it up. With his back to Merrill, he pushed down the map that was poking from the open pocket. He chucked the can in the bed of the wagon.

"I work for the federal government." Merrill was used to the typical reaction as Fred tilted his head and his eyes went from Merrill's clothes, to his Bronco. Merrill handed over his identification.

Fred held the black billfold in his hand, inspecting the seal. It was strange for him to imagine someone in the woods being wanted by a federal agent. The cases he usually dealt with had to do with loggers cutting too much timber, clear-cutting too close to a pond, lake or stream, or running machinery through vernal pools with a total disregard of the necessary habitat for salamanders and frogs.

"Look, there's no sense in us standing out here in the cold. I might have some items in storage back at the office that'll interest you. If you follow me, you can have a look."

While it was true, Fred did have quite a collection of items he had found in the woods, he also wanted to give the ghost a chance at making the pickup. If the past was any indication, whoever he was, he was surely aware, well before Fred, that someone else was poking around.

"All right, ranger, we can do that. I'll have plenty of time to come back out here and do some tracking." Merrill trying to read any hint of concern on Fred's face, did not break eye contact until the ranger swallowed hard and turned to his truck.

⚜⚜⚜

On the walk to the Kakadjo store, Axe mumbled an expletive, and using Heath's back as cover tossed his beer bottle over the snowbank into the ditch.

"Shoot is that the perch police?"

"Yep. Don't say anything stupid."

The snowmobile came to a stop and Axe gave the warden a square, open-mouth grin that showed the stumps of his remaining front teeth. Playing the victim, he gave her a story of how they'd been attacked.

Wanting to put twenty yards between the men and her radio call, the warden walked down the road to talk privately. Kristy keyed her handheld. "Hey, Andy, you in range?"

"Go ahead, Kristy," answered Green.

"What's your 20?"

"Due east of Lily Bay. I'm making a pass over the race trail. Anything wrong?"

Kristy Marsh was a warden from The County. She'd been assigned to help Andy for the Annual New Year's Day North Woods Sled Dog Race. With extra visitors expected and snowmobiles, skiers, and snowshoers, all using the same trails, the department wanted eyes in the air and on the ground. This morning she was on snowmobile patrol near the Sias Hill Cutoff Road.

"Okay, listen. I came across two guys walking – said they are headed to the Kokadjo store. Their story was their truck had been vandalized by a bunch of roughnecks in a logging pit."

Andy didn't respond right away. He tried to think if there was a close place for him to land near there. *"Vandalized? How so?"*

"Broken glass, flat tires. Who knows. Maybe they hit something. One of them was a bit unsteady for this hour of the morning. They are headed to get a ride from some buddies of theirs back to the pit. I'm going to check it out."

Andy banked the plane to head north. *"I'll head that way and circle above. 10-8."*

"10-4. Keep your ears on."

❄✳❄

Pearl was sure she heard something in the conversation between the two wardens. If anyone could read between the lines, it'd be her. With Gerry out with the dogs for a run, she sat at his radio listening to any conversation that came over the airwaves. Her habit of monitoring the radio traffic supplied her with tidbits of gossip to pass along to the other ladies.

She picked up the phone, for she rarely gossiped over the radio; she never knew who might be listening.

"Hi, Dotty. It's Pearl. - - - Oh, Tonight? Over to the Legion? No, we can't. We're full up. People here for the race tomorrow. - - - Listen, dear-ah, you have some contacts down Augusta, right? - - - Yes, that's what I was figuring – through colleagues of Fred's. - - - No, it's nothing illegal to bother Fred with. You think you can see what they know about this warden Kristy? - - - No. No. Not like that. Things like, you know, dear-ah, how old is she? Is she single? Things like that. - - - Well, you see, I think, hearing how she talks to Andy, maybe she's got a thing for him. - - - Now don't be going and saying I'm crazy. I've got two ears and when I have a hunch, I'm usually right. - - - Well, let's just see. You ask around. - - - Oh, I got to go, dear-ah, I need to listen in, I'll call you back later."

❦ ❦ ❦

Flying off to the left of the logging pit, Andy saw two trucks and four men standing around Kristy's snowmobile.

"Warden Marsh, come in." There was a delay. He started into a wide circle.

"Marsh, here. Looks to be all set, Warden Green. These men are ...... some beers ..... expired registration." The transmission was broken up with static.

"10-1, you're signal's weak. I'll make another pass."

By the time Andy came around again, the trucks were pulling out.

"Warden Marsh, come in."

"All set, Andy. They changed the tires and are headed to town."

"10-4. I'm going to continue out over the race trail. Before I head back to base I'm going to put down on Lobster Lake. I need to see Joe Parker."

"10-4. See you back in town. Maybe we can grab a beer and a bite at the Mangy Moose."

Bearing north, Andy answered, "Sounds good. Green out."

Pearl was dancing in her seat. She said to herself, "Now those two are making dinner dates. Wait until Dotty hears this." She switched off the radio and picked up the phone.

❧⁎❧

Making a pass over Lobster Lake for a safe landing zone, Andy didn't see any snowmobiles, ice shacks, or large ice ridges. Turning out over Big Island he heard a loud snap and clang.

He scanned his instrument panel. All levels seemed to be holding. Yet something was loose, he could hear the rhythmic bang – ping . . ping . . ping.

Not knowing what the sound was, he decided he had better try and contact someone before touching down – just in case.

"Mayday. Mayday. Mayday. Warden Green. Putting down on Lobster Lake. Mechanical trouble. Mayday. Mayday. Mayday."

There was no time to wait for an answer; he had no idea if anyone had heard him. He was lined up and descending for a landing.

Ping . . . Ping . . . Ping . . .

When Andy hit the ice, he felt something give and heard a snap. Holding the yoke steady he tried to keep the plane straight during the runout. Something was smacking the right side of the plane. He avoided adding any power to steer and instead let the plane glide over the ice. Slowing down, the plane tilted to the right and skidded into a cove on the east side of Big Claw.

He tried the radio to reach Kristy. Given his location, he knew it was a long shot. There was no response. He called out to Gerry over at the store; same thing, no response.

"This ain't gonna be good." He swung himself out on the ice to have a look.

Moose Sheds

As planned, Don and Linda arrived for lunch at the shack. Sarah watched Joe assemble the sub rolls with ham, cheese, tomatoes, sliced olives, diced onion, green and red bell pepper strips, and pickles.

She reached out and stole a pickle slice. "These pickles are amazing."

"Those are homemade sour dills. My mother's recipe." To the rolls he added olive oil, a drizzle of vinegar.

"You almost done? My mouth is watering over here," stated Don, who was taking advantage of the indoor fishing.

"Almost." Joe shook salt and pepper over each sandwich.

"Linda, can you bring me a pickle please?" asked Don.

Over lunch, Don told them what he and Linda had caught earlier, and Sarah told them about the Lynx family.

"So, what'd you think about the Maine Italian?" Don asked.

Her eyes went from Don to Joe, who told her, "That's the name of the sub."

"Oh. It was good. Although different from our city hero, but good. And those pickles, they were out of this world. I hope you make those all the time, Joe."

"For you, of course."

They fished for an hour and caught two nice salmon that Don planned to use for his contribution to their dinner. After locking up, they drove the sleds along the trail that led to Parker Cabin, and parked.

Realizing they weren't even close to the warm cabin, Sarah asked, "Where are we headed now?"

"We'll make a pass over to Bug Bog," said Joe. "This is the best time of year to explore over that way." Him and Don were already putting on their snowshoes.

"Why's that?" asked Linda.

"It being winter, there are no bugs," Joe answered. He raised his eyebrows at Sarah. "But actually, the bog is a great location for moose sheds."

"Moose sheds?" Sarah asked.

"Antlers," answered Don.

"We might find moose antlers?" Sarah tried to keep pace with Joe's longer strides.

"It's possible. Keep your eyes out on the ground. Moose start dropping their antlers sometime between December and February."

"Dropping?"

Don explained for Sarah. "Well, it's not exactly dropping. For the fall rut, the antlers are needed as a sign of dominance. Once mating season is over, the bulls don't have much use for the antlers. Carrying around a huge rack over the entire winter would burn a lot of energy. To deal with this, the antlers fall off every year. The bone where the antlers grow on the skull begins to dissolve and the antlers start to loosen. The bulls then scrape the antlers on trees, brush, or rocks to make them fall off. If you find one, you can take it back to your apartment and hang it on the wall."

Sarah thought it would be neat to find antlers, but she wasn't so sure about hanging them in her apartment.

When they came to a fork in the trail, Joe stopped. In a whisper, he said, "No talking from here. We're a few hundred yards from the bog. There's always a good chance of a moose sighting in there." He knew Sarah was hoping to see one.

Don mouthed back, "Okay."

They hiked along slowly and at the bog, Sarah read the handwritten lettering on an extra-long bench Joe was brushing the snow from.

In memory of Louise Parker.
She loved her family, these woods,
and the songbirds of Bug Bog.

"Did you build this bench, Joe?" she asked.

"Dad and I. Mom loved to come out here and bird watch."

Glad the moratorium on talking was expired, Don pulled the thermos from Linda's pack. "Who wants a coffee?"

Joe motioned for everyone to sit. Drinking his coffee, he remembered the special times he spent with his Mom at her favorite spot. The bench for her bird watching had been replaced several times over the years, even long after she had passed. Each time Stan and Joe built a new one, from a maple tree on their land, it was more elaborate than the last.

Sarah and Linda were so caught up listening to Joe tell about the time he saw a snowy owl in a tree across from the bench, they hadn't realized Don had walked on ahead; until he yelled, interrupting the peaceful setting, "We got one!"

Linda stood up. "We'd better go see what he's found before he scares off the rest of the north woods."

When they reached him, Don brought his arm from around his back. "Here you go, Sarah. For your home décor." Sarah took one of the antlers and looked it over.

"This is a good find, the pair doesn't always fall off in the same place," said Joe, who examined the other antler.

"Do you think it hurts when they fall off?" Sarah asked.

"I suspect not. They want the things gone, it's all part of nature." Don pointed at the ground where he found them.

Sarah looked down. There was a mangled cage lying in the brush on the edge of the frozen bog. "Do you think he had his antlers caught up in that metal?"

Joe lifted the trap. "He could have used this old beaver trap to shake his antlers loose."

Sarah motioned at the trap. "You trap beavers here?"

"Sometimes. I've had to capture them and relocate them if they are damming up the stream. One year we drove in and the water from the bog here was spread out straight across the road. That old trap is no longer any use to catch anything, you can see there's no doors on it. But if it helps a moose now and then, then I guess it's useful to leave here."

"If you don't want the antlers, Sarah, we can leave them here on the ground. The woods creatures will appreciate it," stated Linda.

"Why?" Sarah's head tilted sideways.

"The squirrels, foxes, otters, bears, and even the deer and moose will nibble on the antlers for the calcium, protein, and other nutrients they contain." Linda ran her gloved hand along the smooth bone.

"That's interesting. Better to leave them then," replied Sarah. "Unless you want them, Don?"

Don reached out to take claim his find. Linda was quicker, intercepted them, and propped them against a tree trunk. "That won't be necessary. We have a shed full of them from Don's antler hunting expeditions."

"Someday I'm gonna do something with all of those."

"When you figure that out, you can collect some more." Linda shot him a glance.

Joe chuckled. "I've seen that shed. Linda's right on this one." He patted Don on the shoulder.

A light snow had begun to fall. Joe contemplated the dark clouds that were visible off to the southwest. He said, "Let's take the trail out to the road and make our way back to the sleds."

"Sounds good to me, I'm looking forward to that left over Italian in the cooler," said Don.

Back in the camp driveway, Joe asked Sarah, "Did you enjoy the hike and fishing?"

"I did. But my toes are getting cold. Three pairs of socks aren't doing the trick. I'm looking forward to warming up by the fire." Nobody could disagree.

"Why don't you ladies go in and get warmed up. Don and I will bring in extra wood."

Once Linda and Sarah were inside, Don stated, "What's the deal? You can't carry a few pieces of wood on your own?"

Joe indicated towards the side porch. "What do you make of that?"

"What are you talking about?"

"Those tracks. Did you walk over by the side porch at all?"

"No. But it could have been one of the girls."

"The tracks don't start over on this side of the cabin. They start in the woods and go right back that way." Joe waved his arm. "Towards the lake."

*
**

*
**

Don shrugged.

Not feeling too comfortable with the tracks, Joe turned, "Let's get inside."

"Everything okay in here?" Joe closed the door behind him.

"Yep, R. C. was glad to see us, or at least he was happy to get a treat," answered Sarah.

Joe walked down the hall. Don followed right behind him.

"Now why do you suppose there are wet spots coming in from this door."

"Good question. "Did you maybe leave this door unlocked?" asked Don.

"Nope. I double checked everything before we left."

"It wouldn't take much to jimmy that lock open. I don't like this one bit."

"Me neither. Let's not say anything to Sarah or Linda yet, no sense giving them a fright until we figure this out. We'd better check the rest of the gear."

After finding nothing missing, the men followed the prints that led off into the woods.

"Whoever was here wasn't concerned about covering their trail," said Joe. It was easy tracking until they arrived at the lake. Joe moved the branches out of his way. "Whoever it was went across the ice."

"This snow is really starting to blow. I'll try Gerry on the radio." Don spun around to head back.

Before Don had even hung up his coat, Linda accused him with a question. "Did you eat all the left-over sausages?"

His hands went up. "No. I packed two for the hike. The rest are on the plate in the fridge. Why?"

"I was going to use them in an egg and sausage quiche in the morning, but there aren't any left."

Feeling hungry, he remembered the Italian sub in the cooler and flipped it open. He sat down on the couch, the cooler next to him.

Joe sensed something was up. "What is it?"

Don pointed in the cooler. It was empty except for the bag of ice.

"Even the whip cream can?" asked Joe.

Don nodded. "Must have swiped it while we were at the bog."

Joe leaned on the counter. "Sarah, Linda." He waited for them to walk closer. "We need to talk."

"What's the matter?" asked Sarah.

"Don didn't eat all the sausages."

"What are you saying, Joe?" asked Linda.

"Don and I found some tracks, leading down to the lake."

"When you say tracks, you mean from a deer?"

"No, Linda. Seems we had a visitor while we were gone."

Instinctively, Sarah jumped up and started checking her backpack. "All my money is still here."

"Whoever it is out here in the woods, wouldn't have much use for money. It seems he only takes the supplies he needs," said Joe.

"Are we safe to stay here?"

Joe had never heard Sarah's voice tremble before. He tried to reassure her. "I don't think we have anything to worry about in that regard. Whoever this is, doesn't want to be seen or come across people."

"One of you mess with the radio setup?" In his hand, Don held the CB mic. The girls both shook their heads.

"What is it?" Joe asked.

"Frequency has been changed and the settings are all adjusted." Don went about testing the equipment.

The snow had changed to a blinding blizzard. The wind had the small hemlocks bent nearly in half. Sarah was on the couch, her legs tucked up under her, and her arms across her chest. Joe knew he was going to have to take her mind off what was going on.

"Sarah, how about you give me a hand whipping up a batch of biscuits – my grandmother's recipe."

She shook her head. "I think I need to have a glass of wine and sit by the fire for a bit."

"Okay, I'll bring you one." When Joe stepped away, the three-successive poundings on the front door were so loud, Sarah screamed. Linda stopped chopping an onion and held up the knife. Joe and Don looked at one another.

The pounding started again, this time with yelling. "Joe, Don, you in there? It's freezing out here."

Joe flung the door open. "Andy, what the heck are you doing out here tonight?"

Warden Green stomped his feet and pushed the door closed. "Wow. What a storm. I can't tell you how happy I was to find the cabin nice and warm earlier."

"Earlier?"

"Yeah, I stopped by looking for you. I had a rough landing out on the lake. I think it's something with the crud cutter rigging. I went back out, but it's too dark now to deal with it."

"You were in the cabin earlier?"

"Yeah, I was cold and I was hoping you'd be here." He saw the look in Joe's eyes. "Well, you always said, if I needed to use the place ... you showed me where the keys were. Remember?"

A forceful breath of air escaped from Joe's lips. "It's not a problem. We thought ... never mind."

"I also had a little snack." His voice was a little low with embarrassment.

A laugh came from Don. "Let me guess. Sausages."

"Um. And a hotcake. Having had your camp cooking before, I knew you must have been on breakfast duty." Andy gave Don a thumbs up.

"Andy, it would have been good if you had left a note or something, to let us know you were here." Linda was still holding the chopping knife up in the air.

"I did." He spun around. "Left if right there on the end table." There was no paper.

"Did you happen to write out the note after you were handling the sausages?" asked Joe.

"Yeah. So?"

"And you left paper, with the smell of sausages on it near a dog?"

Everyone had a good laugh.

Sarah contributed to the clue investigation. "And you used the radio while you were here?"

"Yeah. I had to call down to Gerry, and had him relay to headquarters that I'd be spending New Year's Eve at Lobster Lake." He looked around at the foursome. "Um, if that's okay by you all."

"Of course. There's plenty of room." said Joe. "And this is Sarah. You might remember her from the Fly-in."

"I do. We talked about Henry."

"We'd better get making those biscuits, Joe. We'll need extra." Sarah was in a better mood and headed to the kitchen.

Andy put his hand on Joe's shoulder. "First, I need to speak with you and Don." He motioned with his head and walked over to the side of the room. They followed.

Don asked, "Hey, did you happen to eat the Italian sub from the cooler we left on the sled, too?"

"Sub? What? No."

Don squinted. Joe exhaled.

Andy was getting impatient. "Listen, I've got something important to tell the two of you."

Auld Acquaintance Be Not Forgot

Andy sat down with the guys and told them about Buddy's stolen rifle and how it happened up around near Kettle Lake.

"That is unusual. We've never had these types of problems before." Joe sat with his hands behind his head.

"Not since Red and the bandits." Don reminded him. Joe nodded.

Turning to Andy, Don added, "You know, you could have called on the radio about this, and you wouldn't be spending New Year's Eve with us."

"It's not the kind of message to deliver over the air – you're acquainted with Gerry's sister Pearl, aren't you?"

Don caught Linda giving him the eye from over in the kitchen. "Gotta go. I need to report to the galley."

After Don's appetizer of maple-glazed salmon bites, and a camp dinner of salad, marinated steak tips, and Joe and Sarah's biscuits, they were all seated around the fire. The guys told story after story about their times in the woods.

Prompted by one of Andy's stories about a deer poaching ring, Sarah asked him, "How did you end up being the warden here? Did you take over for Henry?"

Joe and Don both laughed at the same time.

"What's so funny?" Sarah frowned.

Holding back a grin, Andy answered, "No. I didn't take Henry's spot. But he wasn't happy to see me, not at first."

"Why was that?" Sarah lifted her glass.

"I had started with the warden service in 1956, but almost immediately I was called back to active duty. My unit had early involvement in training the South Vietnamese. When I returned to Maine in '63, I rotated assignments. That's when I met Henry. We eventually became good friends and did our share of hunting and fishing together. I learned a great deal working side by side with him. Early on I was assigned a spot down in Knox County."

"For your friendship that was the best assignment that could have happened." Joe handed Andy a beer.

"Thanks. You got that right."

"I don't get it. Then who took over for Henry?" Sarah held out her glass and Joe filled it for her.

"The bosses down in Augusta eventually chose someone to work with Henry until his retirement. That didn't sit well with Ford. And I'll tell you, I would not have wanted to be that guy under any circumstances. He was the one that 'took Henry's job,' at least the way Henry saw it. It wasn't until 1979, when the position was open again and I had enough seniority to get my wish. When I was selected, now mind you, Henry had been retired for over ten years, he still said to me, *'I knew you were always after my job.'*"

Joe raised his beer bottle. "To Henry!"

Don stood up and feeling the evening's mood recited a verse:

> "We two have run about the hills
> And plucked the gowans fine;
> But we've wandered many a weary foot
> Since those times that have gone by."

Joe chimed in:

> "We two have paddled in Lobster Stream,
> From morning sun till dine;
> But waters between us broad have roared
> Since those times that have gone by."

Together they finished:

> "And there's a hand, my trusty friend!
> And give us a hand of yours!
> And we'll take a deep draught of good-will
> For long, long ago."

"Here, Here!"

"Did you two make that up?" asked Sarah.

"Not at all. It's Auld Lang Syne, by the Scot Robbie Burns." Don said proudly.

"I wouldn't have known," stated Sarah.

"Well, over the years we've given it our own spin. Isn't that right?" Joe toasted towards Don.

"Yep. And with my Scottish heritage, it's a poem I know well, even the less popular verses." Don lifted his glass in return.

"You especially enjoy the 'deep draught of good-will' part." Linda's hand came to rest on his leg.

"How about Alice? Is she…," Sarah stopped mid-sentence.

"Oh, no. Not at all. Alice is enjoying her retirement not having to nurse moose, turkeys, or skunks any longer. She flew the coop for warmer weather. She's now down in North Carolina, near her sister, Bonnie," replied Joe.

"The two of them used to make the trip up in the summer, but not the past few years," added Linda.

Sarah nodded. "How about you two? How'd you meet?" She wiggled a finger at Don and Linda.

"To find a bride way up here in the woods, Don resorted to air mail." Joe laughed.

"Hey, that's not how it happened!" Don turned to Sarah. "I was working for the paper company. Back then we worked the woods all winter, much more than nowadays. In the heyday, there were eight or nine pulp and paper plants running three shifts year-round across the state. My first job out of the Air Force was as a pilot for North Woods Paper and Pulp. My main assignment was supply delivery to remote logging operations. With no place to land, I'd buzz the skidder operators to signal them to watch for a drop. I'd circle around and my flying partner would drop a package on a mini parachute. Sometimes the packages contained equipment they needed, but a lot of the deliveries were ham and cheese sandwiches, six packs, and cigarettes. A lot of times we'd land on a lake and taxi loggers and equipment in and out. Then, the bosses gave me a new assignment. It was the greatest of all, but I didn't know it at the time."

Don stopped and finished the slice of cake Linda had given him. He stood and poured himself a brandy.

"Don! What was the great assignment?" His pause was too much for Sarah, she was on the end of the couch cushion.

"He's getting to the good part." Linda knew he was trying to add suspense. She rolled her eyes.

Don raised his glass her way. "You know it." He continued, "The assignment was with a new partner. I thought the company was nuts assigning me to fly around with a female. That just didn't happen back then. The logging industry included a pretty rough bunch of characters. We didn't have what you might say was the cleanest language. So, this girl, a young thing, with a tough attitude was assigned to my plane to take aerial shots of the land. The purpose was for the company to identify future logging locations and to evaluate the regrowth of past cuts."

Sarah turned to her left. Linda smirked.

"On my first mission with this young lady, I flew over a skidder operation. Chainsaw Mike sees me coming and gets on his radio. He lets loose with a dirty joke and some off-color remarks. I responded down to Mike with some off-color remarks of my own. I heard a gasp. I looked to my right, expecting my typical passenger Big Otis Hodges – I had forgotten in the moment who was next to me. Well, her face was a deep maroon. I doubt she ever heard such talk before. Boy, did I feel stupid. I gave my supervisor what for when I got back for assigning me a woman. He told me I had better get used to it as she was going to be working with us and she was going to be my new partner."

"And I straightened him out, you can be sure of that." Linda laughed.

Joe, who had heard the story a dozen times, confirmed, "And that she did."

"Have you always been a photographer?" Sarah asked Linda.

"No, not at all. I studied geography. We were lucky to have an advanced course in aerial photointerpretation that drove my interest trying to apply what I learned. It was around the time when the paper companies were being pressured to be better stewards of the environment and I was offered a unique position. I had to learn my way around aerial photography. I can't say working out here in the woods was easy with all these men, most of which were real cowboys, but I was lucky to fly with Don, he was the best of the bunch."

"Eventually, she fit right in. I didn't want to go back to having Big Otis in the plane – he wasn't as pretty and didn't smell nearly as good." Don winked at Linda. "And to make sure she couldn't back out of the assignment during a mail run one day I proposed to her – a half mile up in the sky."

"That's a different way to pop the question. How'd you slip the ring on her while flying?" Sarah touched her bare ring finger.

"Not so fast, Mr. Flying High." Linda pointed. "He didn't, Sarah. I made him land and ask again, on one knee right there on the runway."

"Yeah, took me a long time to live that down. The guys standing around didn't know what was going on. Buddy told me later at the Junction Bar that his initial thought was I was begging her not to turn me in for a joke I told her or something."

"I'll tell you one thing, his jokes haven't gotten any funnier over the years, but they certainly aren't as dirty as they once were." Linda pecked his cheek.

The hours Don and Linda spent in small planes out over the remote woods of Maine, and how Andy had a disabled plane stuck on a frozen lake, had Sarah wondering. "Other than today, have you ever had any plane, how shall I put it, mishaps?" She looked from Don to Andy.

"Oh, we've had our share." Andy nodded.

"We can laugh about them now. Not so much at the time." Don took a deep breath.

"How about that time I was with you and you turned your Piper Cub into a tree ornament?" Joe rubbed his chin.

"What?" Sarah's eyes were wide.

Shrugging it off, Don said, "Ah, it was nothing. Engine stalled and we glided into some new growth. Plane came to rest, nose down with the wings snagged between two trees."

"This isn't making me want to fly in a single engine plane." Sarah sat back and crossed her legs. "How'd you get down?"

"We had rope, shimmed to the ground and hiked out." Joe put his arm around her.

"Cost me a small fortune to get a road in there and get that plane out." Don looked down.

"All in all, the two of us have seen our share of crashes up this way. Some with not so good endings," said Andy. "August of '56, the summer you were lost, we lost Warden Pilot George Townsend. His plane went down in Maranacook Lake."

Without saying a word, the three men made an almost imperceptible toast to one another and drank.

"Nothing as big as the crash in sixty-three. To the men." This time Don raised his glass high. Joe, Andy, and Linda followed his lead.

"What happened?" asked Sarah.

Don blew out a big breath. "The day the plane went down, we were grounded. The weather wasn't good for flying due to a low ceiling. Linda and I were working in the company field trailer at the airport, going over charts, photos, and planning our next operation."

"The winter was our best time to get photos. The lack of foliage and the snow cover allows for good contrast to the trees, which is necessary for a visual count from the blown-up images," Linda added.

"I'll never forget it, my dad and I were headed up to the lake for the ice fishing derby," Joe said.

"And that was the first time I met Henry." Andy's face tightened and he lowered his head.

A Winter Long Ago

Greenville, Maine
January 24, 1963

"Henry! Henry!"

"What? What is it?" Henry turned on his side and yanked the covers up over his ear.

"Your alarm. It's bounced itself onto the floor again." Alice had been lying with her eyes open before the first ding. She had an internal clock that kicked in the day after graduating high school and she hadn't missed a sunrise in more than thirty-six years; Henry's new clock or not.

Henry, on the other hand, could sleep through a moose knocking over a china cabinet, or one getting his antlers caught on a tent line and wrecking a perfectly good tent. That was a story Henry referred to as, *The Bull at China Lake*, after it happened the October he took new recruits on an overnight for training. The two young men, who were jolted awake by the bull dragging their tent away in the middle of the night (with them in it), traded in their warden hats for desk jobs with the Land Use Commission down in Augusta.

"Is it six already?" He slid his legs over the side of the bed and sat up. After a yawn, he bent over to reach for his wind-up clock. "Son of a poacher!"

"Are you okay, dear?"

"Yeah. If the alarm doesn't wake me up, banging my head on the wall does the trick." He rubbed his forehead with his right hand.

Standing next to the bed, Alice shook her head, pursed her lips to keep from saying something she'd regret, and pulled on her robe. Henry had hit his head many mornings since the Fish and Game Department gifted him the moose alarm clock with the double antler bells for his service anniversary. On mornings he didn't silence it quickly enough, the thing would vibrate off his nightstand. His delay in reaching the alarm before it fell was bound to happen if he had a long night of chasing poachers, rescuing a lost hiker, or on the rare occasions of staying out too late having fun.

Chasing poachers and helping neighbors were the more common occurrences for Henry being out late, versus late-night fun, which he only seemed to do on two occasions – his birthday and New Year's Eve. Last night he wasn't chasing poachers, or helping neighbors. As it was already approaching the end of January, his difficulty getting out of bed this morning had all to do with his celebrating, and not the arrival of the new year.

For his birthday, the Fords had met friends at the Junction Grill for burgers. When Police Chief Bartlett and Town Manager Mike Muzzy insisted on having a round with Henry, he accepted and drank his second beer of the night, which was double the limit he usually permitted himself. Henry was a stickler for always being ready should he need to go out on a call, and two beers were all he was willing to drink, ever. Even last night, when Alice offered to be his designated driver, he replied, "Alice, you're more than welcome to drive home. I'm still only having two beers."

Alice drew back the winter drapes. A thick layer of frost outlined the edges of the window in frozen snowflake patterns. The tiny white prisms scattered the first slivers of sunlight, reflecting reds and yellows on the white of her robe. She rotated her arm to watch the colorful streaks dance on her sleeve. She turned to Henry. "I'll put the coffee on. I know you need to get ready for your big day."

"Hmm." He bent over to reach for his slippers. "Son of a poacher!" He rubbed his head. "Alice, we really need to move this bedroom around."

"Yes, dear." Alice gave him a peck on his stubbly cheek and headed to the kitchen. "Don't be long. I'll get your breakfast ready." She had a feeling he was going to be moving slower than normal, and it had nothing to do with his mild celebrating last night.

Henry sat on the edge of the bed thinking about the day he had ahead of him. From his perspective, today wasn't going to be such a big day, not for him anyway, and certainly not if things were going to turn out as he suspected.

When he got out of the shower, he noticed Alice had hung his new olive-green shirt on the hook of the bathroom door. He didn't think the occasion was worth wearing the only new uniform shirt he had, but he wriggled into it, rotating his shoulders trying to break it in. How he hated the stiffness of a starched shirt. If turning fifty-seven yesterday wasn't bad enough, he wasn't all too happy that his boss had chosen the day after for this new assignment – if that's what it could be called.

In the kitchen, Henry sat down in his chair at the end of the table. Yesterday's paper was lying in the center of the embroidered table cloth. He glanced down at the headline. It was more of the same, Russia and the U.S. holding talks for the enforcement of a nuclear test-ban treaty. For weeks, the papers had been reporting on the letters between President Kennedy and Premier Khrushchev. Henry sighed; he couldn't believe he had to pay eight cents an issue for the same news. He opened to the weather page. The temps were going to remain in the low teens with overcast skies and a chance of flurries every day. The weather was more of the same as well.

Alice placed a bowl of oatmeal in front of him. "Coffee will be ready in a minute."

"Thank you, honey." Henry stared down at the gray oats with slices of canned peaches plopped on top. It had been two years, going on three, since Alice had stopped making him his usual breakfast of three eggs over easy, two sausage links, and home fries with onions. "Doctor's orders," she had told him. Now, he was permitted his favorite breakfast maybe, if he was lucky, once a week, and since yesterday was his birthday, he had six mornings of tasteless mush without any brown sugar, or even any of his own homemade maple syrup, to not look forward to.

Henry stuck a spoon in the center of his oatmeal and waited for it to keel over – it didn't. His left hand fiddled with his warden's log book and with his right he lifted his glass. He downed the prune juice that reminded him of sludge, and tasted worse, made a face, pushed the glass aside, and stuck a spoonful of the mush in his mouth. Slowly he slipped a twice-folded piece of paper from his log. His eyes narrowed as he reread the last few sentences of the handwritten letter on department stationary.

> Henry, I'm sure I can count on you for this necessary assignment. You're one of the best officers in the Warden Service and I know your skills will be highly appreciated.
>
> The assignment will begin on Thursday January 24th. If I don't get to speak with you before then, Happy Birthday.
>
> Sincerely,
> Guilford Hermon Bingham
> Chief District Warden, Piscataquis County Maine

Alice stood near the counter holding the coffee pot, a knot in her stomach sympathetic to Henry's anxiety. When he slid the letter back between the pages of his log, he turned towards the cupboard behind his chair. Alice watched him reach for his usual cup, the one he selected every morning without fail. It was an oversized green ceramic mug, with an image of a trout that he said was lucky. His nephew, Bobby, had given it to him for his birthday two years ago. His sister-in-law, Bonnie, had told Henry how excited Bobby was the day he discovered the mug in the kitchen section down at the Trading Post. Bobby had stood next to Henry's chair as he opened the box and said,

"Doesn't that fish look like the one you helped me catch over on Lily Bay, Uncle Henry? It has the same color spots."

This morning, two years and a day since he opened the gift, Henry paused, his fingers on the mug's handle. He wasn't feeling all that lucky. Alice's lips tightened as she saw Henry's hand move to the left and he picked up a mug from the matching set he had given her for Christmas – white porcelain with sunflower images.

"Don't give it too much thought, Henry. I'm sure it's just routine." Alice placed a matching saucer under the cup and poured his coffee.

"Hmm." He stared into the steaming blackness. "Speaking of routines, I'd better give you a hand with the animals before I go."

"That won't be necessary. You don't have time today, of all days."

"Trust me, Alice, I'm in no rush to start this day. Besides, Bullwinkle might still be a calf, but I'd feel better if I didn't leave you to give him his required shot all alone. While that moose appears to be enjoying the free room and board here at the Ford Wild Game Farm, he doesn't enjoy seeing you approaching him with that needle."

"Fortunately, the vet says he'll only need one or two more of those. His leg is healing nicely. He doesn't seem to mind the shot as much, as long as he has a bucket of carrots and lettuce to eat as a distraction." Alice motioned to the kitchen scrap pail she had ready for her morning rounds.

"That's all great and wonderful, but I'll hold the rope all the same. Once he's healed, I hope that moose is as anxious to get back to the woods as he is for a free breakfast. Since October he must have gained over a hundred pounds on my nickel."

Bullwinkle wasn't the only animal under care at the Ford's. Their garage housed the moose in the large pen, which was coincidently where Henry wished he could be parking his cruiser during the snowy winter months. To the side of that, there was a crate with two racoons, who were found tangled in chicken wire and each had lost a foot. The space under Henry's workbench was enclosed with fencing and was home to an ornery turkey, who had been clipped by a snowmobile. Henry would just as soon throw the bird in the oven than nurse it back to health. But Alice ruled the Ford wildlife rescue and rehabilitation roost, and her number one rule was, and always had been, no eating of those admitted to the facility.

Once the animals were fed, watered, and in Bullwinkle's case, given his medicine, Henry still wasn't his usual hurried self to get out on patrol. He mulled around the garage.

"You'd better be going. I'm all set here." Alice placed the eggs from the hen house in her basket.

"Yeah, yeah, I know. I was just making sure."

"I can handle this. I do it every day. You don't want to be late and have Warden Bingham getting a call."

"I've got plenty of time. The meeting isn't 'til noon. Maybe I'll make a thermos of coffee to bring along in the car."

"I've already filled your thermos. It's on the front seat, along with some carrot sticks and an apple for later."

"Hmm. Same grub as that moose," Henry grumbled low. Ever since his last cholesterol screening, Alice had been cutting back on his allocation of bacon and cheese sandwiches in his lunch box. He walked towards the door, and hung the length of rope he had wound into a tight curl on an iron hook. Leaning over, he kissed Alice on her forehead. "Alright then, if I leave now, I'll have time to check the ice conditions on the lake for the fishing derby before my meeting. I'll be back by dinner."

Alice stood at the garage window and watched Henry drive off. She secretly wished that maybe this was an opportunity for him. Maybe, just maybe, someday soon he'd take more time to relax, he could at least get in more fishing.

She headed back to the house. Halfway up the porch steps, she heard the phone ringing.

"Hello. Ford residence." Alice never knew if the caller would be family, friend, or someone needing Henry's immediate assistance.

"Good morning, Alice."

"Oh, mornin', Bonnie. How are things?"

"Bobby is fit to be tied. He can't wait to get down there for the derby. Wilson is out packing up the truck now. Here he comes, talking a mile a minute. Hold on a second, sis."

Alice could hear Wilson's booming voice through the receiver.

"Delivery guy shorted us loaves of bread again. This time two are missing."

"Have you mentioned it to Henry?"

"What's a warden gonna want to do about missing bread."

"Well, if the driver says he counted the items, maybe the racoons are stealing from us."

"Yeah, sure."

Alice heard a door slam.

"Sorry about that. We've been having trouble with the orders lately. Seems we're always short one thing or another from the early morning deliveries left out on the store porch."

"I see."

"Are we going yet, Mom?"

"A few more minutes. Go and get your boots on. I'll tell you, that boy's been carrying his tackle box since he got out of bed."

Alice laughed. "That kid loves to fish. Henry just left. Said he was going to check the ice. What time are you planning to be at the ice shack?"

"Wilson wants to have lunch out there. He says if nothing's biting, at least he can eat." Bonnie laughed. "We'll be there by ten I'm bringing chili."

"Sounds good. Henry will be pleased with that." Alice paused. "If he even gets to fish with us today."

"Why do you say that?"

"Oh, he has some important visitor due in town. He's meeting the man at the diner shortly. I suspect…"

Bonnie cut her off. "I gotta run, Alice. Bobby's slipped out the back door – no boots or coat on. I swear I need to put a leash on that kid. We'll swing by and pick you up in a couple of hours."

Before Alice said goodbye, the dial tone sounded. She shrugged. "Guess I'll pack up the fishing gear."

Going Fishing

January 24, 1963 – 11:45 a.m.

Offices of The Bangor Daily

Bangor, Maine

"**A**bout how much longer, Joe? I want to get to Greenville before dark." Stan stood at the entrance to Joe's office. It wasn't much of an office, an alcove really, with a folding table along a windowless wall, in the back annex of *The Bangor Daily*.

"I'm just finishing up the hook, Dad. Give me five minutes." Joe moved his eyes from the page in his typewriter, to the clock on the wall. "And it's not nearly noon. We've got plenty of time." He closed his eyes to think. It was his habit to always finish an article and then add a strong opening, to grab the reader, a beginning to pull them in, and keep them reading.

"Okay, I'll meet you in the lobby." Before turning to go, Stan watched his son. He was held motionless by the rhythmic smacking of the keys against the paper, the end of line 'dings,' the slide of the drum back to the left. He felt a sense of pride that Joe had started a job as an outdoor writer for Maine's north woods.

When Joe yanked the paper from the machine, Stan turned for the lobby; passing his own office he pulled the door closed. He paused in front of the window to the main newsroom. A thick fog of cigarette smoke circulated along the ceiling, riding the currents from the heating duct. A dozen reporters sat at their desks, typing, or talking on the phone chasing down leads. Walking down the hall, Stan was full of energy, he felt sad for those who had to work indoors all the time.

Leaning back in his chair, Joe's lips moved slightly as he read over the article. Finishing the last sentence, he slung his bag over his shoulder, and slid the sheets in a manilla envelope. At the copy desk he dropped the package in the brown carboard box, with the word "IN" painted in big black letters.

"Carla, if the boss forgets, as he usually does, remind him I'll be out of contact for a few days. Dad and I will be up at Moosehead covering the ice fishing derby."

"Right, Joe." She pointed to the green board behind her desk. The rectangles with the names, STAN PARKER and JOE PARKER, were under the column labeled, *On Assignment*. "You boys have a good time up there in the arctic."

Joe gave a salute. "See you Monday."

Reaching the lobby, Stan was nowhere to be found. Not that Joe had many places to look. The lobby was a room with four well-worn gold upholstered chairs, a table stacked high with past issues of **The Daily**, and a desk, where sometimes a receptionist sat. Most days, she was off making copies, or filling in in the typing pool, so rarely was anyone at the desk. Joe propped up the cardboard sign, "For Assistance Dial Extension 1043."

A horn beeped twice. Beyond the floor to ceiling glass windows, Stan pulled the truck to the curb. He gave Joe a swing of his arm.

"Got everything?" Joe slid in and pulled the truck door closed.

"Everything I could think of. I double checked we had the most important items – the ice saw, the poles, skimmer, and the tip-ups."

"Sorry about the late start. I couldn't miss that deadline or the boss would have cancelled my trip. He sees it as a boondoggle. The guy has no appreciation for reporting on the outdoors. I doubt he could tell a barbed-hook from a Gray Ghost."

"I understand. That new editor isn't anything like George Smith was. Now, there was a guy who knew his way around a newsroom and putting an article together. Not only the editing, but he knew the Maine outdoors and made contributions to every piece. I sure miss having him around. The Sportsmen's Association is lucky to have him in his semi-retired state. He made the outdoor section of this paper what it is." Stan's lips were tight as he nodded, reminiscing about his old boss, editor, and hunting partner.

Joe knew his dad missed having his life-long friend around the halls of **The Daily**, so he changed the subject. "I suspect it's going to be crowded on the lake this weekend."

"Ah – you know better than that. It's like we're the only ones on the ice, no matter how many people are around."

"Yeah. We're never lacking space." Joe fiddled with the truck's heater that only alternated between pulling cold air in, or blowing hot enough to almost set the vinyl bench seat on fire. "Do you think we'll have a chance to go check on camp?"

"All depends."

"On?"

"On if I catch enough fish. And the weather. When I spoke to Henry the other night, he said with all the snow they've had, it would be tough going to break a trail all the way to Lobster Lake."

"I'm looking forward to catching up with Henry and Alice."

"Henry said Alice has been preparing her gear for the derby for two weeks. You know how much she loves to fish."

"Yep. But last year, she seemed to be playing more host, than fishing. Remember that chicken and vegetable dinner she cooked us? Out there in the ice shack on the woodstove. What a meal to have while on the lake."

"I sure do. Heck of a lot better than opening a can of beans. Ah, but don't worry about her fussing, she loves having company."

Joe stared out the truck's misted side window. The gray sky melted into a farmer's field where withered corn stalks poked through the cover of white. A discarded Christmas tree was lying in the driveway of the farm house, frozen in the plowed snowbank with no hope of getting pulled out until spring. Thoughts of holiday gatherings his family had shared with the Fords when he was growing up played against the snowy background. He felt a nudge from his dad's elbow.

"I made lunches." From a bag on the seat, he handed Joe a sandwich loosely wrapped in a grease-stained brown paper.

Joe could smell his dad's specialty before even unwrapping it. "I wish for once you could keep this combination of yours on separate sandwiches."

"What? You don't appreciate my tuna and egg salad special."

"I don't mind tuna. And your egg salad with the little bits of celery is good – it reminds me of Mom's. I just don't need tuna and egg between the same two pieces of bread at the same time."

"Huh. Suit yourself." Stan took a big bite from his sandwich. The fish and sulfur smell filled the truck's cab. Stan reached over the seat and flipped the metal cover from the rusted red cooler. "You want a chocolate milk?" He held out a small brown and white carton, with a cartoon of a smiling cow under the caption, "*Moo, Moo, Drink Milk.*"

"Oh, Dad." Joe grimaced and blew out a breath.

"What now?"

"You're washing down that sandwich with milk?"

"No." Stan grinned. "It's chocolate milk."

Joe poked around in the cooler. "Is there nothing else in here to drink? No pop?"

"Nope. Just the chocolate milks." Stan grinned wider.

Joe sighed. "Hey – isn't this the fish cooler?"

"Yeah. So? Ain't no fish in it yet."

Joe realized that maybe the smell in the truck wasn't from the sandwiches after all. He fumbled with the radio dial.

> *"In world news, Khrushchev has vowed to West Germany he has no intentions of invading."*

"Yeah, right," mumbled Stan.

> *"The soviet premier stated…"*

Joe turned the dial.

> *"After the Giants loss in the NFL championship game back in December, Gifford's return is in question."*

Joe turned the dial.

"I'll be happier when baseball season starts." Stan wiped a dribble of milk from his chin with his sleeve.

*"You're listening to Bangor's best country. We're expecting a cold snap this weekend. Low teens here in town, colder in the mountains, with more snow on the way. For those of you headed to the ice fishing derby this weekend up on Moosehead Lake, wear your long-johns, it's gonna be frigid out there. Hopefully you'll be in a toasty ice shack with your honey. Maybe I'll see you on the ice. To get you thinkin' fish, here's Hank Locklin with, **We're Gonna Go Fishin**."*

"Leave that one. I like Locklin's pickin." Stan picked up the lyrics and sang along. There wasn't a country song the old man didn't know the words to. They spent the next hour of the drive listening to the radio, with Stan singing mostly off key, and talking about fishing during the commercials.

Been Skunked

Henry pulled his cruiser into a space across from the Lock, Stock, and Barrel. He turned off the engine. Before opening his door, he assessed the cars parked along Pritham Avenue. With no official looking vehicle parked nearby, he pulled on his winter warden cap and crossed to the diner.

It was warm inside, almost too warm, even for a cold winter morning in the north woods. He hung his parka on a hook near the door. Out of habit, he quickly looked at each customer. A few of them were regulars, but this morning, he could tell most were visiting for the annual fishing derby, an event that brought hundreds to the lake each January. The derby was started by the owner of the Trading Post as an economic development idea. For the stores and the few restaurants, it certainly was. For Henry, while he enjoyed the aspects of connecting with those who loved the outdoors, the weekend was full of people getting into situations out on the ice that ranged between being stupid to, in some cases, almost deadly.

He scanned the small dining area for a place to wait for his contact to arrive. All the seats were taken except the booth closest to the woodstove. Four rough looking men, in "his" booth at the back corner, sat staring at Henry. He made a mental note of their characteristics – three had beards, two were wearing trucker caps, one Chevy logo and two Ford, and all of them were wearing army fatigue jackets. The lumber yard crew had pulled two tables together in the center of the room, as they did every day at this time. Everyone in town knew where they were, you couldn't even get a two-by-four until after one o'clock. Henry gave a nod in their direction. "Afternoon, Henry," they returned in unison as he walked by.

A young boy sitting with his dad, asked in a not so quiet voice, "Dad, is that man a cop?"

Buddy turned on his stool. "Hey, Henry, want a seat here at the counter? Buster and I are about finished."

Henry gave Buddy a 'one moment' sign with his index finger and approached the boy.

"Hello, young man. I'm a Maine Game Warden. My job is to protect our natural resources – the fish, the deer, all the wildlife and to make sure everyone is obeying the law. Me and the other wardens also help people if they are lost in the woods."

The boy, who wasn't more than ten, gazed up at Henry with an open mouth. His eyes fell to Henry's side. "Is that a real gun?"

"Yes. Yes, it is."

"Do you shoot people?"

"Son, I think the warden is probably busy." The father pushed the child's plate closer to his son. Only one small bite had been taken from the burger.

"That's okay, sir." Henry took a knee to be at eye level with the boy. His demeanor with children had always been gentle. He took his responsibility to make a positive impression on any future sportsman serious. "What's your name, young man?"

"Gregory."

"I'll tell you, Gregory, no officer goes around with the intention of shooting anyone. Our job is to protect people." The boy shifted his eyes again to the gun. "But sometimes we need to be prepared for danger. Are you going to be ice fishing this weekend?"

"Yup." His eyes opened wide and went from the gun, to Henry's face, to his badge.

"You have fun. Dress warm and listen to your dad." He reached into his shirt pocket and took out two slips of paper. "You can take these coupons to the derby weigh station – over near Folsom's – for free hot chocolate." He handed them to the boy.

The boy held the slips. "Thanks!" He waved them at his dad, who also thanked Henry.

Henry turned back to the father. "The ice around the cove is plenty thick. Stay clear of the channel and the outlet. It's all marked with orange-flagged stakes, but you can never be too cautious."

"Thank you, Warden."

Henry gave a slight nod and walked to the counter.

Buddy went to stand.

Henry's hand went up. "No, no. That's okay. I'm waitin' on someone. I'll stand until he gets here."

"Hiya, Henry. How's Alice?" Karen walked up between the tables with a pot of coffee in each hand.

"She's good. She's keeping busy you know, taking care of the animals."

"Go behind and grab your mug, I'll fill you up on my next pass." Karen went table to table topping off cups.

Buddy watched as Henry searched the shelf.

Buster cleared his throat. "Uh oh." Henry turned to face Buster, who had his hands on a green mug. The image of a bear visible between his fingers.

"You're using my mug?"

"Karen was so busy, she didn't realize it." Buster felt Henry's glare trying to melt him permanently to the stool.

Buddy tried to save Buster from a bear attack. "Henry, you expecting any help out here for the derby? Or are you alone to cover the whole lake again this year?"

Henry turned back to the shelf and picked a cup. "Matter of fact, I'm meeting with a new warden today. My boss gave me the impression the guy might be sticking around for a while. So far, I'm not too impressed. He was supposed to be here at noon and here it is twelve ten. He's late."

A man pushed his way through the door of the payphone stall in the corner. He strode directly towards Henry. "Hello, you must be Warden Ford. I'm Andy Green. I've been waiting for you. I just got off the phone with Warden Bingham getting your home phone number, in case you forgot." He offered his hand across the counter to Henry.

Henry mumbled, "Son of a poacher."

"What was that, sir?"

"Oh, nothing. I said, it's so nice to meet-cha." They shook hands.

Karen hustled by on her way to the kitchen. Henry held out a mug. She lifted the two glass pots. "Sorry, Henry. Lots of coffee drinkers this morning. I'm all out. A fresh pot is brewing. Give me two minutes."

Henry put the empty mug on the counter with a thud. He looked at the young warden. He was maybe all of twenty four, tall, a little taller than Henry in fact; a friendly face, a little too friendly to Henry's thinking anyway; but most of all what bothered Henry is this Green, or Andrews, or whatever he said his name was, was that he was not in uniform. Bingham's letter had informed Henry he'd be meeting a warden. This man had no such characteristics.

"I was under the impression from headquarters, I'd be meeting a warden."

"That's correct. I am."

"Then why aren't you in uniform?" Henry ran his hand over his nose. For some reason, this warden smelled like a bad memory.

"Warden Ford, why don't we go sit down where we can talk. Privately." Green pointed towards the empty booth. The busboy was loading more wood into the firebox.

Green motioned for Henry to lead the way. Henry picked up his still empty mug.

Sitting across from Green, Henry tapped the table. "Did you drive up this morning?"

"Yes, I did."

Uncharacteristically, Henry had no interest in asking anything further. Thankfully, Karen arrived with the coffee and a mug for Green.

"Something to eat, gentleman?" She could have cut the tension and served it on a plate.

It seemed to Henry that all the noises of the diner had stopped. There was no talking, no cutting of sausages, no scraping of butter on burnt toast, no slurping of coffee. The sounds, of course, had not stopped, but to Henry time was standing still. He was deep in thought on where the conversation with this man was going to go.

"Henry?" Karen waved the pot of coffee in front of him.

"The usual for me, please." He didn't look up at her. He knew that Alice had told Karen all about his strict diet.

Karen knew, he knew she knew. "Okay, one Warden Special coming up." She could tell he wasn't having a great day and let the order slide. "Anything for you, sir?"

"Karen, this here's a new warden. I suspect the two of you ought to get to know one another."

She looked at Henry; her eyes making a barely discernable squint. Not wanting to think about the real reason Green was here, she shook the thought from her mind. "Nice to meet you. Welcome to Greenville."

"Nice to meet you as well, Miss."

Karen winced. "Call me Karen."

"Okay, Karen. Hearing you have a Warden Special, make that two. I suspect I need to try that."

"Coming right up." Karen picked up the empty plates from the next table. "Hey, Johnny, stop messing with the fire and take these plates to the kitchen." She handed the busboy the stack of dishes.

Henry took out his handkerchief and wiped his forehead.

"I'm sorry I took you by surprise, not being in my uniform."

"Are you not on duty?"

"I am." Green's voice was flat and direct.

"I don't get it then. Why aren't you in uniform?"

He skated the interrogation and went over Henry's head. "You did get District Warden Bingham's memo – right?"

"I did. It was vague. I even called a buddy down at headquarters in Augusta. All I could find out was more of the same – a warden would be arriving with the details." Rubbing his hands together, Henry's voice raised a little too loud for the small diner. "You may as well cut to the chase and tell me you're planning on taking my job."

Buddy and Buster swung their stools around. This time Henry wasn't imagining it. All the clanking of silverware and the talking at the tables had stopped. Rodney, from the lumber yard crew, whistled an, "Uh-oh," tune. Warden Green laughed – a little too loud for Henry's liking.

Henry's right fist slammed the table. "I knew it." The salt and pepper shakers bounced two inches sideways.

Green sat up straight and responded in a loud, calm voice. He wanted everyone to hear. "Warden Ford, it's nothing of the kind. I'm merely here to learn from you. Warden Bingham thinks extremely highly of you. In fact, everyone I've met in the warden service thinks highly of you. You're a legend. I'm slated to be stationed down in Knox County."

Henry slid back in his seat and rubbed the back of his neck. He noticed Buddy and Buster looking his way. "What are you two stooges looking at?" They lowered their heads and turned back to their eggs and hash. The rest of the customers resumed their own conversations, hoping not to get yelled at.

Henry's cheeks were flushed. "Wow. Hot in here, isn't it." Green held his gaze. Sitting back in his seat, Henry bought himself some time to think. "I'm sorry, what was your name again?"

"Andy, Andy Green."

"I apologize. Warden Bingham's letter wasn't clear at all. But he isn't usually very clear if I'm standing two feet in front of him."

"I see." Andy paused. He rubbed his chin. Then he looked Henry in the eyes. "Rest assured, I'm not here to take your job. I hope we can work together for several weeks, that's all."

"This is all highly unusual. I've trained new recruits in the past, but they've never arrived introduced by an ambiguous letter. Bingham didn't even include your name." Henry cocked his head and motioned at Green's chest with his mug. "And they've never shown up not in uniform."

"Ah, about the clothes. You see, I was on my way here when the car in front of me hit something in the road. I pulled over to find a skunk jammed under their wheel-well. The driver was happier than all heck seeing I was a warden. As my luck would have it, that skunk wasn't dead."

Henry laughed.

"You ever been skunked before, Warden Ford?"

Henry stopped laughing and gave Green a serious look.

Green had a feeling he had hit a nerve. "If you want to check, my uniform's in my trunk."

"No, not at all. I'm relieved that odor isn't your normal cologne. That would have put an end to this here assignment right here and now." Henry crossed his arms and leaned away.

"I'm glad I had this spare set of clothes in the back seat."

Taking a look at the frayed red and black flannel shirt Green was wearing, Henry thought it had seen better days. He wondered why this warden wasn't following the manual that clearly states in the appendix, *"A warden on patrol is well advised to carry a spare uniform and extra civvies in the vehicle at all times."* It was sound advice; a warden never knew what they might run into. There were dozens of times over Henry's career where he had to put on a clean uniform after getting wet or falling in the mud. His regular pants also came in handy when having to be somewhere for a personal engagement without time to rush home and change.

"You should always have spare gear with you," Henry stated. He took a drink of his coffee. "Tell me about what you had in mind? You planning on tagging along on my patrols? You do realize, I can't be waiting around for you. When something happens up here, people are usually in danger and I gotta move – fast."

"No, I certainly won't slow you down. It'd be great to ride along with you when feasible. Maybe I can lend a hand now and then. What I had in mind is more of a school type learning."

The laughter from Henry echoed through the room. Every man, woman, and child, including Johnny the busboy, froze. Henry wiped the tears from his eyes with his red bandana handkerchief.

Then he got serious. His finger tapped the table. The pace of his voice was measured, and loud.

"School type learning? What do you want me to do, draw you stick figures of moose and deer on a blackboard? This isn't a desk job. You learn it by sitting in your cruiser on moonless nights, somewhere on a dirt road, when the temps are below freezing, waiting for a nimrod to light up a field with his headlights. Or by sitting in a wet roadside ditch waiting for a poacher to walk out of the woods on a Sunday evening with a loaded rifle. You earn your paycheck by inching your way across pond ice that is way too thin to be on, to pull a seven-year old girl to safety after she chased after her cat. Your school is getting out of bed five minutes after your head hit the pillow to hike ten miles in the dark to assist carrying out a hiker with a broken ankle. We're in school every day of the year here, it's never the same, and there's no summer break."

Green realized he may have used the wrong words. Nobody in the diner had moved. Everyone's attention was on Green to see what his response was going to be.

"Sir, with all due respect, I have served as a military pilot for the past four years. I've slept in drainage ditches thirty yards from heavily armed Vietnam forces waiting to kill me with machine gun fire. I've carried panicked little girls across rice paddies while bullets flew over my head. I'm not bragging, I've been told you've seen your share of battle when you served our country. I guess my choice of words was poor. It's not typical schooling I need on emergency situations. It's the psychological aspects of the characters you meet here in the north woods. This is a different enemy than I've been fighting. I need to know how to handle them."

The four men in fatigues, focused on Green.

Henry's eyes were wide and he was at a loss of words.

With impeccable timing, Karen arrived with their orders. She placed the plates on the table and from her apron pocket added two sets of silverware. "You men need anything else at the moment?"

Looking up at Karen, Henry asked, "Could you open a window? I haven't been this warm since Alice made me clean out the attic last August."

"The new kid stokes that stove every five minutes. We've never gone through so much wood." She lifted an old wooden-frame window closest to Henry and propped it open with a salt shaker.

Green lifted the top piece of bread from his sandwich. "There's nothing on here but burnt bacon."

His mouth already full from his first bite, Henry reached across the table for the laminated menu that was wedged between the sugar and the napkin holder. He slid it in front of Green. He jammed his index finger three times at the description of the Warden Special, and still chewing, said, "What the heck did you think was on a bacon sandwich."

The corners of Green's mouth turned upward and his head shook slightly as he read the description: '*Warden Ford Special – Six crunchy slices of bacon. Your choice of bread.*'

"You might need more schooling than I thought." Henry picked up the salt shaker in one hand, and the top piece of greasy bread in the other. He dusted the bacon. Seeing Green wasn't impressed with his namesake sandwich, he asked, "You gonna eat that or not?"

Green hadn't taken a bite. He pushed his plate to Henry's side of the table. "Do you have any enemies out here in the woods?"

Henry removed two strips of bacon from Green's sandwich and placed them between the bread on his own. The other four strips he wrapped in a paper napkin and slipped them into his shirt pocket.

"Lesson one, bacon keeps for a long time and comes in handy on the trail. Lesson two, bears can scent that bacon for miles, keep it sealed up. Lesson three, and this is very important, few people out here in the woods are your enemy. A few of them may try to get away with more than they should, but when you make an enemy, you'll know it before I can tell you."

He noticed Green's questioning frown; his eyes still locked on Henry's pocket.

"Bears are hibernating this time of year. On enemies, I've had a few. I'm sure you heard the story of Red and his gang of poachers."

Green tilted his head to the left. "No. I can't say I have. What happened?"

"Are you kidding me? It was only *THE* biggest bust ever to happen up this way." He lifted his mug towards Karen, who was a couple of tables away. "Karen, dear, we're gonna need refills."

"Anything else?" She filled their mugs.

"I'm all set," answered Andy.

"What kind of pie do you have today?"

Karen glared down at Henry. "You know I'm on strict orders from Alice. I could already be in trouble seeing I served you that bacon sandwich." Her voice trailed off and a scowl crossed her face when she realized both plates were in front of Henry. She shook her head at Green.

Green looked from Karen to Henry, trying to figure out what was going on.

"I won't report you. Make it a small piece of apple." He looked across the table at Green. "She makes a wicked good apple pie with a crumb topping."

"Don't try to sweeten me up." Karen picked up the empty plates.

Henry pleaded with her; his eyes wide. He raised his mug. "I need something to go with your delicious coffee. And bring Warden Green a piece, too."

Karen rolled her eyes. At the door to the kitchen she yelled, "Coming in!"

Green stared across the table at Henry. "What's that all about? You on a restricted diet?"

Henry avoided Green's question. "Let me tell you about some of the conniving characters you'll meet out here – starting with Red and his gang, *The Lobster Lake Bandits.*

The North Woods

In the sky, near Moosehead Lake.

"Mayday! Mayday! Mayday"
"Repeat – Mayday! Mayday! She's going down."

No message heard.

Communications were severed.

The ship was tossed in the whirling turbulence.

The pilot struggled to keep the plane level.

The plane lost altitude.

Above the whine of his chainsaw, Spencer felt a rumble in the air. He looked up. The afternoon sky was dulled by a gray overcast that was covering the tops of the mountains.

The ground started to shake. He killed his chainsaw. "Holy crud."

The plane emerged from the thick white cloudy soup above. It was only visible for a second before it disappeared into the side of the mountain. A fireball shot into the air. Black smoke rose against the snow-covered backdrop.

Shocked, the logger couldn't move.

The "dee-dee-dee" song of a chickadee broke the silence.

Spencer dropped his saw, flipped off his scratched orange hard hat, and climbed into his skidder.

"Hey! Hey! Anyone! This is Spence, come in." The CB radio crackled with static.

"Go ahead, Spencer, what is it?"

"Theresa, is the boss around?"

"He's out running the sawmill. What do you need?"

Spencer had been working off Scammon Road for the past week, cutting logs for the loader. Earlier today his partner went home sick. He was the only one at the site.

"I, I just saw a plane crash and explode."

"What? Are you sure?"

"Positive! Call for help."

"Okay, okay, hold on."

Spencer was miles from where the plane crashed. He had worked and hunted these woods for more than twenty years and knew there were no roads leading to where he saw the plane go down. Not that it mattered, the snow was eight feet deep high up the side of that mountain where the unplowed road ended. Nobody was going to be able to drive up there.

He sat back in the taped-up black seat, blew out a deep breath, held his head in his hands, and waited for Theresa. He focused his eyes on where the plane went down. The initial cloud of black smoke had already dissipated in the high winds. His mind raced trying to figure out the fastest route to the top of the mountain. No matter the options, it was going to be a tough rescue. Or more likely this time of year, in these snowy conditions – a recovery. What was taking Theresa so long to get back to him?

The Moosetowner

Greenville Airport

Linda was hunched over the folding table that was the couples work space, lunch counter, and many Friday nights a poker table for Don and the other pilots who hung around the Greenville airport.

"Hey, Don, take a look at this." She was intently studying a collection of aerial photos that were spread out before her.

"What is it?" His back to her, he lifted the top off the coffee percolator and took a whiff. "Yuck."

"That's been sitting over an hour." Linda didn't look up from the photos.

Don put the top back on and pulled the plug. "They should change the slogan; this stuff is only good to the last drop if you drink it right away." He walked over to the table.

"Tell me what you see different between these two images."

Don stood next to her trying to guess what it was she expected him to see. His wife, of a little more than a year, always had a better eye analyzing aerials. Taking the photos and noticing minute details was what she specialized in. He, on the other hand, was a big picture guy, he flew the plane and watched the scenery go by.

Knowing Don would need to study the photos for a few minutes, Linda dumped what was left of the coffee on the snow to the right of the trailer's cinder block steps. She opened the one-pound can of coffee, scooped the grounds into the steel basket, filled the percolator with water, and plugged it back in.

"So, what do you think?" she asked, putting her arm around his waist. She already knew what the pictures were telling her, but she always liked to have a confirmation before reporting to land management of the lumber company what she found.

Don took off his cap, the one with the Cessna logo that he always wore while in the field office trailer, and rubbed his forehead. "Gee, honey, I can't see much in this black and white, the area must be five square miles. Give me a bearing at least, will ya?"

Linda picked up a black marker, and in the white margins she drew an arrow point at the top and another on the right on each photo. Using his two index fingers, Don traced to where the arrows met. He saw nothing out of the ordinary. He looked over his shoulder hoping the bubbling sound of the percolating coffee would save him.

"A watched pot never boils. Look here." Linda tapped the photos.

Don squinted. "Huh, now that looks different." He wasn't really too sure if he saw anything.

"You see it then?" Linda had been studying aerial photos for years. Only recently were manuals starting to be published with techniques to highlight abnormalities. She tried to read each publication to learn when to apply infrared stereograms or panchromatic. From her photos she could now easily pick up the star-shaped white pine crowns, versus the cone-shaped balsam firs; distinctions she still couldn't train Don to see.

"I'm not sure. What do you make of it?" Don asked, stressing the *you*, in his statement.

"The photo on the right is from two years ago. This one on the left, I took last week when we mapped this area again – it's the northside of Allagash Lake." She rocked back and forth on her boot heels; her hands spread on the drafting table.

Taking a seat on a metal steel stool, he held the photo up close to his eyes. "Oh sure, I remember. Looks familiar to me now that I know where I'm looking at. But what do you suppose this blank area is from? A microburst?" The aroma of coffee reached his brain. He walked over, mug in hand, and lifted the pot.

"Let that sit a minute if you don't want grinds in your cup."

"Mmm," he grumped, and sat the pot back down.

"And this can't be from a microburst."

"Why not?" He lifted the top off the pot and looked in.

"Too clean, there's nothing lying on the ground."

Don tapped a teaspoon on his empty cup.

Linda continued, "Looks to be selective clearing. And it wasn't done all that well either. Definitely violates shoreline distances. It's certainly not timber company cutting."

"You have some eye to see that. Looks like a black and white splotch to me."

"When you study these images as much as I do, patterns appear."

"Better you than me. You want me to pour you a coffee?"

"Sure."

"And why would someone cut timber up that way. There aren't any roads to get the lumber out." Don bent over and moved Linda's lenses and drafting instruments on the metal bookcase.

"I was wondering that, too." Linda looked over her shoulder. "Please be careful with that stereoscope. And then I figured they might think that no roads would be perfect cover for such an operation."

"How so? And where the heck is your mug?"

"No roads, means less chance the forestry service inspectors are checking that way." She pointed and raised her eyebrows. "It's right next to the coffee pot."

Seeing the mug on the counter, he shrugged.

When he placed her coffee down on the table, she asked, "What? No sugar. No creamer?"

"Did you ask for sugar and creamer?"

"We've been married over a year now. You'd think you'd know how I take my coffee." She shook her head. At the counter she added her usual two teaspoons of sugar and a tablespoon of powdered creamer.

"What good is cutting the lumber down, if they can't haul it out?" Don shuffled through her other pictures.

Linda tapped her finger on the top of Allagash Lake.

Don frowned. "I'm not following you, maybe I need more coffee."

"They floated it out."

"What?"

"Directly across to this road here." She moved her finger to the east side of the lake. "The way they did it in the old days."

Don sipped his coffee, making a slurping sound that drove Linda nuts. She glared up at him and he moved the mug from his lips. "I doubt that. This isn't 1863."

"Why?" she asked. Her voice had an edge of defensiveness that her theory was shot down.

"Too many campers and hikers. Someone would have seen them taking that much lumber, across a lake, loading trucks, and hauling it out."

Linda sat down in a metal folding chair and held the photo in her hands.

"But you know," Don started and then stopped.

"Know what?"

"Nah, it's crazy."

"Nothing in these woods is crazy. They pay us to fly around, in the middle of winter, taking pictures of the trees. Anything goes. Speak up."

"What if they pulled it across the ice? There's nobody around during the winter that far north."

Linda nodded and wondered why she hadn't considered that. "That's a good possibility. When the weather is clear enough, we'll need to get up there and take a closer look."

"We can, but not until ice out on Allagash Lake. That way we can hike in and assess from the ground. Right now, any evidence is buried under five feet of snow anyway."

"I guess you're right. I'll file the report with the recommendation for a winter monitoring flight and a touchdown in late May." Linda picked up the photos. "I think I'll notify Fred. He's a real stickler. I bet he'd appreciate this case."

"That Moosetowner. You know he would. He grew up in Allagash country. Problem is, he'd want to get up there right away, and I'm not keen on landing there this time of year. A fly-over is one thing, landing and snowshoeing in these temperatures is a whole 'nother level for maybe nothing at all."

Linda placed the photos in the file cabinet. She pulled the next folder needing review and arranged the pictures on the table.

Don poured another mug of coffee and picked up the daily paper. He knew Linda's examination would go on all afternoon. Which was fine with him. With the poor weather conditions, he wasn't planning on flying at all today. While he didn't enjoy trying to spot small differences in photos, he was impressed with her ability to get clear images from the sky and then interpret what she had captured on film. And besides that, she also was the only one he worked with who didn't make a fuss about making a fresh pot of coffee.

He read the first headline, "**All agree. Kennedy's Plan to Lower Taxes a GO!**" Don thought lower taxes would be wonderful, but he'd already heard the plan during the State of the Union Address on the radio earlier in the month. He dropped the paper on the counter and sorted through the pile of magazines for something more recent.

On his way back to his chair, he poured another coffee and switched on the CB.

A screech of static made Linda cringe. "Why are you turning that thing on? There isn't anyone flying today."

"I figured maybe one of the guys might check in."

"They got better things to do than chat on the radio. I'm trying to concentrate here."

"Yes, dear." He flipped the switch off, missing by a second Theresa coming back on the line with instructions for Spencer.

Air Traffic Control

The diner had cleared from the lunch time rush. Workers went back to work; visitors went to claim their square of ice out on the lake. The clanging of dishes could be heard behind the kitchen door. Johnny, the busboy, was on the phone behind the counter. Green, half listening to Henry's story, overheard pieces of the boy's conversation. *"I'll pick you up at eight. – No nobody else will be at the ice shack, we'll have it all to ourselves."* He watched as a delivery driver carried a plastic bin of breads, rolls, and dough and dropped it in front of Johnny. The boy turned away, whispering into the receiver.

Henry cleared his throat. "And that's how Red lost his fishing license and spent thirty days in jail for burglarizing all those camps." Henry leaned back, interlocked his fingers behind his head, and waited for the congratulatory accolades.

Warden Green raised an eyebrow and slowly nodded.

"Don't you think that was one heck of a case?" Henry's hands opened to the heavens.

"I suspect you had to be there. What year was that again?" Green lifted his fork and considered his untouched piece of pie.

"Thanksgiving of fifty-six. You not gonna eat that?"

Green slid the plate across the table.

Holding a forkful of the pie, Henry continued, "We haven't had a surprise snowstorm that early in the season since. That's another thing you'll need to be aware of out here, be prepared for the weather changing at any moment." Scooping up the last bit of crumbs from the plate, Henry had the feeling Green didn't find his story of Red and the bandits all that exciting, which he thought didn't bode well for someone wanting to be a warden in the north woods. He purposely had left out the part of Agent Smith, or Eddy Walsh, if that was the stranger's real name, figuring it wasn't necessary to fill Green in on what was never proven.

The door to the diner flung open. Henry's head swung around to see Rick, from the seaplane base panting near the door.

"Henry, there you are! There's been a plane crash." Rick tried to catch his breath.

"Where?" Henry pushed himself out of his seat.

"Not sure. It came over the radio to Theresa. Chief Bartlett said to find you. He was headed up to the airport."

"Green, you ride with me." Henry shouted over his shoulder. Reaching the door, and getting a whiff of Green, he changed his mind. "On second thought, get your car and follow."

❧∗∗❧

While Linda poured over pictures, most of which showed no abnormal changes year-on-year, Don read an article in **Aviation Week**. When the smell of burnt coffee started to get overwhelming, he stood up to turn off the warmer. He was reaching for the plug when Linda shouted like he'd never heard her yell, other than when a fish got away.

"Don, you got to look at this image of Elephant Mountain! I've never noticed this before. It looks as if someone has …"

The door to their field office opened with a bang against the wall. "Have you heard?" Henry stood in the open doorway.

"Heard what?" asked Don.

"Why don't you have your radio on?"

"Linda likes to work in quiet. Besides, ain't nobody in the air today. The ceiling hasn't lifted in days."

"What is it?" Linda was looking at Henry; trying to figure what was going on.

Green, moved from behind Henry and went directly to Don's radio setup.

"Hey, who are you? Be careful with that." Don moved next to Green to take over operating his radio.

"I'm Warden Andy Green. We have an emergency situation here. You got a plane that can get in the air?"

"Is that so? Where's your uniform? And why do you smell so bad?" Don stepped back.

Green didn't answer, he was busy flipping the radio call book looking for numbers.

Henry placed his hand on Don's shoulder. "We've got a serious situation here. I'm gonna need your assistance. Let Green get on the radio to assess and I'll fill you and Linda in with what I know."

❊✻❊

Stan pulled to the side of the road across from the Indian Store to get out of the way. The town firetruck went screaming by – sirens blaring and lights flashing. "I wonder what that's about?" The vehicle made a right turn onto Airport Road.

"They sure are in a hurry." Joe tapped the side window.

"Yep. I was thinking we'd stop in the diner for a bite before heading up to the airport to meet Don and Linda, but now we'd better go see what's going on." Stan started to pull out and a siren blasted on his left. The ambulance squawked; the red and blue lights bounced off the store window.

"Must be serious." The emergency vehicles were already out of sight up the hill by the time Stan turned the corner.

Flashes of red rotated through the field office's small window. Henry watched the chief of police, fire chief, and volunteer firemen hustle towards the airport traffic control building – a pine log cabin with a two-story antenna structure in the field behind it.

"I'm going over to the control building to coordinate a plan with the chief. You and Andy discuss what it's going to take to get up in the air." Henry pointed at Don.

"Henry, are you kidding? It'll be dark in less than an hour."

"Then there's no time to waste." Henry was closing the door behind him when Stan's truck slid to a stop on the icy dirt.

Joe rolled down the window. "What's all the commotion about, Henry?"

Henry exhaled. The airport was more crowded than he had ever seen. Cars and trucks full of volunteers were arriving by the second. "Plane's gone down. Don will fill you in. I've got to get over to see the chief." Henry strode off.

"I didn't even get to wish him a Happy Birthday." Stan turned off the ignition. "Let's see what's going on." They pulled on their hats and stepped from the truck. Inside, they found Don in a heated conversation with someone they had never seen before.

"I want you to know, I'm a pilot. I have over fourteen hundred hours flying time during my military career. If you can tell me which plane can be ready to go, I'll get her warmed up and in the air."

"Sir, you might be a General in the Air Force, but I have no authority to give you a plane. You know better than that. If I can get up safely, you can fly with me."

"There are men out there in those woods. We need to get there. Now!"

"I understand how you feel. But I fly in this area over two hundred days a year. Even if we could get in the air, we don't even have a location to head to yet."

The young warden was out of patience. "This is ridiculous. I'm headed over to the control building. I'll get someone else to get me in the air." He turned to see two men standing in the doorway. "Excuse me." Joe and Stan moved to one side as Green rushed out the door.

"You two sure picked a heck of a time to arrive." Don fiddled with the squelch knob.

"What's happening?" asked Joe.

"As best as we can tell, a plane has gone down, somewhere east of Prong Pond," said Linda.

"A local?" Stan's face was grim.

"We have no idea. Just got word from Henry before you pulled in," Don shut off his radio.

"Are you going up to take a look? In that?" Pointing, Joe realized he didn't need to direct Don's attention towards the window and the weather outside.

"I haven't been able to think. That warden has got me all turned around." Don pulled on his heavy parka. "Let's all go and see what the chief and Henry want to do."

"Don, put this on." Linda handed him his hat with the fur earmuffs.

Inside the tiny twenty-by-twenty traffic control building, men stood around the radio. A haze of cigarette smoke circled the dim bulbs hanging by wires from the crossbeams. The chief and Henry stood hunched over a topographical map spread on the desk.

Police Chief Bartlett faced the group. "Okay, listen up." He looked over the volunteer crew, all men who had scrambled from their jobs in the middle of the afternoon. To his left were the four guys from the lumber yard. On his right he noticed the pharmacist, the hardware store owner, and the mechanic from the town garage. Against the back wall, flanking the Fire Chief and the town manager, were the volunteer fire fighters, the auxiliary police, and pilots from the seaplane base.

Henry caught a glimpse of the four men he saw in the diner earlier, the ones wearing Army fatigues. They stood at ease; their arms held at their wrist behind their backs. He gave them a single head nod. They returned the gesture.

When the room became silent, except for an intermittent crackling on the radio, the chief continued. "What we know, and don't ask me questions, this is all I know at the moment. What we know is a large, and I mean large, military plane has gone down on Elephant Mountain. Spencer Ackers, from the paper company, many of you know him, he knows these woods as good as the rest of us, he's reported the crash site being on the west side, up near the Woods Road."

The town manager interrupted. "We can't drive anywhere near that location this time of year."

"I realize we can't drive up there, Mike. Not that it matters. We don't know exactly where on that mountain the crash is.

What we've been asked to do, by the command over at the Dow Air Force base in Bangor, is to see if we can locate the crash. They've dispatched a helicopter, but they figure one of our local pilots would have a better idea of the terrain and could do a lower altitude fly-over."

"Don and I will go up." Every man in the room turned towards the woman's voice. Don stood next to Linda, his mouth hanging open. Only some of the men knew who Linda was. What they all saw was a small person swallowed up in a large olive-green parka. She glared back at them. "We know that area as good as anyone. In fact, I was looking over aerial photos of that mountain today."

"What do you say?" Chief Bartlett raised his chin at Don.

Before Don could answer, Andy Green spoke up. "I'll fly with them."

Bartlett's head spun to his left. "Who the heck are you?"

"Chief, let me introduce you to Andy Green, a new Maine warden." Henry whisked his hand in Green's direction.

"Do you know this area, Warden Breen?" asked the chief.

"It's Green. Andy Green. And no, but I know how to conduct search and rescue operations. I'm recently back from a tour in southeast Asia."

"Sir, unless you were in the Vietnam where the land is covered in snow and not rice paddies, I'd rather have those that know the terrain in the air." The chief turned. Henry quickly wiped the smirk from his face. "Can you go up with Don and Linda, Henry?"

"You bet."

"Okay. Spencer's on his way back here. If he's here by the time you are ready to lift, take him with you. Since he's the only eye-witness we know of, maybe he'll narrow the search area for you."

"The rest of you, we've got aircraft coming in. We need fires lit along the runway. This soup of clouds isn't going to lift and those arriving planes, along with Don, will need the beacons. It'll be dark before they have a chance to return."

Stan and Joe, set off with a crew to find kindling and firewood. At camps up and down the road, they dug summer wood from under tarps and loaded their pickup trucks.

Warden Green followed Don and Linda towards a hangar at the edge of the airport.

Henry stopped to talk to the four men he noticed earlier in the diner. "None of you are from around here – are you?"

"No, sir. What can we help with?" They addressed Henry as if he was their drill sergeant.

"We could use your help digging a line of fire pits in that snow." Henry pointed. "Along the runway."

"Yes, sir. We're on it."

Henry nodded. "Thank you." He took long strides to the hangar.

"Linda, you and – Andy, is it? – get the propane heater on the engine while I get things set in the cockpit." Don felt a tug on the back of his coat.

"We only have forty-five minutes of daylight left. Can we even get up there and back?" Linda's voice cracked a little.

Don recognized her concern in the tightness of her lips. "This coming from the woman who volunteered me to fly. You know I won't risk the timing." He turned towards Warden Green. "We ain't got twenty minutes for that heater to run, give it ten."

Along the far side of the runway, Joe was stacking wood into a tee-pee structure when the sky erupted with the vibrating sounds of engines. He looked up. Through the thick gray clouds, he couldn't see one aircraft. He ran to Don's hangar to listen to the radio.

"This is Air Force Grumman Alfa Foxtrot three-seven-fife Mike Echo, AF375ME. Do you copy, Greenville traffic?"

In his pilot seat checking his instrumentation, Don keyed his headset microphone. "Yes, we copy. This is pilot Don Tilton. I'll be your escort towards the recovery site. I'll be flying Beaver Alpha one-three-fife Gulf Mike.'

"Roger. How long 'til you lift?"

"Five minutes. We've got a cold start. Will you wait?"

There was silence. Over at the control building, the police chief and fire captain stared at the radio speaker, waiting for a response.

The Grumman dropped below the clouds and buzzed the airfield. *"Negative. We're heading northeast. See you in the air."*

"Roger. This Beaver has no radar, we're sight only."

"Stay below five hundred feet at all times. AF375ME out."

"Don, this is Chief Bartlett."

"Go ahead."

"We've got word there are two choppers coming in. Five to eight minutes."

"Are they landing?"

"Unconfirmed."

Don switched off his mic. "Great. This airspace is more crowded than the diner for Fish Fry Fridays."

"The pre-warmer is clear." Linda stood at the cockpit door. She was shivering. Partly because it was cold, but mostly because she had had time to consider what they were about to do.

"Okay. Here we go." Don hopped down. With Henry, Andy, and several others he pushed the plane out onto the snow packed runway.

Henry motioned Andy to step behind the rear of the plane with him. "Let me give you a pointer for flying with Don. If you want to learn about the ways of the north woods, it's best to realize you've got two ears and one mouth. Now get in and listen."

Don half turned in his seat. "You two strapped in back there?" Henry gave him a thumbs up.

He looked to his right. "You all set?"

Linda nodded.

Don yelled out the cockpit window, "All clear," and he started his taxi. The sky was getting darker by the minute. The fires along the short airstrip flashed orange and red colors across the windshield.

"Greenville traffic, this is Air Force Rescue, Hotel seven-seven-fife Foxtrot Mike, H775FM, flying Kaman chopper, ninety seconds out."

"Copy, H775FM. Are you landing?"

"Negative. Looking for headings to crash site."

"No known location. You've got a Beaver about to take off, please clear runway airspace, head northeast. AF375ME is already en route."

"Confirmed. H775FM to hold for Beaver. Out."

A black truck, dented like it had been through a hailstorm of rocks, came flying towards the runway. Its horn blared all the way until it pulled alongside the taxiing Beaver. Don slowed to a stop. Without even turning off the truck's engine, Spencer jumped out, yelled to Stan, "Park that for me, will you?" and he grabbed the door to the plane.

"Glad I made it." Spencer looked at the faces in the plane. "Who the heck are you?"

"No time for introductions. Green, move back a row." stated Henry.

"You had me wondering if you'd make it," said Don.

"I had that old truck floored all the way," replied Spencer.

"There's not much room back here," said Green.

"We don't have time to discuss it. Either strap in, or jump out. And give Spencer that headset, quick. You'll find another in the compartment under the seat," Don yelled. He pulled back and the plane lifted into the air.

❋

Joe was helping to move more wood from a truck bed to the signal fires when the repetitive wobble of a chopper drew his gaze to the sky. A helicopter circled wide, flying barely below the cloud cover, and took up the position to follow behind Don in the beaver.

"What do we do now?" asked Joe.

"We help keep these fires going. And we wait. They won't be gone long." Stan glanced at his watch. "They can't be."

Through the trailer window, Joe watched a snowplow clearing additional space for anticipated aircraft parking. Joe and Stan listened between static and drop-outs to the pilot conversations.

⸙⁂⸙

"**O**kay, Spence, where'd that plane go down?" Don asked in his headset.

"Head towards the south side of Elephant Mountain."

"What'd you see? What kind of plane was it? Was anyone with you?" asked Henry in rapid fire.

"I was down off Lily Bay Road. The ground started to vibrate. Even with my saw running and my headgear on, I could hear the roar, but mostly I felt it." Spencer's voice cracked. "I looked up and this plane – a bomber – was flying low, a couple hundred feet off the ground. It was crazy."

"Come on. You're exaggerating. It couldn't have been a bomber." Don banked the plane over Lower Wilson Pond.

"I'm telling you what I saw. It was one of those B52s – I've seen pictures in the paper – had to be over a hundred feet long. It was barely clearing the trees . . . until it wasn't anymore." Spencer shook his head.

"It's possible it was a B52, or what's known as the Stratofortress."

Spencer turned in his seat. "Who are you again?"

"Warden Andy Green. A former Air Force pilot."

Spencer continued to stare blankly at the man.

"I recently finished up my tour in the Air Force. The B52 Stratofortress has been outfitted to fly low. There have been training missions going on lately." Not getting any indication that the logger cared one way or another, Green added, "They've been flying in different parts of the country, testing out new technology."

"Are you supposed to be telling us this?" Spencer angled his head, his eyes narrowing.

"If the plane you saw was really a B52, that would be the second to go down in a low altitude training mission. The first was back in fifty-nine, out in Oregon."

"How do you know all this?"

"As I said, I was in the Air Force and the last accident has already been reported in the news."

Don chimed in. "If that's the case, a B52 is over a hundred and fifty feet long, with a wingspan of over a hundred and eighty feet. That's gotta be some wreck."

"It came in low. You know where that logging road went in a few years back? It had to be right around where they finished the clear-cut in the fall."

"I know where that is, caught some deer poachers up there. Beginning of December." Henry turned toward the rear seat. Green acknowledged with a head nod. Henry went on, "If that's where they went down, at least they are in an area that the plows can get close to. Had they gone down near the summit or over on the backside, we'd have a heck of a time getting in there."

There was only one washboard gravel logging road that made its way along the side of the mountain, a road that didn't even get close to the peak. It was barely two lanes wide with a shoulder that left little margin for error if a motorist ended up in a game of chicken with a logging truck. Not that it mattered now. Once the heavy snows came, that was the end of worrying about logging trucks on the road at that elevation, the crews didn't even bother to plow up that far as it was a losing battle with Mother Nature.

They were silent as they approached the mountain.

Linda had her face close to the side window. "I'd think we'd be able to see smoke." Don banked the wings left and right to give Linda next to him, and Henry in the back, a chance to scan the land off each side of the plane. It was difficult to see any contrast, even for Linda's trained eye. The white landscape was only interrupted by an occasional tall pine that had shaken the snow from its branches.

"Greenville Beaver, this is Kaman chopper. We're off your right. The cloud cover is too thick and we've lost almost all daylight. Command has ordered us to land at the airport. We advise you do the same. We'll pick it up at first light."

"Roger." Don switched back to the internal microphone. "I hate to leave brothers out here, but we don't have a choice. Not in these conditions. Say a prayer." Don turned the plane.

Joe stood in a trance at the window of Don's trailer. The sky to the east was dark, to the west, the outline of the sun was hidden behind the clouds, it would only be a few minutes before it dipped behind the mountains. Crews from the Bangor air base, the State Police, and locals were huddled around the closest signal fire. Near the start of the runway, the lights from the town's fire truck swept a circle of red off the hangar buildings and piles of plowed snow.

The door flung open. Stan threw his gloves on the drafting table, and banged his hands together. "Wow, it's cold out there."

"Did you reach the office?" Joe hadn't taken his eyes from the window.

"Yep. The editor is sending a reporter in the morning. I told him we couldn't be involved in covering the story as I wanted to help in the rescue."

Joe nodded.

Stan blew on his hands and put his gloves back on. "Heck, it's as cold in here as outside. What happened to the heat?"

"The civil patrol collected every propane tank they could find. The chief told them to take all tanks to the hangar for engine heaters. To be prepared for the rescue in the morning."

"Oh."

Joe turned to face his dad. "Don't you think Don should've landed by now?" Joe turned on the CB.

Stan looked towards the horizon. "Don's an excellent pilot and he's flown by instrumentation before. He'll be home free once he gets a visual on the fires and the flashing lights."

The radio static gave way to a voice.

"Greenville traffic, AF375ME, headed back to Dow. We'll return in the morning. Clearing airspace. Copy."

The voice of Chief Bartlett crackled over the radio. *"AF375ME, Greenville traffic confirming."*

"Chief, this is Don. It's like pea soup up here. Keep those fires high. Chopper H775FM will land ahead of me. Copy."

"Okay, Don, the airstrip is clear. Copy?"

"Affirmative."

The chief called out to the chopper pilot. *"H775FM, your landing zone is the east end of the runway. Cleared area is circled by small fires and vehicle headlights. Do you the have visual?"* The chief scanned the sky for the helicopter.

"Affirmative. Sixty seconds to approach."

"Roger. I see you now."

Stan lowered the radio volume. "I wonder if they spotted anything."

"Let's get over to his hangar and find out." Joe pulled his parka hood up over the hat he already was wearing.

By the time they reached the other end of the airport, Don had touched down and was taxiing to the paper company hangar. As soon as he killed the engine, his plane was swarmed with everyone asking questions all at once.

"What'd you see?"

"Did you find the site?"

"Anybody alive?"

"You ever fly that Beaver in the dark before, Don?"

"Back up, people. Let us out. And, no. We didn't get a visual on the site." Henry was agitated and pushed through the crowd.

The chief appeared and walked along with Henry. "You weren't able to find it? A plane the size of a B52, and nothing?"

"Darn it, Chief, it was near zero visibility up there. We only had thirty minutes."

"I understand." The chief looked around the hangar. A sea of faces was staring at him. He spoke as loud as he could. "We've decided to use the school for a command center this evening. The cafeteria will give us more space and the ladies auxiliary is cooking up a meal in the kitchen."

Turning back to Henry, he said, "The military will be housing men over at the railroad depot. I'll need your assistance to help coordinate efforts with the volunteers. I'll see you down at the school."

When the police chief turned to go, Henry caught site of District Warden Guilford H. Bingham headed his way. Henry held his hat in front of his lips. "Son of a poacher."

A Long Cold Night

District Warden Bingham marched across the concrete floor toward Henry. "Ford, what's the situation here? Are we headed up to the site? Who do they have in charge?"

"The plane hasn't been spotted, boss. We are expected down at the school building to devise a plan. As far as I can tell, Chief Bartlett has taken charge. At least up until now." Henry pointed.

A contingent of military personnel from the helicopter were headed towards the police chief. They watched as Bartlett shook and nodded his head to a series of questions.

Bigham turned back, and for the first time noticed the person to Henry's left. "Warden Green, why the heck are you not in uniform?"

"It's a long story, sir. I'll explain down at the command center."

Late in the evening, two local men attempted to locate the plane on their own, snowshoeing through the deep snow. They were found by a man out with his dog on Upper Wilson Pond. The cold had forced them to turn back. One had such severe frostbite on his right foot, it was amputated several days later.

In the auditorium, the commander announced that for the safety of all, no one was to go out searching ahead of his explicit orders. He advised everyone to get some rest as they would need all their energy for the coming day. Some people slept in the auditorium seats; others tried to rest on desks they pushed together in the classrooms. Everyone had a restless night.

To organize efforts, a chain of command was established between the Air Force, the Maine State Police, the Civil Air Patrol, and the Warden Service. Plans were put in place to be up on the mountain by daybreak.

Around midnight it was reported that an orange glow could be seen on the mountain. An area of pines had caught fire from the crash and the flames were visible six miles away in downtown Greenville.

During the middle of the night, a military convoy arrived with diesel fuel, supplies, and a mobile hospital trailer. In the early morning hours, plows from the paper company rumbled down Main Street and headed up Scammon Road. The roads up past Wilson Pond were rarely plowed during the winter, there never was any reason for it. At the highest elevations they pushed through eight feet of snow, with drifts in places as high as fifteen feet. Excavation equipment and dump trucks formed a convoy carting snow from the logging road that wound its way up the mountain. Two trucks slid off a ledge and were abandoned for the time being – so as not to delay the rescue.

At five a.m. the school bells rang to rouse the troops and any of the volunteers who had somehow managed to get some sleep.

On the breakfast chow line, Henry was behind Nate. "Mornin', Nate. Get any sleep?"

"Good morning, Henry. Not much. Spent most of the night up at the airport plowing. How 'bout you?"

"Couple of hours. You heading up to Scammon to help plow?"

"Yeah. Soon as I get some grub. Do you think they'll mind if I pack extra to go?"

Out of the corner of his eye, Henry saw Green enter the cafeteria. "No. You take what you need. Excuse me." He patted Nate on his back and walked across the room.

"It's good to see you in uniform this morning." Henry acknowledged Green's attire with an up and down hand motion.

"Thanks to your wife, Alice. She worked a miracle overnight to get rid of the smell. Said it wasn't her first rodeo dealing with skunk."

Henry's lips tightened. He'd have to ask Alice later exactly how much she divulged on his encounters with his white striped nemeses of the woods.

"Where's the boss?" Green picked up a tray and a plate.

"One thing you'll find about Bingham is he isn't one for waiting around. He's already headed to the command post." Henry got back in line.

"I'm not one for waiting around either. Shouldn't we be going with him?" Green put down his tray.

"Not yet. The commander has a lead unit setting up a post at the gravel pit. Our orders are to help on the snowmobile detail. We need to get the equipment ready. The last report I heard is the plow crew is getting close to the end of the logging road." Henry assessed the serving bowl of fruit cocktail. He moved past it. "From there, we're going in by sled. That snow is deep and fluffy. Breaking trail is going to be rough. I hear they've also got a few dog teams ready to go once the snow is packed down. The wreckage is likely spread out, and we're going to have to cover a lot of ground."

"Then let's go. We can eat on the way."

"You've ever ridden on a snowmobile before, Green?"

The warden shrugged. "How hard could it be. I've flown planes and choppers. Seems to me we're wastin' time and could be on that mountain right now."

Henry shook his head. "Look, the commander in charge is one heck of a planner. Putting snowmobiles in the way of the plows isn't going to get us there any faster. In fact, he knows it will slow the effort if they start sinking in that snow."

Henry scooped a helping of scrambled eggs on his plate along with six slices of bacon. "Men were waiting to start the snowshoe trek as soon as they could this morning. They are stationed at different points on that mountain waiting for word from the surveillance planes. There are already eyes in the sky blanketing the entire side of that mountain."

"How'd you find all this out?"

"I've got two ears and one mouth. Now get your grub and fuel up." Henry wrapped four slices of bacon in a napkin and stuck it in his pocket.

❦✳❦

Even before the sun started to light the sky, Don and Linda were back at the hangar. To prepare, he connected the pre-heater on his plane's engine and Linda scoured her photos of their assigned grid. When Don lined up on the runway, he had flashbacks to his time in the service. The air traffic on the radio was the busiest it had ever been around Moosehead. He taxied, took off, and headed towards Horseshoe Pond. Their assignment this morning was the eastern ridge.

Pilots crisscrossed an area the size of Rhode Island, until finally, a Warden pilot reported a visual on a parachute. A bit after 9 a.m. the main wreckage was spotted. The plows were still miles from the location. Don made a wide circle and Linda snapped photos.

"Beaver A135GM, thank you for your help, please vacate the airspace at this time for recovery aircraft."

"Roger," Don replied.

Linda keyed the internal microphone on her headset. "Before we head back, can you make a pass over the east side of the mountain one last time?"

"Why?"

"I want to verify what I saw on those photos I was examining yesterday."

"What are you talking about? You heard the military, we were asked to clear out."

Linda recalled she never did get to show Don what she had seen. "From the pictures I took last week, there appears to be a tarp camp over that way. It wasn't there in the last set from November." She held up the photo she had brought along.

Don glanced her way, but quickly turned straight ahead. "It's probably something left over from summer hikers. Besides, with all that's going on here, we don't have time for excursions." He pointed the nose back to the airport.

Linda circled the anomaly on the photo with a blue magic marker and slid it back in her envelope.

❦※❦

Henry pulled his cruiser along the snowbank on Scammon Road. Twenty yards ahead, Stan and Joe were unloading snowmobiles from a trailer.

Green pointed. "I've only seen pictures of those machines. Are we riding up the mountain on them?"

"That's the plan." Henry stepped from the car.

"Hey! Henry, I can't open the door. You've parked too close to the snow."

"Lesson for this morning. When stuck in a car, use the window."

Green frowned.

"We need to keep this road clear. If you can't climb out the window, shimmy over to the driver's side." Henry turned, a slight smirk on his face.

"Great." Green climbed out of the window and made his way through the hip-high snow. He approached Henry who was talking with the Parkers.

"Warden Green, this is Stan Parker and his son Joe. These men are two of the finest outdoorsmen you'll come across in the Moosehead region. It'll do you good to heed any advice they give you. They can keep you out of a lot of trouble."

"We kind of met." Warden Green shook each of their hands. "Sorry, things were hectic yesterday. Good to meet you both."

"Understood about yesterday. Nice to meet you, too. Come on, I'll set you up with a machine." Joe gestured up the road.

Stan moved closer to Henry. "A new warden, huh? He looks young."

"Ah, he's okay. A bit green behind the ears, but he'll learn quick."

Stan knew asking why a young warden might be driving around with Henry, was sure to be a sore point – so he didn't. Instead, he asked, "How soon until we head out?"

"I'll go talk with the commander." Henry walked up the road toward the mobile headquarters.

⁂

"These are interesting." Andy gave a red and yellow machine on skis a nudge.

"It'll beat walking." Joe patted a single seat Polaris Sno-Traveler. "Until they break down."

"Break down?"

"Yeah. That's another reason we're waiting until the road is plowed as far as the plows can go." Joe paused. "Doc Pritham, from down in town, has driven a homemade one for years, but these haven't been around long. Hard to tell about their reliability or getting through deep snow."

"Are you saying we'd better bring snowshoes along with us?"

"Unless you're a mechanic and take to working outside in these temperatures."

A cheer, erupting from a group standing outside the command center, drew Joe's and Andy's attention. Henry headed back down the road and yelled, "They've found a survivor! They've got one! He's alive! Wrapped in his parachute. Son of a poacher."

"Imagine that. Out here in minus twenty, maybe minus thirty up on that mountain all night, and someone survived. That must be one tough crewman." Stan slapped Joe on the back.

"That's going to give everyone a boost. We're all gassed up here, Henry. You ready to go?" asked Joe.

"We've been given the all clear to move up to the next clear-out." Henry looked at Green, "You stay close to Joe. He'll show you how to run that machine. You don't want it giving out on you on the side of the mountain."

"Yes, sir." When he was sure Henry was out of earshot, Green looked at Joe and stated, "He's something else."

"Henry is one of the best. You're lucky to be working with him. He's a little rough sometimes, but there's nobody else I'd want to be out here in the woods with than Henry Ford. Now give that machine a choke and pull the rope."

In the airport control building, Linda was taking her turn monitoring the communications. She lifted the side window and waved at Don, who was outside talking to a couple of the local pilots. "Guys, get in here!"

"What is it?" Don stamped his feet on the worn bristle map. They all walked over to the communications table.

"Shh. Come listen."

"Go ahead, H775M."

"Command, ground crew is signaling a survivor."

"Is there an indication on who it is?"

"It's the pilot. They found him hanging in a tree, wrapped in his survival-kit. We're going to lift him out."

"Roger."

"Holy cow!" exclaimed Don. "What a night that must have been."

"I can't even imagine. But then there's hope others are alive, too. Can you three go out there and be sure that chopper's landing space is clear? I need to monitor the radio."

"We're on it." Don and the guys rushed back out the door. On his way out, Don bumped into Fred. "Hi, Fred. No time to talk. Linda's inside."

"Hi, Don. Bye, Don." Fred pulled the door closed behind him.

"Hello, Fred." Linda had first met the local forest ranger not long after she started her job with the timber company. Over the past couple of years, there had been times when she had taken photo evidence of illegal logging operations that she had passed along to Fred. It was in the best interest of her employer to ensure everyone was following the guidelines set forth to protect the north woods. She appreciated Fred knew all the complicated rules and was fair with the loggers when they might misinterpret something; well, he was patient as long as it never happened twice.

"Hi, Linda. Got your message." Fred enjoyed working with Linda, she had earned his respect early on as someone who was a steward of the woods, always looking to do the right thing.

"Thanks for stopping by. It's been crazy – as you can imagine."

"Sure has. Town hasn't been this crowded since Woodsmen's Days this past August. What can I do for you?"

Linda took a folder from her bag and emptied the photos on the desk. "Can I get your opinion on this picture. I think someone illegally cut here." She moved a photo closer to him and tapped the location. "It's on the far shore of Allagash Lake."

"Huh. That's a cut for sure. May I have this photo? Back at the office I can look up permits to see if anyone had permission up that way."

"Absolutely."

"Do you think Don would fly me in there to have a look?"

Linda laughed. "He figured you'd be asking about that. He wasn't too keen on going up there this time of year."

Fred looked down at the other photos scattered on the desk. "I understand." His voice was far off. He picked up one of them.

She noticed what he was staring at. "Now that's an interesting one. What do you make of it?"

Fred's eyes didn't leave the picture. "Is this a camp?"

"So, you see it too?"

"Where is this?"

"Would you believe, it's on the east side of Elephant Mountain."

"I see." Fred opened a topographical map he had in his coat pocket. "Where abouts?"

Linda placed an index finger to the left of Horseshoe Pond. She noticed Fred's map had particular markings he had made.

"Hmm. That makes sense." Fred marked the map with his pencil.

"What does?"

"I've been having trouble with someone, or some people, leaving camps scattered throughout the woods on timber company land. In places that are designated as no camping and certainly no fires. I'm getting tired of cleaning up after them."

"How long has that been going on?"

"It's been happening since before I was on the job. The forester who had this district before me ignored it all. I don't plan to let it go. Besides, things are getting more and more out of control."

"How so?" Linda's gaze was piercing with interest.

Fred lowered his voice, not that it mattered, they were the only two in the building. "Lately, the logging crews have taken to locking their trucks – they've been missing too many lunches."

"Are you serious? Someone steals their food?"

"That's what they say. They go off to cut, come back and they've got nothing but empty lunch boxes. Some of them don't even have their lunch box. Somebody out there is awful hungry."

"And brazen to be stealing from loggers."

"You got that right. You should see the stuff I have collected in a storage unit. Stuff I've found at these tarp camps."

"What kind of stuff?"

"All kinds of things you'd have camping and more. Department policy says I have to store it for five years. Old radios, antenna wire, coolers, newspapers. Always stacks of old newspapers. We burn those. And lunch boxes. Most of those get reclaimed by the logging crews."

He motioned her way with the Elephant Mountain picture in his hand. "Do you mind if I hold onto this one, too?"

"I don't see why not. Don told me I was imagining things."

"You certainly aren't imagining things." Fred slid the photo into his pocket. "I'll let you know what I find out." He tipped his hat on the way out the door.

Linda wondered if he meant about the lumber cutting or the lunch thefts. She didn't have long to ponder it. The radio erupted with traffic.

The rest of the day the airport was the scene of a dozen take-offs and landings – which was twelve more than usual for a Friday in January. The air was also busy with planes from Bangor and as far away as Massachusetts shuffling personnel to the crash scene. The high winds put a stop to the flights and unfortunately, one of the rescuers had to be left on the mountain, to face a night in the cold – alone.

Henry didn't arrive home until well after dark. He collapsed on his bed and fell straight asleep without even having dinner.

Elephant Mountain seen from a frozen pond

Special Mission

❦⁂❦

Saturday Morning

Henry was surprised to see a plate of sausages *and* bacon on the table. Not only that, but Alice had made him three eggs, over-easy. He grabbed her around the waist for a morning hug. "Thank you, dear."

"I thought you could use a hearty breakfast this morning." Seeing him happy, made her day. "Do you need to go back to the crash site this morning?"

"I'm not sure. The commander sent word last night that he wanted to see me."

"What about?"

"Not really sure." When Alice had turned towards the sink, Henry rolled three pieces of bacon in a napkin and placed it in his coat pocket.

"You know, Henry, I can make you a bacon sandwich to take with you."

His eyes went wide, having been caught. "Not necessary, dear. I expect I'll be back by lunch." He finished his coffee, kissed Alice goodbye, and headed to the airport.

He really had no idea why he was summoned. A military aide yesterday afternoon, simply said, *"The commander requests you meet him at o-eight-hundred. At the airport."*

His cruiser vibrated over the corduroy frozen road. After the past thirty-six hours, the silence of being alone felt good. With his left hand he rolled down his window – he breathed in the blast of frigid air. No matter, it was no use. He still couldn't get the smell of jet fuel and burning rubber out of his mind.

Pulling along the airport control building, it seemed strange to Henry for there to be only one military helicopter sitting in the cleared field. After all the activity, for it to be back close to normal so quickly, it felt empty. He noticed Green's cruiser parked near Don's hangar. He wondered why the young warden had decided to be at the airport on a Saturday morning when there was still a fishing derby going on. With long, determined strides, he headed for the building.

Closing the door behind him, he caught Green sitting in a chair near the observation window. Henry started his way, but was interrupted.

"Good morning, Warden Ford, glad you could make it." The military commander shook Henry's hand, and motioned him to a table in the far corner.

"Good morning, sir. How's the pararescue paramedic doing? The one who spent the night on the mountain?"

"Tech. Sergeant Slabinski? He never said one word to complain. He even assisted in recovering a crew member before he was lifted out."

Henry nodded. It never ceased to amaze him how responders put their own lives in harm's way for others. "What was it you wanted to see me about. sir?"

"First, I want to thank you, on behalf of the military, for your professionalism and assistance the past couple of days. You can be sure I will be writing your superiors with my remarks."

"Thank you, sir. But that's not necessary. We were all glad to help."

The commander indicated for Henry to take a seat. "That might be true, but the letter will go out all the same."

He sat across from Henry. Without moving his head, he evaluated the room. There were only a few people in the building. His aide was on the radio communicating their departure time. Another military person was waiting for his turn to use the radio. A third officer was packing equipment. Aside from Henry, the only other non-military person in the building was Green. The commander had argued with his chain of command to bring Warden Green into the conversation on what was happening, but he was denied. The powers at the Pentagon wanted to keep the information as confidential as possible, they reasoned Warden Ford was enough of a risk. And at that, his orders were to brief Ford with only the information he needed to know, no more. At the same time, he didn't see a reason to kick Green out of the control building.

"Sir?" Henry tried to bring the commander out of his trance.

Without acknowledging his pause, the commander continued. "As you must know by now, the B52 was on a training mission."

"Yes, sir, that's what I've come to understand."

The commander gave Henry a glance and then looked towards Warden Green, who was sitting in a wooden chair near the window. Green's gaze was on the activity out on the airstrip. The radio chatter between the pilots seemed loud enough to conceal their conversation, or so the commander thought. "Warden Ford, a military investigator will arrive tomorrow. I want to ask that you guide him to the site."

"Wouldn't it be more appropriate for one of your men to do that, sir?" It wasn't that Henry wasn't willing to assist. It was he wasn't sure how his responsibility fit in with a military plane crash investigation.

"All of my men were pulled out this morning. These days, we are under active preparation at all times." He lowered his voice. "Khrushchev."

Henry nodded. His responsibilities suddenly seemed small.

"You understand. I cannot leave a single man behind. And besides, we can't do much more on that mountain until spring when the snow is melted."

"I heard that an accident investigation crew is already expected. Shouldn't your investigator be part of that team?"

"The accident investigation has a different mission. Along with Boeing, they'll determine if the failure was a mechanical weakness or system issue." He paused and looked at his watch. "The person I need you to guide, has a different purpose."

"I'm not following you, sir. Why is this special investigator showing up? What more does he expect to learn? Who is he?"

The commander noticed Green looking their way. He held his stare until Green turned back to the window. "It has to do with the mission of those men. That's all I can say. I'm simply following my orders to ask that you guide the investigator to the crash site." His eyes narrowed. "And to keep anything you might learn in confidence. That means from everyone." He motioned his head toward Warden Green.

Henry squinted. He didn't feel right about keeping something from Andy, but he didn't know what he was keeping from him anyway.

"Sir, the chopper is ready." The aide stood by the door holding the commander's coat and files.

Acknowledging with a nod, the commander turned back to Henry. "Can I have your word on this?"

"Yes. Of course. I'll do what I can to help."

"Thank you." They both stood and shook hands.

The wobbling sound of the chopper blades vibrated through the small building. Henry and Andy stood at the window and watched the helicopter bank to the south.

"What was the secrecy all about?" Andy didn't take his gaze from the window.

"The commander was very appreciative of all the help we gave him." Henry put on his hat. "I've had enough of this airport – let's go make the rounds at the derby. It'll be good for people to see *two* wardens out and about."

It wasn't that Henry wanted to give Green the runaround, but he had given his word to the commander. That night, he barely slept, wondering about the secrecy of the mission.

❦❦❦

Sunday Morning
January 27, 1963

"**S**on of a poacher!"

"Your head again, dear?"

"Hmm." Henry hung his arm over the side of the bed and captured the bouncing alarm clock. He pushed in the metal post to silence the ringing. "Might be time for a different clock."

"I'll see what's on sale in the Sears and Roebuck catalogue." Alice wrapped herself in her flannel robe. "I was thinking, after church services, we'd have our breakfast out in the ice shack."

"Okay with me." Henry grabbed his pants from the hook behind the door. "I'll need to head to the diner mid-morning."

"What? What for?"

"I need to meet with someone from the military about the accident and take them up to the site."

"I hope it won't take long. I was hoping you'd get to spend time fishing with Bobby today. He's been asking. Besides, you deserve some relaxation time after the past few days."

"I'll have a couple of hours this morning to fish with him. And maybe I'll take him on my rounds to check on the anglers. He always enjoys seeing the fish people have caught, and checking their licenses."

"Can't the new warden, make the rounds today?" She knew immediately that she had used a poor choice of words.

Henry had his pants pulled halfway up his legs when he stopped and responded through his teeth. "He's only here temporarily."

"I didn't mean it as such." She tugged on the bow of her robe belt.

He nodded and gave her a slight grin. "I know it." He pulled her close for a hug. "Let's have our coffee. If Father Paul keeps his sermon short, we'll be on the ice by eight."

"Knowing him, he'll be saying his prayers to win the prize money – again." She pecked Henry's cheek.

"What's he won now? Three years in a row?"

"Yep. The Lord and the togue are with him. That twelve-pounder he landed for first place paid for the new lectern and four candle holders."

"Don't forget the nice new rod he bought himself." Henry was a little jealous.

"Ah, he deserved it." The sound of the phone ringing had Alice spinning around. "I bet that's Bonnie. I'll let her know we'll meet them on the ice." She went running down the hall.

"I'll get the animals watered." Henry headed for the back door to put on his muck boots and field jacket.

⁂

"Good day." Green nodded when Henry sat down on the stool next to him at the counter.

"Hiya, Andy. You already been out on the lake?"

"Sure have. Started at six. I checked West Cove like you asked. I met one guy from out of state, no shack, no license, simply three traps and a lawn chair. He was under the impression that the derby was open fishing."

"Did you cite him?"

"No." Green replied with hesitancy, preparing to be lectured. Sensing Henry expected an explanation, he added, "I sent him over to the Trading Post to get a day permit."

Henry acknowledged the action with a, "Nicely done."

"How about you? Have you made a pass?"

"Oh yeah. Alice, Bobby, and I had six holes going by nine. Around ten, I checked over by Sandy Bay. I found two traps unattended that were tripped. Nobody was around. I pulled them, set the fish free, and put the traps in my sled. People need to be more attentive."

Karen rummaged through the cups on the shelf. She gave Henry a thin smile when she set the bear mug down. "Henry, what's going to happen with that plane wreck on the mountain?" She poured his coffee.

"The military has an accident investigation crew checking it over. I'm going up to the site with one of them this morning."

Andy shot Henry a look.

"Are they going to transport all the pieces out of the woods? This time of year?" she asked.

"I have no idea. I suspect they'll have to wait until the snow melts before they do anything."

"I'll head up with you." Andy gulped the rest of his coffee.

"No, I need you to stay here. Be visible around the lake." Henry avoided eye contact with Andy.

"Why's that?"

"The fishing derby needs monitoring. Go out there and make some friends."

Andy's eyes followed Henry as he left the diner. He wasn't so sure Henry wanted him to count fish, he figured Henry's real motivation was to keep him away from the wreck site this morning. Based on the pieces of the conversation he overheard between the commander and Henry yesterday, he was certain there was something else going on.

Through the window he watched Henry walk to the town dock before going to his cruiser. The photographer from the local paper was taking a picture of an excited boy holding up a large togue. Henry shook the boy's hand. Green left a tip and headed for the ice.

Waiting for the unknown arrival, Henry paced across the cement floor and kept his gaze out the window. He half listened to Don, who was telling him all about the planes and choppers that had been coming and going.

Henry picked up the coffee pot, gave it a whiff, and made a face. "Sorry, bud, it's been there awhile," said Don.

"I can tell." Henry placed the pot back on the hot plate and switched it off.

"How much longer should we be expecting military traffic up here?" Don turned in his chair. Normally, planes communicated amongst themselves to land at the small airport, but with all the extra air traffic, the pilots and civil air volunteers were rotating shifts. This morning, Don was taking his turn.

"It ought to scale back by tomorrow. Not much else left to do – not this time of year anyway."

"Who are you waiting for this morning?"

"Not really sure."

It was obvious to Don that Henry wasn't in a talkative mood. "Well, I hope my relief is on time. I want to get down to the derby. The prize money this year would sure come in handy."

"You'd better hope Alice doesn't beat you to it."

Don laughed. "She's come in second three years in a row. Is it allowable for the wife of the warden to pull in such big fish?"

"Ha! Don't feel bad. She out-fishes everyone. Other than Father Paul."

The pane of glass in the large front window started to rattle. The two of them looked off towards the far end of the airfield.

Nothing was visible in the overcast sky. The radio crackled. *"Greenville traffic, this is chopper LOH369, inbound southeast, requesting clearance to land."*

Don pushed the mic button. "Copy, LOH369. The strip is clear. Do you have a visual?"

"Affirmative. Taking the H on the south end."

"Copy." He turned to Henry. "The guys and I have been talking about making a permanent helipad after this. Keeping that snow painted red has been a challenge."

"Mmm." Henry watched the helicopter land. From the activity the past couple of days, he anticipated a military crew would exit. Not today. Today, one man hopped down to the snow. He held a large backpack over his right shoulder that matched his snow pants, his parka, and his hat – all of which were gray and white camouflage. The man did a three-sixty of his surroundings, pausing to look at the mountains in the distance. When he started to walk towards the airport control building, he blended in with the snowy background.

Henry removed his warden hat and scratched his head. "I wonder who this character is."

"What was that?" Don put the mic back on its hook.

"Nothing. I'll catch you later." Henry's voice faded as the door closed behind him.

The two men met near the runway. Without even waiting for Henry to introduce himself, the man stated, "Warden Ford, I appreciate you taking the time to show me to the site."

"Sure, Mr.?"

"My name is Merrill, Frank Merrill. Did the commander here earlier not give you my information?"

"I don't think the commander in charge knew who was coming." Henry detected a hint of a satisfaction in the man's glance. "That's some chopper. I've never seen one of those before."

"It's a prototype. The brass figures I'll work out the bugs. How will we be getting to the site?"

Henry pointed to his cruiser. "Do you want to have coffee or anything to eat before we go? It will take us two hours to get there and back. Plus, whatever time you need to spend at the site."

"No," Merrill said abruptly. He noticed Henry's frown. "The sooner we get going the better."

"Okay. Let's go then." Henry patted his shirt pocket to check he hadn't already eaten the bacon strips he was saving for a snack.

Merrill took a step back before getting in the car. "Is this car hand-painted?"

"We make do with what we have up here." Henry leaned on the top of the door before getting in.

Merrill ran his hand over the roof. "How'd you get the dents on the roof?"

"Long story."

On the drive to Elephant Mountain, after small talk about the weather, the list of choppers Merrill had experience flying, and how long Henry was a warden, the ride was silent. Merrill sat quietly, staring straight ahead.

In an attempt to learn more about the man's mission, Henry stated, "To tell you the truth, I'm surprised the Air Force didn't leave someone that was here to guide you around." Henry half-turned towards his passenger. He saw the cheek muscles on Merrill's face twitch and tighten.

Realizing, he hadn't asked a question to force a response, he tried a new tactic. "I would have thought one of the officers that was here for the rescue would have wanted to show you the site. Don't you?"

Merrill caught Henry's eye for a fraction of a second, it was long enough to read what Henry was trying to do. He looked away. He squinted against the brightness of the snow and reached into his pocket for his aviator glasses. He had no intention of letting Henry know he didn't need a guide, not even Henry. Merrill had requested someone from the local authorities, someone who might serve a purpose later. While the commander had a choice of who to recommend, he didn't have a choice not to recommend someone, Merrill outranked him. And Merrill certainly wasn't going to tell Henry he didn't want any military personnel around during his investigation. Too many of them had too many connections – inside the organization, and out.

His voice was deep without excuse when he responded. "I suspect everyone returned to the base to piece together the accident details. They will have their hands full preventing another disaster." Merrill went silent again. Finally, he continued. "I'm sure you understand a plane of that size, flying that low, wasn't out sightseeing."

"I caught wind of something about a training mission. Those men had some guts. The man that saw the plane go down, Spencer, said they weren't much more than a couple a hundred feet over tree-line. I don't even like flying that low in a Cessna."

"You can appreciate then why we want to keep the specifics a secret."

"Given you're in Greenville, population not many, give or take this time of year, I can assure you this is the number one topic of conversation around here in the dead of winter – whether they know the secret or not."

"I can imagine. What I meant was, the reason for the mission and the reason for the crash. We're in the midst of a Cold War with Russia and the State Department wants to keep the specific details quiet." Merrill removed his sunglasses, looked at Henry, and waited on a response.

Henry nodded. "Understood." He turned off into a driveway.

"Are we here?" There was an element of surprise in Merrill's voice as he assessed the cabins. "I was told the plane went down in a remote area."

"We've got a ways to go. We're at the North Brook Sporting Camp. This is as far as my cruiser will make it, even if I do have chains on the tires. The department left us two snowmobiles to use. Your commander has some pull. There aren't many of these machines in the entire state."

"I see. The plane didn't come down anywhere close to town then?" Merrill was trying to figure how many nosy people may have been to the wreckage already.

"No. Not at all. You're lucky to get here when you did."

"Why's that?"

"We're expecting another big storm. Once the road up the mountain is snowed in again, there's no getting back up there until the spring melt. The paper company was nice enough to plow once, they aren't going to do it again. Besides, that plane is going to be buried under a whole lot of white by tomorrow night."

"I see. I figured we'd be snowshoeing in." Merrill shot a thumb over his shoulder at the shoes tied to his pack on the back seat.

"You'll need those. Grab your gear." He turned the car off and was about to open his door, when Merrill began to speak.

"I received wilderness training in Maine. West of here. On land the military uses for winter survival skill testing. That was three years ago, come February. I was dropped in the woods, in weather not unlike this, and I had to find my way out with only the limited supplies on my back. Those were four of the most bitter-cold nights I ever experienced."

"What if you got lost?"

A long breath of air escaped from between Merrill's lips. "That was the entire point. The moment I was dropped from the one-engine plane, I was lost. Within twenty minutes I knew the direction I had to head. From then until I was back in the mess hall it was an adventure I will never forget. I saw moose, lynx, and the clearest, brightest night sky I've ever seen."

Henry stared deeply at the man, wondering if he was tough or just a bit nuts. He settled on a little of both. He said, "Let me show you the snow-machine you'll be riding."

"I can't wait to see what that thing can do."

"Don't get your hopes up, it's only a seven-horse engine."

At the crash site, Henry found it odd when Merrill wasn't interested in the path of the destruction. He made his way directly to what was left of the cockpit section. Henry followed.

From inside, Merrill yelled, "It's missing."

"What is?"

Merrill stuck his head near a hole in the fuselage. "I'm here to recover a piece of equipment. And it's not here."

"Maybe it flew out in the crash?" Henry suggested.

"Impossible. A unit doesn't unscrew itself and get cut from the wiring harness in a crash. Take a look, the space in the equipment rack is empty."

Henry hadn't been tempted to get into what remained of the plane, but he squeezed in. It was the first time he got a close-up view of how bad the fuselage was banged up. He bent over to see what the agent was pointing at. "I suspect your military guys removed it already," Henry started to back his way out.

"I'll tell you something, Warden Ford, the people that were here on the rescue and recovery are not the same as the departments that are involved in military technology. Other than the people in my department back in Virginia, and two of those airmen who are no longer able to tell anyone, nobody else even knows that piece of equipment was in the plane. The pilot didn't even know."

Henry coughed. "Are you supposed to be telling this to me?"

Holding the cut wires in his hand, Merrill, blew out a breath that turned to white smoke. "I'm told you know this area better than anyone. I'll need your word to keep this between you and me."

The situation wasn't what Henry had in mind. He was figuring on a quick trip, the investigator would take a few pictures, and then he'd head back to the Pentagon to file a report. Now it sounded as if he was wrapped up in some sort of spying operation.

Henry nodded slowly. "Sure thing. I don't know what 'it' was that you're missing, but if that's all you came for, let's get out of here. I'm freezing."

"You go on ahead. I'm going to look around."

Henry wasn't sure what to do. He felt somewhat responsible for the agent's safety up on the mountain. But then again, if the man was some sort of survivalist, he most likely would be fine on his own.

"Suit yourself. I need to go check on things down at the lake – we've got a fishing derby wrapping up." Merrill made no indication he was listening and was already making his way through the mangled fuselage.

Henry dragged himself out, calling back over his shoulder, "I'll meet you later at North Brook, where we picked up the sleds. Stick to the trail and you'll end up right back there. I'll be there by dark."

The man was already walking in widening circles around the fuselage; he raised a hand, indicating he understood. "Thanks, Ford. You've been extremely helpful."

Henry shook his head and mumbled low as he pulled the cord to start the snowmobile. "And I thought the Warden Service was a crazy place to work."

Mountain Man

❈❈❈

North Brook Sporting Camps

With the sun going down, an orange tinge outlined the edges of the clouds beyond the lodge's windows. Henry sat enjoying a cup of hot cider with Stan and Joe. The lodge's five-foot-wide fireplace, built from massive stacked slabs of granite with a mantel from local black slate, was burning logs that took two men to load.

"I hope to never see a weekend like this again – ever." Henry put his feet up on a wood ottoman.

"I'm surprised so many people turned out for the derby – given the circumstances and all." Stan's hand dropped to his leg.

"A lot of the folks were already here, or headed up before they heard about the plane. Like us." The white ball pinged off the end of the cue Joe was holding.

"Did Bobby catch a big one?" asked Stan.

"He was happy with the two-pounder he pulled out. Alice spent an hour cleaning and cooking that tiny fish and he ate two bites of it."

"I'm glad they didn't cancel it. Gave folks a distraction from thinking about what was going on." Joe banked a ball into the corner pocket.

"As they say, the show must go on. The town rallied and came together once again – in more ways than one. Mike Muzzy submitted a plan to host a recognition dinner at the American Legion to thank everyone."

"What a great idea..."

The front door banged open. Merrill had icicles running down his beard and the snowshoe poles in his hands appeared to be frozen to his gloves. Stan looked at Henry and noticed he was barely holding back a laugh. Merrill walked directly towards the fireplace and turned his rear end towards the flames.

"Cold out there. Isn't it?" asked Stan who was sitting in a rocker, not knowing who the man was. Merrill said nothing.

Henry put down his mug and stood. "I didn't hear you drive up?" Quicker than a bobcat, Henry was at the window. "Where'd you park it?"

"Tha, tha, that, THAT darn machine almost near got me killed." He flung the poles to the floor, pulled off his gloves, and stuck his hands over the fire.

"What happened?" Henry crossed his arms.

Merrill draped his wet coat on a hook next to the mantel. "What a hike back. Wasn't planning on that, or the sleet."

"Hike? Where's the sled?" Henry didn't even want to imagine having to explain to Bingham something went wrong.

Joe filled a mug from the kettle. "Would you care for a cup of warm cider?"

"Ah, thank you." Merrill lowered his voice, "Do you think you might round up some bourbon?"

"I'll see what I can do." Joe walked towards the bar.

"What happened with the department's snowmobile?" Henry walked closer to Merrill.

"It's out there." He pointed towards the mountains. "In the snow, up on the trail."

"Out where?" Henry demanded. He got no response. Taking a breath, he took a seat and tried to calm down. "Why don't you explain what happened?"

Merrill dragged a well-worn leather chair close to the fire. He sipped the cider, made a face, and set the mug down on the floor.

"You going to tell me where the department's property is? Or do I need to go out searching for it?" Henry put his hands on the arms of the chair to rise.

Merrill cleared his throat. "After you left, I tried to make sense of," he paused, taking note of Stan, "with what I was showing you. There were a lot of tracks. But I noticed something that didn't look right."

Joe returned and handed the agent a glass. "On me."

The agent downed the drink in one gulp. "Thank you. I needed that." He looked at Joe. "Any chance there might be one more? Have the bartender run me a tab. No ice this time."

Joe reached for the glass, nodded, and disappeared down the hall.

"What didn't look right?"

"As you can imagine, there were boot prints, snowshoe prints, and I came across more than a few deer prints, even moose."

"Nothing abnormal." Henry shrugged.

"Give me a second, my brain isn't even thawed out yet." Merrill pulled off his boots and stretched his feet towards the hearth. "Ah, that feels good." Seeing Joe entering the room, a hint of a smile was barely visible behind his wet beard.

"Bucky's getting dinner ready." Joe handed him the bottle of bourbon. "He'll settle up with you later."

"That's my kind of hospitality." He re-filled his glass and this time sipped it more slowly.

Henry was getting impatient. "And?"

"What I noticed was an odd set of tracks."

"Odd how?"

Merrill shot a glance at Stan and Joe. He realized he was divulging information to two people he didn't know. "Maybe we ought to talk somewhere more private, Warden?"

Henry's eyes moved from Merrill, to Stan, to Joe, and back to Merrill. "These men are two of the closest friends I have." Henry motioned at them. "This is Stan Parker and his son Joe."

"We're staying here at the North Brook camps for the fishing derby," added Joe.

Merrill raised his glass in their direction. He turned to Henry. "As this is a confidential matter, I'd rather keep it between us."

Stan could see Henry was about to say something on their behalf. He stood up. "Joe and I need to go cover our gear in the truck bed. Right, Joe?"

"Sure." Joe wanted to hear the story, but went along.

Henry turned back to Merrill. "You haven't said what happened to the sled? Where is it?"

Merrill poured a drink and took a long sip. Henry was tapping his fingers on the arm of his chair.

When Stan and Joe were out the door, Merrill stated. "It's out there. But not around here."

"What happened?"

"I'm trying to tell you! The tracks I saw were snowshoe tracks that were different from the rest. Someone with a homemade pair."

"That's not uncommon."

"What was different is that these tracks came in from the east and left towards the east. Not with the others."

Henry blew out a deep breath. He didn't care anything about tracks unless they were from the snow machine. The department only had six of them and Bingham was adamant Henry was responsible for the two that had been left in Greenville. "What are you getting at?"

"I followed the tracks down the opposite side of the mountain. I followed them for almost three miles, until I came to…"

"Are you gentlemen going to be having dinner with us tonight?" Henry and Merrill turned to see the owner, Bucky, who was also the chef, and barkeep, wearing an apron with a moose head on it, standing in the doorway.

"No, no, Bucky. Alice will be expecting me." Henry held up his hand, wanting to get back to his conversation.

Bucky motioned towards Merrill with a flick of the head.

"Whatever you're cooking smells pretty good. I could eat. Would you have an extra room here as well?"

Bucky took notice of Merrill's fatigues. "You're in luck. A bunch of your buddies checked out this morning."

"Great. Put me down for the week. And thanks for the bourbon. I'll take the bottle."

Henry's head snapped around. He thought, *A week? What was this guy going to be doing for a week.*

"I'll bring you a room key after I serve dinner. And we're having moose steaks and corn chowder." Bucky turned back towards the kitchen.

"Now that chow sounds good. Sure you can't stay, Warden?"

Henry exhaled, getting impatient. "What did you find?" He threw his hands in the air. "And where's the sled?"

"I found a camp."

Henry's mouth dropped. There was silence. He started laughing hard and slapped his legs.

"What's so darn funny?"

"You walked for three miles, in negative ten degrees, through five feet of snow, and you think it's news that you found a camp? Out here in the woods? A camp?" Henry laughed louder.

"Warden Ford! This wasn't any typical camp."

Henry stopped laughing. His eyes narrowed. "How do you know that?"

"And, it was recently occupied. Coals in the pit weren't even covered over with snow. Whoever was there, left in a hurry."

The story of a hermit camp immediately interested Henry. For years, he had a suspicion someone had been living in the area, someone that had never been seen. Odd things had gone missing every now and again from cabins and campsites. A knife, a razor, some pots. During the winter, locals would sometimes whisper quietly that the fruits and vegetables they canned in the fall were disappearing quicker than they could possibly be eating them. Henry had heard the stories of hermits in the woods nearby. Jim Whyte of Monson was one of them, but he'd been dead for more than thirty years and wasn't so much of a hermit in the end. The Whyte rumors had started about when Henry began his Warden career. The FBI had shown up a number of times looking for Whyte, but they never told Henry anything more than they found him and spoke to him. Then there was the hermit Bill Hall. He wasn't anywhere near as friendly as Whyte. Hall didn't want anything to do with anyone, but in 1945 he helped the wardens find fugitives they were searching for. Hall had since left the Maine woods. As far as Henry knew, he had gone south in search of a warmer climate. Over the years, stories of hermits came and went. Locals sometimes made hermits out of some homesteader who simply didn't have much interest in socializing. Henry always took the stance to let people be. Yet, lately there were more and more reports of missing items, closer to Greenville. Last spring, a Massachusetts resident filed a complaint that someone had lived in his cabin most of the winter.

"What else did you see?" Henry crossed his arms.

"I found these." Merrill reached down in his pack that was next to the chair and took out a stack of folded newspaper clippings. He handed them to Henry. "These were in a wooden box wrapped in canvas. I found it stashed in the snow, not far from the tarps. I think someone intended to retrieve it. They had camouflaged it with pine branches."

"These are from the late nineteen forties." Henry thought for a moment, and then said, "Why would anyone have papers that are almost twenty years old out here in the woods?"

"I have a pretty good idea. Have you heard the story of…" The door swung open and a blast of cold air entered the room.

"I'll bet you, Dad, the Bombardier model goes a lot faster than the Polaris."

"You're on. If you can convince him." Stan stomped his boots on the mat.

"Hey, Henry, any chance you'd let Dad and I have a race with those snowmobiles?"

Merrill stared in Joe's direction. "That might be a problem, you see the snowmobile I was using, well, it went off a cliff."

"WHAT?" Henry jumped to his feet.

"Supper is served men!" Bucky passed through the lounge and near the stairs he yanked the cord on the dinner bell. "Chow Time! Chow Time!"

"It's like the old west around here." Merrill reached for his boots.

Stan put his hand on Henry's shoulder. "I'm sure there's plenty of grub. If you can stay." He was smiling, knowing there was no way Henry was leaving without finding out about his sled.

※

Monday January 28, 1963
Lock, Stock, & Barrel

"Here he comes now." Buddy nudged Buster.

"Morning, Henry."

"Mornin'." Henry walked behind the counter for his mug. "Where's Karen?"

"Back in the kitchen. The busboy dropped a whole dish pan of plates. She's mighty sore this morning. Ain't she, Buddy?" Buster snickered.

"Whatever you do, don't call her *ma'am*," Buddy added.

"Hmm." Henry walked over to the coffee pots and filled his mug. He took a seat at the end of the counter, leaving two stools between him and the guys.

"Ask him." Buster's head motioned toward Henry.

Buddy shook his head. "I ain't asking him."

"What are you two arguing about? I can't read this paper with all your bickering." Henry half turned towards them.

"Nate was in earlier and…"

"And he told you about the sled. Is that right?"

Buster looked down at his plate of scrambled eggs. "Yep." He let out a snicker.

"It's true. And I don't want to hear any more about it. Nate will have it pulled out of there soon enough."

"What? The military guy can't handle a few horsepower?" Buster laughed.

Behind the guys a throat cleared. They turned to see the towering stature of Frank Merrill. His black eyes were focused directly on Buster. He was still wearing his winter fatigues, an issue they had never seen before, making him look even larger than he was.

"You were saying, gentleman?"

Buster swallowed hard.

Henry let out a slight chuckle. "Morning, Merrill."

"Morning, Warden."

"Have a seat." Henry gestured to the stool next to him.

Merrill looked at the small stool and the little space between each thinly padded red seat. "How about we take that table?"

"Fine." Henry picked up his coffee. "I suspect I'll see you two out on the ice later?"

"Yeah. See you later." Buddy turned to Buster and whispered, "By-gosh, Nate must have been telling the truth. That mountain of a man really threw the sled off the cliff." Buster didn't stop shaking his head as he watched Henry and Merrill walk to the opposite end of the diner.

"What are your plans today?" Henry leaned back in the chair.

Picking up the salt and pepper shakers, Merrill placed them on the chair next to him. He then spread a map on the table. "I figure the person I'm looking for wanted to get away from that area. He had a nice hideaway going. Until a B52 dropped from the sky and fifty people showed up."

"A hermit, if that's who's living back there, if he's anything like those I've met, they tend to be solitary. What does this person have to do with your equipment?" Henry paused. "Those tracks you found could have been from any one of the volunteers. And that tarp camp you found, left from some hunters in the fall."

"That's one theory. Yours. I'm going with mine. And mine is my equipment is missing and those tracks led me to that camp. I have to get that ..." He stopped when Henry turned his head slightly and looked beyond Merrill.

"Good morning, men." Karen placed a mug in front of Merrill. "Regular or decaf?"

"Regular, please, ma'am." Merrill gave her a warm smile.

Karen's eyes went wide. Henry braced for the lashing.

"My name is Karen. What can I get you two?"

"Usual for me." Henry pushed his cup her way for a refill and traced his finger over the map Merrill had placed on the table; trying to avoid eye contact with Karen.

She knew it was useless to police the warden's diet. "And you, sir?"

"I'll have the same."

Karen started to walk away.

Merrill continued, "And three hotcakes, three eggs, over easy, and a thick slice of Canadian bacon."

Karen tilted her head, slowly, and said, "Al-righty then."

"Hungry, are you?" Henry asked.

"No more than usual." Merrill shrugged. "What I was saying is I need to find that equipment. There were other pieces of electronics missing as well."

"Look, are you one-hundred percent certain none of the military personnel took what you're looking for? There is no one out here in the woods that would have a clue what to do with any of it anyway. Especially a hermit – they don't usually have places with electric, you know."

Merrill looked around. Buster and Buddy and most of the diners had already left. "Henry, look, I've heard good things about you."

"You have? From who?" Rubbing his chin, Henry started to wonder who this Merrill was. He thought, *He's been in town for less than twenty-four hours, how could he know anything about me.*

"You have an impeccable record. You served our country. You're well respected around here."

"Thank you, but what does this have to do with the equipment you're looking for."

"What I'm about to tell you, is classified. I'm going to tell you because this is your jurisdiction and your eyes and ears out here in these woods are instrumental."

"This is beginning to sound very unusual."

"The person who stole that equipment, may not know exactly what it's for, but I can tell you, he is brilliant and this could be a matter of national security."

"This person is someone you know? And how is this related to national security?"

"What if I told you, this person has been living out in the woods for almost twenty years?"

"Around here? Everyone lives out in the woods."

"No. You know what I mean. This person is living in the woods in a way nobody knows he's there."

"I think I'd know if someone was living in the woods in my district." Henry's voice dropped off a little too quickly, exposing his doubt.

"Would you?" Glancing at his watch, Merrill said, "Look, it's almost oh-nine-hundred, I have to make a call to headquarters to report in. I'll be back in five minutes to fill you in." He rose and went to the phone booth in the corner. By the time he maneuvered into the small space, his back was pressed up against the bifold glass door.

Henry rubbed the back of his neck. Maybe there was something to the rumors. He sat remembering all the odd stories people had been telling.

The door to the diner banged against the wall.

"Henry! Henry!" Buddy was huffing.

Henry jumped up and took three long strides to him. "What is it?"

"It's Bobby." Buddy gasped for air. "He's fallen through the ice."

"Where?"

"Town dock. Andy Green said to get you." Buddy was bent over trying to catch his breath.

Henry glanced toward the phone booth. Merrill couldn't hear or see a thing going on behind him. There was no time to waste.

Henry ran out the door.

Buddy followed.

A Toast

Lobster Lake – Parker Cabin
Close to Midnight – December 31, 1988

A piercing cry from outside in the darkness made R.C. jump. The fur on his back stood up, his tail curled upright, and he stood growling, keeping his distance from the door.

"What was that?" Sarah's head drew back and her eyes were wide. "Sounded like a child screaming."

"Okay, boy. It's fine." Joe ruffled R.C. on the back. "Probably a red fox."

"Yep. Those screams can set you on edge," Andy agreed.

"What makes them scream?" asked Sarah.

Andy walked to the window. In the darkness there was nothing to see. "It's how they communicate to one another." He turned back to Sarah. "However, it will be unfortunate if you're a light sleeper, seeing the females are most vocal between one and three in the morning – it is mating season after all."

"You'll get used to them and sleep right through it." Don yawned.

"This from the man who would sleep through a Maine Central freight going through the bedroom." Linda gave him a raised eyebrow.

Sarah thought that while she could sleep through the blast of sirens outside her city apartment, she wasn't so sure she'd not bolt awake from a silence-shattering scream. Remembering where they were in the story, she asked, "What ever happened with Bobby falling through the ice?"

"Oh, he turned out fine." Joe nodded. "What happened is he slipped near the outlet over by Pritham Ave. The water was only two feet deep there. Still was enough to get him good and wet. Bonnie wouldn't take him home, she wanted to fish and teach him a lesson. He had to sit in the ice shack wrapped in a blanket near the woodstove until his clothes dried. He didn't leave her side for weeks after that."

"Hey, it's almost midnight!" Linda said.

"Wait, I bought champagne." Joe went to the kitchen and came back with a bottle. Sarah followed him carrying five jam jars.

"Joe, don't be offended, but I'll stick with my beer." Andy raised his bottle.

The cork popped as Don and Linda led the countdown, "5, 4, 3, 2, 1."

"Happy New Year!"

"Joe, that's the worst champagne I ever tasted." Don grimaced.

"Ah, well. It was on special up at the Trading Post."

Everyone put down their unfinished drinks.

Sarah was still curious about the accident. "It's amazing to me that a B52 was flying over Maine."

Don put his hands behind his head and leaned back in his chair. "You have to realize, the crash happened back during the cold war. The Berlin Wall had been built less than two years earlier. The Cuban Missile Crisis happened the prior October. It was a tense time all around."

He poured the rest of his beer into his glass and continued, "The mountains here were a main purpose of the flight. The crew was being trained on operating new equipment. It was necessary to practice low level flight to prepare for Soviet air defenses, which had developed advanced radar. It was a routine training mission, until they hit that turbulence from the winds off the lake."

"Wouldn't it have been safer to fly in a warmer climate?" Sarah asked.

"I don't think the climate was a concern for their training. They were interested in mountain terrain. And the USSR isn't exactly the climate, or the flatness, of the Arizona desert, now is it?" injected Joe.

"I suppose you're right. I'm grateful for the men and women that do these jobs to secure our safety," said Sarah.

"I second that." Joe raised his beer in Don's direction, and then to Andy, in recognition of their service.

"That must have been some tough rescue in freezing conditions." Sarah reached for her wine glass.

"It certainly was. Many locals came out to help." Don blew his nose, obviously choked up.

Linda said, "Still gives me shivers thinking about those men on the mountain with no shelter at all, for the entire night."

Sarah sipped her wine and stared at the flickering flames as Joe poked the wood in the stove.

"Did they discover the reason for the crash?" asked Sarah.

With a serious tone, Andy filled in the details of the tragedy. "The B52 was designed as a high-altitude plane, to drop nukes. The military decided to test the planes at low altitude to fly under radar. That meant flying low, very low, under five-hundred feet or so. To do that, and stay airborne, a plane must fly fast. As a pilot, I can tell you low altitude flying puts immense stress on a plane, the whole thing just shakes, rattles, and rolls. Those men were trying to stay low, fly fast, and maneuver over mountains in a plane that's wider than a football field. Even in the best of circumstances, those are tough requirements.

"The accident investigation team was at the site by the weekend. I read the report that was issued. They determined there was a structural failure in what is known as the vertical stabilizer. Flying at low altitude doesn't give the crew much time to react in such a monster plane if something does go wrong, and without the stabilizer the pilot had little control. He held the plane as long as he could."

Lifting his beer bottle, he finished it off and cleared his throat. "Only the three crew members on the upper flight deck had ejection seats. The pilot, Dan Bulli, ejected and was found the next morning thirty feet up in a tree. Luckily, his survival kit stayed with him through the fall. The navigator, Gerald Alder, had some special luck indeed. His chute never deployed and he fell to the ground attached to his seat. Somehow, he survived the fall and the impact with the ground at many times the force of gravity. They found him almost two-thousand feet from the wreck. He was banged up with broken ribs and a fractured skull. He survived the cold by wrapping himself up in what remained of his torn parachute. The temperatures during the night on that mountain were estimated to be minus thirty. How a parachute kept him warm enough is amazing. The co-pilot did not survive. The crew members on the lower deck would have had to parachute out from a door or a hatch. At the altitude they were flying, none of them had a chance."

There was silence in the camp. Joe opened a journal, and passed it to Sarah. She read the article that was taped to the page out loud for everyone to hear.

Bangor Daily

Sunday January 26, 1963

Elephant Mountain B52 Crash

The B52 crash on Elephant Mountain on Thursday afternoon, claimed the lives of seven servicemen. It may be months before the reasons for the disaster become apparent. The military has sent words of gratitude to the local volunteers who assisted in the search, rescue, and recovery.

The two survivors, the pilot Colonel Dante E. Bulli, and the navigator, Captain Gerald J. Adler, are reported to be in serious, but stable condition.An accident investigation team is working with the military and the National Guard as they continue to piece together the facts of the accident.

The men that died in service to our country:

Major William W. Gabriel

Major Herbert L Hansen

Major Robert J. Hill

Captain Charles G. Leuchter

Major Robert J. Morrison

Tech. Sergeant Michael F. O'Keefe

Lieut. Colonel Joe S. Simpson Jr.

See full story in special insert.

She exhaled and passed the book to Don.

"That crash site is sacred ground," said Don. "Originally, they hired a salvage company to take away the metal. That was discontinued after a time. It's now treated as a memorial."

"Dad took these photos the following summer." Joe handed Sarah a leather-bound book. Sarah sat in silence examining the faded pictures and reading the hand-written captions.

"Joe, did Henry ever mention anything to you about that special investigator that showed up?" asked Andy.

"Not to me. Maybe to Dad, but Dad never said anything."

"That investigator, he was an interesting fellow." Andy rubbed his chin. "Henry was tight lipped over the whole thing. Seemed all very secretive."

"I remember meeting him the night he came back to North Brook Camps, up at Wilson Pond, after he crashed Henry's sled. Dad and I could tell whatever the reason for his visit, he didn't want us to know about it." Joe gathered the empty glasses and put them near the sink.

"Sarah, if you want, we can ride the sleds over to Elephant Mountain," said Don.

Her head tilted. "What's there to see after all this time?"

"You'd be surprised. Pieces of the wreck are still there." Don looked down and swallowed hard. "We could go up tomorrow, after the start of the dogsled race and be back in time to see the finish." Don was ready to sell the adventure. "What do you say, dear?" He looked at Linda.

"It's okay with me, but right now, I'm going to bed." She looked at Joe, Sarah, and Andy, "Happy New Year, everyone. Good night."

The woodstove popped and crackled. Joe added three pieces of oak to burn through the night. R.C., sensing the routine, barked at the door.

"Okay, boy. Let's get your leash." Joe grabbed his coat and a flashlight. A wave of bitter cold air swept across the room when he opened the door. He turned back. "Snow has stopped and the skies are clearing. Andy, grab some blankets and a pillow from the hall closet for the couch."

Andy's hand went up. "Will do." The door banged shut.

"Don, do you think you'll be able to give me a hand to get the ski fixed in the morning? I need to be in the air to watch for any trouble a dog team might have." He threw a pillow on the couch.

"No problem. We'll get you pieced back together in a jiff. We can get over to your plane at first light. 'Night." Don lifted his arm on the way to the bathroom.

⁑

Curled up in bed, under two heavy blankets and a top quilt his mom had made with north woods animal fabric, Joe asked Sarah, "Are you enjoying winter at camp?"

"It's been terrific spending time with you. Certainly different from my typical New Year's Eves. Except..."

"Except?"

"This craziness – with things going missing. It has me on edge."

"A city girl like you? Worried about a backwoods thief? It's nothing."

"You might be right, but I'd certainly feel a lot better if it wasn't happening at all. It's creeping me out knowing someone might be stalking around outside."

"Don't you worry, I'll protect you. And R.C. will bark while he's hiding behind the couch if anyone comes around."

Sarah squeezed his hand, knowing he was trying to make her feel safe.

"I hope Don and Andy didn't raise your fear of flying with the story about the B52."

"No more than usual." Sarah pulled the heavy quilt up around her neck and snuggled close to Joe.

🌱✳🌱

Joe woke to see R.C.'s flickering eyes next to the bed. The dog was letting out a low rumbling growl.

"What is it boy?" Joe looked at his watch. "It's three o'clock. You'd better not have to go out now." He opened the drapes to peer out.

The moonlight was reflecting the shadows of the trees down on the snow cover, painting a winter night landscape in the camp dooryard. All of their earlier footprints, from the porch to the sleds, had been covered over. He pulled the curtains closed.

He whispered at the dog, who had already flopped back down on the floor, "You must have heard a fox. Go back to sleep."

When Joe slid back under the covers, Sarah rolled towards him. "Everything okay?"

"R.C. got spooked by an animal, that's all."

"Oh," she said, not opening her eyes.

Kettle to Kettle

❧✳✳❧

When Sarah woke up, she reached for Joe, but the space next to her was empty and all the warmth had escaped from his side of the bed. Slipping from under the covers, she was quickly reminded that the bedroom had no heat, other than what migrated from the woodstove over the walls that didn't reach the ceiling. She was glad she slept in her socks. From a hook by the door she took Joe's flannel shirt and put it on over her sweatshirt.

At the sound of the door creaking open, Joe gave her a cheerful, "Good morning."

She kissed him and went to pour coffee. "'Morning. You're up early." Her head was not yet clear.

"Didn't you hear Andy and Don head out this morning?" he asked.

"No, I didn't. Did they wake you?" she asked.

His pencil paused above the sketch he was working on. "To not hear Don in the morning would be a miracle. The guy has one volume – loud."

"Huh – I didn't hear him at all. What are you drawing?"

His pencil stopped moving. He wasn't quite ready to show her yet. "Oh, it's nothing."

"Let me see." She bounced from the chair to stand behind his rocker. "Is that me? It's so good!"

"I'm glad you like it. I wasn't sure . . . well, if, you'd be okay with it."

"I love it." She could see he was a bit uncomfortable. "But you know, you're supposed to be sketching me a picture of sled dogs racing – for the magazine."

"Yeah. I'll get to that later today."

"By the way, what time does the race start?"

"The way the Kettle to Kettle race goes, the starts are staggered. If we get over to Kokadjo we can see the first teams starting. We can then ride up to Elephant Mountain and be back to see Gerry finish." Joe rolled up the blankets Andy had used on the couch.

"Kettle to Kettle? Why's it called that?" Sarah picked up the camp journal. "I'm writing about my camp adventure."

"Ah." He was glad to see she was feeling at home, and she was leaving memories in the journals. "The race starts at the Kokadjo Store, near what is now Roach Pond. The Indian name for that pond is Kokadjeweemgwasebem, which means Kettle Mountain Lake. The course then passes between Spencer Pond, for which the Indian name means Kettle Mountain Pond, and Little Spencer Mountain, which is Kokadjo or Kettle Mountain."

"Why so many kettles?"

"The mountains and ponds, get their names from a legend having to do with Mount Kineo. I have to gas up my sled, but take a look at this." He opened *Woods and Lakes of Maine* and handed her the book. "The Indian legend about the kettles, is explained in here."

"This is an old book."

"Yep, it's an original. It was published in the 1880s. It belonged to my grandfather," said Joe, as he pulled on his hat and stepped outside.

Sarah gently turned the aging pages. She was about finished scanning the chapter when Linda emerged from the bedroom, still in her pajamas and wearing a robe.

"Is everything all right?" Sarah placed the book on the table.

"I'm not feeling all that great. Seems it will be a puzzle and reading day for me."

Secretly, Sarah thought that sounded like a very good day – reading by the fire, looking out at the snow. "Oh, sorry to hear that. Can I get you anything?"

"No. I'm going to stretch out here on the couch and cover up." She spread out the blankets Joe had rolled up.

Standing by the gas tank, Joe was perplexed. There was no way in one day they had used over fifty gallons of his reserve. He screwed the cap back on his tank as Don came sledding up beside him.

"That was quick. What was wrong with Andy's plane?"

"The crud cutter had snapped. Luckily, those planes have an extra rig kit. It wasn't too bad to get it corrected, but it's freezing out there. My fingers were about to fall off. He flew back to the Fish and Game hangar to get it looked at." Don reached for the gas pump handle to fill his sled. "Wow – this was full when we pulled in two days ago. How did we use all that gas?" With his gloved hand, he flicked the tank gauge.

"We didn't." Joe's facial expression said it all.

"What are you thinking?"

"I'm thinking how we didn't see or hear someone carry off that much fuel!"

"Had to be some brazen fool to do that while we're in the camp thirty yards away."

"Could have been while we were out."

"There's something else." Don sat back down on his sled.

"What's that?"

"It took me longer to help Andy than it should have."

"Why's that?" Joe pulled his gloves back on.

"We had some investigating to do." Don gave Joe a serious look.

"Investigating of what?"

"There were some sled tracks going across the lake. Out over to Big Island." He pointed, as if Joe didn't know which direction the lake was.

"So? Could have been anyone out for a ride, or ice fishing."

"Yeah. But we found a spot on the ground that was used for a campfire. They had kicked snow over the fire pit, but it was recent."

"Are you sure it was recent?"

"There was also a depression in the snow where a tent had been up." Don noticed Joe was still suspicious. "And Andy found a squirrel pelt along with the skeleton thrown to the side."

Joe made a face. "Really? Do you think someone cooked it?"

"That's what it appeared to be. And..." Don paused.

"And?" Joe was agitated.

"Andy made the comment that whoever it was had to have been there after the snow stopped last night. The tracks were fresh."

Contemplating why R.C. had growled in the middle of the night, Joe exhaled. "Let me get a padlock for this tank. Go ahead and let the girls know we're ready to head over to the starting line."

⚝✻⚝

The two snowmobiles cruised down the trail towards Kokadjo. The sky was a deep blue, a perfectly clear winter day, with the temperature hovering around 20, and almost no wind. It was a dog-sledders dream for race weather. Cold enough to hold snow, not slushy; and warm enough to make it fun, not unbearable for man or beast.

After finding out Linda wouldn't be going, Don was relieved to get the all clear he could go out for the day. R.C. on the other hand seemed to be happy to have someone to stay home with him, especially since Linda allowed him to crawl up on the end of the couch with her. The feeling was mutual as he kept her feet toasty.

Five minutes into the ride, Don was missing Linda. He called on a new partner to chat with. "Joe, do you know what they're serving up over at the start line this year for food?"

"Bobby mentioned he'd be helping Mitch dish out barbeque pork, chili, and brisket."

"Mmm, Mmm, I love that barbeque from Trailside. We'd better put the hammer down, I don't want to miss out on that."

Don wasn't kidding about speeding up. Sarah wondered if they were in a race she wasn't told about. Joe felt her arms holding onto his waist a little tighter. She was relieved when they stopped alongside a line of parked snowmobiles.

Bobby waved them over to the bonfire where spectators had gathered. "Hi. Happy New Year! Where's Linda?"

"Happy New Year. She's a bit under the weather. So, she's back keeping R.C. company," answered Don.

Bobby nodded.

"Anyone start yet?" asked Joe. The waiting dogs were barking something fierce.

"Not yet. The team from up near Millinocket is lining up," said Bobby. "Behind them will be the sled from Canada. They have some strong team. I'm thinking they may take home the three grand."

Don shot Joe a glance. With a bob of his head, Don indicated to Joe to look over to his left. Leaning against a truck with dog kennels in the bed, was Axe, who raised his beer to Joe.

Joe turned back to Don, "Guess his buddy Heath is the musher?"

"Good thing. I'd pity the dog team that had to pull that lard around." Don pointed his thumb in Axe's direction.

"They're starting." Bobby pointed up the line.

Dogs were yelping. People were cheering. Snow went flying.

Between starts, Don went to the chow wagon and brought back lunch for everyone, even though it was not yet eleven.

After they watched Gerry's team start, Sarah asked, "How long until they get back?" She moved behind Don and Bobby.

Joe's glance went from Sarah, to his left to see Axe was sitting in his running truck, staring their way.

Looking at his watch, Bobby said, "First team should be back in four to five hours." He held up a race map to show

Sarah. His finger traced the course. "They start here at Kokadjo, go up between the Spencers, then along Lobster up to the carry, before they turn back towards Spencer Pond."

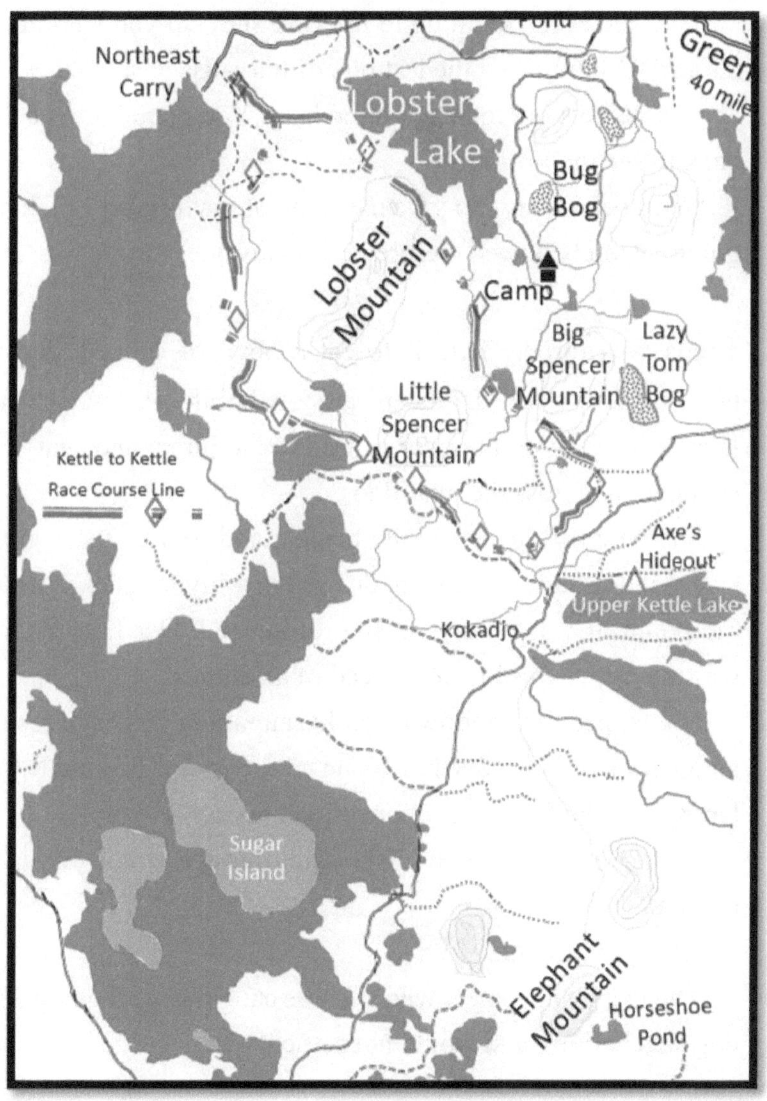

"Will we be back by then?" Sarah wrapped her hands around a steaming cup of hot chocolate.

"Oh sure. It's only a twelve-mile ride," Joe answered.

"Where you all headed?" asked Bobby, curiously.

"We're taking Sarah up to the B52 site. Do you want to go along?" Don finished the last bite of his sausage sub.

"Can't. I've got to help around here. You planning on being back to see the finish?"

"You bet. Be sure to save me some of that brisket Mitch has going." Don bellowed, before pulling away.

🌲*🌲

Linda was forcing herself to eat a bowl of canned chicken noodle soup, when she heard a snowmobile. A few seconds later, a banging on the door caused her to jump, and sent R.C. stampeding across the pine floor.

She wrapped herself in the blanket and peaked through the side-window curtain. A man, dressed in army fatigues stood on the porch. It wasn't anyone she recognized. Her first thought was maybe he was lost or in need of assistance.

She tapped the window to get his attention. His hand rose in an open wave. She gave him a one moment sign. Taking R.C.'s leash from the hook, she clipped it on his collar.

"Yes? May I help you?" She said, through a narrow gap of the door.

"Are you, Linda?"

The fact that he knew who she was caught her off guard. The dog was barking and would not settle down.

He took a knee, and without any fear, opened his hand. "Easy, boy." The dog immediately calmed down. "Sit." R.C. obeyed.

The man, scratching R.C. behind his ears, looked up at Linda. "My name is Frank Merrill. Fred, the forest ranger, I believe you know him, told me I might find you here."

"I know Fred. Do you work with him?" She asked with surprise. She didn't take the man for a forest ranger.

He stood back up. She had to tilt her head back to see his face. "No. I don't work with him. I'm with the federal government. He's helping me with a case."

"What kind of case?" She fought back a cough.

"I can explain, but you should get out of the cold. Might I come in?"

"Oh. Um..." She was intrigued on why someone from a federal agency would have any interest in the kind of work Fred did, why he'd be out on New Year's Day at Lobster Lake, but mostly she was concerned about letting someone in while she was alone.

Merrill noticed her hesitation. "Here's my identification." Linda reached for it.

"And this is from Fred." He handed her a yellowing photograph. The paper was dry, and the edges were crumbling off.

Holding the photo, Linda's lips rose slightly in recognition. "I see. Come in, Mr. ...," she looked down at the identification again, "Mr. Merrill."

When he sat in Joe's rocker, she had a feeling the arms were going to split off, they strained outward.

"I haven't seen this picture in many years. Why'd Fred give this to you?"

"He had it on a shelf in his storeroom. He told me it would come in handy as a calling card."

"Why, I guess it did. How can I help you?" She grabbed a tissue and sneezed. "Sorry, I must have caught something."

"That doesn't sound too good. Taking anything for it?"

She touched a spoonful of soup to her lips. "Chicken soup. But it's cold." She dropped the spoon back into the pot.

"Here, let me heat that up for you." As he stood to pick up the pot, the rocker lifted off the floor, stuck to his hips. He pushed the chair down. "You know, I first visited Greenville around the time you gave Fred that photo."

She thought back to when she took the picture. "This picture was taken not long before a plane crashed close to this location on the mountain."

He stirred the soup. "I know." He turned to see her frown. He continued, "Henry Ford took me to the B52 crash site, which is the purpose of my investigation."

She shivered. The story they all had relived last night, her old photo, and the man's visit was an odd coincidence. "My head is all fogged up from this cold. I'm not sure I'm following you, or how I can help."

He turned off the burner, and placed the pot on a towel.

"Thank you. You didn't need to do that."

"Not a problem." Glancing at the rocker, he decided instead to sit in the recliner.

With difficulty, Linda swallowed a spoonful of soup. "Can you tell me what this's all about?"

He glanced around the room; his gaze stopped on the radio equipment. Not wanting to risk something being said over a CB, he didn't want to say too much in the way of specifics. "Fred mentioned, with all the pictures you take for logging operations, maybe you might have captured other camps on film."

Linda sniffled and made an attempt at a laugh. "Don, my husband, said I was making more of it than it was. He told me those camps were left by irresponsible hikers. I tried to make him fly me around – to convince him. We saw a few over the years, randomly when we were flying for the company. I don't have any of the photos anymore."

"Could you remember where the camps were? Or did you notice any patterns to the chosen locations? Someplace good for a hideout?"

"I see the woods in my sleep, I've studied photos of trees for so many years, all I see are patterns."

Merrill took Fred's hand-drawn map from his pack. "Any of these locations bring back any memories?"

"Where'd you get this?" She immediately recognized the logging company boundaries.

"Fred."

She stared at him; her eyes narrowed.

"He's been keeping records of where he found camps over the years."

"That figures. I always suspected Fred wanted to find the person 'littering up his woods,' as he put it." Studying the diagram, she ate her soup. "These two here. I remember those locations. I had Don fly in low. They were in places not easy to land near or hike to." She looked up, "Only a forester who likes sleeping out in the woods might have the patience to go searching that deep in the forest."

He nodded, thinking to himself, '*or a special agent on a mission.*' Instead, he said, "Turns out, both Fred and I have been searching for this person for different reasons. Mostly, Fred. I gave up back in the early seventies. I haven't been back to Maine since. I figured it was hopeless." He took a piece of bacon from his shirt pocket and took a bite.

A sound came out of Linda more as a cough, than a laugh. "What?"

"You just reminded me of Henry Ford. He always had bacon in his pockets."

Merrill nodded. "You know, it's a habit I picked up after hiking around with Ford. And it's better than packaged jerky."

"What made you come back? What's so urgent to be here on New Year's Day."

"There was a radio call. The agency still listens to all frequencies. They passed it on to me based on the message."

He moved Fred's map closer to her. "I realize you're not feeling well, but you see, this is the best clue I've had in years. What I need is your educated guess on where he is."

"What makes you think I know?"

His index finger ran down the center of the map. "Think. Think about these locations, considering where you spotted camps in the past. Where might you put a camp close to here, in the vicinity around Lobster Lake, based on what you know about the woods, the logging operations, the past locations. It'd have to be within a half-days hike from the store."

Linda studied his face. He seemed tired. Worn down. But, behind his leathery, wrinkled skin and the unkept beard, she saw something in his eyes – a kindness, a soft spot to help someone. She took a deep breath. Tasting a spoonful of soup, she chewed the rubbery chicken pieces, and tried to squint away her headache.

"Here." She drew a tight circle with her finger.

He handed her a pencil. The mark she made was smaller than the circumference of the eraser end.

"Why there?"

"Nobody goes there. No loggers. No campers. Lazy Tom Swamp is useless for wood or fishing or hunting. It's quiet. It's also close enough to get to Gerry's in a couple of hours on foot."

"That's what Fred was thinking."

"What else did Fred say?"

"He mentioned the network of streams and brooks in that area would make it a heck of a lot easier to travel without leaving tracks."

"That's a good point. It's all frozen solid right now."

He looked at her empty bowl. "You want any more soup?"

"No. Thank you." She shook her head. "Are you going out looking for him? Tonight?"

"I have to, before he moves again. Winter is the best time to track, it's easier to see through the bare trees. And maybe, I'll get lucky and find some tracks in the snow."

She nodded, she was familiar with winter tracking for her photography habit and took plenty of unobstructed aerial photos during the winter months.

He stood to go. Looking around, he realized they were alone. "I was here once before. With Henry. He was helping me track one winter and we stayed here for a night. Here and a number of the remote warden camps. Is Joe Parker around?"

Linda twirled a loose piece of thread on her sweater. "No. My husband, Don, and Joe actually, took the sleds up to the B52 memorial."

His head moved slowly, up and down. He exhaled. "I've been back there a few times over the years. I met Joe and his dad once too." He pulled on his coat. "I appreciate your time."

They shook hands. "Will you let us know if you find him?"

"No." He paused at her look. "I won't have to. It'll be in all the papers. Thank you for speaking with me."

She latched the door and watched him drive off.

Her head was aching. She read the label on the cold medicine again. *'Do not take more than four capsules in twenty-four hours.'* She looked at R.C., "Doesn't say I can't take four in less than four hours." She slid under the covers on the guest room bed. In less than ten minutes she was sound asleep.

Memorial Ride

❦❖❦

Winding up the mountain, Sarah was finally getting used to the feel of riding on a snow machine. It was the first time in three days she was less concerned of falling off and was actually enjoying the ride. It was also a different experience to get a wave from every sled going the opposite way. She couldn't think of a time she was waved at in the city from a stranger, unless it was the one-finger salute.

Joe's voice filled her helmet. "Don, which trail you planning on taking?"

"We'll stick to the logging roads, then we can avoid Avalanche Pass."

"Avalanche Pass?" Sarah's voice cracked.

"Nothing much to worry about the way we're headed. Avalanche Pass is a steep slope on the backside of Prong Pond Mountain. Sometimes, snow slides down and bugs up the trail. Don's being dramatic."

"That's because you're not the one out here with the trail crews clearing it," Don said.

"And we appreciate all you do. But, so you know, Sarah, there are places where big avalanches happen up this way. What was it, Don, four or five years ago, up on Katahdin those men were buried?"

"Buried?" Sarah was even more concerned.

"Yep." Don answered. "They were hiking, high up, when the snow gave way. All five were buried under the snow. Luckily, one of them dug himself out and helped one of the others break free. With their equipment buried, they couldn't free any of the other three men. The least injured made his way back to the ranger station. Unfortunately, by the time help arrived they were only able to rescue one other. Two men died."

"And you're certain there's no danger the way we're going?" Sarah asked to confirm.

"Along the trails we're taking there are few areas that encroach where a slide can occur. All the same, you always have to be aware, know where you're going, and be prepared at all times. This is the wilderness." Don signaled with his right arm that a turn was coming up.

Sarah kept her eyes turned upward at each ridge rising to her left or right. She wondered if Linda was having a relaxing time.

At a fork, Don veered to the left.

"Where you headed?" Joe wondered why Don was not heading directly to the B52 location.

"You'll see."

When he stopped in a logging clearing they had a view south beyond Greenville and to the north clear to the ridges west of Northeast Carry.

"Wow! What a view of the lake from here." Sarah was obviously impressed.

"I figured you might like this." Don was glad to see his secret viewing location was appreciated.

"All the other ponds nearby really show up with the snow-covered ice. I had no idea there were so many." She took out her camera. "How big is the lake?"

"It's not that easy to put a number on it, given the shape," Joe answered. "Think about it this way, Manhattan Island is thirteen miles long and two miles wide. Moosehead Lake is about forty miles long and at its widest point it's ten miles wide."

"Another interesting fact," added Don, "is that Manhattan might have four million people on it, at least on a weekday, right now, in all the area we can see, for miles in all directions, there might be at most four thousand people."

To not be out done on north woods facts, Joe added, "That might be true for people, but there are over ten thousand moose and fifteen thousand deer out there." His arm swept across the horizon.

"Okay, explain something else to me. I understand that Moosehead was named because of the shape of the outline. And Lobster Lake was named because it resembles a claw. But this Elephant Mountain you're taking me to, that isn't an animal I'd associate with Maine. Is it the shape of an Elephant?"

"Somewhat." Joe nodded. "An elephant head and back, anyway. I have pictures at camp. I'll show them to you later."

Don pulled his helmet back on. "Let's move out. We only go a little ways farther on the sleds, then we snowshoe in."

At the path leading to the crash site, Don stopped his sled; he was ticked off. "Now who the heck drove down there!"

It was obvious snowmobiles had gone from the logging road down the narrow foot-trail. The snow was packed down and a line of new-growth tree saplings had been flattened.

Putting on his snowshoes, Don was getting winded. "This is a memorial site, they're not supposed to drive down there. The pieces are strewn all around, they'll be driving over them." He was headed down the path on his own before Sarah even had one of her snowshoes buckled.

"I'll wait for you. Take your time." Joe handed her the second shoe.

"He sure is in a tizzy."

"As president of the snowmobile club, Don negotiated access with the timber company a long time ago to keep this path open. If anyone messes up, they could shut it down."

Sarah and Joe arrived a minute behind Don at the main debris location. He was spewing all sorts of expletives.

"Would you look at this!" he pointed.

It didn't take Joe long to see what had happened. The snow was dug over and it appeared someone had dragged out parts of the wreck.

"Who would have done this?" Don threw a stick at a tree.

Joe looked at Sarah. He turned to Don. "I think I have a clue. I came across a couple of guys with lots of scrap metal in their truck the other day. Canadian plates."

"Do you think they're metal thieves?"

"Could be." Joe examined a long metal rod that had been sawed off.

"We had better get back to camp. I need to call Chief Robley. And maybe Andy Green. Whoever did this was probably hoping snow would bury their tracks before anyone was here. Sarah, may I use your camera?"

"Absolutely." She handed Don her Kodak.

While the guys took pictures, Sarah wandered around. A light snow had started to fall, and she could not imagine what the two surviving crewmen had gone through on the night they spent in the woods. There were large tires, axels, and pieces of plane fuselage scattered throughout the woods. Her mind ran through the story about the crash. She shivered. It was a sobering experience to see pieces of metal and rubber left there on the mountain.

On the walk back to the sleds, she asked Joe, "Why would someone do that?" Her hands indicating the dug-up ground.

"These low-life thieves sell metal by the pound," he answered. "Maine is making it difficult to sell, but maybe these guys found a way to get it across the border. We'd better catch up to Don before he heads down the mountain without us."

With Don, uncharacteristically, not being his chatty self talking into the headset, Sarah thought about all that was happening around camp. What she anticipated to be a quiet winter get away, was turning out to be a mystery in the north woods. Bouncing along, she took her mind off of it by running through the adventures she had ice fishing, the sled race, finding moose sheds, and the lynx sighting – all the experiences she wanted to include in her magazine article.

Suddenly the sled jerked to the right. A loud clang came from below the seat. Sarah's helmet hit the back of Joe's shoulder and the sled froze in place.

"What is it?"

"Not sure. Hey, Don, we've got a problem. Swing back."

He was driving so fast, Don was almost out of range. "Wha... hap..en..?"

"You're breaking up. Turn around."

By the time Don circled back, Joe was lying in the snow examining the sled. "What is it?"

"Track split." Joe stood up and walked around the other side to see how bad it was.

After contemplating the break, the guys knew they didn't have the parts or tools needed to fix the sled out on the trail.

"I can try and tow you," said Don.

"Not with a torn track you can't. You take Sarah to camp and bring back a tow-behind. We'll load it up and I'll ride back with you."

"You're going to stay out here? Alone? It'll be dark soon."

Joe tried not to laugh at Sarah's concern. "No big deal. You go get warm back at the cabin."

Don yelled, "I'll be back in two shakes."

Joe gave a wave into the shower of sleet-snow that had started. Watching them drive away, and realizing he'd be waiting over an hour for Don to get back, he decided to build a fire. Off the far side of the trail he noticed a stand of dri-ki out in a frozen bog.

Stepping to break off a dried branch, his leg plunged through the ice, quickly filling his boot with ice water. "Great. This is what I need right now."

With a fire going to be even more critical, he hustled to collect the kindling. Being careful where he stepped, he made his way back up to the trail.

⁂

"**D**arn, Leon, it's a good thing you saw those sleds."

"Yeah. Lucky we happened to hit that clearing to see them when we did." Leontel opened the trail map. "This side trail connects back down below."

The brothers had been on their way back to camp, towing behind each of their sleds a load of their latest haul, when Leontel spotted the headlights from Don and Joe's sleds winding up the mountain.

Napolin took the map. "Are you sure? It looks narrow."

"Better to try, than risk running into that group, or any others with this load. Let's get moving."

They followed the trail for thirty minutes when it dead ended in a sand pit. The trail that exited on the far end was covered in four feet of snow, with not even a moose track through it.

Napolin stood, his helmet in his hand, and spit. "I'm not risking breaking trail towing this haul."

Leontel considered their predicament. "We've burned a lot of gas going this far out of our way."

Napolin looked at his fuel gauge. "We'll be all right."

"What if we run into those sleds?"

"Little odds of that." Napolin spit again. "And if we do, we'll handle it."

They turned back out of the pit the way they came. Back on the main trail, they opened up their engines to make up lost time.

Joe dropped the wood and birch bark a few yards behind his sled. A yelp from a coyote somewhere on the mountain echoed through the pass; at least he hoped it was a coyote. By now it was dark, the light on the front of his sled was fading out, the battery near dead. He was not only going to need the fire to keep him warm, but it would be a good safety signal should a sled come around the bend.

He stepped to the side as a snowshoe hare came running right at him, and then veered off to the right. The tree branches parted and a fisher bounded onto the trail in pursuit. The carnivorous mammal of the weasel family, realizing he had lost his dinner, stood still, and considered his next move.

Over the years, Joe had seen fishers many times. Their fear of humans usually meant they made for a quick getaway. This one was three feet long and due to the heaviness of its sheen coat of dark brown fur it looked to weigh twice as much as its probable twelve pounds.

Although startled, the fisher decided to fight another day and he walked off into the woods in the direction of the hare prints. Joe exhaled. He thought, *I guess I was in the right place at the right time for that rabbit.*

Stacking the wood into a tee-pee, Joe heard the growl of sleds coming his way. He stood off to the side. When the two men coasted to a stop, they lifted their face shields. Joe recognized them immediately; what was worse, he saw they recognized him.

"Look at this, Leont. If it isn't Mr. Good Samaritan from the Trading Post." Napolin coughed several times.

Leont snickered and lit a cigarette. "Got some trouble, mister?"

Joe considered his situation. He didn't know what the two guys were all about, but he had a good hunch. Pieces of metal extended from the rear of the tied down tarps on the sleds they were pulling.

Napolin noticed Joe's stare and moved between him and their haul. "You broke down?"

"A little bit of trouble. I'm waitin' on a buddy of mine. He went to get a part."

"Is that so?" Leont got off his sled and blew smoke in Joe's direction. He kicked at the broken track. "You'll be needing much more than a *part*."

Joe's eyes narrowed.

Napolin touched Joe's sled with the palm of his hand. "Engine's cold. Been here awhile? Maybe your buddy isn't coming back." Walking around the far side of Joe's sled, his heel knocked over the woodpile. "We could give you a lift." He flicked the gas cap.

"Nah. Not necessary. I don't need you to hang around."

Following Napolin's lead, Leontel nodded. "Maybe not, but seeing as you're not going to be riding this sled anywhere, you might lend us some of your gas then? We could just siphon a few gallons. Seeing we're running low." The grin on Leontel's face widened, showing the space where he was missing two bottom incisors.

Joe couldn't recall how long Don had been gone. His demeanor changed quickly as his adrenaline rose and he changed to offense. His hand reached for the latch on the cargo holder mounted to his sled.

At the same time, Napolin moved his hand under the tarp of his cargo sled. "I've got a siphon hose in here we can use." A gust of wind ripped down the narrow trail. The tarp on the tow-behind was flung up exposing the gray metal parts.

"Hey! Those are B52 parts from up the mountain." Joe made a move for the tarp and pulled it off. He felt a cold rod hit the back of his neck. Falling to the ground his vision went from the white of the snow, to the black of a tunnel.

⁂

"Stove's almost out. Can you check on Linda, while I get this started?" Don shoved pieces of starter wood onto the coals.

"Linda?" Sarah peeked into the guest room. R.C. was curled up at the foot of the bed. Linda's breathing was steady as the blankets rose and fell. Sarah gently closed the door.

Don was already on the radio trying to get a hold of Gerry. She sat down and listened.

"This is Eagle One, is anyone on over at Northeast Carry, come in?"

"Hello, Don. This is Pearl. We missed you over this way to watch the dogs finish. What can I do for you?"

He sighed. With Pearl monitoring the communications, he knew this conversation was going to take twice as long as he had time for. And the worst of it would be the information would be spread from Fort Kent to Moxie Falls within five minutes.

"Listen, Pearl. I've got a situation. Joe's sled broke down pretty bad. I've got to go and get him. Maybe try and tow his sled on a flatbed. Or we'll leave the sled until tomorrow."

"Doesn't sound too bad. As long as you're back before the storm rolls in."

"What storm?"

"Some kind of lows, or highs, I don't understand it, colliding. Stirring up a surprise wallop. They expect we'll be getting close to an inch of ice, then a foot or more of heavy wet snow. Gonna be a mess. Blew up kinda sudden. Last I heard was it should hit around five."

Don looked at his watch. He didn't need more squirrels thrown at him today. "Pearl, there's more. Joe being stuck out there on the trail, that's not the worst of it."

"Oh?" Pearl's voice rose in anticipation.

"We think someone has stolen some of the B52 wreck."

"The plane? How do you know that?"

Trying to conserve time and get back to Joe, Don relayed as little to Pearl as she needed to know. He finished with, "As I said, get a hold of Andy, or any wardens you can reach, or Chief Robley. Call out to whoever you need to. - - - I'm well aware it's New Year's Day. Tell them what I told you. I have to go."

He clicked off the radio and when he turned, he saw Sarah sitting on the couch, still in her snowmobile suit; a small puddle surrounding her boots.

"Linda's sound asleep." She indicated towards the bedroom with her head.

"That's probably best." Don had his hand on the doorknob, ready to leave.

"I want to go back out with you." Sarah's voice was firm.

Don's head turned quickly and he went to snap something, but stopped.

She stood. "I can ride Linda's sled."

"I really don't think that's a good idea. I'll be back with Joe in a couple of hours. I don't want to risk something else going wrong. Not tonight. And not with a storm coming."

Sarah looked out the window. A sliver of sun was piercing through a break in the clouds on the horizon.

Behind her, Don continued, "It'd be better if you could keep the fire going and be here if Linda needs anything." They both turned at the slurping sound. R.C. was licking up the puddles. "And take care of R.C., I bet he needs to eat." He could sense she still was torn.

She looked at the dog. "All right. But can you show me how to work the radio?"

He blew out a breath. "Okay, grab a pen. Write this down."

Making a Getaway

Coming to, Joe coughed, causing him to take in a deep breath. He gagged at the stench of whiskey, beer, cigarette smoke, and burned fish. He couldn't lift his head. He was wedged on the floor under a counter that was pushing down on the back of his neck, forcing his chin into his chest. His eyes were covered with a mothball-smelling cloth. With his hands tied behind his back, his fingertips felt the smoothness of a wooden post. Through a slit between the blindfold and his cheek, he noticed the floor was spotted in melting snow, pooling up around his legs.

In the background, he recognized the cough from one of the guys that had hit him. The next voice he heard was Axe's.

"And you decided to bring him here? Didn't you think his buddy was going to come back, see his sled there, and go searching for him?" Axe flipped the table he was sitting at. Glass shattered and beer cans rolled across the floor.

Napolin and Leontel looked over to Heath, hoping he'd agree they took the only choice they had. He offered no parley.

Based on the body-odor and a beer opening, Joe could tell Axe was standing close. He could hear him chugging the beer.

Axe's plan had been to be lay low for a day, and then travel in the early morning hours before daybreak. He had it all worked out – where they would store their haul in the woods on the American side, how they would sled it across the slash, that twenty-foot-wide treeless swath at the border, and when they were to make the final drop to the scrap metal buyer back in Canada. He even had a dealer waiting for a piece of the B52 memorabilia, willing to pay top dollar. Now his plans were in jeopardy because his partners had to go and knock out a local. He threw the almost empty can at Joe's legs.

"We gotta get out of here. You idiots load up the trailers and stuff in the haul. I'll get the dogs crated." The splitting of wood Joe heard, next to his right ear, was Axe's boot going through the maple cabinet door of the kitchen island.

Once the trailers were hitched to their trucks, Axe conferred with Heath. "We got to ditch those two." His head jerked towards Napolin and Leontel. "After this goes down, this is the last time we haul with them."

Heath nodded. "What about that guy in there?" He thumbed back towards the cabin.

"He'll be fine. We'll call in a tip once we're over the border at a bar in Lac Etchemin." Axe could tell Heath wasn't sure about leaving Joe tied up. "Look, his buddy will probably find him long before that. We got to bolt. This weather is either going to give us cover, or strand us before we can get to Hurricane Pond Hill."

The last sound Joe heard was from the plows on the two trucks scraping their way down the gravel driveway. Once Axe's yelling and the dog barking had stopped, it was dead quiet and Joe had time to realize how bad his head was throbbing. He tried to free his hands, but the constrictor knot around his wrists and the post pulled tighter the more he struggled. His legs were wrapped in rope from his knees to his ankles, from which a long anchor line stretched to the legs of the cast iron woodstove, which the gang hadn't even bothered to load up to keep the cabin warm. Not that it mattered.

Axe had been the last of the gang to walk out. From the corner of the dirty rag covering his eyes, Joe could see Axe's boots, covered in dog crap, when he came to say farewell. "Maybe that pretty blond will come save you. If not, you can be sure I'll look her up sometime."

Joe let fly a string of curses at Axe, who laughed on his way out. "Try to stay warm." And without pulling the door closed behind him, Axe flicked the lights off and walked out. The door swung wide open. Sleet flew across the room hitting Joe in the face.

He knew to fight the onset of hypothermia he had to stay awake. Thoughts of Don searching gave him hope and kept him alert – for a little while. He thought about his mom. His dad. Under the mask his eyes closed – he thought of Sarah.

❦⁂❦

Don swung around at the sound of snowmobiles.

"Where's Parker?" Andy waved his flashlight in a large circle. Kristy swung her sled around to keep a light in the opposite direction.

"I wish I knew. I left him right here," Don said, his hand indicated the broken-down sled, "A little over an hour ago."

Since getting back, Don had spent the last five minutes walking in circles, disturbed Joe was missing, and wondering what to do next.

"Andy, take a look at this." Kristy was kneeling on the ground, close to where Joe had stacked the wood.

"He probably was planning to warm up, but for some reason didn't light that," said Don.

"Not the wood. This." Kristy pointed to a pipe sticking out of the snow. Andy reached for it. He shined his flashlight along the metal. "We'd better have a look around."

"I've been through here for the last thirty minutes. I can't find anything, not even footprints." exclaimed Don.

"We'll take a quick pass, all the same." Andy looked at Kristy and tightened his lips. She knew his meaning; he had wished Don hadn't stomped all over any traces of prints or evidence they might have found.

"It's been snowing pretty hard. I doubt we'll find anything." stated Kristy. She continued, "You know, yesterday when I ran across those four Canadians who had the two flat tires, the skinny one mentioned they were staying over on Roach Pond. That's not far from here. Maybe they've seen something."

Don was suspicious. "Four Canadians? Was there a big guy with the skinny one?"

"Yeah. How'd you know? The skinny one took a punch to his back when he answered my question about where they were lodging." she stated.

"Joe said he came across two Canadians with lots of odd metal in their truck. We also ran across the fat one and the skinny one a couple of times. Could be they are all together if it's the same four," said Don.

"Let's get a move on and go check the places over there." Andy was already mounting his sled.

"There are dozens of camps over that way. Where do we start?" Don threw up his hands.

"We need to check each one. Together *and* in silence." With a look he made sure Don got his meaning. "We'll park the sleds on the ice and make our way around on foot."

Smoke burning his nostrils caused Joe to open his eyes. A wall of flames was feet from his face. He went to pull on his ropes, but realized he was free, and he wasn't in Axe's cabin. He pushed himself up, wanting to run from the fire. A wave of dizziness forced him back down. Lying on an old army blanket stretched over the cold ground, he noticed he was in a lean-to made from hemlock branches. A campfire was crackling, a stack of wood was neatly piled near his feet out of the snow, and a can of beans stood open in a pot.

"Hello? Anyone here?" he shouted.

He stretched his neck; a shooting pain ran from the front of his head to his lower back. His right hand felt the crust of dried blood on the back of his neck. Slowly he pulled himself up enough to sit on a log. He looked around. If it were July, he would have thought nothing strange of the camp he was in. But in the dead of winter, in the middle of a storm, it wasn't a place he wanted to spend the night.

He called out again. "Is someone here?"

In the firelight he noticed a tarp tent. It was surrounded by three large boulders and old-growth pines of tremendous circumference at the edge of the narrow clearing. A roof over the tarp was constructed of intertwined pine branches balanced over the rocks, providing perfect cover from the sky above.

He parted the tarp. "Hi there. Anyone here?" It was too dark inside to see anything. From the fire, Joe picked out a burning stick and walked back to the tent.

Sticking his head through the crude door, he held up the burning stick. A small propane heater was situated in the center of the space that was no bigger than a car. There was a cot piled with blankets, next to clothes stacked on shelves made from branches tied together with string. Under a hanging lantern, books, magazines, newspapers, and electronic equipment wired to car batteries, were covered in plastic on a plank table balanced over four logs. A fifth log sat upright for a stool. He untied the lantern and lit it.

A green log book on the cot caught his attention. The cover was labeled, "Maine Forest Service – Squaw Mountain." He opened it and flipped the pages. The first few entries were observation notes from the 1960s. Scanning the pages after that, Joe squinted. His head was throbbing too much to make sense of the German handwriting.

Outside, he searched the inner perimeter of the small clearing. The remaining sides of the camp were enclosed by a crisscross of blow-downs. The trees were packed tightly together, and had he passed by the camp from the outside, he would have never known there was a small clearing in the center. He followed a narrow path between two trees that dead ended at a covering on the ground. Taking a breath, he lifted the piece of wood. He got down on his knees, lowered the lantern, and peered into the hole. The pit contained canned goods, sodas, and some boxes of pasta.

Another beaten path led into a thicket where an open-air outhouse seat was fashioned from an old back-less kitchen chair. Behind that was what appeared to be a garbage dump of old cans, propane tanks, and cardboard.

He stood by the fire. His single focus was on getting out, to get into the woods. His problem was he could find no obvious path between the trees or boulders.

His other problems were, it was dark, it was snowing hard, and he had no idea where he was exactly. Worst of all, he had no idea who's camp he was in, how he got there, if the person was friendly, or even if the person was coming back.

Then again, here at the camp there was a fire, blankets, and food.

His fingers slipped through his snow pants and pulled on the clip he had attached to the beltloop of his jeans. On his key chain he looked for the small compass his dad had given him. It was missing from the thin metal loop. He looked at his watch. More than four hours had passed since he parted with Don and Sarah.

Forcing himself to think through the pain, he tried to calculate how far someone could have transported him, most likely on foot, but he really had no idea. He had to determine whether he was north or south of Parker Cabin. The only way to do that was to start walking to find a place he might recognize. If he could get to high ground by daybreak, he figured he could recognize a mountain peak.

Realizing he was likely going to spend the night out in the woods, he took the blanket from the lean-to, and used it to wrap up the pot, the can of beans, a soda, and a few newspapers to use for kindling.

He started to climb over a downed tree trunk, when he quickly turned back. Along the side of the tent he picked up an old pair of snowshoes he had spotted. Seeing them in the light he realized they were handmade. He was impressed, until he rotated them around. Carved in the side of the wood were the initials SGP.

"Son of a poacher!" Joe heard himself say out loud. He was annoyed he had not seen his dad's snowshoes missing.

Tucking the shoes under his arm, he turned to go. From his left, a deep voice froze him solid.

"Hold it right there."

❧❋❧

The wardens and Don had checked a half-dozen camps, all of which were closed for the season. Not one of them had considered stopping their search for the night, not while Joe was still missing. When they came upon sled tracks and boot prints that led from the pond, they made their way cautiously around the side of the property, hidden behind the trees.

"Door is wide open," whispered Don from behind a pine tree.

One tree over, Andy held a finger over his lips. He motioned to Kristy that he was going around the side and for her to circle the other way. They both slowly walked tree to tree, keeping out of sight of the windows and doors of the cabin.

Meeting at the front door, Andy and Kristy disappeared inside.

The instant Don saw the beams from their flashlights turned on, he made a run for the cabin.

"Anyone here?" he yelled, running through the door.

"No. It's empty," answered Kristy. "Andy's checking out back."

"This place is trashed." Don kicked around the beer cans that were all over the kitchen floor.

Andy came through the backdoor. "You should see the boathouse – looks as if wolverines were set loose in there. Even the walls are chewed over."

"Someone was tied up here." Kristy picked up a coil of rope.

"This is Joe's!" Don held out a small compass he picked up off the floor; the face was smashed.

"This doesn't look good." Andy shined his flashlight on drops of dried blood. "Let's get over to Parker's cabin. I need to use the radio. We're going to need more manpower."

Bourbon. No Ice.

❄☀❄

Joe slowly turned, the flames from the fire shimmered across the face of a man who somehow had quietly squeezed through the trees without making a sound. His frame was wider than the hundred-year-old pine behind him. Ice hung from his beard blending into his white and gray army fatigues. His dark eyes evaluated Joe.

"Guten Tag Herr Johannes von Heinrich."

"Huh? My name is Joe Parker."

"Joe Parker? I'll be." The man stepped closer.

"Who are you? Have we met?" By now, Joe was certain he had seen this person before.

"You bet we have." Merrill reached out his hand to Joe. "Frank Merrill. I was here in sixty-three, with Henry Ford. At the lodge. You brought me a drink."

Joe laughed. "I remember. Bourbon. No ice. That was the night you had a mishap with one of Henry's snowmobiles."

"That's right. The old man was pretty sore about that." Eyeing the blanket wrapped over Joe's shoulder and the old snowshoes leaning against his leg, Merrill's voice changed. "What the heck are you doing out here, Parker?"

"Any chance you know where *this* is?" Joe swung his arms around.

"Yeah, we're in a boggy swampy area close to Lazy Tom Pond."

Given the isolation of the camp, Joe would have never guessed he was a mere five miles from Lobster Lake and had he walked in the right direction, he'd have hit a snowmobile trail within several hundred yards. It was an area he knew well, at least in the daylight and not after being knocked unconscious.

"How'd you find me here?"

"Long story. I've been tracking the fugitive that lives here. Did he take off?"

"I have no idea. I never saw him. I was knocked out by a bunch of low-life metal thieves,"

"Ah, those Canadians?"

"You know them?"

"I came across them yesterday – deflated their hopes for stealing my winch. I was tracking my suspect and ended up at the cabin that gang was using for a hideout. The tracks led me this way. I tell you something, that hermit was more concerned for your life than me finding him. He's never left a trail before. This time I could tell he was dragging something heavy, the impressions in the snow must have been you."

"How do you know he was concerned for my life and he's not waiting in the dark to kill us both?"

Merrill's eyes narrowed. His head went left and right. "Nah. He's a recluse. He may be stealing things to survive, but I don't take him for a killer."

Joe noticed Merrill's stance become more alert, his right hand moved inside a deep coat pocket.

"Besides, that hermit knew I was going to be able to track you here. He dragged you from that cabin in that." Merrill pointed to the toboggan Axe had failed to pack in his rush to leave. "Finding him now, out on his own, is going to be another issue." Merrill investigated the paths within the small camp.

"You think you could point me in the direction of a road or snowmobile trail? I need to get back to the cabin. My buddy Don is probably out in this storm searching for me."

"I can walk out with you. But first I need to look for something." Merrill flipped on a high intensity flashlight and ducked into the tent. Joe followed.

Merrill had to stay on his knees to fit in the low space. His immediate focus was on the pile of electronic equipment.

Wondering if there was anything else of his in the camp, Joe poked around. He shook his head when he saw sitting on a crate next to the cot, a deck of Alaskan Air playing cards. Reaching down to pick them up, he noticed a wooden tackle box on the floor. It was a box he had made, years ago. Last he saw of it, it was in the shed. He pulled it out and flipped open the metal clasp.

"Son of a poacher!" Both Joe and Merrill exclaimed at the same time.

"What'd you find, Parker?" Merrill was flipping through the log book.

"Oh, an old tackle box of mine." Joe closed it; he didn't figure Merrill needed to know what was inside it.

"Hmm." Merrill lifted a gray metal box with wires hanging from it.

"What do you have there?" Joe slipped the cards into his coat pocket.

"A piece of equipment of mine that has been missing for over twenty-five years."

"What's so interesting about that radio?" asked Joe.

"Oh, this is no radio. It's useless now, but back in 1963 it was highly classified military equipment."

"Why would a *hermit* steal that?"

"I'll explain as we hike back to the trail."

⁂

Kristy, Don, Linda, and Sarah were crowded around the radio listening to Andy talking to Border Patrol.

"The one who goes by the name Heath, is showing a couple of my men where they hid the B52 parts and the stolen metal over on the far side of Hurricane Pond. They had planned to sled it across the slash later in the week. Once we uncovered two sets of books one of them was keeping, and the stolen rifle they started squealing on one another like you wouldn't believe. You planning on flying up here in the morning to transport these suspects back?"

"All depends on the weather." Andy switched to his main concern. "What have they told you about Joe Parker?"

"One of the agents is interrogating the leader, the one going by the name Axe, right now to get the specifics on how they left him. He swears he planned to call in the location of the cabin as soon as they were over the border."

"We found that cabin. Parker wasn't there."

When the door opened, Sarah screamed, "Joe!" She rushed to hug him.

"Hey, Gary, let me get back to you tomorrow. Parker just dropped in." Andy exhaled and shook his head in Joe's direction. "He doesn't look all too bad. Can you call out and let the others know they can stand down."

"Great news. Will talk to you tomorrow. Out."

"Where the heck have you been, Parker?" asked Andy, both concerned and relieved. He gave Joe a look over.

"Long story. I need to get into some dry clothes." Joe turned, "And this is . . ." His face went blank. He spun around and scanned the room.

"What is it? asked Sarah.

Linda whispered to Don, "Do you think he's okay?"

"I'm fine. Did he not come in behind me?"

Sarah shook her head. "Who?"

"Maybe you'd better sit down." Andy pushed the rocker close to Joe. Joe sat, looking confused.

"We'd better clean up this wound," remarked Kristy, who was examining Joe's neck. "I think it's a surface cut. I'll get the first aid kit from my sled."

Once Joe was changed and his cut bandaged, he put his feet up on a stool close to the fire. They all listened as he explained his encounter with the four Canadians, the hermit he never saw, and Frank Merrill, who had disappeared into the night.

When he finished, he went over to the door where he had left the snowshoes. "The hermit had these." He dragged a kitchen chair over to the wall near the loft stairs, stepped up, and placed the shoes on the nail. "There. Back where they belong."

"Son of a gun. I didn't even realize those were missing," said Don.

"Don't feel too bad. I didn't either," replied Joe. He then handed Don the pack of Alaskan Air playing cards.

"So, *he* took the cards!"

"But there's more." Joe smiled.

"Like what?" asked Linda who was wrapped in two blankets, still not feeling her best.

With a secretive look, Joe picked up the tackle box and placed it on the coffee table.

"Fishing tackle?" Linda's nose scrunched.

When Joe opened the lid, Sarah exclaimed, "Ew. What's that smell."

"Mold." Joe dumped the contents of the box on the table. Linda, Don, and Andy pushed around the dark green and black bits of paper.

"Is this money?" asked Andy.

Nodding, Joe removed the center of the tackle box to reveal the lower compartment. He flipped it and two canvas bags fell out.

Linda reached for one and smoothed it out flat. "Is this a Brink's bag?"

Joe cocked his head and flashed a big grin.

"Get out!" Sarah picked up the second bag.

"I'm confused. Why would the hermit have the Brink's loot?" asked Don.

"I have no idea. Wait until you see that camp. The guy was a hoarder." Joe took a long drink.

"Fred always said the hermit abandoned the camps and left stuff behind. He was always ticked he had to clean them up."

Linda poked around through the pile of wet bills that were falling apart.

"Maybe the hermit left stuff he didn't want or need. But the items he felt were important, for whatever reason, he must have moved with him from camp to camp."

"Why would he have the Brink's money? Was he one of the bank robbers?" Andy pointed at the bags.

"No, he wasn't one of them. But I have a feeling he's been the eyes in these woods for a long time. He probably knows more of what people do around here than anyone – except maybe Pearl. Merrill said the hermit has been hiding out since the late forties."

"Where is Merrill anyway?" Andy's arms flung open. This was yet another time the agent had given him the slip.

"He was right behind me, at least until I walked in the camp. I have a feeling he went looking for the hermit. He's been tracking him for decades and has never been this close to finding him."

"Did Merrill say who this hermit was?"

"Yep." Joe looked off out the window. He put his feet back up on the stool.

When his glass was close to his lips, Linda shouted, "Who was he!" Joe's spilt his drink down his shirt.

"Okay, okay." Joe wiped the bourbon with his hand. "This hermit, was a German spy."

"Get out." Linda sat back and crossed her legs.

"It's true. He escaped from the prisoner of war camp over on Spencer Lake."

"There's no prisoner camp over there," Linda stated with a confident smirk.

Andy coughed. "Not anymore. But during World War II there was. It wasn't too far from a logging camp. There were some buildings still there back in the sixties. Eventually, the feds destroyed them. Most of the prisoners were eventually sent to France or England."

Joe took up the story. "Turns out, this hermit was one of the four prisoners that escaped."

Andy interrupted. "No. There were only three. I remember that. We were told about it during training. Maine Wardens had tracked them down."

Joe's hand went to his chin and his head moved slightly up and down. "There was a fourth. Merrill said they never caught him. They kept it from the papers – obvious reasons. His name is von Heinrich, or something. The escape was planned at the highest levels of the German spy network to get Heinrich free. He was an electronics expert who had stolen some of the American plans. The other three escapees were counting on him to get in radio contact with the German U-boat that was supposed to pick them up off the coast. But the botched escape, and the delay hiding in the woods from the searchers, left him stranded.

"A few weeks after the escape, he broke into a radio station, stole parts of a transmitter, and built radio equipment. But by the time he tried to contact the boat, it was long gone. The Navy had ramped up patrols out in the Gulf of Maine, effectively scaring off any German ship, if there ever was one to begin with.

"So, Heinrich was stranded. He wandered around Maine for decades. A few times he located a place with a ham radio and sent out a call. Not that it mattered, the only people listening were ham operators and sometimes the government. After the B52 crash, Heinrich stole a crucial component from the cold war technology era – he knew something was different about it to be savvy enough to swipe it. Merrill figures he planned to get back to Germany with it. Merrill returned to Maine a half-dozen times over the years to track the spy each time a radio signal or clue was found. He even worked alongside Henry tracking the hermit."

"I never heard about any of this." Andy frowned.

"Amazing." Sarah shook her head at yet another Maine mystery.

"Wait a minute. The picture I had of a camp over on the far side of Elephant Mountain, was this hermit living there back then?" Linda shot Don a look.

Joe shrugged. "Could have been. Seems to line up. Anyway, once the cold war was over and the stolen technology was worthless, Merrill's personal mission has been to find Heinrich, to get him home. But he's been impossible to locate. In fact, Heinrich had pretty much disappeared. Merrill figured him for dead. Until a coded German message was sent from Gerry's ham radio. Recent news events had him come out of hiding."

"That explains the Springsteen article Gerry found in his kitchen." Linda slapped the arms of her chair.

"I was thinking about that," said Joe. "The article about the Berlin Wall must have given the hermit cause to try and make contact once again."

"Why'd he start stealing things then?" asked Sarah.

"I can only guess survival isn't as easy in his old age. Merrill figures he's pushing mid-sixties."

"I've read a lot of Maine hermit stories, this one is the most mysterious," Linda said.

Someone banged on the door. R.C. barked. Everyone jumped. Andy's hand went to his sidearm.

Being closest to the door, Don opened it. "Hey, Gerry!"

"Wow. Guess we've found the party."

"We?" asked Joe.

Buddy and Buster pushed in behind Gerry.

"Hi All!" Buddy was in great spirits. "Warden, I hear you found my rifle."

"How'd you hear that?"

"We were over at Gerry's after the race. Pearl told me. She heard a call a bit ago between Border Patrol and Chief Robley about his report on a stolen rifle with the initials "BB." Pearl called Fred's wife, who called the Mrs., which put me in a lot of hot water because I hadn't told her the rifle was stolen."

The laughs echoed through the cabin.

"Your rifle is safe with the border patrol. It's evidence now."

"What?" The smile faded from Buddy's face. "You mean I'm not getting it back?"

"In due time. We need to be sure that gang gets prosecuted for all the damage they did."

"Not to mention kidnapping and assaulting Joe." Don was still seething.

"That'll be the first priority to charge them with," said Kristy.

"What about this?" Gerry pulled an envelope from his coat pocket. "That Canadian won the sled race. They didn't show up for the post-race awards dinner to collect their check."

Warden Green reached for the envelope. "I'll take care of that. I know an elderly couple who are going to be grateful for this donation from Axe. They'll be needing it to fix up their cabin."

Free Agent

❦✳❦

"**H**ow's Joe doing?" Linda was hunched over a cup of tea at the kitchen counter.

"He's groggy, but was good about staying awake. Thank you for sitting with him to give me a few hours of sleep."

Linda nodded. "Not a problem."

Sarah looked back at the living room that was strewn with the overnight guests. Buster had claimed the couch, Buddy pushed two easy chairs together, and Gerry made a bed roll on the floor with R.C. snoring right alongside him. The stories went on late into the night and the storm stranded everyone at Parker cabin.

"That bump on the back of his head is going to sting for a while." Linda stated as she poured Sarah a coffee.

"Sure will. He isn't too happy about having to go to the hospital for an x-ray, but I've convinced him it's the right thing to do." Sarah opened a journal.

"What are you reading?" asked Linda.

"I found this journal in the bedroom nightstand when I was looking for something to read. The stories are not about Lobster Lake, but someplace called Pemaquid. Do you know where that is?"

"It's over on the mid-coast region. I remember Joe talking about his grandmother's place over there. You'd have to ask him about it." Linda's head turned and looked up.

"No, you go first."

"No, you. I insist."

"Oh, okay."

Linda and Sarah looked toward the ladder to the loft to see Kristy coming down ahead of Andy.

"You two sleep okay up there? Not too chilly?" asked Linda.

"Are you kidding me. Buster must have been stoking the stove every hour on the hour. I had to open the window." Kristy headed down the hall to the bathroom.

"But the window was on my side of the loft. She froze me out." Looking at Linda, Andy asked, "Where's Don at?"

"He's out in the garage looking over Joe's sled. He was up at five and went to fetch it. Said he couldn't sleep knowing it was out there on the trail."

"Ah. I'm gonna use the radio to make sure the flight's all set to get Joe to the hospital."

An hour later, Don, Andy, and Sarah were standing next to a plane on Lobster Lake.

Joe was seated in the back, worried about leaving the cabin close-up to Don. "Now are you sure you know how to drain the pipes and button everything up?"

"I don't need to know. Gerry's there. He's your caretaker, isn't he? And Buddy and Buster are going to transport your sled into town to be fixed up. Don't you worry, Linda is packing things and we'll meet up with you in a few hours."

"Keep R.C. on a leash – I don't want him running off."

"Yes, I'll make sure of that," Sarah said.

"Did I give you the keys to my truck?" he asked her.

"I have them. I'll get your truck to town. Stop worrying, we've got this." She reached in for a kiss.

Finally, Joe accepted that his camp, his dog, and his truck were in good hands. He exhaled. "See you in a few hours then. I'm looking forward to doing the two-step with you over at the Junction Grill."

"Two-step?" she frowned, not sure what that was.

"Okay, Sarah, they need to go. Joe, an ambulance will pick you up at West Cove." Andy banged on the side on the plane. "All set, Roger."

Roger gave a thumbs up, Andy closed the door, and the engine started up.

By eight, the Junction Grill was packed. Almost the whole town had arrived for the fundraiser concert to support everyone Axe's gang had robbed of pipes and camp supplies.

At the table along the back wall, the chief was sitting with the wardens. "I'll tell you, I'm glad crooks are dumb. The records they kept of each location they stole from is going to make a conviction as sure as black-fly bites in May." Chief Robley took a gulp of his coke.

"We can only hope." Andy nodded. "And we were fortunate enough to stop that Elephant Mountain Gang before they took the stuff across the border. The B52 parts that were taken are already over to the Civil Patrol hangar."

Kristy added, "Don has organized volunteers to haul them back up the mountain tomorrow. I'll be going up with them. Do you want to go along?" She raised an eyebrow at the chief.

"Um, sure. I think my calendar is free. Any word on that fed?" Robley's eyes narrowed.

"None at all. He disappeared . . . just like the hermit." Andy took a bite of his burger with extra crispy bacon.

"Hmm," said the chief.

"Hey, the bands back for another set. And there's old Fred — ready to do his *Elvira* part," exclaimed Buddy.

With the whole joint singing the *mow mows*, the place was rocking.

When the dance contest was announced, Joe grabbed Sarah around the waist. "Come on, honey. It's time to two-step. This fiddle player does a heck of a cover of the *Orange Blossom Special Hoedown*."

"Whoa, cowboy. I'm not sure. I'm from the city."

"What? You never saw *Urban Cowboy*? Follow my lead."

"Are you even supposed to be dancing?"

"Ah, Doc gave me a clean bill of health." He took her hand to take a spot on the dance floor that was filling up with couples stepping and spinning around the floor.

Don twirled Linda over to Joe and Sarah, "Lookin' good, city slicker!"

Buster was dancing with Karen, and Buddy and his wife, who had forgiven him about the rifle, were hooting along the outside circle next to Kristy and Andy.

Pearl nudged Dot, "See, there goes those two wardens. Dancing together. In uniform no less! What'd I tell ya, dear-ah."

☙✻❧

Bangor Airport

The Bangor airport was nearly empty and the click of Sarah's boots on the tile floor beat a slow rhythm down the concourse. The bounce had gone out of her step; the week had gone by too fast.

Joe held her around the waist.

"Sorry about all that went on out at camp. It's not nearly that unusual most of the time."

"I live in New York City – unusual is an hourly occurrence. I was able to experience an adventure in the north woods, along with a little mystery. I caught a togue, which I had no idea was the same as a trout. I got to snowmobile and see a sled dog race. And we watched the northern lights." She squeezed his hand. "Are you kidding me? This was a great trip. I wish I could have stayed longer."

Joe had to talk through his grin. "You know, Lobster Lake is a great place to write in the summer. Do you think you could get approval to work from Maine?"

She sighed.

"What is it?" he asked.

"The magazine owner wants me to do some coastal Maine stories." She caught the corner of his mouth sag. "But I'm certain I'll be able to visit you here at camp. I still want to hike Katahdin. Besides, I'm sure we'll see one another way before then."

He nodded and was about to say something, when ...

"Northwoods Air is announcing the final call for flight 1121 to New York's JFK airport. All passengers should now be on board."

"Guess that's me." She hugged him one last time and whispered, "Valentine's Day is only a month away. Let's meet someplace warm."

"You got it." He watched as she handed the agent her ticket. She looked back once, waved, and disappeared down the jetway.

Joe stood at the window until the plane taxied away. Back in the truck he pushed in a Haggard tape and held the fast forward button until he found the song.

His voice filled the cab, "Silver Wings..."

R.C. groaned.

🌲✳🌲

Late Spring – 1989

Fred's mission this morning was to assess the fire danger, which is always an issue in early spring before the leaves and greenery reappear in the woods. After checking the clearings of recent logging operations and making his notes, he veered northwest.

It wasn't too difficult for Fred to come across the camp; he simply triangulated based on an old copy of his map. The camp was set behind a swampy area, a place nobody would normally bother venturing near. It was abandoned, and from the looks of it, it hadn't been used in months.

The typical array of trash had been left. A few propane tanks, empty cans, radios, batteries, a tarp, a cooler – all items someone camping would use, and likewise a woods hermit might acquire at a new home. Assessing the situation, he began separating what he could take care of immediately. For the larger and heavier junk he'd have to return with an ATV, which would only get him as close as the old fire warden's cabin anyway. He wasn't pleased he'd still have to haul the trash out by hand.

From along the wood-line he heaved a rock into the center of the camp. "I'm getting too old for this," he said out loud. He heaved a dozen more football-size rocks towards the first. He then built a foot-high stone circular pit in the clearing. When he was done burning all that could be burned, he reached into his pocket. On the coals he placed his map, watching it flare up in an orange flame.

Taking his foldable shovel off his pack, he buried the ashes in six inches of sandy dirt. Making a trip to a nearby brook, he filled his fire pump and drowned the dirt with water.

At the edge of the clearing he sat on a log to rest. He picked up the fly he had set there earlier and looked it over. It was a mix of black, white, and green feathers. He had never seen one tied like it before. He found it in a clear plastic bag securely nailed to a tree at the perimeter of the camp. Inside the bag was a ripped page from the fly-fishing book he had left months ago as a gift. The fly was a variation of the one displayed, however, the name had been crossed out and above in neat block print, it was labeled, "Smokey Ghost."

Fred slipped the fly back into the bag. He removed a letter that was also in the bag. He read it again.

United States of America

State Department

Johannes von Heinrich:

Be it known you are hereby exonerated of spying offenses (1940 – 1945), prison escape (1945), and theft of property of the United States in 1963. The war has ended, you are to return home. The United States will pay your expenses back to Germany. Provide this letter to any officer of the law for them to contact us at the below number.

You are free.

Sincerely,

Secretary of State

At the bottom of the letter, two handwritten notes were added. The first, signed by Frank Merrill read:

Johannes – I have tried to find you for twenty five years. You are an expert woodsman. But you no longer have to stay out in the woods. Come in. It's over.

The message was repeated in German.

The second written message, in very broken English, was from the German.

> Ranger – Your friend left this letter the day you left me the new boots. He will not find me, but I knew you would. Tell him message received. Now leave me be.
>
> To other friend, Parker man, tell him the money I never used. I hide it because the man who left it in 1952, it was not his. I watched. They were bad men.
>
> J.v.H.

A ripped section of an old newspaper article about the Brink's robbery was left with the letter. Striking a match, Fred held the article down in the firepit with his boot and lit it. His heel ground the ashes into the dirt and he emptied the rest of the water from his pump over them.

He placed Merrill's letter with the note from the hermit in his bag. Before turning to leave, he knocked in the rocks surrounding the pit.

From the top of the small hill to his right, a raven let out a cry. But to Fred's trained ear, he knew better. Swallowing the last of his Moxie, he meandered down the trail back to his wagon.

When a twig snapped in the woods behind him, the momentary change in his stride was barely noticeable.

He did not turn back to look.

Don't Look Back

Afterword

Spoiler alert.
Do not read this before reading the book.

While this book is fictional, as are the characters, many of the locations and some of the events are real.

The setting for the book is known as the Maine Highlands – which extends from Bangor in the south to beyond Baxter State Park in the north. It includes the state's highest peak, Mt. Katahdin; longest river, the Penobscot; and the largest lake, Moosehead. It's a region within Maine that is almost as large as the entire State of Massachusetts.

There are two mountains by the name Elephant in Maine. One is part of the Mahoosuc Range, in the Rangeley Lakes region. The Elephant depicted in this novel is in Piscataquis County, near Greenville Maine.

The avalanche in Baxter State Park where two climbers died happened in 1984. Since 1963 over a dozen hikers and climbers have died on Katahdin from falls, lightning, or exposure to the elements.

Metal theft happens more than you might think. Although nowadays, there are statutes and penalties that are proving to be a large deterrent. To also counter theft, newer camps use waterlines made from plastic tubing, which has no value to thieves. Scrap yard dealers are also more attentive to the metal they buy. As the metal is often returned to the owners, it is the metal dealer that ultimately loses out.

Maine has had more than a few famous hermits. I will post stories from time to time about the Maine hermits on my blog. Follow me there.

The Spencer Lake Prisoner of War Camp in Western Maine, and the escape of three men is a real story. I have no knowledge of a fourth prisoner eluding capture. This is a novel. However, the entire time period of Maine POW camps is a fascinating piece of history.

Usually, snow permitting (yep, sometimes we don't have enough snow in the north woods) there is a sled dog race in Greenville. From the starting line, or places along the hundred-mile wilderness course, you can watch as sleds are pulled by awesome teams of dogs. There's a bonfire, food, and an all-around good time. Pack your ice fishing gear, snowshoes, and make a weekend out of it.

Lastly, and certainly the most somber part of this tale, is the true crash of the B52 into the side of Elephant Mountain on January 24, 1963. I highly recommend a visit. The first time I visited, it was late in the month of August. Streaks of sun shone through the trees. I was the only one walking the trail. I sat and stared at the parts of the plane. I read the crew member names from the large piece of slate that has been gifted as a memorial. A light breeze stirred the hundreds of small American flags that visitors had left amongst the wreckage.

We must always remember that serving our country is dangerous and full of sacrifice. Thank you to all the men and women that serve in the armed forces of **The United States of America**. To those that made the ultimate sacrifice, their stories need to live on.

As this book is a work of fiction all the names and details with respect to the January 1963 B52 crash are not intended to be one-hundred percent accurate. I encourage readers who are interested in the actual event to review the published articles and books about this day in military history.

B-52C-40-BO Stratofortress
Mission Call Sign – Frosh One Zero
Final Service January 24, 1963

Names and Mission Responsibility:
- Major William W. Gabriel – Master Navigator
- Major Robert J. Morrison – Co-pilot
- Major Herbert L. Hanson – Navigator
- Major Robert J. Hill – Radar Navigator
- Captain Charles G. Leuchter – Radar Navigator
- Technical Sergeant Michael F O'Keefe – Gunner
- Lieutenant Colonel Joe R. Simpson – Command Pilot

Survivors:
- Colonel Dante E. Bulli (1922-2016) – Pilot, Aircraft Commander
- Captain Gerald J. Adler (1931-) – Navigator

Selective Further Reading

1. Fox News, with contributions from The Associated Press, "Seat from 1963 B-52 Crash Found in Maine." 22 May 2012. <www.foxnews.com/us/seat-from-1963-b-52-crash-found-in-maine>

2. Joseph, Ron, "Escape from Spencer Lake." *Downeast Magazine,* December 2014. <downeast.com/history/escape-spencer-lake/>

3. Hubbard, Lucius L., "Woods and Lakes of Maine – 2020 Annotated Edition," Burnt Jacket Publishing, 2020. A reference on the Moosehead Lake region and the North Woods of Maine.

4. New England Aviation History, "Elephant Mountain, Maine – January 24, 1963." May 19, 2018. <www.newenglandaviationhistory.com/tag/lt-col-joseph-r-simpson-jr/>

5. Ricker, Nok-Noi, "Survivor Of 1963 B-52 Crash That Killed Seven in Maine Dies After Years of Military Service." Bangor Daily News. January 31, 2017. <bangordailynews.com/2017/01/31/news/piscataquis/survivor-of-1963-b-52-crash-that-killed-seven-in-maine-dies-after-years-of-military-service/>

6. Swopes, Bryan R., "1963 Elephant Mountain B-52 Crash." This Day in Aviation - 24 January 1963. <www.thisdayinaviation.com/tag/1963-elephant-mountain-b-52-crash/>

7. Wax, Joseph R., *"Final Mission – The North Woods."* Independently published, 2019. This book includes stories about the crew members personal lives and families.

Acknowledgments

I want to thank you the reader for choosing my book to read. It is the encouragement, the prodding, the asking about the next book from you that made this a reality. Writing is a hobby of mine and I am glad you enjoy my stories. Maybe by reading this series you will find yourself wanting to visit the Moosehead region. If you go, please leave a comment on my social media posts to let me know where you visited and what you did while there.

Please keep in touch on Facebook, my blog, or through reviews – those 'stars' matter a great deal, so please click a few.

I thank my early readers, beta readers, and those that assisted with editing. Special thanks to Marisa, Mary Lou, Gina, Rebecca, Amy, Fred, and George for their comments and corrections.

Why, the most important people are always listed last in such public thank you notes, I don't know. I am grateful to my wife, Meredith, who provides me with so much support of my sometimes-consuming hobby. She reads the early drafts, she proofs, and she makes my bacon extra crispy, just the way I like it.

Dear Reader:

Thank you for reading. I hope you enjoyed this novel.

Please keep in touch. You can find me on my social media pages.

Lastly, please share what you thought about, "The Elephant Mountain Gang – Mystery at Maine's Moosehead Lake," with a review or by sending me a message.

See you on the trail,

Tommy

For books and links visit:
www.tommycarbone.com

About Tommy Carbone

Tommy Carbone lives in Maine with his wife and two daughters. He studied electrical engineering and earned a Ph.D. in engineering management.

He writes from a one room cabin, on the shores of a lake, that is frozen for almost six months out of the year, and moose outnumber people three to one.

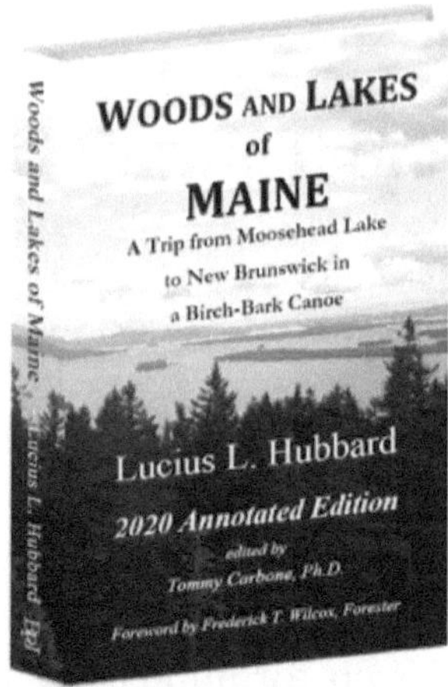

A memoir of a wilderness excursion in Maine.

A guidebook with history of the Moosehead Lake Region.

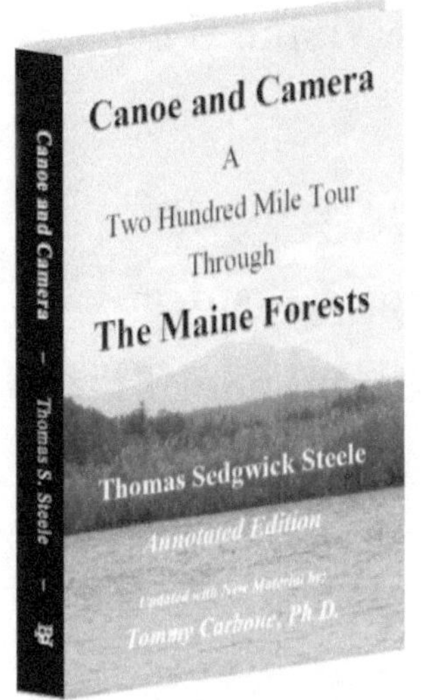

Canoe and Camera

Annotated Edition

of

Steele's first memoir

from Moosehead Lake

to Medway.

Paddle and Portage

Annotated Edition

of

Steele's second canoe

trip memoir from

Moosehead Lake to

Caribou.

Also available in a combined two-book hardcover edition.

Exploring The Maine Woods

**Based on the writing of
Fannie Hardy Eckstorm
this memoir is a wonderful tale of the Maine
woods and history from the 1800s.**

www.ingramcontent.com/pod-product-compliance
Lightning Source LLC
Chambersburg PA
CBHW020916110726
47900CB00001B/159